LILY OF THE
VALLEY

To Kellyn—

May you always listen to God's leading.

Faith Oliver

~Jude 10~

HYMNS OF THE WEST SERIES

LILY OF THE VALLEY

Faith Blum

Paperback Edition
November 2015

ISBN-13: 978-1517358679
ISBN-10: 1517358671

Cover by Perry Elisabeth Design
        perryelisabethdesign.blogspot.com
Images (c): Unsplash, Andi_Graf
        pixabay.com;
Massonforstock, pastordavisjunocom
        canstockphoto.com
Layout: Penoaks Publishing
        penoaks.com
Editing: Kelsey Bryant
        kelseybryantauthor.weebly.com/editing.html

To Lydia

Through the work of writing this, my longest novel yet,

you kept me going.

Your excitement to see what happened next was contagious.

Thank you!

TABLE OF CONTENTS

I charge you, O daughters of Jerusalem,
Do not stir up nor awaken love
Until it pleases.
Who is this coming up from the wilderness,
Leaning upon her beloved?
I awakened you under the apple tree.
There your mother brought you forth;
There she who bore you brought you forth.
Set me as a seal upon your heart,
As a seal upon your arm;
For love is as strong as death,
Jealousy as cruel as the grave;
Its flames are flames of fire,
A most vehement flame.
Many waters cannot quench love,
Nor can the floods drown it.
If a man would give for love
All the wealth of his house,
It would be utterly despised.

Song of Solomon 8:4-7 (NKJV)

PROLOGUE

Micah threw the pad of papers on his desk. The thud echoed in the small room and he scowled. He'd been staring at the same sentence half the day trying to understand what the person was proposing for his business loan. He had yet to succeed because each time he started the second paragraph and read the words "family business," his son would come to mind and he would start to dream up his own family business. Then the memory of his wife's death would tear all the dreams apart. He could never start something like that without his wife, without his supporter, without someone to give him more ideas.

He closed his eyes and whispered, "God, what am I doing here? Why...? Why did all this have to...?" He buried his head in his hands. A year had passed since Edith's death. He should be over the worst of his grief and yet it seemed like it had just begun.

Maybe he needed a change. If he changed jobs, maybe Jeremiah would stop doing things to get his attention. To do that, he'd have to leave Chicago. His breath caught as an idea formed in his head. He could go West. He could start fresh. He could make new friends who wouldn't bring up his wife's death every hour.

Micah jumped from his chair and pulled out his pocket watch. Quarter to five. It was a little early, but he knew his boss wouldn't mind. He neatened his desk and waved at his coworkers as he hurried outside.

He breathed in the fresh air and almost choked. Yes, he needed to get out of this city. The factories made the air unbreathable. As difficult as his childhood had been, at least he'd had real air to breathe instead of coal smoke.

Micah stopped in front of the large, ornate door to his huge house. When he'd bought it for Edith, he hadn't thought it was huge, but he had also been hoping to fill the house with children. Another dream that had died with Edith. Now all he saw was wasted space and expense. He would talk to Seth in the morning and see if he was still interested in the house.

With a steadying breath, he opened the door and nearly got bowled over by an excited little boy.

"How are you today, Jeremiah?" Micah asked as he picked the boy up.

"Fine, now that you're here," the five year old said.

"Did you behave for Mrs. Gold?"

"No," he replied with an impish grin.

"No?" Micah asked with a frown. "Why not?"

"I didn't want to." Jeremiah leaned back and crossed his arms.

Micah sighed and set Jeremiah down. "You should always do the right thing whether you want to or not. Especially when your father gave you exact instructions to behave."

"That was yesterday," Jeremiah protested.

Micah closed his eyes and prayed for patience. When he opened them, he saw Mrs. Gold walk in, pulling her gloves on with a scowl on her face.

She looked up at him. "After what that boy did today, you're lucky I need the money and am willing to stick around. But I'm warning you, one more day of this, and I will quit."

Micah raised an eyebrow and looked at Jeremiah. "Go to your room, Jeremiah. Wait for me on your bed. No toys or books."

Jeremiah ducked his head. "Yes, Sir."

"At least someone gets respect from him around here," Mrs. Gold huffed.

Micah crossed his arms. "What did he do today?"

"He went into the garden without telling me and without putting his coat or shoes on. He found some frogs and scared the cook half to death by having a frog race in the kitchen."

Micah fought a smile at the thought of the uptight Helga watching the frogs in horror.

"When I told him to play nicely in his room, he destroyed the place, forcing me to clean all of it up and still keep an eye on the boy. I swear, Micah Carson, that boy needs a good, firm hand to the backside every day to teach him to behave. I know Edith's only been gone a year, but that boy needs a mother. And a wife wouldn't hurt you any either."

Micah stiffened and put his arms by his side. He forced himself to breathe calmly and not react. "That will be enough, Mrs. Gold. There is no need for you to meddle in my personal life.

"Next time Jeremiah destroys his room, perhaps you should make him clean it up instead. That might be more effective than a 'firm hand to the backside' once I finally get home. If you'll excuse me I have some things to discuss with my son. Good day, Madam."

He brushed past Mrs. Gold and left her to let herself out. He knew it was rude, but he wasn't in a gentlemanly mood right now. First his so-called "friends" and now Mrs. Gold. He would never remarry because he could never love another woman as much as he had loved Edith. He knew it was unfair to Jeremiah, but better for Jeremiah to grow up motherless than with a mother who didn't love either of them.

Micah ran up the steps two at a time and took his suit jacket off as he went. He threw the jacket into his room as he passed by and unbuttoned the top button of his tight, collared shirt.

He knocked on the door to Jeremiah's room. "May I come in?"

"Yes."

Micah pushed the door open and stepped in. "Jeremiah, we need to talk."

Jeremiah looked up at him with wide eyes. "I stayed on my bed."

Micah chuckled. "I see that. Thank you for obeying me. That's not what I need to talk to you about. The way you treated Mrs. Gold today was uncalled for and wrong and you know it. Tomorrow, I want you to apologize to her."

"Yes, Pa."

"I also want you to listen to her and obey her tomorrow and every other day she is here."

"Yes, Pa."

Micah sat on the bed next to him. "Do you know why disobedience is wrong?"

Jeremiah shrugged. "Kinda."

"Why?"

"God says not to."

Micah smiled. "That's right. Why does God say not to?"

Jeremiah wrinkled his nose. "I don't know."

"Disobedience to parents is disobedience to God. God tells children to 'obey your parents in the Lord for this is right.' If you disobey your parents, or those in authority over you, that is sin."

"Sin is bad. Preacher says so. If you sin, you go to that hot and spicy place." Jeremiah shuddered.

Micah bit his cheeks to keep from smiling. "That's right. It's not spicy, but I think you get the picture. I don't want to have to punish you and neither does God."

Jeremiah hung his head. "I know." He sighed. "I'm hungry."

Micah smiled at the abrupt change in conversation. "So am I, Cowboy. Which reminds me, you should apologize to Mrs. Helga."

Jeremiah smiled sheepishly. "Yes, Pa. I'll do that now."

A few months later, Micah had sold his house, quit his job, and packed as few belongings as he could. What he wouldn't need, he gave away to charity houses. He kept a few of Edith's things to remember her by, but the rest, he reluctantly gave away.

He still had no idea where he would go, but decided to take the train as far west as possible and then look at the stagecoach destinations. Jeremiah didn't care as long as they went west.

Micah kept an eye on Jeremiah as he watched the scenery hurry by outside the train window. He had let Jeremiah have the window seat so he could get lost watching the scenery instead of running up and down the aisle. Even while looking out the window, Jeremiah alternately stood, sat, and squirmed.

A smile crept onto his face as he remembered the many times Edith had complained about how much *his son* moved and how little sleep she got.

"Whatcha smiling about, Pa?" Jeremiah's voice cut into his thoughts.

"You and your ma," Micah replied.

"Tell me?" Jeremiah begged.

"What do you want to know?"

"Did she love me?"

Micah's eyes misted over. "Yes, she did. She loved you very much and hated leaving you behind."

"Did she love you?"

Micah nodded.

"Then why'd she leave us?"

Micah sighed. "God decided He needed her more than we did." If only he could believe his own words.

7

"But I still need her."

Micah pulled Jeremiah into his lap. "I know. So do I, but if God thinks we can live without her, we'll have to try."

"Can I have a new ma?"

Micah tensed. "Why?"

Jeremiah shrugged. "I'd like one."

Micah kissed the top of his head. "We'll see."

The stagecoach came to a stop. Micah looked at the sleeping boy in his lap. Should he wake Jeremiah or not? He waited for Gage Bradford, the stagecoach driver, to open the door.

As he stepped out, carrying his son, he looked around the small town. Although small, it looked tame compared to some of the other towns they had passed through.

"Do you know where I could find lodging, Gage?"

"There's a hotel up the street a bit. The saloon is next door, but at least they aren't attached like in most towns."

"Thank you, Gage," Micah said.

Gage nodded. "Not a problem." He brushed the lock off Jeremiah's forehead. "This little guy reminds me of my boys back home."

Micah smiled as Gage pulled his hand back and hefted the bags off the stagecoach.

A young lad about twelve walked past and Micah stopped him. "Young man, would you be willing to help me carry my trunk to the hotel? I can carry the bags if you take the trunk."

The boy gave him a looking over that Micah found a little disturbing, but the boy must have been satisfied with what met his eyes. "Sure, Mister."

The boy lifted the trunk as if there was nothing inside. Micah raised an eyebrow in surprise as Gage helped him get the carpetbag in his hand.

"Thank you again, Gage. It was nice meeting you."

Gage nodded and Micah smiled as he followed the boy carrying his trunk. At the hotel, he set the carpetbag on the floor and dug in his pocket while he held Jeremiah in his arms. "I'd toss it to you, but with Jeremiah in my arms I can't."

The boy grinned and took the coin out of Micah's hand. "That's all right. Thanks, Mister."

"What's your name?"

"Lou. Are you plannin' on staying around Cartersville?"

"I hope to, Lou. Thank you for your help."

Lou shrugged. "You're welcome, Mister. What's your name, anyway?"

"Micah Carson."

"I was glad to help, Mr. Carson. My pa says I should always help if I can. I didn't realize all that stuff was yours when I walked by or I'd've offered right away."

Micah chuckled. "I guess we did bring quite a few things, didn't we?"

"Not as much as Mr. Wilson and his family did. Now they brought a lot of stuff, including some real fancy Eastern doohickeys I don't understand the purpose of."

Micah failed to hide his amusement and Lou looked suddenly embarrassed.

"You ain't from the East are you, Mr. Carson?" Lou asked.

Micah bit his cheeks. "Kind of. I'm from Chicago, but I came out West to live like a Westerner, not an Eastern dandy."

Lou grinned. "I like you, Mr. Carson. When you're settled in, I'll ask Pa to have you over." He put a finger to his chin. "Unless I can talk him into letting you come today. I think you'll like it here. The town's small, but we're growing. The land out here is real good for ranchin' if you've got money and willpower to stick to it."

"What about farming?"

Lou grimaced. "Maybe. The best farmland's been taken, though." He shrugged. "You'd have to ask around."

"It sounds like we'll get on in this town just fine. Now, I need to get a hotel room reserved and my son in the bed before my arms fall off."

"How's 'bout you set him here on the sofa and I'll keep an eye on him until you get the room reserved? Then I can help you carry your stuff upstairs."

Micah looked at the sofa and back at Lou. "That is an excellent idea. Thank you."

Five minutes later, Lou left the hotel and ran home to beg an invitation out of his parents. Micah chuckled to himself as he unpacked a few of his belongings into the small dresser. The boy seemed so excited to have new people in town.

A knock sounded on the door shortly after Lou left. "I wonder who that could be," Micah muttered to himself. He opened the door to see Lou standing there.

"Hiya, Mr. Carson. I hope you don't mind, but I brought you an invitation from my parents." He handed Micah a piece of paper and pencil.

Micah smiled while he read the invitation. "They sure went to a lot of trouble just to invite a stranger to their house for supper."

"Maybe, but they like to pretend sometimes that Cartersville is more civilized than it really is."

"Here you go," Micah said as he handed the reply back. "Can you be here at a quarter to five to show us the way to your house?"

11

"Sure! See ya later," Lou said as he ran back home.

Later that night, Micah collapsed into the bed next to his sleeping son and sighed with contentment. Not only had Jeremiah made new friends, but so had he. And he had a job already. It wouldn't be very much, but he would look for something else in the morning.

Lou's parents, Simon and Carlotta Lancaster, were ranchers and neither could keep the books well. When Micah had mentioned he used to work at a bank, Simon asked if he could take over the bookkeeping. Micah had quickly accepted.

The Lancasters had six children: an older girl, Lou, two more girls, and then twin boys Jeremiah's age. Micah smiled as he remembered how well Clem, Chancy, and Jeremiah had gotten along. They were finally home.

CHAPTER ONE

Jeremiah ran to catch up with the two boys walking down the street. "Clem! Chancy! Wait up!" The twins turned around at the same time with matching grins on their matching faces.

When Jeremiah caught up to them, Clem spoke, "Hi, Jeremiah. How's the sheriff's son today?"

Jeremiah stuck his tongue out at Clem. "Running late, obviously. Either that or you two decided not to wait for me."

"We waited," Chancy said with a mischievous grin on his face.

"Yeah, and for how long?" Jeremiah demanded.

"Long enough," Clem said. "Let's go or we'll be late for the first day of school."

They talked as they strode quickly to school.

"It's gonna be strange to have Ruth...I mean, Miss Brookings, as the new schoolteacher," Jeremiah said.

"Yeah. And it'll be hard to remember to call her Miss Brookings, too. She's always been Ruth," Chancy protested.

"And she's only nine years older than us!" Jeremiah exclaimed.

"Yeah, but we're only ten, so she's also almost twice as old as we are," Clem pointed out.

"I suppose. Well, here goes nothin'," he said as they entered the schoolyard.

Clem slapped his arm. "Don't have such a grouchy attitude about it, 'Miah. It won't be that bad."

"Says you. Pa and Ruth are real good friends and talk a lot. Now with 'Miss Brookings' bein' my teacher, they'll talk about me even more." He shrugged as he scanned the schoolyard. "Hey! There's John and James! Let's go welcome 'em to school!"

Ruth looked around the classroom from the back of the room and shook her head in amazement. A few years earlier, she would never have accepted a position that forced her to be in front of anybody for any length of time. When she'd first moved to Montana, she could barely talk to her new best friend, Annabelle. In the last few years, Joshua, her parents, and God had worked hard to get her out of her shell.

Over the last year, she had gained more friends, including Micah Carson and William Steele, and her friendship with Annabelle had blossomed to where Annabelle now took advice from Ruth and Ruth enjoyed being with Annabelle. As she walked up the aisle, she thanked God for the opportunities and influence she had on Annabelle and the children in Cartersvi— She shook her head. It wasn't Cartersville anymore. It was Castle City. She really had to get that change through her head. It may have been over half a year since the change, but she still wasn't used to it.

Ruth stopped in front of the stove and scrunched her eyebrows together. Heat already came from it. She glanced around and saw the note on the chalkboard.

"Decided to warm the school up for you while I was on my rounds. Hope you don't mind. Micah."

Ruth smiled and shook her head. Leave it to the sheriff to think of something like warming up the school before she arrived. If he wasn't careful, starting the fire might end up becoming part of his job description.

She whistled a nameless tune as she erased Micah's message and wrote her name on the board along with letters, words, and sentences, a few page numbers, and a few math problems of various levels. When the board had everything written on it, she opened the ledger on her desk and skimmed it. She knew all the names either from town socials or church.

With a glance at the clock, she took one last look around the classroom. Everything seemed to be in order and ready for the children. Ruth breathed a quick prayer for strength, stamina, and creativity. She already knew she had at least four ten year old boys in her class and one of them was a known troublemaker. He had been trouble when she first arrived and he had been only six then. He was also Micah's son.

Ruth looked at the clock again. Time to ring the bell. She picked up the small bell from her desk and walked to the door. The schoolyard was full of playing children. A couple of the girls caught sight of her and made their way toward the schoolhouse.

Ruth smiled as she rang the bell and greeted each child as they walked into the schoolhouse and put their lunch pails in the coatroom. Each of the students took a seat at a desk and Ruth was glad she had already made her own desk arrangements. The four boys she thought would be the most trouble were sitting together and whispering together.

"Good morning, Class," Ruth said as she walked up to the front. "I am Miss Brookings and will be your teacher this year. I'm glad each of you were able to come this morning. The first thing we are going to do is set a few rules and then do some new desk assignments." She turned a stern eye to the four boys who were still whispering together.

"Clem, what is the first rule at this school?"

Clem's head snapped up at the sound of his name. "Pay attention when the teacher is talking."

Ruth nodded her approval. "Chancy, what is the second rule?"

"Be courteous to the other students."

"And is whispering to your friends being courteous to the other students, John?" Ruth asked.

John ducked his head. "No, Ma'am."

Ruth held eye contact with each of the four boys for a few seconds. "Jeremiah, what is the third rule?"

"I don't know," Jeremiah said, crossing his arms and looking defiant.

"You don't know or you don't want to say?"

"I don't know," Jeremiah said with a glare.

"Can you read?"

"Yes, Ma'am," he conceded grudgingly.

Ruth stepped to the side. "What does it say on the board after the number three?"

"Behave during recess and lunch breaks," Jeremiah muttered.

Ruth looked around the room. "Suzanna, what is the fourth rule?"

"Speak clearly when asked to answer a question," Suzanna replied.

"Thank you."

Ruth went through the rest of the rules and then told each of the students where they were to sit. There were just enough boys in the third reader to have the four potential troublemakers split up and Ruth breathed a sigh of relief when the desk seating went without any problems.

The first day flew by without any further issues and after the children were dismissed, Ruth walked to her new home with a bounce in her step. During the week, she would stay in the cottage set aside for the schoolteacher and on Friday afternoon, she could go home until Sunday night.

She swallowed hard and tried to keep her breathing normal as she approached the house. Her stomach rolled and jumped as she thought about the next few nights she would spend alone. At least Micah had promised that he and his deputy would keep a close eye on the place both day and night. His promise to stop by occasionally to check on her helped to calm her nerves a little.

She rested her books precariously on her left arm as she put the key in the lock. The lock snapped and she gripped the doorknob. As she turned the knob, a boot thumped on the bottom step behind her. Ruth spun around and her books crashed to the porch as she faced the intruder.

"I'm sorry. Did I startle you?" Micah asked.

Ruth put a hand to her heart as if making sure it hadn't left her chest. "Yes, you did." She laughed nervously. "You need to stop practicing your Indian walking."

Micah grinned sheepishly. "Sorry about that. I thought you saw me. You must've been lost in thought under that big hat of yours."

Ruth huffed. "I'll have you know this hat was specially made for me by Joshua. He knew I didn't like bonnets because they shade the sides of my face too much."

Micah smiled as he bent down and helped Ruth pick up her books and papers. "I know. I just like teasing you about it. How'd the first day of school go?"

"After a minor problem at the beginning, the day went very well."

"A minor problem?" Micah asked as he picked up the last book and straightened. "This wouldn't involve my son, would it?"

Ruth cleared her throat. "Um, yes, it would."

Micah frowned. "What did he do this time?"

"Nothing needing discipline, just a little correction. And it wasn't just him; John Jenkins, and Clem and Chancy Lancaster were also to blame. I took care of it and hopefully most of their classroom antics will be avoided by splitting them all up during class."

Micah raised his right eyebrow. "I hope so. Let me know if Jeremiah causes too much trouble."

Ruth looked up at him with a smile. "I plan to. Just like I plan to tell any of the parents if their child gets to be too much trouble."

Micah chuckled. "Thank you, Miss Brookings. I'd better get back to the office to make sure Obadiah isn't getting into trouble." He handed her the stack of books and papers.

"Your deputy is causing trouble?"

"Nah. He just likes to think he's the sheriff and do some of the paperwork. Then he messes it up so much I end up spending twice as long fixing it than I would if I'd done it to begin with."

Ruth laughed and shook her head. "Then you'd better get back fast. I have school assignments to figure out anyway, so I have plenty to work on tonight as well."

Micah tipped his hat at her. "Talk to you again soon, Miss Brookings."

"Same to you, Mr. Carson."

CHAPTER TWO

October 6, 1879
Dear Diary,

The good part about living in town is I get to see Annabelle more often. The bad part is I don't get to see Mother and Father or talk to them, and I've noticed that I'm overly suspicious. I know Castle City (I actually remembered to call it that this time!) is more civilized and I trust Micah and Obadiah to keep everybody safe, but there are still rough men around and many of them go to the saloons. Lord, help me to trust You!

On another note, I've discovered it is really hard to cook for just one person. I don't think I've ever cooked for fewer than five people except when Joshua and I got stranded in the wilderness.

But that doesn't count since we didn't even have much food to cook.

I've taught for two weeks now and I think it's going well. I also had an idea on what to do with my extra food. The Hale children rarely have food to bring for lunch because Mr. Hale is out of a job and they don't have money for food. I'm going to bring some of my extra food today to give to them.

It's time for me to go get the schoolhouse ready.

The sun rose warm and the sky was clear of clouds when Ruth walked to school. As she entered the schoolyard, she waved at the early students who played in the yard. Since the day was warm, the fire was not needed and Ruth felt a twinge of disappointment that she didn't have to erase a note from Micah this morning. As soon as the thought came, she scolded herself for being so silly and hurried up to her desk.

On the desk sat a piece of paper with some pencil scrawlings on it.

Howdy Teacher! You don't know me, but my kids talk bout you a lot. I been lookin fer a wife and mother fer a few years and was wonderin iffen we cood meet and get to no each other a bit. Ill come after skool to git yer answer.

Grover Miller

Ruth grabbed the edge of the desk to steady herself. If she didn't know him, that probably meant he didn't go to church. And if the kids outside were his, she knew they had an older sister a little younger than her. What kind of man would ask to court her through a note? And couldn't he have gotten Samantha or Otis or even ten-year-old Olive to check his spelling? Especially since it was written to a schoolteacher. Ruth shook her head and threw the note into the woodstove wishing there were coals to burn it right away.

Shaking off the uncomfortable feeling she'd gotten from the note, Ruth turned to the blackboard and tried to concentrate on writing what was needed there. Maybe she could get Micah to be here... No, she would have to do it alone and outside where the children could see everything. She just hoped Mr. Miller wasn't too intimidating.

Everything had been written on the blackboard and Ruth took a deep breath. "God, help me forget the note until after school and help Mr. Miller graciously accept my rejection or at least be willing to talk to Pa." After her prayer, she picked up the bell, pasted a smile on her face, and strode to the door to ring for the children to come in.

School went fairly smoothly, but Ruth knew the children wanted to be outside in the warm weather. At lunch, Ruth went outside with them to eat. She sat on the steps and opened her lunch pail. She scanned the yard for the Hale children. Her eyes caught sight of Jeremiah walking toward them.

Paul, Callie, and Richard Hale sat off by themselves, watching everything going on in the schoolyard. Jeremiah said something and Paul shook his head. Jeremiah shrugged and walked back to his group of friends.

Ruth tapped her foot. She may as well go now. She took her lunch out of the lunch pail and set it on the step. Picking up the lunch pail, she made her way to the Hale children.

"I realized I have too much to eat and really need to get back inside to prepare for the afternoon. Would you three mind helping me out?" Ruth asked.

Paul looked up at her. "You bein' honest, Miss Brookings?"

"Yes, I am. I'm not used to only cooking for one person, so I keep making too much," Ruth replied.

Paul looked from her to his siblings and held out his hand for the lunch pail. "I'll return this after school. Thank you, Miss Brookings."

Ruth smiled. "You're welcome. Thank you for helping me out."

She turned away and caught Jeremiah's eye. They smiled at each other.

The afternoon went well and as Ruth erased everything from the blackboard, she suddenly remembered Grover Miller's promise. Maybe he would forget. As she thought it, someone cleared his throat and from the deep sound, it wasn't one of her students.

Ruth turned slowly with a prayer in her heart. She recognized him, but could tell he'd cleaned up and put on some of his best clothes; which wasn't saying much.

"Miss Brookings?" the man asked.

Ruth took a step toward her desk, keeping the desk between them. "Yes. And you must be Mr. Miller."

"Yes, Ma'am. Have ya thought about what I said?"

"Yes, Mr. Miller, I have. But I'm afraid if you want to court me, you'll have to talk to my pa."

Grover Miller took a few steps forward until he stood in front of the desk. It took all of Ruth's resolve to stand her ground. Why hadn't she asked one of the children to help her clean the blackboard today?

"I don't have time to go all the way out to the ranch, Miss Brookings."

"You could come to church on Sunday and talk to him then."

Grover scowled and rubbed his beard. "I cain't. I have things to do."

Ruth didn't even want to imagine what kinds of things he did. "All right. Then I'll give you the answer I'm sure Pa would give you. The answer is no."

A flash of rage crossed Grover's face. "No need to get all hoity-toity, Miss Brookings. You just don't realize how bad I need ya. I got no wife and haven't fer a long time. Samantha's gettin' married next week and then it'll be just me with the little 'uns. Olive ain't old enough to take over fer Sam."

"I'm sorry for your troubles, but there is nothing I can do about it," Ruth said. "There are plenty of other women in town. Try asking one of them."

"I already have. You were my last hope."

Ruth didn't know whether to feel insulted or relieved. She decided on relieved. Just as it looked like Grover would try to go around the barrier between them, the schoolhouse door slammed shut and Paul walked in with his siblings in tow.

"Here's your lunch pail, Miss Brookings." He stopped and glared at the man standing in front of her desk. "Sorry if I interrupted anything." His eyes said he wasn't sorry at all and that he had intentionally come in right then.

"No harm done, Paul," Ruth said, forcing a smile. "This gentleman was just leaving. Thank you for returning the lunch pail."

Grover looked from the boy, who was almost as big as him, to the schoolteacher and decided to leave.

"Callie," Ruth asked as Grover left, "would you like to help me clean the blackboard? Unless you need to go home right away." Out of the corner of her eye, she watched Grover leave. Jeremiah ran in as soon as Grover was gone.

"There you are, Paul. I was lookin' for you," he exclaimed. He turned a curious glance to Ruth. "What did that man want?"

"He wanted something I couldn't give him," Ruth replied. "Thank you, Paul, for coming in when you did."

"I thought he mightn't have good intentions and he'd been in here long enough," Paul said with a shrug.

Ruth nodded. "If he comes again, either of you have my permission to come up with any excuse to come in here. If all else fails, you can come in to help me clean the blackboard."

Paul smiled. "Yes, Ma'am. Callie, Richard, it's time to go. Ma's waiting for us."

Callie pouted. "Can I help Miss Brookings first, please? She did ask."

"All right. But, Richard, you stay here with Callie and walk home with her. Thank you for the lunch, Miss Brookings."

"Anytime. I'm just glad to get rid of some of the leftovers."

Paul left and Ruth handed Richard and Callie each a rag. Jeremiah trailed after Paul and Ruth hurried to catch up to him.

When they were out of the schoolhouse, Ruth looked at Jeremiah. "Thank you, Jeremiah, for offering your lunch to the Hales."

"How'd you know?" Jeremiah asked.

"I saw you go up there."

"Oh." He shrugged. "Weren't nothin'."

Ruth grimaced. "When will you start using real English, Jeremiah?"

Jeremiah grinned. "When it stops buggin' you so much when I don't."

Ruth tried to glare at him and failed. "Run off home now. I'm sure Mrs. Tucker is wondering where you are."

28

"Nah. She's used to me bein' home at all sorts of hours."

Ruth tapped her foot in agitation. "She shouldn't have to be. She worries about you, you know."

Jeremiah shrugged. "She ain't my ma. And you ain't my ma, neither, so you can't tell me what to do either." He turned and ran down the path to the road.

Ruth sighed and prayed for wisdom. With a deep breath, she made her way back into the schoolhouse.

"Good job, Richard and Callie! I think that's the fastest that blackboard has ever been cleaned. Thank you."

Callie curtsied. "You're welcome, Miss Brookings."

The red in Richard's cheeks darkened. "Glad to help."

"I'll see you tomorrow," Ruth called after them as she gathered her books and papers and hurried home. Micah wasn't waiting for her today, so she put a small pot of stew on the stove and thought through what needed prepared for the next day.

As she finished her last bit of planning, she looked around and stood up. She didn't like being around a lot of people, but this quiet was driving her just as crazy. She grabbed her shawl off her bed and left the house to take a walk.

As she neared the General Store, she caught sight of a familiar pink dress. "Annabelle!"

Annabelle turned and when she saw Ruth, she grinned. "Ruth, what are you doing?"

Ruth caught up to her friend. "Taking a walk. The house was getting too quiet."

Annabelle gave her a hug. "I thought you liked quiet."

"I do, but not all night, every night. And on the ranch it never got that quiet."

Annabelle and Ruth continued walking as they talked. "How have you been, Annabelle?"

Annabelle shrugged. "Fair, I guess. It seems like you are the only person who wants to talk to me. I know I wasn't the most pleasant person to be around, but I have tried changing. Why can't people see that?"

Ruth nodded. "I've noticed they avoid you, too." She fought a mischievous smile. "Anybody in particular you want to notice the change?"

Annabelle blushed. "Yes, but he doesn't even acknowledge my existence, so it's pointless."

Ruth raised an eyebrow. "*He* doesn't? Oooh."

Annabelle swatted Ruth. "Stop it!"

Ruth laughed. "Sorry. So, who is this blind man?"

Annabelle stopped and looked at her with doubt in her eyes.

Ruth laughed. "You don't have to tell me if you don't want to."

Annabelle looked around and sighed. "William," she whispered.

"Our ranch hand?" Ruth clarified.

"Shh!" Annabelle hissed. "Not so loud."

"Sorry. Why don't you think he acknowledges your existence?" Ruth tried to think of a time when William had ever been rude, especially to a woman, and couldn't think of anything.

"Because he only notices you, Ruth. Didn't you know that? You're the prettiest of the two of us..."

"I am not!" Ruth protested. "You are far prettier than me."

"Maybe on the outside," Annabelle agreed, "but men like William don't just notice the outside. They see the inside, too, and that's where I'm lacking."

The wide expanse of the land stretched out in front of them and they stopped walking. Ruth looked around to make sure nobody could hear them. "You can change that, Annabelle, with God's help."

"I've tried and I manage to do it for a few days, but then I go back to the way I was before."

"I'll help you," Ruth offered.

"How?"

"We'll do a Bible study together. I usually don't have anything to do in the evenings. If your parents agreeable it, you and I could do a Bible study every weekday evening except Friday."

Annabelle stared at the grassy fields. "Are you sure?"

"I'm positive. It will help me, too. I haven't done well with my own devotions, so this will help me since I'll have to do a little preparation before we get started. We can help keep each other accountable."

"Can you do it and your teaching?"

"Most of my school preparation isn't very hard. If I can't do it one day, it's not like you live so far away that it is a waste of time for you to walk to the house and find out we can't study that night."

Annabelle smiled. "Thank you, Ruth."

"You're welcome."

They parted ways and Ruth made her way back to the house. As she walked along, she stopped in front of the sheriff's office and paused to look at the mountain behind. It always amazed her that the snow stayed on the peak year-round. A gust of wind threatened to blow her hat off and she put her hand on top of it until the wind died down. Looking both ways, she hurried across the dusty street to see if Micah was in his office.

She opened the door and stepped inside.

"Miss Brookings!" Micah exclaimed in a pleasant voice. "What brings you here?"

"Restlessness and a desire to see my friend," Ruth replied with a smile.

"At least it wasn't Jeremiah's antics," Micah said.

Ruth laughed. "Not this time. He's been very well behaved so far." She looked around the office. "Where's Obadiah?"

"At home. He was on duty last night so I let him go home and get some sleep."

Ruth nodded.

"You look like you want to ask something. What is it?"

Ruth smiled. "You know me too well."

Micah stuck his tongue in his cheek and shrugged. "Nah. It's my business to know people. What is it?"

"Do you know a man named Grover Miller?"

Micah put his foot on the chair and propped his elbow on his knee. "Yes. Why?"

"He came to the schoolhouse today after school."

Micah's elbow slipped off his knee and he straightened. "Anything happen?"

"No, nothing happened. I just wondered about him." Ruth avoided his eyes.

Micah ran his fingers through his dark brown hair. "He's not a good man to be loitering around the school. He has been a drunk since his wife died. I've had to toss him in jail a few times to sleep it off."

Ruth's eyes widened. "Oh."

Micah cleared his throat. "What did he want?"

Ruth shook her head. "I'd like to talk to my parents about it first."

Micah nodded. "Let me know if you have any trouble with him."

"I will."

Micah smiled. "You mentioned restlessness. Why are you so restless?"

"I'm not used to being alone so much. There's only so much you can do by yourself. Annabelle is going to help with that, though."

"Really? How?"

Ruth smiled. "We're starting a Bible study together. She really wants to change and I offered to help her."

Micah grinned. "I'm glad you're going to help each other."

Ruth looked around. "Me, too. Well, I suppose I should let you get back to work and I should make sure my stew isn't burning."

Micah sat down behind his desk. "I do have some papers to fill out and wanted posters to sift through."

Ruth opened the door. "Bye, Sheriff Carson. Have a good night."

"You, too, Miss Brookings."

CHAPTER THREE

William twirled a straw stem in his hands as he sat on his bunk. Thoughts ran through his head faster than a buffalo stampede. The straw fell out of his fingers, but he kept moving his hands.

"He must be thinkin' hard," Peter said.

"Yep," Wyatt drawled.

"What should we do 'bout it?" Flynn asked.

"I dunno. Maybe borrow his gee-tar?"

William's head jerked up. "Nobody touches my guitar. And just because I'm thinking doesn't mean I can't hear you talking."

"We knew that," Peter laughed, slapping his hat on his knee. "That's why we was teasin' you."

William sighed and shook his head. "Sure you were."

"What were you thinking so hard about anyway?" Flynn asked.

"Nothin'," William said, his cheeks warming.

"Oh ho, ho!" Peter exclaimed. "He's been thinkin' about a girl!"

William took a deep breath and willed the redness and heat off his face. It didn't work, so he reached down and slid his guitar case from under his bunk. When the lid was open, he lovingly caressed the mahogany wood. The bunkhouse went silent and William sat down and gently strummed each string to check their tone.

"Any requests?" William asked as he strummed random chords.

"What's the name o' that one hymn yer always playing?" Peter asked. "Something about lilies and friends and things like that."

"'The Lily of the Valley,'" William replied as he plucked out the first few notes. He hummed along with the tune for the first verse.

"Could you sing the words while you play?" Flynn asked.

William nodded and in his quiet baritone voice, sang along.

I've found a friend in Jesus, He's everything to me,
He's the fairest of ten thousand to my soul;
The Lily of the Valley, in Him alone I see
All I need to cleanse and make me fully whole.
In sorrow He's my comfort, in trouble He's my
stay;
He tells me every care on Him to roll.

He's the Lily of the Valley,

the Bright and Morning Star,
He's the fairest of ten thousand to my soul.

He all my grief has taken, and all my sorrows
borne;
In temptation He's my strong and mighty tow'r;
I've all for Him forsaken, and all my idols torn
From my heart and now He keeps me by His
pow'r.
Though all the world forsake me,
and Satan tempt me sore,
Through Jesus I shall safely reach the goal.

He's the Lily of the Valley,
the Bright and Morning Star,
He's the fairest of ten thousand to my soul.

He'll never, never leave me, nor yet forsake me
here,
While I live by faith and do His blessed will;
A wall of fire about me, I've nothing now to fear,
From His manna He my hungry soul shall fill.
Then sweeping up to glory to see His blessed face,
Where rivers of delight shall ever roll.

He's the Lily of the Valley,
the Bright and Morning Star,
He's the fairest of ten thousand to my soul.

When he finished the last verse, Peter snored softly and Flynn and Wyatt looked about ready to fall over in their chairs. William smiled and put his guitar in the case. He would always be amazed how music affected people.

"Good night, y'all," William said in a loud whisper. He had drawn the straw for the first night watch, so he pulled on his coat and stretched as he walked to the door.

"Stay safe out there," Wyatt called.

William raised a hand in acknowledgement and stepped into the cool night. As he saddled his horse, he knew tonight would be a long night of prayer.

He had always wanted to marry and had chosen to wait for God to tell him when His timing was right. During his last night watch almost a week ago, God had laid the desire on his heart stronger than ever before. He wanted to have a wife he could talk to and who would understand him even when he couldn't find the words to say what he meant or wanted to. The other ranch hands and his boss were good friends, but not like he envisioned a wife being.

William swung into the saddle and started his long ride around the pasture. With a sigh, he tried to think of the few Christian women in the area. Ruth and Annabelle were the only young women of marriageable age who weren't already engaged or married. Of the two, Ruth was the only one ready to be married. Annabelle was too flighty. Though, she did seem to be changing for the better.

"Heavenly Father, I'm sure You already know what I'm gonna say. I need Your wisdom. I want to get married and start a family, Lord, and I know You want this for me as well. But who am I supposed to marry?

"Ruth is...well, Ruth is a great friend. And she's also my boss's daughter. Isn't there some kind of law against that? Maybe not, but somehow it still seems wrong to ask her to court a simple ranch hand who may never own his own spread. I know she wouldn't care, but it still doesn't seem right. And I'm not really sure we could be more than just good friends, anyway.

"The only other young lady in the area that I know of is Annabelle. She's certainly grown up the last couple years, but she's still infatuated with Joshua and she has a lot of spiritual growing she needs to do before she can really be a good wife to anybody. Would she even want to marry a simple ranch hand? She seems like a city girl with expensive tastes."

He looked up at the stars. "'O Lord, our Lord, how excellent is Thy name in all the earth! who hast set Thy glory above the heavens. Out of the mouth of babes and sucklings hast Thou ordained strength because of Thine enemies, that Thou mightest still the enemy and the avenger. When I consider Thy heavens, the work of Thy fingers, the moon and the stars, which Thou hast ordained; What is man, that Thou art mindful of him? And the son of man, that Thou visitest him?'

"Why are You so mindful of us, Lord? We are but sinful creatures who spite You and use You for our own gain. We forget to give You the praise when You do something for us. We are miserable creatures whom You have decided to bless for some reason I have yet to understand. Lord, what am I to do?"

His horse snorted and William chuckled. "Tired of me talkin', Ol' Boy? How does singing sound to you instead?" The horse moved his head up and down in a horse version of a nod. "All right, let me think of a song to sing. How about the one I've got stuck in my head and happens to be Ruth's favorite?"

William lifted his eyes to the stars again and sang the hymn he'd just finished singing. He spent the rest of his watch singing hymns of praise to his Savior.

As he rode back to the bunkhouse for some much needed sleep, he realized he still didn't have an answer to which young lady to court. All he had was peace, and although it was a blessed relief, it wasn't exactly what he was looking for. He settled into his bunk and his last thoughts were of stars, Ruth, and Annabelle. Those thoughts might have had something to do with his strange dream in which Ruth and Annabelle floated with him among the stars and he had to figure out who to marry. He awoke before he found out which young lady he chose.

A few hundred miles away, Joshua Brookings lay outside under the stars, trying to sleep. When he couldn't, he asked God whom he was supposed to pray for. As soon as he did, an image first of Ruth, then later Annabelle, and finally William popped into his mind.

"God, I'm not sure why, but I can't sleep. You seem to want me to pray for Ruth and her two friends. I don't know what to pray, so I pray they will follow Your paths and that You will lead them where they are supposed to go. Help them as they continue to grow in their relationships with You."

Joshua sighed. "Help Ruth as she teaches those children. And for Annabelle, I pray she will see what she needs to change in her life and that You will give her the grace she needs to change them. I pray for William, that he will stay strong in his faith in You and not stray in his path. And since

I'm praying, Lord, could you please help me find this outlaw and the little boy he kidnapped? And please keep me safe while I do so. In Jesus' name I pray, amen."

He took a deep breath and rolled onto his side, stirred up the fire, and put another piece of wood on. When the fire was tended to, he covered himself with his blanket and closed his eyes.

October 28, 1879
Dear Diary,

It's been three weeks now. Harvest time is almost over and I'll soon have the older children to teach as well. Will they be good or bad influences on the rest of the children? Time will tell, I guess.

I'm really having problems. My priorities are mixed up. When I get up, I do my school prep, eat breakfast, and then if I have time, I do my personal devotions. I'm telling you this because then I'll have really admitted it. My prayer is that this will change by the next time I write.

I hereby resolve to do my school prep last in the mornings and put God first. Lord, I need You to be my scheduler. I can't do it on my own. Between devotions, school, school prep, keeping the house clean, and having Bible study with Annabelle, I feel like I have too much to do. Direct my paths, Lord. If there is something I should not be doing, let me know somehow what it is. Thank You for always being there for me. Especially when Grover Miller was at the schoolhouse. Thank You for sending Paul in at just the right time.

Well, it's time for me to get some sleep. Good night.

CHAPTER FOUR

William knew Ruth wouldn't be home until the next evening, but he still felt like his heart was trying to hammer through his chest. He wiped his sweaty palms against his denim pants as he stepped onto the porch and knocked on the front door.

As he waited, he turned to look up at the stars. One thing he loved about autumn was how clear the stars showed up in the frosty air.

"Good evening, William," Mrs. Brookings greeted. "Do you need something?"

William spun around. "Um, I was wondering if I could speak with Mr. Brookings."

Harriet smiled. "Of course. Come in. You can go into his office. He'll be glad for the interruption. He's working on the accounts and you know how much he dislikes working with numbers."

William smiled. "That's why Joshua always did them."

Harriet sighed. "Yes, but Joshua's not home often enough to save Daniel the trouble and Ruth is too busy now."

William shrugged. "I'm sure he'll do fine."

Harriet reached up and rubbed William's shoulder. "He's in there."

"Thank you, Ma'am." William tipped his hat at her.

"You're welcome."

William knocked on the door to the study and waited.

"Come in." The voice on the other side of the door sounded as if it came from between clenched teeth.

William turned the doorknob, took a deep breath, pushed the door open, and stepped inside.

Daniel set his pencil aside and leaned back in the chair, folding his hands behind his head. "What can I do for you, William?"

William took his hat off and spun it around in his hands. He swallowed a few times and took a deep breath. "I came to talk to you about Ruth."

Daniel leaned forward and rested his elbows on the desk. "What about her?"

"I...I was wondering if you would allow me to come calling on her. I know she's only here on weekends and I don't wanna take away from your family time too much..." his voice trailed off.

Daniel stared at William for a few seconds. "I've been expecting this for some time now."

William looked up sharply. "You have?"

"You two are really close and I thought perhaps one of you might have more than brotherly or sisterly feelings toward the other. Why do you want to court her?"

William cleared his throat. "We're good friends and I'd like to see if there's more to it than just that. The Lord has laid on my heart the desire to marry soon and I'm not sure who to marry. The only other person I'd possibly consider is Annabelle and she isn't ready yet."

"So you want to try a courtship with Ruth," Daniel said.

"Yes."

Daniel nodded. "I'll pray about it and when Ruth gets back, I'll talk to her and have her pray about it as well. I'll try to have an answer to you by the end of next week."

William took a deep breath and smiled a little. "Thank you, Sir."

Daniel smiled. "You're welcome, William."

Harriet and Daniel sat at the table, sipping their coffee. "How did the accounts turn out?" Harriet asked.

Daniel grimaced. "The only good thing about the accounts tonight was the interruption I had and the end result. We're still making money. We won't be the richest ranch around since we sell our horses at fair prices, but we won't be destitute either."

Harriet nodded and asked the question she'd been dying to ask all evening, "What did William want?"

Daniel grinned. "You can probably guess. He would like to court Ruth."

"I wondered how long it would take him. You told him yes, didn't you?"

"I told him we would pray about it, especially after we told Ruth."

Harriet blinked her eyes. "Why?"

Daniel sighed and swirled the coffee around in his cup. "I'm not sure Ruth wants one more thing to do right now. If she's willing, I will give my blessing, but I don't think Ruth is the girl for William and William isn't the man for Ruth. They are too much alike and I don't think either of them will ever develop a love for each other besides that of a brother and sister."

"Who else is Ruth supposed to marry? Or William for that matter? It's not like there are many Christian options around here."

"From what William said today, he does have another option and I think he already likes her, he just doesn't think she's ready."

"Who?"

"Annabelle."

Harriet felt her coffee cup slip a little and set it down carefully.

Daniel fought a grin. "The way he talked about Annabelle made me think there's already some feelings between them, but he either doesn't know it or doesn't want to admit it."

"Why do you think she's not ready?"

"I didn't say she isn't, William did."

Harriet nodded. "Sorry, I missed that." She sighed. "I guess we just have to wait and see what Ruth says."

"And pray."

"Yes. Praying is always a good idea."

Daniel made sure he was at home and on the porch when Ruth arrived. "How's my girl?" he asked as he enveloped her in a tight hug.

"Ready to be home for the weekend." She pulled away from him. "I never thought I'd say this, but I miss the noise everybody makes. It's too quiet and dull at that cottage. And I absolutely cannot make food for just one person. Which ended up being a good thing since three of my students can't bring their own lunches and I was able to feed them."

Daniel laughed. "That doesn't surprise me. Have you ever cooked for fewer than five people?"

Ruth raised an eyebrow and cocked her head. "I don't think so."

Daniel smiled and changed the topic. "Sometime tonight we need to talk about something. Do you want to get settled in and see your mother first?"

"And die of curiosity? I don't think so. What is it?"

Daniel sat on the porch swing and patted the seat next to him. When Ruth joined him and snuggled into his shoulder, he continued, "William came to my office yesterday and asked to court you. I didn't give him an answer yet because I want you, your mother, and me to pray about it for a week first."

Ruth drew in a deep breath. "I'll pray about it."

"That's it?" Daniel asked. "That's all you have to say? Do you have any sort of opinion right now?"

Ruth smiled and put her arm around her father's shoulders. "I hadn't ever thought about it, so no. I need to pray about it before I can state an opinion."

Daniel sighed. "I hoped you would have a little bit of a reaction for me."

"Sorry, Pa."

"It's fine." He stretched his legs. "I suppose we should go inside before your ma wonders what happened to us."

"I got another offer of courtship this week."

Caught in the act of standing, Daniel collapsed back onto the swing. "What? Who? And why didn't he ask me?"

"The father of three of my students. Apparently I was the last woman on his list. He doesn't have time to come out here or to go to church, but he has plenty of time to spend in the saloon."

"That's a flattering reason for him to ask you," Daniel stated dryly. "What's his name?"

"Grover Miller. He has a daughter a couple years younger than me who's getting married next week, and he needs a wife to feed him and help him take care of the five younger children."

Daniel raised both of his eyebrows. "I take it you weren't impressed."

"I was in one respect. He actually took a bath and tried to clean up a little before coming to ask. But after I said he should talk to you, he tried to get out of coming here and I finally told him I wouldn't want him to court me anyway."

"Did he still persist?"

"Yes. The Lord certainly took care of me, though. That was the day I brought my extra food for the Hale children and they came in just as I was wondering what Grover would do. The Hales returned my lunch pail and after Grover left, the eldest, Paul, told me he purposely waited until he thought the man had been in the schoolhouse long enough."

Daniel smiled. "How old is Paul?"

"I think he's thirteen."

"Would you thank him for me on Monday?"

"You could thank him at church."

Daniel nodded. "True. If Grover becomes a problem, tell me or Micah and we'll talk to him."

"I will, Pa. Thank you."

"You're welcome, Sweetheart. Now, we really better get inside so your ma can see that you survived another week alone."

Ruth grinned. "Yes, Sir."

54

CHAPTER FIVE

With the first few weeks of school over, Ruth expected the next week or more to be a trial. The children were now comfortable with her and could start testing her limits.

During the time when Ruth worked with the youngest students on their reading and the older students did their assigned math problems, Ruth heard a suspicious noise and looked toward the back of the room.

"Jeremiah Carson!" Ruth said sharply.

Jeremiah flinched and looked at Ruth. "Yes, Miss Brookings?"

"What do you have in your hand?"

"Nothin'."

Ruth stood up, a stern look on her face. "Open it," she demanded as she approached him. The eyes of all the students were on the two of them.

Jeremiah opened his hand and a large frog blinked at her. Ruth forced herself to hold her ground while the girls closest to Jeremiah screeched and moved away from the frog.

Ruth put her right hand on her hip and pointed toward the door with her other hand. "Get it outside right now. And get back in here as soon as it is."

Jeremiah tried to keep the grin off his face. "Yes, Ma'am."

The rest of the morning went as smoothly as it could after the rude interruption. During lunch, however, a scream from outside sent Ruth racing out the door.

One of the girls' lunch pails was on the ground and a very unhappy frog hopped away from the pail. Ruth locked eyes with the laughing Jeremiah and she marched out to him. Jeremiah looked around trying to find a place to hide, but he was surrounded by his friends. Jeremiah tried to get their attention, but by the time he did, Ruth had gently moved John out of the way. She grabbed Jeremiah by the ear and pulled him out of his group of friends.

"What was that for?" Jeremiah asked when Ruth let go of his ear. He rubbed the ear and glared at her.

Ruth kept her stern gaze on Jeremiah's face. "Did you put the frog outside when I told you to?"

Jeremiah swallowed hard. "No, Ma'am."

"Why not?"

"I thought it would be more fun..."

"More fun?" Ruth interrupted. "More fun to scare a girl half to death and ruin her lunch?" She put her hands on her hips and closed her eyes. "Have you eaten your lunch yet, Jeremiah?" She looked into his face.

Jeremiah's eyes grew wide. "No..."

Ruth looked around. "Go get your lunch and give it to Grace right now. And I will be watching you the entire time. When you give her the lunch, apologize to her and make it sincere. Then come with me to the schoolhouse and sit in the first row with a desk. When I'm ready, I'll talk to you and figure out how else I should punish you."

As Jeremiah walked to the pail next to Clem's feet, his stomach grumbled and he scowled. A whole day without lunch. He gave his lunch pail to Grace and mumbled an apology, then trudged next to Ruth back to the schoolhouse. Once inside, he chose the front row desk farthest from Ruth.

Ruth slowly finished her lunch and read some of the essays the children had turned in. When she got to Jeremiah's, she picked up the piece of paper and flipped it over. She glanced at Jeremiah and saw him picking at a scratch in the desktop. She looked back at the piece of paper and set it aside.

After finishing the last of the essays, Ruth stood up, picked up Jeremiah's essay, and sat in the desk next to him. "Can you explain your behavior this morning?"

Jeremiah shrugged. "No."

"So you have no idea why you brought the frog inside or ruined Grace's lunch?"

"I wanted to."

"Why?"

Jeremiah grunted and crossed his arms. "Grace is annoying. She's always acting like she's better'n everybody else."

Ruth tapped her fingers on the desk. "Who made you the judge of that?"

Jeremiah wrinkled his nose, but didn't answer.

Ruth sighed. She would have to talk with his father about this and let him deal with it. "And how do you explain this?" She held the paper with his name on it.

"It's invisible ink."

"Even invisible ink leaves indentations, Jeremiah." Ruth sighed. "You will stay here after school and sit in your desk writing your essay as well as a note to give to Grace tomorrow. The note will have an apology and also say three nice things about her. And make sure those nice things are things she would think are nice."

Jeremiah looked up at Ruth with wide eyes. "Miss Brookings, please..."

Ruth held up her hand. "No, Jeremiah. You are not getting away with this. I will also have a talk with your pa this afternoon. When your essay and note are finished, we will both walk down to the sheriff's office together."

"Miss Brookings..."

"Nothing you say will deter me from this punishment."

"But I had plans to study with Clem and Chancy."

"You'll have to do it another time," Ruth replied as she stood up. "Go ring the bell, please."

Jeremiah bowed his head and obeyed in sullen rebellion.

The remainder of the school day went by without incident and when the other children were dismissed, Jeremiah pulled out his blank essay paper and started scribbling furiously. Ruth sorted her desk and stacked everything for easy grabbing. Then she read through each essay again, making suggestions and corrections to each.

"Done," Jeremiah announced five minutes later.

"Bring them both up here, please," Ruth said without looking up. She finished reading an essay before looking at him and taking the two pieces of paper from him. She scanned the page Jeremiah handed her. After a minute, she handed the essay back to him. "Read it out loud to me, please."

Jeremiah cleared his throat and opened his mouth. He tilted his head and closed his mouth, staring at the page for a few seconds. "Do you have another piece of paper?"

Ruth bit her cheeks to keep the smile off her face and opened the drawer to her left. She pulled out a piece of paper and handed it to him.

Jeremiah took it and sulked back to his desk, writing more carefully this time.

While he rewrote the essay, Ruth read the note to Grace and smiled. At least he'd taken more time with this. When Jeremiah came back a few minutes later, Ruth handed him the note.

"This is very well done. You can give it to her tomorrow." Ruth picked up the new essay and read it. "This is much better. Thank you, Jeremiah." She placed it on her stack and picked up the stack.

"I'll carry the books, Miss Brookings."

"Thank you. We're going to stop by the cottage before heading to the sheriff's office."

Jeremiah sighed. "Do you have to talk to Pa?"

"Yes, I do," Ruth answered.

Jeremiah's shoulders slumped and he walked toward the door. When they were both outside, Ruth locked the schoolhouse.

After putting her school items on the kitchen table at the house, Ruth and Jeremiah walked toward the sheriff's office.

Jeremiah dragged his feet the closer they got and stuck his hands deep in his pockets. Ruth ignored the disgruntled boy at her side and marched into Micah's office.

"Mr. Carson, are you in here?" Ruth asked.

Micah came in from the cell area. "Miss Brookings, Jeremiah. What a pleasant surprise!" His eyes narrowed when he saw the dejected look on Jeremiah's face. "Or is it going to be pleasant?"

Ruth shook her head. "I'm afraid this is not a leisure visit."

Micah dropped into the chair behind his desk. "What did you do now, Jeremiah?"

Jeremiah shrugged. "Just brought a frog to school."

Micah cleared his throat. "Was it a day when you could bring something like that to school?"

Jeremiah shook his head.

"And did you scare some of the girls?"

Jeremiah nodded. "A little. But not as bad as when Grace opened her lunch pail."

Micah closed his eyes. "Why?"

Jeremiah stood up straight. "Miss Brookings told me to put the frog outside, so I brought it out of the schoolroom and put it in Grace's lunch pail. Can I go home, Pa? I'm almighty hungry."

Micah leaned his elbows on the desk and looked from his son to Ruth and back again. "Is there a reason you're so hungry?"

"Miss Brookings made me give my lunch to Grace."

Micah fought a smile. "Good. You may not go get something to eat. You won't eat anything until dinnertime and if I hear even one complaint, I won't let you eat supper either. I raised you to be more of a gentleman than this. You should treat girls and women with respect and gentleness. That means no frogs or bugs or anything like that. You will sit in that chair," he pointed to the chair across the desk from him, "until I am ready to go home with you and then you and I will visit the woodshed."

Jeremiah glared at his father, but stomped to the chair and sat down.

Micah turned his attention back to Ruth. "Is that all he did?"

"I think so," Ruth replied. "But I would like to talk to you if I can."

Micah nodded. "Go ahead."

Ruth looked at Jeremiah, debating whether to bring the conversation up in front of the boy. "I admire the way you have raised Jeremiah so far and your desire to teach him to be a gentleman. However, there is something lacking."

Micah grimaced. "I am not getting remarried. I've done fine so far."

Ruth shook her head. "I agree. To a point. Today was a good example of that. Jeremiah can be a perfect gentleman when he wants to be and when he thinks about it. But he is also only ten. He needs an example, not just instructions. The best way for him to have an example, and to practice, is if you have a wife and he has a mother. Plus, his mother would hopefully be able to help curb some of his wild behavior and soften some of the rough spots in his character."

Ruth held up a hand before Micah could interrupt her. "Don't answer now. Just give it some thought and a lot of prayer. I don't expect you to go out and ask to court the first girl who walks past this office. Just pray about it." She took a deep breath. "You and Jeremiah will continue to be in my prayers."

Micah opened and closed his mouth a few times and Jeremiah took the opportunity to cut into the conversation. "I don't want just anybody for a ma."

Micah looked at his son. "I think that will be my decision, Son, not yours. You can pray about it, but I'll make the decision. If I decide to marry at all."

Jeremiah ducked his head and Micah turned his attention back to Ruth. "I'll think and pray about it. By the way, I like the way you disciplined Jeremiah today."

Ruth grinned. "You only heard part of it. I also kept him in from the rest of lunch and made him stay after school to finish the essay he didn't write, but had turned in. He also wrote a note of apology to Grace with three things he likes about her."

Micah chuckled. "Yep, I like the way you handled it. Thank you for being such a caring teacher and for talking to me about it. I'll have a good talk with him tonight."

Ruth nodded. "Thank you. And thank you for praying about a wife. Please try to be open to God's leading and not just go by what you would prefer."

Micah bit his lip. "You know me too well."

Ruth laughed. "No I don't. I know you just well enough. Talk to you later, Mr. Carson." She turned toward the door and waved at Jeremiah. "See you tomorrow, Jeremiah."

Jeremiah huffed and crossed his arms.

"Goodbye, Miss Brookings," Micah called. "Stay safe."

Ruth turned her head toward him and grinned. "Isn't that what you're here for?" she teased.

Micah tilted his head back and laughed, the sound filling the small room.

CHAPTER SIX

After tucking Jeremiah into bed, Micah left on his nightly round through the town. He went the opposite way he usually did. Instead of starting near the schoolhouse, he ended there.

"God," he prayed as he started his patrol, "keep Ruth safe tonight, from both human beings as well as from bad dreams. Thank you for sending her into my life." As he walked, he kept a sharp eye out for anything illegal. "Ruth has been such a help and encouragement these last two years, but especially since Joshua left."

Micah sighed. "I just don't know what to think about what she said today. Get married? If I ever get married again—and that's a big if—I want to marry for love. There are maybe three women who go to church who aren't already married. One of them has five children and the other two are at least ten years younger than me. Is marriage really something you want me to consider, Lord? I just don't know what to do here."

For the rest of his stroll around town, Micah waited and listened for God's leading. As he approached the cottage Ruth lived in, he paused. "Lord, I know You order our footsteps. Please guide me."

As he climbed under his blankets a few minutes later, he realized his prayer would take a long time to get a real answer. "Heavenly Father, if You want me to get married, give me the desire for marriage and the desire to love someone. I know I could write a mail order bride, but I really don't think that would work for me."

He rolled over to his side and closed his eyes.

There were no more incidents at school that week and Ruth was thankful for that. After spending a half hour in prayer and personal Bible study in the morning, preparing for and doing Bible study with Annabelle, plus teaching and trying not to get worried while living by herself, Ruth felt too pressured to concentrate on punishing any of the children.

When Friday morning rolled around, Ruth suddenly remembered she was supposed to have an answer for her pa today about William. As she prayed before school, she knew what the answer had to be. The brisk air cooled her off without being too cold and the sun shone brightly. As she walked to school, she knew everybody, including herself, would be anxious to be outside. After almost an hour in the afternoon of not learning anything, Ruth dismissed school an hour early. She scurried around the schoolroom, straightening everything up for church on Sunday, when all she really wanted to do was run home to be with her parents.

As she locked the door, someone cleared his throat behind her. Ruth turned around, trying not to look as impatient as she felt. When she saw Mr. Miller, her heart sank. "What would you like, Mr. Miller?"

"Have you considered my proposal?" he asked.

"I have and I told you my answer last week."

"But Miss Brookings, the kids and I are starving. With Samantha gone, we don't have anybody to cook for us except Olive."

"So eat at the café or learn how to cook."

Grover grinned. "Would you teach me?"

"No," Ruth said abruptly. "If you want to learn how to cook, ask Micah Carson or the cook at the café. Now if you'll excuse me, I need to go home."

"May I escort you home, Miss Brookings?"

Ruth glared at him. "No, you may not. You wouldn't make it that far."

Grover scratched the stubble on his cheek. "Don't you live in the cottage over there?"

"Only during the week. On the weekends I go to my parents' ranch." Ruth straightened her back and marched down the steps, trying not to brush against the man as she walked past him.

She got to the bottom step before he grabbed her upper arm. "Please, Miss Brookings?"

"How many times do I have to tell you?" Ruth asked, trying to get her arm out of his grasp. "The answer is no and it will continue to be no, no matter how many times you ask or how often you ask it. I won't give you cooking lessons, I won't let you escort me home, and I certainly will not marry you. Now let go of me or I will scream and..."

"You heard the lady," another male voice cut in. "Let her go right now, or I will arrest you for assault."

"A-what?" Grover asked.

"Assault. It would land you in a prison yard for a good, long time," Micah said in a dry voice.

Grover let go of Ruth's arm as if it had suddenly become too hot to touch.

"Thank you," Micah said. "If I ever see you coming near the schoolhouse again when school is in session, I'll have you arrested and locked away for as long as I possibly can." He turned to Ruth. "Are you all right?"

Ruth took in a shaky breath. "Now that you are here, yes."

Micah smiled. "Go on home. I'll make sure Mr. Miller stays here."

"Thank you, Sheriff."

"You're welcome, Miss Brookings."

Ruth quickly gathered what she needed from the cottage, then hurried home. She knew Micah would keep his word, but she didn't want to risk Grover catching up to her. Hopefully with Micah's threat, Grover would leave her alone now.

When she reached Double B Bar Ranch land, she breathed deeply and ran the rest of the way to the house. This time, Harriet sat on the porch waiting for her.

Ruth ran straight into her arms and gave her a big hug. "It's good to be home, Ma."

Harriet kissed the top of Ruth's head. "It's good to have you back."

"I wish the ranch was closer to town so I could stay here instead..."

Harriet pulled her closer. "I know, Sweetheart. So do I."

Ruth tried to hold back the tears, but the worry, exhaustion, and events of the week suddenly crashed down on her and she sobbed into her mother's shoulder. Harriet gently led her to the porch swing and sat down.

"Shh, shh, Ruthie. What's the matter?"

After two minutes, Ruth pulled back and wiped her cheeks. "Is Pa inside?"

Harriet nodded.

"Can we go inside and I'll tell you both?"

Harriet and Ruth walked into the house and to the study.

"Ruthie's back!" Daniel exclaimed. He jumped up from his chair and came around his desk. "You've been crying." He glanced between Ruth and Harriet. "What's going on?"

Harriet shrugged. "I don't know; she wanted to tell both of us."

Ruth sank into a chair and her parents also sat down. "I told you about the Bible studies with Annabelle, right?"

"Yes," Harriet said.

"Those are going very well and I enjoy having an adult to talk to every day. But the Bible study is pretty much the only thing that's gone well this week. With the warm weather, the children aren't behaving well. Then Jeremiah exacerbated the problem when he brought a frog into school. I told him to put it outside and thought he had. At lunch, I found out otherwise. Do you remember Grace Johnson?"

Daniel and Harriet nodded.

"Jeremiah put the frog in her lunch pail."

Harriet gasped and held back a laugh. "I can imagine how that went over."

70

Ruth grimaced. "I made Jeremiah come inside for the rest of lunch and give his lunch to Grace. The essay he'd written that morning was blank, so he also got to stay after school and rewrite it." Ruth sighed. "After he was finished with that, we went to the sheriff's office to talk to Micah. Jeremiah told Micah what he'd done and I confirmed it. I also challenged Micah to pray about getting married. I truly believe Jeremiah would behave better if he had a mother. Ever since that talk, I haven't seen or heard from Micah until today and that was only because he was doing his job."

"Why is that such a worry?" Harriet asked.

Ruth shrugged. "He usually talked to me at least once a day in either a note or stopping by to make sure I'm doing fine."

"What day did you challenge him?" Daniel asked.

"Monday."

Daniel raised an eyebrow. "And he didn't stop by at all?"

Ruth shook her head.

"Hm. Why did you talk to him today?"

Ruth closed her eyes and took a deep breath. "Grover came over again. I dismissed school an hour early and he came by just as I locked up the school. He wanted to know if I had reconsidered.

When I told him no again and tried to walk past him, he grabbed my arm."

Daniel stood up, a fierce expression on his face. "What?"

Ruth smiled sadly. "Micah came by just then and told him to let me go and warned him not to come near the schoolhouse or he'd get arrested. I came home as fast as I could after that." Ruth hugged herself. "It's all been too much for me this week. I want to be able to spend more time in prayer because they all need so much prayer, but I have less than a half hour each morning and even then I feel rushed after I'm done."

"Do you think Micah's warning will keep Grover away from you?" Daniel asked.

"I hope so. If not, I'll tell you."

"You're sure?"

Ruth drew in a deep breath. "Yes."

Harriet stood up and moved behind Ruth to massage her shoulders. "I don't like it."

Daniel sighed. "I don't either, but what can we do?"

"Nothing," Ruth said. She took a deep breath. "About William. I'm flattered by his request, but I can't do it. I need to concentrate on my walk with God, helping Annabelle, and teaching. Adding a suitor right now would be too much." She looked up with a smile. "And Annabelle is in love with him, or at least close."

Daniel fought a smile. "Did she tell you that?"

Ruth shrugged. "Kind of. That's one reason she wanted to do the Bible study. She really wants to change and needed encouragement to do so."

Daniel looked up. "I'll tell him tonight."

"Am I making the right decision?" Ruth asked.

Daniel smiled at her. "I think so. If you had chosen to have him court you, I would have supported you, but I'm glad you decided not to. I love William like a son, but you two are too similar."

Ruth sighed. "I just hope he's not the only man left in this town who would marry me. When I told Annabelle about William, she was jealous at first, but when I told her I planned to say no, she thought I was crazy. Apparently, I'm already an old maid and should have jumped at the chance."

"Don't let what other people say influence you, unless they're your parents," Harriet chuckled. "You don't want to marry the wrong man. If God wants you to be married, you will get married in His timing. Look at Anna. She didn't get married until she was thirty and is glad she waited."

Ruth nodded. "I know. It's just hard. And I don't want to disappoint William, either." She looked up at Daniel. "Make sure he knows it's nothing against him. I think he is a wonderful friend and substitute brother."

Daniel nodded. "I will."

Harriet stopped massaging Ruth's shoulders. "Would you like to help me make supper?"

Ruth looked up, glanced over her shoulder, and smiled. "Yes, I would."

Harriet and Ruth left Daniel to his paperwork. Before he continued, Daniel laid his head on the desk. "Lord, help me when I talk to William. And, Father, I need wisdom about what to do with Grover. Right now, all I want to do is go over there and threaten him, but I know that wouldn't be the right thing to do." He sighed. "Give me patience, Lord."

CHAPTER SEVEN

"You wanted to see me, Mr. Brookings?" William asked.

"Have a seat, William," Daniel said. When William had settled into the chair across the desk from him, Daniel cleared his throat. "After much prayer, thought, and discussion with Ruth and Harriet, I have decided not to allow you to court Ruth." He raised his hand. "Please hear me out before reacting.

"There is nothing wrong with you. I would personally love having you as a son-in-law. If I had another unmarried daughter besides Ruth, I would gladly let you court her. However, I don't think you would accomplish anything during a courtship.

"You will make someone a wonderful husband someday, of that I am sure. However, your bride will not be Ruth. You and Ruth are too similar and would never survive a marriage together. Unless I am mistaken, there is someone else in the area you already have feelings for, but you are either afraid to admit it, or you don't realize it."

William swallowed and drew in a deep breath. "Thank you, Mr. Brookings. You're right about Ruth and me being too similar. I knew that even before I asked. I...well, to be honest, I don't really know why I asked."

Daniel smiled. "I'm guessing you wanted to know for sure that this door was closed."

William nodded. "Probably. As for what you said about someone else, I don't know if you're right there or not. I guess I'll keep praying."

"Harriet, Ruth, and I are also praying for you. And if you ever want to talk about anything, I'm always available to you to either listen or give advice. Especially if I'm in the middle of book work."

William smiled. "Thank you, Sir." He bowed his head for a few seconds before meeting Daniel's gaze. "Can I talk to Ruth for a couple minutes?"

Daniel nodded. "She's in the kitchen."

William strode out of the office and into the kitchen. Harriet was nowhere in sight. "Ruth?"

Ruth spun around, a worried look on her face. "Hi, William."

William walked around the table until he faced her from a few feet away. "Thank you for saying no."

Ruth let out the breath she'd been holding and a tentative smile tickled her mouth. "You aren't upset or hurt, are you?"

William shook his head. "No, I'm not."

"Are you sure?"

William nodded and waited until Ruth looked up at him. "I'm sure. I knew before I even asked we probably wouldn't ever be anything more than brother and sister." He let go of her and Ruth smiled.

"Good. We can continue to be friends, right?"

William chuckled. "I don't know what I'd do if I lost my friend."

Ruth grinned. "And when you find your bride, I'll be right here praising God."

William nodded. "I'd like that. And when your groom comes, I'll be here making sure he treats you right, too."

"While we wait, would you like to help me finish the dishes?"

William looked from her teasing face to the counter and back again, then shrugged. "Why not?"

On Sunday, Ruth walked to church with her parents. It was their turn to open up the schoolhouse for church and make sure the fire was lit if it needed to be. She chose to wait outside while her pa went in to light the fire. She had only waited a few minutes when she saw Annabelle coming toward the schoolhouse and rushed to meet her.

After a quick hug, Annabelle raised an eyebrow. "How did William take it?"

Ruth smiled. "Very well. He was very gracious and we're still friends."

"I still think you're crazy to turn him down."

"He and I both knew it wouldn't work for us to get married anyway," Ruth answered.

"Then why did he ask?"

Ruth shrugged. "He didn't tell me."

A group of horses bearing riders came into view. Annabelle grabbed Ruth's arm. "Here he comes! And we're all alone."

Ruth shook her head and shrugged Annabelle's hand off her arm. "You'll be fine. Remember what we learned this week in Bible study?"

Annabelle took a deep breath and let it out. "'Be anxious for nothing, but in everything by prayer and supplication with thanksgiving let your requests be made known to God. And the peace of God, which passeth all understanding, shall keep your hearts and minds through Christ Jesus.' Philippians 4:6-7."

"Exactly!" Ruth exclaimed. "I'm proud of you for getting that memorized. Now you just have to put it into practice."

Annabelle groaned. "I know. That's where I have the most trouble—remembering the things I learn."

"What's two plus two?" Ruth asked.

"Four," Annabelle responded, her face scrunched up in confusion.

"Who was the fourth president?"

"James Madison. What are you doing, Ruth?"

"What do they call the study of rocks?"

"Geology," Annabelle responded. "What purpose does this quiz serve?"

Ruth smiled. "One more question. What is Genesis 1:1?"

"'In the beginning God created the heaven and the earth.'"

Ruth nodded. "Repetition is the key. You remember things better than you think, you just need to keep repeating them until it becomes natural."

"I can attest to that," William cut in. "Mornin', Ladies."

Ruth turned and smiled at him. "Good morning, William."

"Good morning," Annabelle parroted.

"How are you two lovely ladies this fine morning?"

"I'm doing very well, thank you," Annabelle replied.

"Besides not wanting to go back to the schoolteacher's house this evening, I'm doing just fine," Ruth answered.

William frowned. "Why don't you want to go there?"

"I miss my family and the ranch hands," Ruth replied. "And do you know how hard it is to cook for just one person?"

"Don't you have one of them fancy iceboxes?" William asked.

"Yes, but it doesn't work very well and when I make something, even when I try to keep it small, I still make more than I need for the week."

"Hm," William responded. "Do you feel safe there?"

"No, she doesn't," Annabelle said. "She keeps the door locked even when she knows I'm coming over."

Ruth looked down at her feet. "I'm just overly nervous. I know Micah and Obadiah will keep me safe, but I still feel too cautious."

Daniel approached them. "You aren't too cautious, Ruth. I'm glad you keep the door locked." He looked at William. "Can I get your help moving the desks?"

"Yes, Sir. I'd be glad to help."

As they walked away, Annabelle opened her mouth to say something, but another voice spoke first. "Good morning, Miss Brookings and Miss Wilson."

Ruth and Annabelle looked over at the two people who had come up to them. "Good morning, Mr. Carson and Jeremiah," Ruth said.

Annabelle nodded to them.

"Can I go play, Pa?" Jeremiah asked.

Micah looked around the yard. "Just don't get dirty."

Jeremiah rolled his eyes and ran off to join John, James, Clem, and Chancy.

Ruth watched as he got the other four boys into a huddle and they had an animated discussion about something. She wrinkled her eyebrows when Clem and Chancy both turned their heads to look in their direction.

"Ruth?" Annabelle asked, nudging her.

"Huh?" Ruth started.

"Mr. Carson just asked you a question. Where were you?"

Ruth looked at the group of boys again and then back to Annabelle and Micah, her cheeks warming. "Sorry, I was watching the boys. They look like they're up to something."

Micah chuckled. "That's all right, Miss Brookings. I saw the powwow, too, and have my own concerns about what it means. What I asked wasn't important and it appears to be time for church now."

Ruth's cheeks grew warmer. "I'm sorry I didn't pay attention to what you were saying."

Micah waved his hand as they headed for the door. "Like I said, it wasn't important."

Ruth nodded as they made their way up the steps.

CHAPTER EIGHT

"There's the line cabin," Flynn said.

"Mmhm," William replied.

"You've been awfully quiet on this ride," Flynn mentioned.

William glanced up. "I'm sorry."

Flynn laughed. "Don't be. It's just strange."

"I'm usually quiet, aren't I?"

Flynn nodded. "I suppose, but you usually at least sing or something on long rides."

William's face grew warm. "I didn't realize anybody heard me."

Flynn smiled. "We do. So...whatcha been thinkin' about?"

"How best to word the question I want to ask you."

Flynn raised an eyebrow as he jumped off his horse. "Does it matter how it's worded?"

William dismounted. "I suppose not."

"What's the question?"

"I know you've listened to a lot of what Mr. Brookings has said and I guess I'm just curious if you've accepted Jesus' gift yet?"

Flynn leaned against the rickety fence. "Not yet." He straightened quickly and looked at the sky. "If we want to finish and get back before supper, we'd better get to work."

William nodded. "Can we talk while we work?"

Flynn frowned. "I suppose."

William took the hammers and nails out of his saddlebags. "Why haven't you accepted His gift?"

Flynn shrugged. "Don't see the need to."

William inspected the steps for loose boards before stepping on them. "Why not?"

"I've done more good than bad. God'll see that."

William motioned to the door hinges and Flynn tested them.

"The hinges are all right," Flynn said.

William nodded. "Doing good things won't get you to heaven."

"Why not?"

"No sin can enter heaven. If you have even one sin to your name, you can't enter heaven. Only through the washing of Jesus' blood can you be saved."

Flynn took an offered nail and pounded it into the doorframe. "The boss has said that before."

"Then why do you still think your good things can get you into heaven?"

Flynn shrugged. "I just never thought it was that important. I figured I'd do something about it on my deathbed."

William sucked in a breath and turned the doorknob. "Let's see what's in here..." He paused. "Wait a minute. What would happen if an angry grizzly bear charged out of this cabin when we opened the door, ran straight for you, and killed you before you had a chance to do anything, including repent?"

Flynn's eyes went wide. "I don't know."

"Where would you go if that happened?"

Flynn gulped. "Hell."

William nodded. "Doesn't that scare you?"

"A little."

William pushed the door open. "None of us can guarantee we'll have a chance to make a deathbed confession." He nodded to the pack horse. "I'll check the cabin and start sweeping while you get the supplies."

Half an hour later, the cabin was clean and the supplies all organized in the cupboards. As they swung into their saddles, William gave Flynn a searching gaze. "Going back to the grizzly bear scenario, let's change it some. What if the bear charged out of the cabin, but I jumped in front of you and I was killed? Because of the time it took the bear to kill me, you got your rifle and shot it before it could kill you. What would you think of me?"

Flynn jabbed his heels into his horse's sides and trotted alongside William. "I'd mourn your loss and thank you every day for saving my life."

"Jesus Christ died in your place on the cross. Shouldn't you do the same for Him?"

William spurred his horse into a canter, leaving Flynn to his thoughts while he prayed for him.

November was almost over before Ruth began to feel like she could finally breathe again. The children at school behaved for the most part, the Bible study with Annabelle continued to be productive, Grover had stayed away from her so far, and her relationship with God had strengthened.

The only thing that concerned her was Jeremiah's growing rebellious streak. She didn't know what to do about it except tell Micah and he had avoided her at all costs for almost a month.

After school, she asked Jeremiah to tell his father she needed to speak with him. Jeremiah grudgingly agreed to pass it on.

Later that evening, a knock at the door interrupted her Bible study with Annabelle.

"I'm sorry, Annabelle. I asked Jeremiah to tell Micah to come talk to me as soon as he could," Ruth apologized.

Annabelle smiled. "That's fine. I need to think about the last question you asked anyway."

Ruth grinned, walked to the door, and grabbed her shawl. "Good evening, Micah," she said as she opened the door.

Micah frowned. "I'm interrupting something, aren't I?"

"Your coming gives me time to think guilt-free," Annabelle called.

Micah shrugged and stepped back so Ruth could step out onto the porch.

"What is it this time?" Micah asked as he crossed his arms.

Ruth took a step to the side to get a better look at him in the moonlight. "You look as rebellious as your son."

"What do you mean by that?"

Ruth breathed in. "Jeremiah is doing well learning what he needs to at school, but his whole attitude has changed slowly ever since the day I made him stay after school and challenged you. Now after seeing you for the first time in almost a month, I think I know why. What's the matter,

Micah? Why haven't you been to church? Why are you avoiding me? And why are you ignoring your son?"

Micah's head snapped up. "How did you know?"

Ruth shrugged. "About you ignoring your son? It was a guess. The rest of it could have been observed by pretty much anybody."

Micah scowled. "It's none of your business."

Ruth crossed her arms. "When it affects one of my students, I think it is. I have also considered you a friend for over two years and consider one of the duties of a friend to be pointing out error when I see it. Do you want to know what I see?"

"No, but that's not gonna stop you, is it?"

Ruth smiled. "Not this time." She took a deep breath. "I see a man who is fighting God because he doesn't want to do what God is leading him to do. I see a man whose rebellion against God has affected his son's behavior and attitude. As Jeremiah's schoolteacher, I will let his silent rebellion slide for now, but if it becomes worse, I'll have to ask Pa to talk to you." She sighed. "Micah, you are a dear friend and I have missed talking to you the last month. I don't like seeing you like this and I certainly don't like telling you this. You know me well enough to know that I hate confrontation, but..." her voice trailed off. "I couldn't let this slide."

She swallowed the lump in her throat and watched Micah put a mask of rebellion and impassivity on his face. "Good night, Micah. Annabelle and I will pray for you and Jeremiah, and as soon as I get back to the ranch, I'll be asking my parents to pray for you more as well." Ruth glided quietly into the house leaving Micah behind with his thoughts.

With a heavy heart, she sank into her chair. "We need to pray for Micah and Jeremiah tonight."

Annabelle looked up at her, concern in her eyes when she saw Ruth's downcast face. "Why?"

Ruth sighed. "They're both rebelling; Micah against God and Jeremiah against authorities."

"Is that why they haven't been at church?"

"Probably."

"Any idea why they are rebelling?"

"I have a guess, but I don't dabble in gossip," Ruth said with a sad smile.

"You know what I think?"

"No, but you're going to tell me anyway," Ruth teased.

Annabelle stuck her tongue out. "He needs a wife."

Ruth forced herself not to react. "And who is he going to find out here?"

"There's a couple of widows at church."

Ruth huffed. "Right. Mrs. Nelson is old enough to be his mother and Mrs. Kincaid has five children."

"What's wrong with Mrs. Kincaid having five children?" Annabelle asked.

"Nothing, I guess," Ruth conceded. "Hm. I wonder if Grover Miller asked her."

Annabelle stared at Ruth in astonishment before bursting into contagious laughter. Ruth and Annabelle laughed until the tears rolled down their cheeks.

When Annabelle caught her breath, she held up two fingers. "I see two problems with that. One, Mrs. Kincaid wouldn't marry someone who doesn't at least go to church. Two, Grover wants a pretty young woman, not a woman who's old enough to have actually mothered his children."

Ruth's forehead wrinkled. "How do you know that?"

"All the women who have talked about Grover are Samantha's age or a little younger or older. Not that there are many of those."

"Hm. Maybe I should ask Pa to talk to him and tell him to try asking someone a little older."

"Or maybe he already has and they just don't talk about it," Annabelle suggested.

"Maybe," Ruth said as she picked up her Bible. "Shall we continue?"

"Would you mind if I just answer the question you asked before Micah came and then we can wrap up?" Annabelle glanced at the clock on the mantel. "It's getting late."

"That's fine. How can you apply First Peter 3:1-4 to your own life?"

"Well, I'm obviously not a wife yet, so I can't be subject to my husband, but I can practice by listening to and obeying my father. And maybe I can win my father to the Lord by my obedience?" Annabelle looked sheepish. "I'll be the first to admit I'm rather strong-willed, so this whole subjection thing is hard for me to put into practice. If Cheyenne or Helena were closer, I would probably join the suffrage movement and be fighting for women's rights. Instead, I'm here in a Bible study trying to learn how to give input, but let my father make the final decisions."

Ruth smiled and nodded, encouraging Annabelle to continue.

"As for the rest of that passage, we shouldn't wear fancy clothes simply to attract attention. That's the hardest one for me. I've always been the type to wear something just to get attention, especially when Father and Mother are too busy to notice me. I think I should go through my wardrobe and get rid of, or remake, a lot of them. I can still be stylish, but not flaunting.

"And I need to also work on the meek and quiet spirit. Some people are born with that, like you. I wasn't. I was born speaking my mind without caring what others thought, and doing what I thought was best regardless of other people's opinions and commands. I think that part will be a long journey of baby steps starting with thinking before speaking."

Ruth clapped. "Annabelle, you have come so far already. I hardly recognize the stuck-up girl I met almost four years ago. When I met you, I wasn't even sure if I could become your friend. Of course, I was also painfully shy at that time. Now, you and I can actually get along and you are learning so quickly, I am almost jealous."

Annabelle shook her head. "Don't be. If I would have listened to you earlier, I wouldn't have to learn all this now. Speaking of which, could you come to my house sometime to help me go through my wardrobe and purge it?"

Ruth smiled. "I would love to. It sounds like a lot of fun. What about tomorrow after school?"

Annabelle nodded. "Perfect! You could stay for supper, too."

"You mean I wouldn't have to fail at cooking for just one person? I don't know if I can handle that."

Annabelle giggled. "You are too funny, Miss Brookings."

"And you love it, Miss Wilson."

Annabelle stood up. "Yes, I do. Oh! I almost forgot that we still need to pray." She sat back down. "We need to pray I can apply this passage and also pray for Micah and Jeremiah. Anything else?"

"Those are the main prayers for now."

"What about you? Should we pray for wisdom and creativity?"

Ruth smiled. "I suppose that would be acceptable. Who wants to start tonight?"

"I will." Annabelle folded her hands in her lap and bowed her head. "Dear Heavenly Father, thank You for allowing Ruth and me to get together again. She has been so wonderful with this Bible study. I don't know what I'd do without her. Lord, would You please bless Ruth with wisdom and creativity as she teaches? I know children can be hard to deal with, so she needs all the help she can get. I also pray for Micah and Jeremiah, Lord. I don't know what their problem is, but You do. Help them to follow what You want rather than what they want."

"Dear God," Ruth prayed, "thank You for giving us this wonderful time of study tonight. The study has been such an encouragement to me. I might be the teacher here, but I think I'm learning just as much as Annabelle is. Lord, help Annabelle as she puts what she's learned into practice. Help her think before she speaks, figure out what clothes are pleasing to You, and not rebel against what her father tells her.

"Lord, You know my heart and You know even better than I do what Micah is fighting against. Father, give him understanding and an open heart to do what is right, even if he thinks he doesn't want it. And for Jeremiah, show him that just because his father is acting this way doesn't mean he can, too. If John, Clem, and Chancy can help out at all, give them the desire and wisdom to do so. In Jesus' name, amen."

Annabelle took a deep breath. "Thank you, Ruth."

"You're welcome," Ruth replied as she stood up. "Thank you for coming over and making my time less monotonous and also for the invite to supper. I'll see you tomorrow after school."

Annabelle stretched. "Yep. See you tomorrow!"

That night, as Micah finished his rounds through town, he stopped outside the gate to Ruth's house. He had tried to push what she'd said out of his brain, but it all came back again. Could he really be the cause of his son's erratic behavior? Why was he fighting God so much?

Micah sighed and trudged away from the little house. "God, most men want to get married or even remarried. Why am I fighting this so much? Is it because the woman I think I might love doesn't see me in that way? Is it because I can't keep Edith out of my head? Is it because I'm a coward? Is it because I don't know what Jeremiah would think? What's the matter with me?"

He looked around. "I know. I can talk to Miles tomorrow. He might have some ideas."

He took another scan up and down the main street. No criminals were around and it was time for bed.

CHAPTER NINE

"Ruth!" Annabelle exclaimed. "I didn't expect you this early, but I also lost track of the time. Come in! I can't wait to get started on this."

Ruth smiled at Annabelle's enthusiasm. "I didn't expect to get here this early, either, but there isn't much school prep to do."

Annabelle beamed as she led to way to her room where she already had some dresses laid out on her bed. "I'm thinking these can be remade a little to make them both stylish *and* modest."

Ruth walked to the bed and fingered the material. "These two could, but I don't think there is anything we can do with this dress except make a blouse or skirt out of the skirt and toss the rest of it."

Annabelle bit her lip. "All right." She picked up the offending dress and threw it on the floor. "Done. What about the rest of these?"

For the next hour, Ruth and Annabelle looked through every dress, skirt, and blouse Annabelle owned and either put it back in the wardrobe, disposed of it, or put it in a pile to be remade. When they were finished, they folded the dresses that needed work. After those were piled, they took the disposed of dresses and folded them to be made into blouses.

By the time they were finished, supper was on and they ate with Annabelle's parents, laughing many times at the jokes Mayor Wilson made. Ruth walked home with a bounce in her step. She stopped abruptly when she saw the gate open and someone standing on her porch.

The man on the porch stepped forward when he saw her. "I've been waiting for you to get home."

Ruth furrowed her eyebrows. "Is something wrong, Sheriff?" She walked halfway to the porch and Micah stepped off the porch.

"No, I just wanted to talk to you. Where were you?"

"At Annabelle's house."

Micah nodded. "Well, I came here to tell you that you were right. As usual. I need to stop fighting God and do what He told me to do. God does want me to get married and now I just have to figure out who He wants me to marry."

Ruth drew in a deep breath and smiled. "I'm happy to hear you decided to listen to God. I'll be praying for you to have wisdom."

"Thank you. I told Jeremiah. He said he knows who I should marry, but he'll let me figure it out first. If I pick wrong, he'll do something about it."

Ruth laughed. "That sounds like Jeremiah."

"That's not all he said, either. He said John, Clem, and Chancy all agree with him. Which means he knew I should get married before I told him I was thinkin' on it."

"I think most people in town knew you should get remarried, you just fought it. Why did you do that anyway?"

Micah sighed. "I loved Edith with all my heart and didn't want to let her go. I thought if I considered remarrying, that would mean I had to stop loving Edith. I talked to Miles today and he said he'd thought the same thing until he met Anna. Then he realized his love for Anna was different than for his first wife and he could love them both. He can love the memory of Rebekah and love Anna in the present. After all, you can love more than one child, so why not more than one wife?"

Ruth looked up at Micah. "It sounds like you had an eventful day."

Micah nodded. "I did. I'm just glad there weren't any big crimes committed. I don't know if I would have been able to concentrate enough on my job to take care of it." He looked around. "I should let you take care of things and get to bed. I just wanted to thank you for your push and prayers."

"You're welcome. I'm always glad to pray for you. And anybody else."

Micah touched the brim of his hat with his fingers. "Good night, Miss Brookings."

"Good night, Mr. Carson."

"Pa finally decided to get remarried and he doesn't know who to marry," Jeremiah said.

"But you know who, right?" John asked.

"Of course. I can tell Pa likes her and I don't think it's just because I want her as my ma."

Clem nodded. "He likes her. And I think she likes him, but she hides it better."

"I agree," Chancy said. "So what are we going to do about it?"

"I have some ideas," Jeremiah said. "Most of them have to do with me misbehaving so she has to talk to Pa a lot. Which means I have to get punished a lot, too."

"But if it means they realize their need and love for each other, it'll be worth it, right?" John asked.

"Maybe," Jeremiah said. "I think I'll wait another week or more first and see if Pa asks her father anything. If he doesn't go out there, we just might have to resort to stronger measures."

"In the meantime, we could all pray about it," John suggested.

Clem looked at John. "That's a good idea. And that'll probably work better than anything else, anyway."

"Then it's a plan?" Jeremiah asked. "We'll pray for a couple of weeks and if nothing happens, we'll go to plan B?"

"We'll go to plan B?" Chancy asked. "What do you mean by 'we'?"

"Well, for a couple of my ideas, I'll need some help from someone."

"So we'll have to get punished so you can get your ma?" Clem asked.

"No!" Jeremiah exclaimed. "I'll claim all the blame so you won't get anything more'n a ruler to the hand."

Chancy looked doubtful. "She's pretty hard with that ruler."

Jeremiah crossed his arms and glared at Chancy. "If it gets me a ma..."

John bit his lip and scuffed his toe on the grass. "All right. I guess we could do that."

Jeremiah grinned. "Thanks, guys. You're the best!"

Four days had passed since her talk with Micah. As she prayed for Micah to have wisdom in his choice, God kept impressing something on her, but she couldn't figure out what it was. When Friday came, she couldn't wait to get home and dismissed school early again since the children were as antsy as she was. She had to talk to her mother.

Instead of taking the road, Ruth cut across the land and ran part of the way home so she could get there faster. By the time she reached the front door, she was out of breath and exhausted, but it felt good.

Ruth opened the front door. "I'm back!" she announced.

Harriet came out of the kitchen with her hands full of flour. "I'm making bread if you'd like to help."

Ruth grinned. "I'd love to! Let me get changed and wash up; then I'll be right in."

Five minutes later, Ruth entered the kitchen and took a deep breath. "It smells heavenly in here."

Harriet smiled. "Thank you, Ruth. There is some dough there ready to be kneaded."

Ruth uncovered the ball of dough and sank her hands into it. "I think this is the thing I miss most. I don't have time during the day to make bread."

"More than you miss your family?" Harriet asked, a twinkle in her eyes.

Ruth wrinkled her nose and smiled. "No, I meant besides that."

They kneaded in silence for a few minutes before Harriet spoke up. "You have something on your mind, don't you?"

Ruth sighed. "Yes, I do."

"What is it?"

"Do you remember when I said I'd told Micah he should get married about a month ago?"

"Yes, I remember quite vividly. He missed the next few weeks at church, too."

"That's because he was fighting God. He admitted to me on Tuesday night that I was right; he does need a wife and is now praying for wisdom on who to court."

"What does this have to do with what is on your mind?"

Ruth took a deep breath. "I don't know exactly. Ever since Micah finally talked to me again on Tuesday, I've been praying for him to have wisdom and when I do, I get this feeling that God is trying to tell me something, but I can't figure out what. Has that ever happened to you?"

Harriet punched her ball of dough a few times and covered it with a towel. "Many times."

Ruth stopped kneading her bread. "What did you do?"

"Asked my mother what to do."

Ruth shook her head with a smile. "What did she say?"

"She told me to wait. 'God will reveal it to you when He is ready to. Just wait and be ready to obey when He lets you know,' she said. I've never forgotten that advice and it has gotten me through many tough times."

Ruth bit her bottom lip and went back to her kneading. "That's a lot easier said than done."

Harriet chuckled. "I know it is. I'll add patience for you to my list of things to pray for."

Ruth laughed. "Thank you, Ma. I don't know what I would do without you."

"I don't know what I'd do without you, either, Ruth. As much as I would love for you to be married, I dread the day of your wedding."

Ruth looked up. "Why?"

"You're the last to leave home, Ruthie. You're my baby. All my other children are either married or off gallivanting around the countryside chasing criminals and desperados. Although, I wouldn't mind spoiling a few of my grandkids more. That was the one thing I did not like about moving out here."

"Maybe they can come visit sometime," Ruth suggested. "The train should be coming this way soon. If it hasn't already."

Harriet smiled sadly. "I hope so."

"The bread has been kneaded, Mother Dear. What's next?"

Harriet looked at her doughy hands. "How about we clean ourselves up and sit out on the porch with a cup of tea?"

"That sounds wonderful!"

When they were sitting on the swing outside, Harriet spoke. "How is your Bible study with Annabelle going?"

"It's wonderful, Ma. We are both learning so much and Annabelle is truly changing. Just wait until you see her on Sunday. She has totally transformed her wardrobe. And her attitude is changing, too. If you hadn't seen her since the day we met, you wouldn't recognize her. She is completely different. I know she was a Christian before, but now she's truly living it."

"I'm so glad to hear that," Harriet said. "I've been praying she changes. But what do you mean about her attitude?"

"She's always been really headstrong and kind of snobby, but she is truly trying to change that. For example, on Monday, we read First Peter three about having a meek and quiet spirit and she started to put it into practice right away. You won't believe the change it's made in her."

"I can imagine and look forward to seeing her on Sunday."

They both sat silently sipping their tea for a few minutes, in the silence, Ruth's thoughts drifted to Micah. *Lord, I don't know what Micah's going through or if he's truly resolved everything, but please keep him in Your Almighty hands.*

"Howdy, Ladies!" a voice called.

Ruth started and opened her eyes. Where had he come from?

Micah rode up from the woods at the side of the house.

"Good afternoon, Micah. How are you doing?"

"Better since I accepted what God was tellin' me to do," Micah replied.

"Sometimes you have to learn that the hard way," Harriet said.

"Is Daniel around?" Micah asked.

"I'm sure he is, I just don't know where. Would you care to stay for supper?"

Micah leaned forward, resting his hands on the saddle horn. "I wish I could, but I didn't make arrangements for Jeremiah to stay somewhere else for supper, so I should go home and make somethin' once I'm done talking to Daniel."

Ruth glanced at her mother. "Stop by the house before you leave and we'll send something home with you for your supper."

Micah tipped his hat. "Much obliged, Ladies. I'll do that."

As Micah headed away from them, Ruth stood up. "We should start making supper anyway."

Harriet stared out after Micah. "I wonder what he needs to talk to Daniel about."

Ruth shrugged. "When Pa comes in, he'll tell us if we need to know."

"Hm." Harriet shook herself. "Well, let's get supper made."

CHAPTER TEN

"How big of an age gap do you think is too much for a married couple?" Daniel asked his wife as they got ready for bed.

Harriet sat on the bed and raised an eyebrow. "Who's the older one?"

"He is."

"Hm." She paused to think. "Fifteen years for sure."

"What about ten years?"

Harriet looked up at him. "Lots of people get married with larger gaps than that. I don't think that's too much depending on the couple. Love can definitely bridge any gap."

"And if he has a child only nine years younger than she is?" Daniel asked.

Harriet's eyes grew wide. "Why are you asking all these questions?"

"I'll tell you in a minute."

"All right." She sighed. "That would make things a little trickier, but I still think it would be acceptable as long as the child is supportive of the marriage."

"And if the young lady is your own daughter?"

Harriet put her hands down beside her on the bed to steady herself. "What?"

"Micah asked to come courting Ruth," Daniel said, watching Harriet from the corner of his eye.

Harriet took a deep breath. "And you think the ten years between them is a problem?"

"I don't know what to think. When I think of a husband for Ruth, I always think of someone who is similar to, but slightly different than William. Someone closer to her age. Micah is a wonderful young man, but is he right for Ruth?"

"Are you going to tell Ruth?"

"Not yet. I want time to pray fervently about it first, especially after his time resisting God. Plus, she's already praying for him. I told Micah I would have to pray for a while and talk to you and Ruth first. He's willing to wait as long as we need."

"He is?"

"Yes. As anxious as he suddenly is to get married, he also thinks—and these are his words— that 'God is crazy to even think about him marrying Ruth because they are so different and so far apart in age.' End of quote."

Harriet slapped a hand to her mouth. "He really said that God is crazy?"

Daniel chuckled. "Yes, he did."

Harriet shook her head. "I don't see why it's so crazy. It isn't that unusual for two people to marry when they are of very different ages. And why would you have a problem with Micah becoming our son-in-law?"

"He's Matthew's age!" Daniel protested.

"He's at least two years younger than Matthew," Harriet corrected.

Daniel sat next to her. "You really don't have any problems with it?"

"No, I don't. If they love each other, ten years is not that big of an age gap, even with Jeremiah in the picture. And they are such good friends, I don't think they will have any problems."

Daniel sighed. "You're probably right."

"Probably?" Harriet asked, an eyebrow raised.

Daniel grinned. "I'll pray about it."

"What are we doing for Thanksgiving this year?" Ruth asked the next weekend.

"I was thinking we could invite the Jenkins family over. With Anna so close to having her baby, it would be best if she didn't have the stress and worry of cooking."

"Good idea," Ruth replied. "I'm assuming we'll have the ranch hands as well."

"Of course. Unless they are invited elsewhere."

Ruth grinned. "Ooo! I wonder if Annabelle could talk her parents into inviting William for Thanksgiving."

Harriet shook her head and laughed quietly. "Mayor Wilson might not want a simple ranch hand coming, but you could suggest it to Annabelle. Are you trying to play matchmaker?"

Ruth laughed. "Maybe."

"Good for you. I think William might need a slight push."

"I'll talk to Annabelle on Sunday."

"Should we invite Micah and Jeremiah as well?" Harriet asked.

"If he'll come. I think I've gotten on his list of non-friends for some reason."

Harriet stopped stirring the cornbread. "Really? Why do you think that?"

Ruth shrugged. "Before I confronted him, he would sometimes start the fire before I got to school and leave a note for me, but he hasn't lately. He would occasionally stop by when the children left school to make sure everything went well. And most nights when he did his rounds, he would start near the schoolhouse. It was comforting to see him walk past every evening. Now he must go past there last after I'm in bed. He still does all of those

112

things once in a while, but not nearly as often as when the school year started."

She sighed. "I miss talking to him, too. He seems to avoid me whenever I'm walking in town. The only times we talk now are at church for a few minutes or if Jeremiah does something wrong and I need to tell Micah about it. Even after he said he accepted what I'd said, he still seems to avoid me."

Harriet forced herself not to smile. "I wonder why he changed so much."

Ruth shrugged. "The only thing I can think of is my challenge to him to find a wife so Jeremiah can have a mother. I can't think of anything else I might have done, unless he doesn't like the way I punish Jeremiah."

"I don't think the last one is the case. Didn't you say Micah really liked your creativity in the first punishment?"

"Yes, he did like it," Ruth replied.

"Would you like your pa to talk to him?"

"No, I don't think that's necessary. I mainly just want to be able to talk to him about more than just the weather and Jeremiah. Maybe find out how he is really doing?"

"I'll see what your pa Daniel thinks."

Ruth smiled and gave her a hug. "Thanks, Mother."

"You're welcome, Ruthie."

"Annabelle!" Ruth called out as she walked into the churchyard with her parents.

Annabelle hurried to her, holding her arms wide.

Ruth hugged her then pulled back. "I had an idea. Do you think your parents would invite William for Thanksgiving if you ask them to?"

Annabelle held onto Ruth's arms and her eyes grew wide. "They might. But why? Isn't he going to be at your house?"

Ruth grinned mischievously. "He'll be invited, but welcome to go elsewhere. I just thought you might want to invite him over."

A deep voice broke into their conversation. "Good morning, Ladies," Micah said. "How are you two this fine morning?"

Ruth took a deep breath. "I'm doing well. How about you?"

Micah smiled. "Excellent. I'm doing very well. I feel like a load is off my shoulders."

"Why?" Annabelle asked.

"I finally listened to God and did what He told me to do," Micah answered.

"Does this mean you'll finally start talking to Ruth again?" Annabelle questioned. "She's missed your conversations, you know."

Ruth elbowed Annabelle and glared at her.

A crease formed between Micah's eyebrows. "She has?"

Annabelle nodded. "Yes, she has. And since I value my ribs, I won't say anything else."

Micah chuckled and Ruth's face reddened.

Ruth cleared her throat. "I am glad to hear you listened to God."

"Me, too," Micah replied. "I also had a talk with Jeremiah. He should behave better now."

Ruth shrugged. "We'll see. Boys will be boys, you know."

Micah laughed. "I know. I was one of those who misbehaved growing up."

"And now?" Annabelle asked.

Micah put his hand on his heart and tried to look angelic. "I act my age and am fully grown up."

Ruth smirked. "I don't believe you."

Micah opened his eyes and feigned shock. "What? You don't? Why not?"

"Your son talks about you," Ruth replied, quirking an eyebrow and somehow keeping a straight face.

"What did he tell you?" Micah demanded.

Ruth grinned and gave her best imitation of a haughty look. "A lady nevah tells on her friends."

Micah shook his head and sighed. "Fine. I'll have to ask him, then."

Annabelle looked at Ruth, then at Micah, and back again. "I'm lost."

Ruth laughed. "Sorry, Annabelle. We should have included you a bit more."

Annabelle shrugged. "It's fine. Didn't you have something to ask Mr. Carson?"

Ruth blinked. "How did you know?"

Annabelle winked. "Your mother is trying to get your attention."

"Oh." She turned to Micah. "Micah, do you have any place to go for Thanksgiving dinner?"

Micah raised his eyebrows. "Um, no, I don't think so."

"Would you and Jeremiah like to come to our house and celebrate with us?" Ruth asked.

"Yes!" Jeremiah exclaimed.

Ruth swiveled to her right. "Where did you come from?"

"I was hiding and being quiet," he replied. He turned to Micah. "Please, Pa? Can we go to Ru...Miss Brookings' house for Thanksgiving?"

Micah swallowed. "If it's all right with her parents."

"Ma's the one who came up with the idea," Ruth said.

"Will the ranch hands be there?" Jeremiah asked.

"Probably," Ruth replied. "Unless they're invited elsewhere." She glanced at Annabelle out of the corner of her eye.

"What about Peter?" Jeremiah questioned.

Ruth raised an eyebrow. "He'll probably be there."

"Good!" Jeremiah exclaimed. "I like him. He tells funny stories."

Micah shook his head as the bell rang, beckoning everyone into the building. "He has a good point there."

Ruth nodded as they all turned to walk into church. "I know he does. That is one thing Peter excels at."

"Meaning ranching isn't?" Micah teased.

Annabelle laughed and Ruth shook her head.

"I didn't say that, did I?" Ruth replied.

Micah fought the grin trying to spread its way across his face. "Not exactly."

Ruth caught sight of her parents. "I'll talk to you after church. Maybe, anyway."

Micah waved. "Yes, Ma'am. I hope we can." *More than you know.*

CHAPTER ELEVEN

Ruth and Harriet spent the day before Thanksgiving in the kitchen preparing for the Holiday feast. They baked the rolls, five different pies, peeled potatoes, baked the squash, and plucked and gutted the turkey Daniel had shot. For the first time since moving there, it was cold enough for them to leave the turkey outside in a container without worrying about it going bad.

"Mother?"

"Yes, Ruth."

"Why do we put so many things in the brine?"

Harriet smiled. "To make the turkey more flavorful."

"So the rosemary, thyme, and salt are just for flavor?"

"Hm. I think the salt makes the turkey more tender as well, but I'm not sure."

"How long have you been using the brine?"

"Since before I can remember, so it must have been something my mother did."

Ruth nodded. "Are we doing glazed carrots this year?"

"That's a good idea. I forgot about those." Harriet put her finger to her chin. "We should. I'll go get some carrots from the root cellar. We can at least have them peeled and cut ahead of time."

By the end of the day, Ruth and Harriet were exhausted and couldn't wait to go to bed. Daniel and Flynn took pity on them and did the dishes while William, Wyatt, and Peter tried to make the ladies laugh by telling outrageous and exaggerated stories. When even the funniest stories and jokes didn't make them crack a smile, they gave up and told them to go to bed.

Ruth woke up at the crack of dawn. After dressing, she went to stand on the porch and watch the sunrise. She knew she should put the turkey in, but decided everybody could wait an extra fifteen minutes for their Thanksgiving meal.

The sun came up in brilliant colors: golds, pinks, reds, and oranges all mixed together in a glorious display.

"Thank You, Lord, for all You have given us. Your mercies truly are new every morning. You fill and sustain us more than we will ever know.

Thank You for giving us this special day of Thanksgiving to You. And thank You for allowing President Lincoln to make this day a national holiday. May we truly be grateful for all You provide for us.

"Father, I pray for Your grace today as we celebrate. Give those who have nothing, or very little, a thankful heart despite their circumstances. And for those who have plenty, may we truly be grateful for all You have provided, and remind us to share with those who have less than us.

"I pray for the Hale family, Father. Help them be grateful today, despite all they are going through. And Lord, please help Mr. Hale find a job soon.

"Thank You for giving us this beautiful day for our Thanksgiving celebration. May we honor You in all we do today."

The colors of the sunrise were gone by the time she finished praying, and she went back inside to get the pan ready for the turkey.

"Hiya, Miss Brookings!" Jeremiah exclaimed as he climbed off his horse.

"Happy Thanksgiving, Jeremiah and Micah! I'm glad you could come today."

"Me, too!" Jeremiah said. "Is Peter here?"

"Yes, and so are Flynn and Wyatt," Ruth replied.

Jeremiah turned to his pa. "Pa, can I please go to the bunkhouse?"

"Yes, you may," Micah said.

As Jeremiah scurried off, Micah asked, "Are they even in the bunkhouse?"

Ruth laughed. "Yes, they are. If they hadn't been, I would've said something."

Micah nodded. "I notice you didn't say William was here. Is he or isn't he?"

"He's having Thanksgiving dinner with the mayor's family."

Micah raised an eyebrow. "How did he manage to get an invitation over there?"

Ruth ducked her head and smiled shyly. "Someone might have suggested that Annabelle ask her parents to invite him."

Micah bit his cheeks. "I see. Is there another matchmaker in town?"

Ruth wrinkled her forehead. "Another one?"

Micah rolled his eyes. "I think there are five boys playing matchmaker. I might be wrong, but they seem to be hinting an awful lot."

"Who are they?"

"John, James, Clem, Chancy, and my son."

"Dare I even ask what they're hinting at?" Ruth asked.

"They're trying to get me married off," Micah said.

Ruth's eyes went wide. "Really?"

"Yes. I think Jeremiah liked your idea of marrying me off and decided to take matters into his own hands with help from his four friends."

Ruth grinned. "Well, John and James did it once before and it worked..." She let her voice trail off.

"Ha ha," Micah said without a smile. "Very funny. I think John knew his father better than he knows me."

Ruth shrugged. "I don't know. I think he might do a satisfactory job of it."

"Or maybe they could just leave it up to me. I might already have some ideas or I might have already asked a young lady's father if I can start courting his daughter."

Ruth's eyes opened wide again and she took a deep breath. "Really?"

Micah grinned. "A gentleman tells no secrets he's supposed to keep. Especially when he doesn't want to tell on himself in the first place."

Ruth shook her head and smiled. "That's all right. I should go inside and see if Mother needs help."

"I'll join you," Micah said.

Ruth paused with her hand on the doorknob. "What?"

"Is there something wrong with a man helping in the kitchen? Or do you have some other reason you don't want me in there?"

Ruth opened the door. "The only reason I wouldn't want you in the kitchen is so you don't snitch before dinner."

"I wouldn't snitch the food!" Micah protested.

"Yes, you would," Harriet said as they walked into the kitchen.

"Beset on both sides. What shall I do?" Micah asked in a melodramatic voice.

Harriet picked up a bowl and handed it to him. "Here are the potatoes and a masher."

Micah took the bowl in his hands and stared at it. "What am I supposed to do with this?"

Harriet chuckled. "Mash the potatoes with the milk and butter until there are no more chunks of potatoes left."

Micah set the bowl on the table and raised an eyebrow. "Are you sure you want me to do this? I might ruin it."

Harriet shook her head. "The only way you'll ruin them is by not mashing them or by putting them back on the stove."

"As long as you're sure," Micah said.

"I'm sure."

Ruth shook her head with a smile. "What can I do to help, Mother?"

"I need gravy made and your father to carve the turkey. Where's Jeremiah?"

"In the bunkhouse seeing Peter," Micah answered.

Harriet sighed. "Ruth, before you start the gravy, go out and find either Jeremiah or your father. If you find Jeremiah first, ask him to find your father and tell him he needs to carve the turkey."

"Yes, Mother," Ruth said as she headed out the door.

As soon as she was out of hearing, Micah asked with a lowered voice, "Does she know I asked to court her?"

"Not yet. Daniel isn't going to tell her until he is settled in his mind. Why?"

Micah breathed a sigh of relief. "Something I said today made me think she didn't and I wanted to make sure."

Harriet nodded. "Do you want her to know yet?"

"No, not until Mr. Brookings is ready for her to know. He must have told you, though."

Harriet smiled. "Yes, he did. He wanted my opinion."

"I hoped he would."

Harriet turned back to the table full of food and went through her mental checklist of things she needed to remember.

Ruth came back a couple minutes later. "Jeremiah's off to find Pa."

"Thank you, Dear," Harriet said. "I have everything out for the gravy."

"You're welcome. And thank you for getting the fixings out," Ruth replied. "How are the potatoes coming, Micah?"

"They're just about ready, I think."

"How have you gone five years without mashing potatoes, Micah?" Harriet asked.

Micah shrugged. "Mrs. Tucker makes them once in a while."

"I guess you can make them for yourself now."

"Maybe."

A knock on the front door interrupted them. "Oh, that will be Miles, Anna, and family." Harriet hurried to the door to let them in. "Good afternoon, Miles and Anna!" She peeked around them. "Where's John and James?"

Miles smiled. "Good afternoon. John and James saw Jeremiah and decided to stick with him for now."

Harriet nodded. "That doesn't surprise me. Come on in. We're almost ready to eat, so you had perfect timing."

Miles cleared his throat. "Do you mind if I head out back and see the ranch hands?"

"Don't want to be in a kitchen full of women?" Anna teased.

Miles smiled. "Nope."

"Micah's in there, so it's not just women."

Miles raised an eyebrow. "Why is Micah in the kitchen?"

"I wanted to help out!" Micah shouted from the kitchen.

Miles shook his head. "More power to you. I'm going out if the hostess doesn't mind."

"Go ahead," Harriet said.

Miles left and Harriet took Anna's arm. "How are you doing?"

"I feel huge," Anna said as she waddled to the kitchen with Harriet. "I'm praying this baby comes soon. It's getting to the point where I can't seem to do anything. And I'm ready to hold my baby in my arms and see what he or she looks like."

"I remember those times. They were both wonderful and hard at the same time," Harriet said with a dreamy smile.

"Hello, Mrs. Jenkins," Ruth said.

"Happy Thanksgiving, Ruth and Micah," Anna said. "Is there anything I can help with?"

"I think everything is ready," Harriet replied. "Thank you for the offer."

When Daniel, Jeremiah, John, and James trooped into the kitchen a few minutes later, everything else was ready and Jeremiah was sent out to gather the rest of the guests.

By the time everybody was in the kitchen, all the food had been crowded on the table.

"Is it just me, or does it look like the table's sagging in the middle?" Peter asked, mischief in his voice.

Harriet slapped his arm playfully. "It is not. Weren't you the one who made this table? And didn't you make it so it wouldn't sag?"

Peter cleared his throat. "Um. Maybe?"

Micah chuckled. "I remember helping you carry it in here to surprise them, Peter. You can't deny it. If William were here, we could get a second witness."

"I saw him makin' it," Wyatt commented.

Micah pointed at Peter. "See? You can't win here. You've been caught."

"I don't know about the rest of y'all," Daniel said, "but I'd rather not stand here gabbin' when I could be eating. All this food looks good enough to eat."

Everybody moved around and took a chair out, somehow managing to make sure Micah and Jeremiah surrounded Ruth. Jeremiah pulled out her chair and, with a little help from Micah, pushed it in for her when she sat down.

When Ruth and Micah weren't looking, Jeremiah winked at the ranch hands and Jenkins boys and mouthed a "thank you" to them.

After everybody was situated and seated, Daniel folded his hands and closed his eyes. "Heavenly Father, we come to You today with thankfulness in our hearts. Our year has been successful and productive in many ways and for that we thank You. Nothing we have succeeded in would have been possible without You. As we gather today, we want to remember those less fortunate than ourselves and pray that You will provide for them, and if You want us to do anything to help them, give us willing and open hearts.

"Thank You, Lord, for giving us family, friends, food, and good health. Thank You for blessing this ranch with wonderful, productive men to help run it. I don't know what I would do without Peter, William, Wyatt, and Flynn. They have been a huge blessing to me. Thank You for the Jenkins family. Their ministry to this town has made an impact already. I pray their little one will arrive safely.

"And Lord, thank You for Micah and Jeremiah. Jeremiah's antics make almost everybody laugh. You have gifted him greatly. And Micah has been a blessing as sheriff. Lead them down the paths You want them to go.

"I also want to thank You for Harriet and Ruth. Lord, they are such a blessing. I don't know where I would be without them. Thank You for allowing me to provide for them. Thank You also for all of our absent family members. I think of Matthew, Martha, and Esther and their families as well as the families each around this table have left behind. They may not be perfect, but they are family and we love and miss them. Thank You for sending them into our lives. I also thank you for Joshua. Lord, keep him safe today and always.

"Thank You for sending Your Son to die on the cross for our sins and then raising Him again from the dead. Your gift of salvation is truly the greatest miracle ever given.

"And last, but not least, thank You for the hands that prepared this meal and the work that went into it. Bless this food and our conversation today. May we honor You in all we do. In Jesus' name, amen."

"Amens" echoed throughout the room and all was quiet while plates were dished up.

"Mmm!" Ruth exclaimed as she savored a bite. "Ma, we should have Micah mash the potatoes more often. These are wonderful!"

Micah's cheeks grew warm. "How does the way I mashed them make any difference? Your mother put the milk, butter, and salt in them."

Ruth clenched her teeth to force herself not to smile, and Jeremiah noticed her struggle when he glanced at her. A small laugh escaped his mouth.

"What are you laughing about?" Micah asked.

"Nothing," Jeremiah said as the laugh escaped fully.

Peter looked from one to the other. "I think he's laughing because Ruth is trying not to smile while she teases you, Micah."

Micah shook his head. "Fine. Laugh if you want to."

"Sure smells good in here," a voice from the entryway interrupted the conversation.

Ruth's eyes widened and her breath caught as Harriet rose from her chair.

"Did you leave any food for me or do I need to go to town for some?" Boots clomped toward the kitchen and a brown-haired head with an impish grin popped into the doorway.

Harriet, Ruth, and Daniel all hurried from the table toward the intruder as he stepped fully into the kitchen.

The four family members embraced and whispered together as their guests looked on with happy smiles.

Harriet forced herself to step away from her son. "I'll go find another place setting. Could someone please get another chair?"

131

Micah's chair scraped against the floor as he stood up.

It took a couple minutes, but Joshua was soon seated at the table and had a plateful of food in front of him. He looked around the table, soaking in the face of each one. "Where's William?"

"William is at the mayor's house today," Daniel answered.

"What?" Joshua asked as he took a bite of food, nearly dropping his fork.

Daniel shrugged. "He was invited over and decided to go."

"Hm. Interesting."

Silence reigned while everybody ate their meal. John broke the silence after his plate was half empty. "How is being a detective?"

Joshua grinned and set his fork down. "I love it! Of course, there are some things I don't like, but those are few and far between. I rescued a little boy who'd been kidnapped and brought the kidnapper into the U.S. Marshal's office. That was my first solo job. Otherwise, I've mostly been learning how to be a detective and getting all the rules, regulations, and methods down."

"Can I help you sometime?" Jeremiah asked.

Joshua looked at Micah and shook his head. "I don't think so. Most of what I do is too dangerous for you to be along."

Jeremiah pouted, sticking his lower lip out.

"If you're not careful," Anna said, "a bird might make a nest on your lip, Jeremiah."

Jeremiah glared at her and Joshua laughed.

"What's it like having my sister as your teacher?"

Jeremiah pulled his lip back to his mouth and chewed on it. "It's fine. It'd be easier if Pa and her didn't know what the other person was thinking all the time, though."

"What?" everybody said at the same time.

Jeremiah chuckled. "All together now!" He cleared his throat. "Well, they both seem to know when I've done something I shouldn't and they don't even tell each other sometimes. They read each other's minds. It's kinda scary."

"We do?" Micah said. "I didn't know that. Although, it could come in handy."

"Especially if you could read the mind of the criminal you're tracking so you knew where they were and what they were planning to do," Joshua said.

"Or when you are sharing the Gospel with someone," Miles put in. "That way you could know if they were truly sincere."

Micah laughed. "That's true. But it would also mean you could read more than you really wanted to know."

Peter shook his head, his eyebrows squishing together. "Changing the subject... How'd you manage to get here today, Joshua?"

Joshua grinned. "Thanks, Peter. That conversation was getting a little strange. I found the little boy and asked if I could take a week off to come home for Thanksgiving."

"I'm glad you could," Flynn said. "We could use an extra hand 'round here right now."

Wyatt jabbed his brother with his elbow. "Be nice, Flynn."

Flynn put a forkful of squash in his mouth. "Why?"

"So we can put him to work and make him think it was his idea," Wyatt said. "And you shouldn't talk with your mouth full. There's three impressionable boys sitting around this table."

"Who? Am I one of them?" Joshua asked.

Daniel choked on the water he had just taken a drink of. "No joking when a man's trying to take a drink."

"Sorry, Pa," Joshua said.

"No you ain't," Peter replied. "No tellin' lies here. Especially with the preacher at the table."

"You shouldn't lie whether I'm here or not," Miles said.

"I know that. Just like I shouldn'ta used the word ain't with the schoolteacher here," Peter teased.

"I am so glad I don't have to teach you at school, Peter," Ruth said.

Peter took a fake bow while staying seated. "My pleasure, M'lady."

Jeremiah looked from person to person, trying to figure out whether to laugh or ignore everything. When he heard John's stifled laugh, he couldn't help himself and started a chain reaction of laughs around the table.

When the laughter settled down, Ruth looked around at the empty plates. "Is everybody ready for dessert?"

"Definitely!" Peter exclaimed.

"Did you make pumpkin pie, Sis?" Joshua asked.

"Of course I did," Ruth replied.

"I'm more than ready for that," Joshua exclaimed.

"I'm ready for a piece of everything," Jeremiah said.

"Me, too!" John echoed.

Micah, Miles, and Anna looked at each other. "I have no idea where they put it all," Anna said.

"In my mouth," John answered.

James nodded vigorously.

"Same here," Jeremiah echoed.

Ruth pushed her chair back. "I'll go get the pies if you would kindly stack the plates and move some of the food out of the way."

"If it means we get pie sooner, I'll gladly help," Flynn said. "Did you make some of your famous lemon meringue pie?"

Ruth's cheeks grew warm. "Yes, we did. We tried to make everybody's favorites. As long as we remembered correctly. We made a lemon meringue, chocolate, apple, and two pumpkin pies."

From the lip licking and satisfied noises coming from around the table, Ruth decided she had chosen correctly.

Five minutes later, conversation lagged while the pies were savored.

Flynn was the first to lick his plate clean. "You should open a bakery, Ruth."

Ruth's cheeks warmed again. "I would never be able to teach school and run a bakery at the same time."

"So quit teaching and open a bakery instead," Wyatt suggested.

"Who's going to fund it?" Ruth asked.

"I'll help," Peter said. "I've got some money in my savings."

"Me, too," Wyatt and Flynn said together.

Ruth shook her head. "No, the children need a teacher more than you need to get fat and poverty-stricken by buying my pies."

"We might die poor, but we'd sure be satisfied," Flynn teased.

Ruth rolled her eyes. "Not unless you want to teach school."

Flynn's eyes grew as big as the plate in front of him. "No, Ma'am. Not me. I don't have the patience for it. I'd either kill myself or the students on the first day."

Joshua laughed. "I highly doubt that."

"I would!" Flynn insisted.

"Well, I guess I know who to go after if any of the students end up dead," Micah said grimly.

Flynn snapped his fingers. "Oh, shoot! I forgot there was two lawmen and a preacher in the room."

Ruth laughed. "Flynn, I think you're just trying to make us wear off some of that meal by making us laugh."

"Just don't make me teach those kids," Flynn warned.

Ruth shook her head. "I don't think Micah or the school board would let me."

"I know I wouldn't," Micah said. "It would be a threat to the community." He stretched his arms over his head. "I don't know about the rest of you, but I'd like to take a bit of a walk."

"Miss Brookings could go with you, Pa," Jeremiah spoke up. "I'll stay here and help the rest of the guys clean up. Oh, and Mrs. Brookings and Mrs. Jenkins could go, too."

Micah stopped mid-stretch and stared past Ruth's head at his son. "You might want to ask the 'rest of the guys' if they're all right with being volunteered and letting me shirk my duties."

"You won't be shirking your duties, you'll just be doin' your job as a sheriff by keeping them safe while they take a walk," Jeremiah argued.

Harriet laughed. "I would be just fine with letting Jeremiah and 'the guys' clean up, if it's all right with them. And a handsome escort like Micah would be wonderful."

Ruth still had her eyes narrowed as she stared at Jeremiah. "Why not Pa instead?"

"He's not a lawman," Jeremiah said.

Ruth cocked her head. "Then why not Joshua?"

"Joshua's on vacation from peacemaking and Pa wanted to take a walk," Jeremiah insisted.

"Joshua might, too," Ruth said, a smile working its way to her mouth.

Jeremiah clamped his mouth shut for a few seconds. "I ain't sayin' why."

Micah put a hand on Ruth's shoulder. "Let's just go unless there are major objections from the others. I think I know and I'll explain it on the walk."

"The only objection I have is being called 'a guy,'" Daniel said.

"Fine," Jeremiah huffed. "The gentlemen and gentleboys shall clean up whilst the ladies and sheriff take a leisurely stroll."

Micah stood up and pulled Ruth's chair out. Together, they walked to the door where Harriet and Anna met them.

CHAPTER TWELVE

Micah offered his arm to Anna and she waved him off. "If it's all right with you, I think I'll just sit out here on the porch. I wanted to stay out of the kitchen, but I don't think I have the energy for a walk."

Ruth smiled. "I don't have a problem with it."

"Me either," Harriet said. "Enjoy the fresh air and quiet."

Micah nodded and offered an arm to each of the Brookings ladies.

As they strolled to the creek, Ruth said, "You were going to tell me why Jeremiah wanted you to come with us."

Micah sighed, but didn't say anything for a little while. "He's trying to match the two of us up."

Ruth stopped walking, causing her mother and Micah to stop. "What?"

Micah forced a smile on his face. "Yep."

"I didn't think he liked me that much."

"I don't know what he's thinking," Micah said.

"He sees you two have a good friendship and thinks you would work well as husband and wife," Harriet cut in.

Ruth shook her head. "I guess I never really considered it."

Micah cleared his throat. "How long do you think they'll take to clean up?"

"A while. Why?" Harriet responded.

"I was thinking we could go see the horses in the pasture," Micah replied.

Ruth took her arm out of Micah's. "We'll have time. Especially since they don't really know what they're doing."

"Yes, but there are nine of them," Micah said.

"That just means eight more people to argue with the person who comes up with the idea."

Micah threw his head back and laughed. "Too true. Let's go see the horses."

An hour later, the laughing threesome returned to the house to find Anna missing, and when they stepped inside the kitchen, it was spotless. Harriet put her hands on her hips and turned in a slow circle. "This looks amazing. But where are the culprits who did this?"

Micah looked around. "Probably in the bunkhouse."

"Let's go out there to thank them," Ruth suggested.

When the kitchen was cleaned up, the men all went out to the bunkhouse and Anna joined them.

"They won't think to look for us there," Jeremiah said.

"I think they will," Daniel replied. "But we can do it anyway."

"Actually, I was hoping you wouldn't come with us," Jeremiah said.

"Oh? Why not? Because you want to do some matchmaking?" Daniel asked.

Jeremiah's jaw dropped. "How'd you know?"

Anna laughed. "It was pretty obvious how you worked things out so Ruth and Micah had to sit next to each other during dinner."

"And I saw right through your attempt to get them on a walk with just the two of them and a chaperone," Daniel answered.

"It worked, didn't it?" Jeremiah protested.

"Yes, it did," Daniel conceded. "I'm just wondering why you want to match them up."

"I want a ma and Ruth's the only one I want as my ma," Jeremiah replied.

"Why's that, Kid?" Peter asked.

"Even though she's tough on me," Jeremiah started, "I like Ruth as my teacher. And I see that as a step just below being a ma, so she'd be about the same, I think. I don't really remember my first ma or much of Chicago, even. I just know Pa was real sad for a long time. Now he seems to be better, but he's missing something."

"And you think he needs a wife," Joshua stated.

"Doesn't every man need a wife?" Jeremiah asked.

"No," Peter said. "I've lived this long without one. But some do."

"And besides, Miss Brookings told Pa he needed a wife," Jeremiah protested.

"And what Ruth says is always right," Miles said.

"No, but I think she's right this time. And I think Pa agrees," Jeremiah said.

"If you say so," Daniel answered.

Knock, knock. "Can we come in?" Micah's voice could barely be heard through the solid wood door.

"Come on in!" Joshua invited.

The door creaked open and Micah's face peeked in. "Is it safe for the ladies to enter?"

"I hope so since I'm in here," Anna called.

"Long as they don't mind a little mess."

Ruth's silvery laugh filtered into the small bunkhouse. "We had a house full of people before they all got married or moved out. I don't know if our house was ever perfectly clean until Joshua left."

"Hey!" Joshua protested.

Harriet smiled as they walked into the bunkhouse. "She's right and you know it, Joshua."

Joshua crossed his arms and pretended to be cross. "Humph."

Harriet shook her head. "We came in to thank you for cleaning up. The kitchen looks beautiful. Thank you all."

"You're welcome's" were muttered around the room.

"Now what?" John asked.

"Now I need to go back to town so my deputy can have his Thanksgiving dinner," Micah said.

"Aw, Pa! Do we have to?" Jeremiah asked.

"Did I say anything about you?" Micah asked. "If they're willing to have you and bring you back to town, you can stay here."

A huge grin showed up on Jeremiah's face. "Really?"

"Is that all right?" Micah asked Daniel.

Daniel looked at Miles. "Would you mind taking Jeremiah to town when you leave?"

Miles smiled. "I'm sure we could manage."

"He can stay," Daniel said.

Micah waved to everybody. "If you've got time, Joshua, I'd love to visit with you sometime."

"I'm sure I'll make it into town while I'm here," Joshua said.

Micah nodded. "So long, everybody. Thank you for a wonderful Thanksgiving."

After Micah left, everybody else dispersed to their own activities. Peter, Wyatt, and Flynn rode out to check on all the stock and the Brookings and Jenkins families, plus Jeremiah, went inside to play some parlor games.

After a light supper, Miles and Anna decided it was time to leave. They said their goodbyes and left the Brookings family to themselves.

A week after Thanksgiving, Joshua left and Ruth had taught a full week of school. She was glad to be back home again.

At supper that evening, Ruth looked around. "Why aren't the ranch hands here?"

"I made them fend for themselves tonight. I needed to talk to the two of you alone."

"About what?" Ruth said, curious what he would say.

Daniel ate a few bites of the meal, then looked up. "Ruth? What would you think about marrying someone who is ten years older than you?"

Ruth's fork paused on its way to her mouth. "Um. I don't know. I hadn't thought about it. Why?"

"I was just curious," Daniel said, as he put a large bite of roast in his mouth.

Ruth narrowed her eyes as she set her fork down. "You are rarely curious about something unless there's a specific reason for it."

Daniel chuckled. "You know me too well." He shoved his plate back and leaned back in his chair, folding his hands and putting them behind his head. "Micah asked if he could court you."

Ruth's body went still and shock shot through every part of her. "He did what?"

"He asked..." Daniel began.

"I know, I heard you; I just didn't think I heard correctly." She took a deep breath and glanced at her mother. "When I challenged Micah, even after the talk at Thanksgiving, I never expected him to ask to court me."

"Why not?"

"Because...I don't really know why. I just didn't expect it." She picked up her fork and pushed the food around on her plate. "What do you think?"

"About what?" Daniel asked.

"Me marrying a man ten years older."

"I asked you because I want to hear your opinion before you hear mine," Daniel replied.

Ruth's eyes flickered over to Harriet before settling on her father. "I don't see why it would be a problem unless you have a problem with it. Not that long ago, it wasn't unusual for young ladies to marry someone old enough to be their father. It even still happens sometimes."

Daniel chuckled. "That's true. It still happens, if I recall correctly. What about Micah in particular?"

"The only thing I'm worried about is Jeremiah. Micah said Jeremiah's trying to match the two of us up, but he doesn't seem to like me much as his teacher. What will happen if I become his stepmother?"

Harriet smiled. "I don't see that as a problem. He might test you a bit, but as a mother, I've learned that the children who test you most are the ones who love you most and want to be around you most. And the children you discipline love you more than those you don't."

"And Jeremiah told us at Thanksgiving that he wants you as his ma," Daniel said.

Ruth nodded slowly. "I would like to pray about it first though."

"I expected you would," Daniel said. "I'll tell Micah on Sunday that I'll give him an answer around Christmastime."

Ruth nodded. "That sounds fair."

"Can I ask what you're thinking right now about it?" Harriet asked.

Ruth swallowed hard and met her mother's eyes. "You can ask, but I don't think I can even answer that question yet. I have no idea what I'm really thinking. When I challenged him to find a wife, I never dreamed he'd ask me. We're good friends, but I never thought we would even think about going beyond that. And I'm too young to even be Jeremiah's mother. I'm not sure I can be a good mother to him, which is why I challenged Micah in the first place."

When she paused, Harriet stopped her from speaking further. "You are already a better mother to him than he's had since his mother died and that is just during the school day when you teach him. I am amazed at how creative you have gotten with punishments for all the kids there. A ruler to the hand can work in most cases, but sometimes they are too hardened for it to work."

Ruth smiled. "I prefer a punishment that fits the crime than one universal punishment used for every crime."

"And that is why I think you will make an excellent mother."

"Thank you, Ma." Ruth turned her attention to Daniel. "What do you think of the age difference?"

Daniel leaned back in his chair. "After my initial reservation, I came to the conclusion that age doesn't matter—in most cases—and that it is mostly about their love for each other. If you two can love each other, I have no problems with it."

Ruth smiled. "Thank you, Pa."

Daniel pushed his chair back. "Well, I suppose I better check on things out there. Thank you, Ruth. Let me know when you have an answer."

"I will," she replied.

CHAPTER THIRTEEN

Snow covered the ground for the first time that year. Ruth sighed as she shoveled her paving stones. This was another reason why she hadn't wanted to live in town. Shoveling was her least favorite job to do. Maybe she could hire Paul Hale to do it for her. She wouldn't be able to pay much, but his family needed any little bit they could get.

As she lifted the next shovelful of snow, a hand reached out and took the shovel from her. "I'll take care of this, Miss Brookings," Clem said. "Can I take the shovel to the school, too?"

Ruth stared at him. "Yes, you may."

Clem grinned. "Thank you, Miss Brookings."

Ruth put a hand on his shoulder and smiled. "No. Thank *you*!"

"You're welcome."

Ruth watched as the boy shoveled much faster than she could have. She shook her head. The energy those boys had. She went into her house and gathered her things. While she waited, she wrote a note for Paul to bring home to his parents asking if she could hire him to shovel her sidewalk and the walk to the school every day there was new snowfall. She hoped they would say yes.

When the note was written, she picked up her things and stood up. "Lord, help me get through today. My mind is going a million different directions. Help me concentrate only on what is needed today. May everything I do today be pleasing to You. Amen."

With a deep breath, Ruth opened her door and stepped out onto the shoveled walk. With a smile, she followed the shoveled path all the way up to the schoolhouse steps where Clem waited for her. "Thank you, Clem. That was very kind of you to shovel for me."

"Ma thought of it. And since I was ready first, I got to come do it instead of Chancy."

"Would you please thank your mother for me?"

"Yes, Ma'am. Should I come every time it snows?"

Ruth unlocked the door and opened it. "I'm not sure. I'm going to ask Paul if he can do it. If we get a really heavy snow, I'm not sure you would be able to do it."

Clem nodded. "Okay."

At lunch, Ruth approached Paul. "Paul, I have a favor to ask you."

Paul stood up and brushed the crumbs off his pants. "Yes, Ma'am?"

"I need to hire someone to shovel the walk from my house to the road and from the road to the schoolhouse every time it snows unless there is no school. Would that be something you would be interested in? You should make sure your parents are all right with it, too."

Paul nodded. "I would be interested in that. I'll ask as soon as I get home this afternoon. Can I let you know in the morning?"

"Yes, you can. If it snows tonight and your parents are fine with you coming, just show up about a half hour before school and knock on my door so I can give you the shovel and the money."

Paul smiled. "Thank you, Miss Brookings."

"I also have a note for your parents asking them about this," Ruth said.

Paul took the note from her. "Thank you."

"You're welcome," Ruth replied. "Has your father found work yet?"

Paul nodded. "Yes, he did. He's helping out at one of the ranches. Not great pay, and it's only temporary, but better'n nothing."

Ruth smiled. "I'm happy to hear that. He's a good man. I can't figure out why no one will hire him."

"None of us can, Miss Brookings. Least of all Pa."

Ruth sighed. "I'm sure the Lord has some reason for it. I'll let you get back to your lunch. Thank you again, Paul."

"You're welcome."

"Good evening, Annabelle!" Ruth exclaimed as she opened the door. "It's been such a long time."

"I know!" Annabelle said as she flopped into a chair. "Ten days is way too long to go without seeing you."

"How was the trip to Helena with your mother?"

Annabelle sighed. "Dreadful. Mother complained the whole way there, and then she tried to get me to buy these awful dresses. And worst of all, I couldn't find a Christmas present for my best friend. Everybody else, but not you. Despite all of that, I tried to find things to be thankful for."

"And did you find anything?" Ruth asked.

"Yes. The carriage wasn't robbed, it didn't rain or snow on our way there or back, I found presents for everybody else, I kept Mother from buying me anything I wouldn't wear, and the bed at the hotel was heavenly."

Ruth smiled. "That sounds much better."

"What did you do while I was gone?"

Ruth shook her head. "All the normal things except my Bible study with you. It just didn't work without you there." She winked at Annabelle. "Of course, Thanksgiving was in there, too, as well as a few days of no school. I mostly spent our Bible study time in prayer. A lot happened while you were gone, actually."

"Really? Like what?" Annabelle asked.

"First, tell me how Thanksgiving was with William. He's not talking about it."

Annabelle blushed. "Well, I think it went well. After dinner, Mother went upstairs to nap and Father sat in the parlor reading his newspaper. That left just William and me to do whatever we wanted. William, being the outdoorsman he is, asked if we could sit on the porch swing to talk instead of sitting in the parlor. Father gave his consent, so we did. We were both silent for a while. I had no idea what to say and could tell he was thinking about something. When he finally spoke, he asked why I was so different recently. He actually noticed before coming to Thanksgiving dinner!

"I told him about my desire to be a Christian who does God's will instead of just listening to it. I also told him how you've been helping me with the Bible study and keeping me accountable. All he did was nod which was a little disappointing, but I

155

found out he needs time to think before he responds.

"After a couple of minutes of thinking, he spoke again. Ruth, did you know he'd been wanting to court me, but didn't think he should because he didn't think I was ready to marry him?"

Ruth shook her head. "No, I didn't know it exactly. I hoped he would, but I didn't know for sure."

"Well, he did. When he said it, he immediately covered his mouth and said he shouldn't have said it before he asked my father." Annabelle giggled. "So I told him I would try to forget it until right after Father told me about it. After that, we just talked until he decided to go back to the ranch."

"Has he asked your father yet?"

"I don't know!" Annabelle exclaimed. "Father hasn't said anything to me, but I did just get home last night."

"I guess we'll just have to be patient," Ruth said.

"You'll be the first to know," Annabelle said.

"I know."

Annabelle leaned forward, a twinkle in her eye. "You said a lot happened while I was gone. What kinds of things?"

"First, Joshua showed up just as we were starting our Thanksgiving meal and stayed for almost a week. That was absolutely wonderful! He loves his work, but I think he misses us, too. Then I had a week of school to teach. The children were a little more squirrely than usual, but nothing I couldn't handle."

She took a deep breath and swallowed. "Then on Friday at supper, Pa asked me the strangest question. He asked, 'What would you think about marrying someone who is ten years older than you?' I had no idea what to say to that. It turns out that Micah Carson asked Pa if he could court me."

Annabelle's eyes grew wide. "Really? He finally did it?"

Ruth's eyes narrowed. "What do you mean by that?"

"I've thought for a long time that you two would be perfect for one another," Annabelle said.

"You have?"

"Yes. You're really good friends, you like each other, you like Jeremiah and he likes you. It's perfect! What was your answer?"

"Nothing yet. It's only Monday. I don't know what to say yet."

"Just say yes, he can court you. If it doesn't work, you can tell him so sometime during the courtship."

Ruth shook her head. "No. Jeremiah would never forgive me for that."

"What are you talking about?"

"Jeremiah is set on having me for his stepmother. He doesn't know Micah asked to court me and he is trying to play matchmaker."

Annabelle grinned. "Good for him."

"The point is, I want to be absolutely sure I would actually be willing to marry Micah if he courts me."

"I'm not sure I understand."

"I want to know God's will for me after I'm finished teaching school. I want to know that I could say yes to Micah after getting to know him more without going out of God's will for me."

"Hm. I guess that makes sense."

They sat in silent thought for a little longer. "Well, I suppose we should start studying the Bible," Ruth said.

Annabelle smiled. "Yes, we should. It's been too long."

CHAPTER FOURTEEN

William's knees knocked together as his hand rapped on the door. He knew Annabelle would be at the Jenkinses' house, so at least he wouldn't have to face her right now. Talking with her father would be hard enough.

"Good morning, Sah," a young black man said. "How may I help you?"

"Is Mayor Wilson in?" William asked.

"Yes, he is. What is your name?"

"William Steele."

"Ah yes, come inside, Mr. Steele."

"Thank you, Mr...."

"Thomas. Just Thomas." Thomas motioned to a bench just inside the door. "Wait here please."

William looked around at the wide open room with vaulted ceiling and chandelier. Who was he to be asking to court Annabelle? Why would Annabelle ever marry a ranch hand like him who would never be able to afford anything even remotely like this? He was about to slip out the front door when he heard Thomas speak.

"Mr. Steele, the mayor will see you now."

William stood up and hesitantly made his way toward Thomas. As he came alongside the butler, Thomas put a hand on his arm.

"Don't worry about Miz Annabelle. She just wants a loving husband, not a rich one."

William's head snapped toward the man. "Why do you think that?"

Thomas paused. "Miz Annabelle has changed in the last few years. She wants what God wants now. It's as plain as the nose on yer face she likes you. As long as her father's seen it and isn't too greedy, he'll let you court her."

William took a deep breath. "Thank you."

Thomas nodded and opened a door to his left. "Mr. William Steele, Sah."

"Come in, William," Mayor Wilson said, not looking up from the piece of paper he was reading.

William stepped into the room and waited for Mayor Wilson to be ready to talk with him.

Mayor Wilson looked up from his paper a minute later. "You really are as quiet as they say. Have a seat." He motioned toward the ornate chair across from him. "I suppose I can guess why you are here."

"You can, Sir?"

Mayor Wilson smiled. "When my daughter asked if we could invite you over for Thanksgiving dinner, my suspicions were confirmed. I watched you two, you know."

William furrowed his eyebrows. "What?"

"After dinner that afternoon when you were on the porch swing. You probably don't realize it, but you two are already half in love with each other. My only concern is how you will support a wife. You work on the Double B Bar Ranch, correct?"

"Yes, Sir."

"And live in the bunkhouse, I assume."

"Yes, Sir. I plan to get a place of my own soon, though. Mr. Brookings already offered to sell me a few acres of his land to build a house on."

"How do you plan to pay him and buy the materials for the house?"

William sat up straighter. "I have a good sum of money saved in the bank, Sir. I also plan to build a house in sections starting with just what is needed and adding on when we need to."

Mayor Wilson nodded. "And your pay is enough to support a wife and future children?"

"Yes, Sir."

He named the amount he made every month and Mayor Wilson raised an eyebrow. "That's quite a bit more than most men pay their ranch hands."

"Yes, Sir, but it's pretty normal for foreman pay."

"You're the foreman?"

"Yes, Sir."

"How did the youngest ranch hand on the Double B get to become foreman?"

William smiled. "It isn't necessarily age or experience that makes a foreman, it's how he handles men and leads them."

Mayor Wilson nodded. "You have my permission to court Annabelle. Just don't end up like some of her other suitors or you'll get a backend full of buckshot."

"Her other suitors? I didn't realize she'd had any."

"Not for a while. Not since she started changing. Most of them were after her money."

William blinked. "What money?"

Mayor Wilson chuckled. "Her dowry. When she marries, Annabelle will have a substantial dowry."

"I didn't realize that."

"I noticed and that's a good sign. Now, would you like to tell her or shall I?"

William swallowed hard. "I can unless you would prefer to do so."

Mayor Wilson glanced at the clock. "She should be returning any minute now. We could tell her together."

"Whatever you prefer, Sir."

Mayor Wilson stood up and walked around the desk. "No more of this 'Sir' business, William. You and I will most likely become father and son soon. You can either call me Mr. Wilson or Gilbert."

William smiled. "Thank you, Mr. Wilson."

The front door opened and they heard distant voices.

"That would probably be Annabelle. I'll go get her if you are ready."

"What?" William asked.

"Since she is home, we can tell her together."

William sank back into the chair. "All right."

While Mr. Wilson was out of the room, William breathed a quick prayer. "God, I am doing the right thing here, aren't I? I don't want to be out of Your will in anything I do, but especially not marriage."

"What are you talking about, Father?" William heard Annabelle ask.

"You will see, Annabelle."

The door whooshed open and William stood up. "Good morning, Annabelle." He reached up to tip his hat only to realize his hat was in his other hand.

Annabelle blinked and looked from one man to the other. "Good morning, William. What are you doing here? Father hasn't talked you into taking the secretary position, has he? Because you would hate it."

"No, I haven't," Mayor Wilson said. "Would you please have a seat, Annabelle?"

"Sure." She stretched the word out as long as possible as she sat in the chair next to William. "What's going on?"

Mayor Wilson looked at William. "You or me?"

William opened his mouth to speak, but nothing came out.

"Father, you're intimidating him," Annabelle protested.

William sat up straighter and turned toward Annabelle. "Miss Wilson, your father has given me permission to court you, if you are interested."

Annabelle's eyes snapped to William and back to her father. "Really? I expected you to tell him no because he's 'beneath me.'"

Mayor Wilson shrugged. "He can support you if you don't spend too much. And he's moving up in the world. I also want you to marry someone you like. Although he isn't who I would have chosen, he's better than most of the other options in town."

Annabelle smiled and turned to William, her grin widening. "My answer is yes, I would be honored."

William smiled shyly and let out the air he'd been holding in. "Thank you. Will Wednesday evenings work for your family, Mr. Wilson?"

Mayor Wilson nodded. "Yes, Wednesday evenings are usually the only day that will work."

Annabelle smiled. "I'll have to tell Ruth, but I'm sure she won't mind skipping one night a week for our Bible study."

William stood up. "I should get back to the ranch. Thank you, Mr. Wilson, for fitting me in this morning."

"My pleasure," Mayor Wilson said as he stood up. They shook hands. "You are welcome anytime, William."

William jammed his hat on his head. "Thank you, Miss Wilson, for allowing me to come calling." He tipped his hat.

Annabelle stood up with a smile. "Thank you for finally asking. I'll see you out."

As they left the study behind, Annabelle spoke up, "Father wasn't too hard on you, was he?"

"No, he wasn't. He was actually very nice. I wasn't expecting it."

"Good." They stopped at the front door. "I'll see you on Wednesday then."

William nodded. "Yes, Ma'am. What time?"

"Would six o'clock work? You could join us for dinner."

William looked up at the chandelier in thought. "That should work just fine. If it doesn't, I'll let you know."

Thomas was suddenly next to them. "Are you leaving then, Mr. Steele?"

William smiled. "Yes, Thomas, I am. And you may call me William."

Thomas nodded. "Very well, William."

"Oh, and Thomas," Annabelle said, "William will be joining us every Wednesday evening."

Thomas grinned. "Good for you, William. It's about time someone took Miz Annabelle and swept her away."

William laughed and headed out the door.

"Miss Brookings!" John exclaimed as he ran toward her.

"Yes, John?" Ruth asked.

"Ma had her baby while we were at school!"

Ruth stopped her progress toward the store. "She did?"

John nodded. "She's wondering if you can come over to help get supper on."

"I'll do more than that," Ruth said. "John, could you please go to Annabelle's house and tell her I'll be at your house helping out?"

"Sure."

"Thank you!" Ruth called as John ran to the mayor's house. Ruth shook her head and turned around, hurrying to the parsonage.

She knocked on the door before opening it. "It's me, Ruth," she said as she walked into the house.

Miles walked in from the hallway. "Come on in, Ruth. Meet my precious little daughter, Rebekah Marie."

Ruth smiled as she stepped up to him and looked at the bundle in his arms. "She's adorable, Pastor Jenkins! How is Anna?"

"Tired, but very happy," Miles said.

"I think I'll go peek in on her and then get supper ready."

Miles nodded, but said nothing.

Ruth shook her head and resisted the urge to ask if she could hold the baby. Miles was too infatuated by his little girl to share her right now.

Ruth rapped on the bedroom door.

"Come in," Anna's voice said.

"Hello, Mrs. Jenkins," Ruth said as she walked into the room. "Little Rebekah is beautiful."

"Her father is completely besotted," Anna laughed.

"I know. I just came in to see if you need anything, but since James is here, I guess he could get you what you need."

Anna nodded. "I'll be fine. I'll probably take a short nap soon."

"Good. I'll take care of everything except feeding Rebekah. And I'm hoping to ask Annabelle if she can come over in the morning to help you."

Anna shook her head. "That isn't necessary."

Ruth put her finger to her lips. "I know it isn't, but I'm going to do it anyway. The more rest you get, the sooner you'll be feeling like your normal self."

Anna smiled. "All right. Just know that I'll remember this and force you to do the same when your time comes."

Ruth laughed. "It will be a while before that happens. If it happens at all."

Anna raised an eyebrow. "We'll see."

Ruth shook her head and went to the kitchen to cook.

"Father?" Ruth asked a couple weeks later.

"Yes, Ruth? What is it?" Daniel set the ledger aside, grateful for yet another interruption. He really needed to hire someone to keep his accounts.

"I have an answer about Micah."

Daniel motioned for Ruth to sit down and searched her face. "Why do you sound so hesitant?"

Ruth looked away and took a deep breath, clenching her hands together. "Because this is a really big decision for me and I'm afraid I'm making the wrong one."

Daniel frowned. "Why is it so big?"

"Jeremiah is trying to match Micah and me up because he wants me to be his stepmother. I don't feel right saying yes to a courtship with Micah if I'm not also ready to say yes, Micah is the man God wants me to marry."

Daniel took a deep breath and nodded. "I hadn't thought about that. I wondered why it was taking you so long to decide."

Ruth smiled sheepishly. "I'm sorry."

"Don't be," Daniel said. "You had a good reason. What is your answer?"

Ruth swallowed hard and tried to catch her breath. "Yes."

Daniel watched Ruth's face, trying to find any shade of doubt, resignation, or hesitation. "And you are sure about this?"

"Yes and no." Ruth drew in a deep breath. "I think so. Every time I say yes, I second guess myself." A laugh forced its way out of her. "It's not a good idea for me to be alone too long. I think too much and don't have anybody to talk it over with.

Even though I've been at the Jenkinses house often, it still hasn't been enough."

"I'm here now. Would you like to talk it through?"

Ruth sat up straighter. "Yes! Please!" She kept silent for a few seconds as she gathered her thoughts. "I love Jeremiah and would be honored to be the woman who molds him into a gentleman. I missed Micah's friendship when he refused to talk to me about anything other than Jeremiah and the weather for a few weeks. Although, that does concern me some. Will he retreat like that if he's confronted about something else?

"I don't know if I love Micah or what love even feels like. I also know that love is a choice and not just a feeling, so maybe I don't even really have to worry about that. I do know that I like him and it's different from the way I like William and Joshua. What *does* love feel like?"

Daniel smiled. "If I could answer that, I could probably become the richest man in the world. Love is different for everybody, so I can't answer your question. I might be wrong, but it is entirely possible that what you're feeling now is the beginning of a deeper love for Micah. It is definitely a good foundation for it, at the very least."

Ruth nodded. "Thank you, Pa. That does help me. And my answer is still yes. My only concern is my job. As a schoolteacher, I'm not supposed to court or be in the company of young men."

Daniel leaned back in his chair. "I'll talk to Mr. Jensen and see what he thinks. We might have to tell Micah to not come calling until after school is out for the year. But I won't talk to Mr. Jensen until after we tell Micah." He got a mischievous look on his face.

"What are you thinking, Pa?"

"Micah and Jeremiah are coming for Christmas, right?"

"Yes," Ruth said hesitantly.

"What if we wrap up the answer to Micah's question for his present? He'd only have to wait an extra week or so."

Ruth chuckled. "That would be kind of fun. And we could see how he handles embarrassment because I'm sure Jeremiah will insist he read the note out loud."

Daniel laughed and slapped his thighs. "We're doing that. If he doesn't listen to his son, I'll get Joshua or or your ma to goad him into reading it."

Ruth grinned and stood up. "Thank you for always being here for me, Pa."

Daniel stood up, walked around the large desk, and hugged his daughter. "You're welcome, Ruthie. I wouldn't have it any other way and I hope you are very happy."

CHAPTER FIFTEEN

Micah breathed deeply as he entered the ranch house. The smell of apples, pine trees, and baking ham combined into a fragrance that embodied Christmas. He couldn't think of a better smell in the whole world.

"Like the smell of something?" Joshua asked.

Micah opened his eyes and smiled. "Yep."

"Anything in particular?"

"All of it. Or rather, the combination of it all."

Joshua grinned. "I agree."

Micah looked around at the pine boughs, holly, and popcorn ball strings decorating the entryway. "Is William going to be here?"

"Yes. Mayor Wilson wanted a Christmas all to themselves this year since it'll probably be the last time."

"Does that mean William's courting Annabelle?" Micah asked.

"Yes, it does. And they're both ecstatic," Ruth said as she walked in. "How are you this afternoon?"

"Well, besides having a very impatient son all morning, I'm doing fine. I should've gotten a deputy without family to go to for holidays. I'm just glad you were willing to work with my schedule."

"Me, too," Joshua said. "Christmas would be lifeless without you and Jeremiah."

"Why?"

Joshua shrugged. "Ever since you and I became friends, you two have been here for Christmas. You're practically family."

Micah's eyes flicked to Ruth then back to Joshua as he shrugged.

"Speaking of Jeremiah, where is he?" Ruth asked.

"Bunkhouse," Micah replied. "Probably getting everybody to come in here so he can open presents."

Ruth laughed. "Instead of standing in here, would you two like to join us in the parlor?"

"Sure," they said together.

By the time they were settled into chairs, boots stomped in the room off the kitchen and a minute later, Jeremiah bounced in with four ranch hands trailing him.

"Which presents are mine?" Jeremiah asked.

"How about you greet our hosts first, Jeremiah?" Micah suggested.

"Hi," Jeremiah said, still looking under the tree. "Thanks for having us here today."

"Jeremi..."

Harriet put a hand on Micah's arm, interrupting him. "He's already waited all morning. And he's only ten."

Micah smiled faintly. "I suppose."

Ruth stood up and walked to the tree. She knelt down, her dark green and red plaid skirt billowing out around her. "They should all be labeled. Joshua? William? Would one of you like to help hand presents out?"

Joshua jumped up. "I will."

After the presents were handed out, Daniel asked, "How do we want to do this?"

"It's your house," Micah said. "You decide."

"You've always had us open from oldest to youngest," Jeremiah said. "Why would you change it?"

Daniel shrugged. "I thought perhaps someone might be too impatient to wait to be last."

"Not today."

Daniel grinned and nodded at Peter. After all the presents were opened and being oohed and ahhed over, Daniel disappeared for a minute. He came back carrying a large box. Ruth turned her head away from Micah in an attempt to hide the grin trying to work its way onto her face.

"Micah, there is one present left for you to open," Daniel said when he stood in front of the lawman.

"Me?" he asked. "Why do I get singled out?"

"Yes, you," Daniel replied, handing the box to Micah.

Micah hefted the box. "It's heavy. Can I shake it?"

Daniel sat down and nodded.

Micah shook the box and something shifted heavily inside. "Hm. It's acting like a rock."

"Open it, Pa!" Jeremiah exclaimed.

Micah shrugged and set the box in his lap, ripping the brown paper off the box. He lifted the lid and pulled out a large rock with a string tied around it. With a cocked eyebrow, he turned the rock over in his hands until the note attached to the string was in front of him.

His eyes scanned the note and spots of red grew on his cheeks.

"Read it out loud, Pa!" Jeremiah said, bouncing up and down on his knees.

Micah shook his head and clamped his lips shut.

"Aw, come on, Micah. You can't go disappointing your son on Christmas Day, can you?" Joshua teased.

"Do you know what's in this note?" Micah asked.

"Nope, but it must be embarrassing to turn you so red," Joshua said with a grin.

Micah shook his head. "No, I won't read it out loud."

"It can't be that bad," Harriet put in.

Flynn leaned his elbows on his knees. "Yeah, come on, Micah."

Micah sighed. "All right." He tore the note from the string and set the rock at his feet. "'This paper certifies that one Micah Carson hereby has the permission of Daniel and Harriet Brookings to court their daughter, Ruth Ann Brookings, as soon as the school board should allow such an event to take place. Signed, Daniel and Harriet Brookings.'" As he read the note, he felt his cheeks burning hotter and hoped his beard covered most of it.

"I'm glad I didn't get my permission that way," William said with a chuckle.

"Does that mean Ruth's going to be my stepma?" Jeremiah asked.

"Not yet. We have to court first..." Micah started.

"Why?" Jeremiah interrupted. "Don't you know enough about each other already?"

"No, we don't," Ruth said. "There's lots of things men and women don't talk about unless they are thinking about marriage or are married to each other."

"And we need to talk about some of those things," Micah continued. "We also have to decide other things."

"Like what?" Jeremiah asked.

Peter put a hand on Jeremiah's shoulder. "There are some things you don't need to know about until you're older, Jeremiah, and you just have to accept that."

Jeremiah pouted, but recovered quickly. "But this does mean you might become my stepma, right?"

"Possibly," Ruth said. "If we both believe God is leading us on that path."

"How long does a courtship take?" Jeremiah asked.

"That depends on the couple and the parents," Micah replied. "And in this case, the school board as well since we might not be able to start courting until after the school semester is over. I'll talk to you about it later, all right?"

Jeremiah shrugged. "Fine. When's supper?"

Ruth laughed. "Which presents are mine and when's supper. Do you ever think about anything else?"

"Yes. You and pa getting married before planting season," Jeremiah replied with a grin.

Micah shook his head and Harriet saved them both from responding. "Ruth, let's go see what needs to be done for supper yet."

"Gladly," she replied.

In keeping with tradition, after the Christmas dinner was eaten, Daniel read the story of Christmas from Genesis to Revelation.

When Daniel said the last word, William leaned back in his chair. "I remember the first time I heard that story from you, Mr. Brookings. It struck a chord in me and I've never been the same. In a good way, of course."

Peter nodded. "I remember that day, too. Ruthie was just a shy, young girl at the time. She's sure grown up since then. Joshua was a quick-tempered young man, trying not to outgrow his legs; I was a hardened old man; William was a confused and quiet boy; Wyatt and Flynn haven't changed much, but what has changed has been for the better. Each year, I get somethin' else outta the story, that's for sure."

Daniel closed his Bible. "What did you get out of it today?"

Peter cleared his throat and rubbed his forehead. "Shoulda known better'n to open my big mouth. Well, I learned that God must've known what He was doin' when He told those prophets to make those predictions. You said they all came true?"

"Yes, they did," Daniel said. "At least the ones I read. There were some I didn't read that will be fulfilled when Jesus comes back again." He looked around the table. "How about we go around the room and say one thing we learned or got from the reading today?"

"I'll go next!" Jeremiah volunteered. After a nod from Daniel, he said, "I decided I wouldn't wanna be Jesus' brother. He was perfect and it's bad enough having a pa as sheriff and have everybody think you have to be perfect. I could see myself being the total opposite of perfect, just to be rebellious."

Micah laughed. "Don't you already?"

Jeremiah scrunched up his nose. "No."

Micah winked. "I put myself in Joseph's shoes. It would've been hard to endure the looks the people gave him and Mary. And then to be responsible for raising the Son of God? I cannot imagine it."

There was silence for a few seconds.

"I'm confused about something," Flynn said. "I don't understand why Jesus had to come to earth to save sinners. I realize we needed a sacrifice, but weren't the Old Testament sacrifices enough?"

"No," William said, "they weren't. If it had been, you're right, Jesus wouldn't have come as a babe to live among us. The Old Testament sacrifices were just a picture of our need for a real sacrifice. Only a person who was sinless and perfect could truly save us. An animal sacrifice was only a temporary thing and had to be done every year. Jesus died once for all."

Flynn nodded. "Hm. Thank you."

William smiled. "The part of the story that stood out to me was the sacrifice Joseph made. He was looked on with scorn for marrying a woman who was expecting. He had to see all the looks Mary got. And it is entirely possible he had to be the midwife when Jesus was born. As I contemplate marriage, it's sobering to realize that marriage really is about complete sacrifice of self."

Wyatt shook his head. "All I could think was 'there is no way I could have done it.' I couldn't have been Jesus, I couldn't have been Joseph, and there's no way I would've survived as one of those prophets."

"Many of those people probably didn't think so either, but God's grace would have gotten you through," Joshua said. "Which is what I saw. God's grace is sufficient no matter your circumstances. His grace was sufficient for the prophets, Joseph, and Jesus Himself. And His grace is sufficient for us today."

"I saw God's power," Ruth said. "No human could have caused Mary to become pregnant in that way. No mere human could have been perfect like Jesus was perfect. No human could have raised Jesus from the dead. No human could have caused Jesus to ascend to heaven and sit at the right hand of God. Only God could have done it all."

Harriet chuckled. "That is funny. I was kind of thinking the opposite, Ruth. As you read, Daniel, what stood out to me was Jesus' humanity. He showed us His weaknesses. He didn't try to hide them like so many of us do. Even though He was perfect, He still struggled."

Daniel smiled. "It's truly amazing how each of us can see different things. The one thing that really hit me was God's judgment. He is the righteous judge and will judge you if you don't accept His Son. Rejection is an option, but it's an option that will only send you straight into the fire and brimstone and eternal separation from God's love. That is truly a sobering thought and one that makes me want to share the Gospel with more people."

Murmurs of agreement went around the table.

After a couple minutes of reflection, Peter slid his chair back and stood up. "Thank you for a wonderful afternoon and meal. I have to be up early tomorrow to check the herd, so I'm gonna head to the bunkhouse for some shuteye." He looked around the table. "It was nice seein' you all again."

Jeremiah jumped up and ran around the table to hug Peter. "Thank you for the carved horse. I love it!"

"You're welcome, Kid," Peter said, patting him on the back. He waved as he walked to the door.

As he disappeared outside, Flynn and Wyatt stood up. "We should turn in, too," Flynn said.

Wyatt nodded. "Thank you for the gifts and wonderful dinner."

"Are you going to leave, too, William?" Jeremiah asked.

"Yes, I am," William said, "but I thought I'd go to town to give Annabelle and her family the gifts I got for them."

"Can I come with you?" Jeremiah asked.

William shook his head. "I'd like to do this alone."

"Maybe Joshua could do something with you," Micah suggested. He looked at Joshua with a questioning glance.

Joshua grinned. "I have the perfect idea, Jeremiah. How about sledding in the moonlight?"

Jeremiah's eyes went wide. "You can do that?"

"If there's enough snow and moonlight you can. And I think there's just enough of both tonight."

Jeremiah looked around the kitchen. "What about cleanup?"

Micah cleared his throat. "I had an idea for that. If Ruth is willing, I thought the two of us could clean up the kitchen while Mr. and Mrs. Brookings cleaned up the parlor."

Daniel smiled. "I like your idea, Micah. Go ahead and have fun with your new sled, Jeremiah. Joshua, we'll let you know when it's time to come in."

Joshua nodded. "All right, Pa. See ya later."

Jeremiah and Joshua bundled up and raced outside.

CHAPTER SIXTEEN

"Are you busy, Micah?" Daniel asked as he stepped into the sheriff's office from the blustery, cold weather.

Micah looked up. "No, I'm not. Just doing some paperwork that can wait."

Daniel took his mittens off and rubbed his hands together near the stove. "It's cold out there."

Micah nodded. "I know. If the temperature drops much more, I'm gonna head to the schoolhouse and tell Ruth to send the children home."

"Good idea. Before you do that, I did have something to discuss with you."

"I figured that's why you were here." Micah smiled.

Daniel turned to face Micah. "I just came from my discussion with Mr. Jensen. He said he can't give anybody preferential treatment. The rules say a schoolteacher can't be courted and he won't bend them. I figured that would be his answer, but I was hoping..." Daniel sighed. "Well, I guess my main purpose in coming here was to tell you that and ask if you're willing to wait."

Micah leaned back in his chair. "I'm willing to wait. I don't know about Jeremiah, though. It'll be hard to wait. When's school done?"

"May sometime, I think."

Micah winced. "Winter's usually my slow time."

Daniel chuckled. "I can't imagine why."

"Oh, something about criminals not liking to freeze to death any more than the rest of us."

Daniel shifted his feet. "Well, I'd better get home before the temperature drops any more. Does your thermometer outside work?"

"Until it gets under twenty below zero, then it has a hard time dropping further."

Daniel peeked out the window. "I'll stop by the schoolhouse on my way out and tell Ruth to send the children home. The temperature has dropped five degrees while I've been in here."

"What's it at?" Micah asked.

"Two below."

Micah nodded. "Stay safe on your way home."

"Thank you for waiting."

"She's worth waiting for," Micah said, looking Daniel in the eye.

Daniel smiled. "See you Sunday."

"See you."

"Just as we were settling in for a mild winter," Ruth muttered, "we would have to get a blizzard the second week of February. Lord, I know I'm complaining, but if we're going to get a blizzard, couldn't it wait until I for sure have time to get to the ranch instead of sneaking in on a Friday afternoon?"

She glanced up at the darkening clouds and debated whether to attempt the trek to the ranch or not. From the look of the sky, the blizzard would reach the ranch before she could get there.

"Miss Brookings!" a deep voice called as she unlocked her door to get inside the cottage.

Ruth turned to see who had called her. "Hello, Sheriff."

Micah stopped running when he reached her porch steps. "You aren't going home are you?"

Ruth shook her head. "No, I'm not. I thought about it for about two seconds, but it isn't worth the risk."

Micah took a deep breath and let it out. "Thank the Lord! Do you have enough wood and food to last a few days?"

Ruth nodded. "I should be set. The only thing I won't have is someone to talk to once in a while."

"What about Annabelle?" Micah asked.

"I'll be fine."

Micah bit his lip in concentration. "Jeremiah?"

Ruth shook her head. "I appreciate your help, Micah, but I really will be fine. I might get a little spiritless and stir crazy, but so will everyone else."

Micah searched her face in the darkening light. "As long as you're sure."

Ruth smiled sadly. "I'm sure."

"All right. If I can, I'll check on you tomorrow."

"Don't risk your life to check on me," Ruth said.

"I won't."

"See you after the blizzard then."

"Yeah. See ya." Micah watched as Ruth disappeared into her cottage. A weight settled on his chest. He knew he should be worried about the others in town, but they all lived with someone else as far as he knew. If only he had noticed the clouds sooner and gone to the school, Ruth could have gone home instead of being cooped up in a small house by herself.

He knew she liked being alone, but blizzards could do a lot of damage and be scary to listen to if you didn't have someone to help keep your mind off of it. Plus they could last almost a week. Not often, but they could. And she'd never been alone that long as far as he knew.

Micah hurried to his office the long way to make sure everybody was inside. "Jeremiah. Coat and mittens now. We need to get home and bring lots of wood in."

"Why?"

"A blizzard's coming. That's why Ruth sent you home early. It looks like it'll be a bad one."

"How bad?" Jeremiah asked as he stuck his arms in his coat.

"I don't know, Son. Hopefully not as bad as the old timers are predicting."

"Why?"

Micah pulled his mittens on and opened the door. When Jeremiah went through, Micah closed and locked it. While they walked the three blocks to their home, Micah answered Jeremiah's question. "The old timers are predicting over three feet of snow in a three-day period. That's the low estimate. The highest estimate was more than six feet of snow over five days."

"Five days?" Jeremiah exclaimed. "That would mean it would snow until..." He paused to count. "Wednesday!"

Micah nodded, a grim look on his face as he glanced upward.

Two houses down from their house, Jeremiah stopped suddenly. "What about Miss Brookings?"

"She has enough food and wood to last five days."

"You talked to her?"

"Yes."

"But she'll be all alone."

Micah sighed. "I know. She said she'd be all right. If at all possible, I'll go check on her during a break in the storm at the first opportunity."

Jeremiah put one foot in front of the other until he reached the front door. "Couldn't I go stay with her?"

"I offered and she said she'd be fine. I'd prefer you be with me anyway."

Jeremiah scowled. "Fine. I'll go get some wood while you unlock the house."

"Thank you, Jeremiah."

February 15, 1880
Dear Diary,

It is day two of the blizzard and barely over twenty-four hours since Micah left. I am already getting antsy. Since I finally have the time and have no one to talk to, I decided to talk to you.

I've decided to stay in the room with the fireplace because it is the only room that has stayed remotely warm. My bedroom door is closed to keep the draft from coming in here. I took all the blankets off my bed and brought them and a change of clothes in here. I already keep my book and Bible in here, so at least I didn't have to bring those with me.

Right now, I'm curled up on my easy chair, wrapped in a blanket writing in you with a pencil so I don't have to worry about dripping ink on anything. I keep the fire blazing all day and night, waking up every couple of hours at night when I start to get chilled. I need to mention to the school board that they should do something to keep the drafts out. I shouldn't have to freeze in here when the fire is going so well and so hot. I'm afraid I'll start the house on fire.

I am so thankful I had Paul Hale fill my lean-to with wood last week. If he hadn't... Well, I won't go there. Let's talk about other things. Oh yes, I need to update you on the last two months. So much has happened and I haven't had time to write.

Three weeks before Christmas, Pa told me Micah had asked to court me. I was stunned to say the least. After what I had told him a few weeks before about his need for a wife, he asked if he could come courting me? After spending three weeks hardly speaking to me, he asked to court me? He did tell me his reasons for avoiding me after Pa gave him permission to court me. He avoided me because he didn't want to give away that he was thinking about courting me or that he was interested in me at all. So he avoided me instead. Especially when he was fighting against God.

To continue the story, Micah asked Pa shortly before Thanksgiving. Pa prayed about it and discussed it with Ma. Pa had an issue with Micah being ten years older than me which is why it took so long. He finally decided he would give permission if I was agreeable to the courtship.

Well, as I said, I was stunned to know that Micah had even asked. I told Pa I would pray about it. And I did. Micah has a son, as I'm sure I've told you before, and he really wants his pa to get married. I took two weeks to decide how God was leading, not because of the age issue, but because I needed to decide that I could become his wife unless something major came between us. For Jeremiah's sake, I needed to know for sure I could say yes if Micah asked me to marry him.

Five days before Christmas, I was home for the weekend and holidays and finally had my answer. Yes, dear diary, unless something comes up, it looks like I could be married before next year. I'm excited, scared, and overwhelmed all at once. Am I doing the right thing? How will I know when I'm in love with Micah, if I even end up loving him? Or am I already?

The hardest thing is that we can't start courting until after the school term is finished in May because of the rules of a schoolteacher. Some of those rules are just plain silly, I think, but I'm sure there was a reason for them. What concerns me most is living here in town during the week. Will that create temptation for either of us or can we keep being just friends until May?

Today. Or was it yesterday? Whichever it was, he was really sweet. Just before the blizzard, he made sure I wasn't going to try to get home before the storm hit. I'm glad I didn't. He then made sure I had enough food and wood and company. When he asked if I wanted Annabelle or Jeremiah to stay here, my first thought was, "No, I don't want either of them, I want you here with me." Is that bad of me? I know it would have been utterly wrong for him to stay here. But his courage, strength, and calm comfort me much like Joshua has done in the past.

Ah, Joshua. I haven't kept you informed about him, have I? He came for Thanksgiving and again for Christmas. He surprised us on Thanksgiving, but the Christmas visit was planned. The job he had between the holidays took only three weeks and he ended up getting to the ranch before I did! I have to admit, I was a little jealous.

Joshua loves what he is doing and when he arrived here, there was a sweet letter from the parents of the little boy he rescued. He now has a place to stay if he ever goes near Phoenix, Arizona. I miss having him around, but Micah and William have become older brothers to me as well. I can tell both of them pretty much anything.

The thing I miss most about being stuck in this house during this blizzard is teaching. I really do love teaching. Even when the students don't do what I tell them to, misbehave, or have problems of some sort, I love what I'm doing. I wouldn't want to do it my whole life, but I do love it right now for this season of my life.

I'm grateful we have a lenient school board. They allow me to choose the school days and let school out early if I decide to for whatever reason.

The howling of the wind is driving me crazy. Between that and the cold... I try to read, but the howling wind is horrible for concentration. Writing in you has helped tune it out some, but not enough. I wish I had a victrola. At least then I could turn on some music to help drown the noise out. Praying is about the only other thing I can do that keeps the wind from making me go *insane. But I'm afraid most of my prayers are complaints right now.*

Well, I can't think of anything else to say right now. I think I'll continue trying to read "Little Women." If this blizzard lasts much longer, I'll finish it again. This is only my fifth time reading the book since Mother gave it to me for Christmas four years ago. Meg, Jo, Beth, and Amy are calling my name.

Thank you for listening so patiently.

Micah gritted his teeth as another gust of wind shook the house. He glanced at Jeremiah. He was picking at his food.

"Not hungry?"

Jeremiah shrugged. "I'm hungry, I just don't feel like eating. The sound of the wind is too unsettling."

Micah nodded. "After three days of this, I agree."

"I think I'll just go to bed. At least when I'm asleep I don't hear the wind as much."

"All right," Micah said. "I'll clean up supper."

Micah moved slowly around the small kitchen and

took a deep breath. At least now he didn't have to pretend as much. He had tried to stay calm and unworried around Jeremiah, but every night when Jeremiah was asleep, Micah paced up and down, up and down. When the last dish was clean, Micah looked around the house. Pacing didn't solve anything. But what else could he do?

"Lord, I need Your peace. Help me to not worry about the people in this town and Ruth in particular. I know she's in Your hands and You will take care of her. Even though I know this, I worry that she isn't warm enough and that her wood and food won't last long enough. God, if she is in need of anything, please let me know so I can do whatever I can to help her.

"Heavenly Father, You are the Comforter, the Prince of Peace, the Creator and Protector of the world. Keep everybody in and around Castle City safe and inside their homes. If they need to care for their animals, give them what they need to stay safe while they do so. And if You wouldn't mind, please take this worry away from me. Or at least help me worry less. Thank You, Lord. Amen."

After his prayer, Micah realized just how exhausted he was. He climbed into bed without taking his clothes off. At the last second, he bent over to take off his boots. He was asleep before his head hit the pillow.

Sometime during the night or early morning, Micah woke with a start. Was it a noise? Micah lay still trying to remember. He listened for a minute before realizing the wind had stopped. He jumped out of bed, pulled his boots on, and raced for his son's room.

Shaking Jeremiah awake, Micah whispered, "The blizzard stopped, at least briefly. I'm going to check things outside."

Jeremiah sat up and rubbed his eyes. He cocked his head and a slight smile touched his face. "Okay. I can't come, can I?"

Micah shook his head. "If I'm not back by the time you get up, put some wood on the fire and stay warm. I'll try not to take long, but I'm sure the drifts will be hard to get through."

"You're gonna check on Miss Brookings, right?"

Micah nodded and stood up. "Yes."

"If I came with you, we could both shovel through the drifts," Jeremiah suggested.

"No. If the storm comes up suddenly, we would both be stuck out in it. With just one person, there is more of a chance of that person making it."

Jeremiah huffed. "Fine. I guess I'll stay here and pray."

"Thank you. I'll be back soon, Jeremiah."

"I hope so."

Micah left his son's room and put his coat, scarf, and mittens on. As he grabbed a few leftover biscuits, he prayed, "Lord, bring me back safely, please."

He looked out the window, but it was too dark outside to see anything. Grabbing a shovel, he swung the front door open, thanking whoever had built the house for making the door swing inside. He stared out the door and his mouth gaped. In front of him was a wall of white with just a thin sliver of darkness showing at the top. When he got his wits back, he closed the door and trudged upstairs.

Micah opened the window above the lean-to roof and climbed out onto the snowy roof, keeping a close grip on the windowsill so he didn't fall before he was ready. Micah threw the shovel down and it landed with the handle almost half deep in the snow. That was a good sign. He hoped. He sat on the edge of the roof and took a deep breath.

"Here goes nothing," he said as he pushed himself off the roof. He landed an arm's length away from the shovel and sank past his knees in the snow. With a shaky breath, he straightened and reached for his shovel.

It took him an hour to shovel out the lean-to door and the path around to the front of the house where he dug out the front door. From there, he shoveled himself a path out of his yard and to the sidewalk. The snow was at least two feet deep and in many places, over four feet deep.

When he reached Ruth's house, he paused for breath just outside the gate. Glancing at the sky, he couldn't tell if the clouds were dark because it was early in the morning or because another storm was blowing in. He hoped it was the former. With renewed vigor, he finished shoveling the path to Ruth's door. The wind must have been blowing from the west since the porch railing and roof didn't stop the snow from burying her door.

He knocked loudly three times, waited a few seconds, then knocked again.

"I'm coming," a sleepy voice said.

The door cracked open. "Who is it?" Ruth asked.

"Me. Micah," Micah said.

"Micah? What are you doing here at this hour?" Ruth asked.

"I came to check on you. I didn't know how long the storm would be done and wanted to take advantage of the break while I could."

"I'm fine," Ruth said. "Now get out of here before someone sees you and thinks something awful."

Micah chuckled. "Sorry. I didn't think of that. But I've been out here for over two hours and haven't seen another soul and they wouldn't be able to see out of the windows."

"I don't care," Ruth said. "Thank you for checking on me. I'm doing fine. Now please go home before another storm hits. If one does."

Micah nodded. "Stay warm."

"I am," Ruth replied as she closed and locked the door.

Micah stared at the closed door. This side of Ruth was new. He sighed. But she did have a point. And as a schoolteacher, she had to exemplify morality to her students. He turned away and made his way back to his house along the opposite side of the street.

An hour later, he was home and his son was happy to see him. After shoveling out a window, Micah listened as the wind picked up again. He looked outside. It was lighter out now and he could see the snow starting to fall again.

"Lord, let this be a light snow, and not another blizzard."

"Amen," Jeremiah said. "I've had enough of this. How bad was it, Pa?"

Micah walked to the front door. "There was snow piled up to here." He stretched his hand up until it was an inch below the top of the door.

Jeremiah stared at him in amazement. "I don't believe it!"

Micah smiled. "The snow drifted like that almost everywhere I saw."

"Did you get to Miss Brookings?"

"Yes," Micah said. "She's all right."

Jeremiah cocked his head and chose not to comment on the odd look that crossed his father's face.

"When can we leave the house?" Jeremiah asked.

Micah sighed. "When I'm sure this snowstorm isn't another blizzard."

"When will you know that?"

"A couple more hours, probably."

Jeremiah sighed. "Fine. I guess I'll go finish up that history assignment."

Micah fought a smile. "Sounds like a good idea."

CHAPTER SEVENTEEN

February 16, 1880
Dear Diary,

Help me! I'm going crazy. I always wondered what it would be like to be all alone for a few days with just my Bible, a book, God, and you. Now I know. It's horrible. I've always enjoyed praying. At least recently. I love praising God and praying for people who need it. Yesterday, I barely managed to pray for fifteen minutes before I had to stop because I caught myself complaining.

Reading "Little Women" has helped, but it's even hard to concentrate on that with the wind howling through the house. It sounds like a cougar crossed with a wolf. Sleep has been hard to come by. I either wake up because the fire is starting to die, or I can't get to sleep because of the wind slamming things into the wall or just howling and screeching through the cracks.

God, I need You. I need Your strength. Please let this blizzard leave us soon. I'm not sure how much longer I can stand it in here.

February 17, 1880
Dear Diary,

It's now Tuesday morning. The blizzard has been blowing through since Friday night. To say that I want out of here would be an understatement. It has been three days since I last talked to a real person. Well, until early this morning, that is. The storm stopped for a while and I woke up because it was so quiet.

A couple hours later, I was dozing when I heard a knock on the door. I don't even really know what time it was. I opened the door just a crack, even though I knew it was Micah. Oh, how I wanted to invite him inside for some tea and a long talk! But it was risky enough with him standing out in the cold with me inside.

I think I might have hurt his feelings by shooing him away the way I did. I'll have to make amends when the storm is over. Micah must have shoveled out my window. Either that or it didn't drift as much there.

It is snowing again, but this time, it seems to be a light snow. I've seen a few brave souls venture out to shovel themselves out.

I've lived here almost five years, but this is the highest I've ever seen snowdrifts after just one snowstorm. Most of the drifts go all the way up to the lower sills on the windows if not higher.

I wonder what it's like out at the ranch. How are the horses surviving? Did they find shelter? Are the ranch hands all safe? Are my parents safe? Are any of them snowed in? I wish I had a way to find out, but I don't. I'm stuck here with just my own thoughts, a semi-warm fire, you, and God.

I'm going to have to figure out what to do about school. It will take at least from now to the end of the week to dig everybody out. Right now, I'm thinking I'll give the students another week off. It probably won't be safe for at least half the children until then anyway.

If the snow and wind don't pick up in the next hour or so, I'm going to go visit Annabelle. If I get stuck there for a couple days because another blizzard blows in, I don't care. I'd rather be stuck there with them for a couple days than be here by myself any longer than I already have been.

My mind is going a million different directions in an attempt not to go crazy. Thoughts of school, the children, the people in town, my family, my friends are all jumbled up. I'm sorry if I keep hopping from one topic to another, but that's the way my brain is working right now.

Well, I suppose I should get something to eat and maybe by the time I'm done with that, the snow will have stopped. Thank you for being here for me. Not that you had much choice.

An hour later, Ruth bundled up in her warmest coat, a shawl, scarf, and mittens. Before opening the door, she took a deep breath. As much as she had hated being stuck in this house, at least she'd known she was mostly safe inside. Outside, even though the wind had died down and the snow appeared to be slowing, a blizzard could blow in very quickly.

She opened the door and stepped out onto her porch. Micah had obviously shoveled her porch off earlier in the morning. She could see that snow had been there, but it was now gone. With a shrug, she locked the door and hurried down the steps.

"Hi, Miss Brookings!" a cheerful voice called as she passed the General Store.

Ruth looked around and spotted Jeremiah shoveling snow off the streets into a pile almost twice as tall as he was. "Hi, Jeremiah! How are you doing?"

"Better now that I can be outside."

Ruth smiled. "I know what you mean."

"Where ya headed?"

"I'm going to Annabelle's house to visit with her," Ruth said. "Where's your pa?"

"He's somewhere around shoveling something. You might see him on your way to the Wilsons'."

"Thank you, Jeremiah," Ruth said with a smile. "Have fun shoveling."

Jeremiah grinned. "Oh, I will!"

Ruth skirted around a pile of snow spilling out of an alley. She looked up at it as she walked past. The amount of snow was mind-boggling. As she approached the Wilsons' mansion, she heard raised voices coming from around the snowbank between her and the house.

"I'm telling you, the good-for-nothing ran away and probably got stuck in the storm!" Mayor Wilson's voice rose to a pitch Ruth had never heard from him before.

"Mayor Wilson," Micah's calming voice said, "I'm sure he just went home to his family. I will go check to make sure he is safe at home. If he isn't, I will gather a search party and we will look for him. In the meantime, I suggest you do something productive to work off some of your nervous energy. Maybe you could grab a shovel and help the men clear the sidewalk and roads."

Ruth walked around the snowbank and approached the house. As she came up to the gate, she heard the mayor's gasp.

"I will not stoop so low! I have servants for that purpose."

"It would help your political aspirations if you showed you care for the people by helping them out. As mayor, you don't have to do it, but if you do it anyway, it would show you have a kind heart."

Mayor Wilson glared at Micah until the creak of the gate caught his attention. He glanced at Ruth, then turned back to Micah. "Let me know when you find Thomas. And tell him to come here right away." He turned back to Ruth. "Are you waiting for something?"

Ruth gulped. She saw why Annabelle didn't like getting on his bad side. "I...I was hoping to talk to Sheriff Carson a few minutes before visiting with Annabelle."

The mayor nodded. "Annabelle and her mother left an hour ago to check on the Jenkinses."

Ruth forced herself to smile. "Thank you, Sir. I'll go join them there."

"I'll escort you so you can tell me what you wanted," Micah said.

"Thank you, Sheriff," Ruth replied.

They left Mayor Wilson behind and walked toward the parsonage.

"I wanted to apologize," Ruth said. "My attitude this morning wasn't very good and I was rather snippy toward you. I'm sorry."

"You had a right to be snippy. I should've thought how it would reflect on you. If anything, I should apologize for not thinking beyond my 'need' to make sure you were doing all right."

Ruth smiled. "So shall we both forgive each other and be done with it?"

Micah glanced at Ruth, a smile forming on his face. "Yes. I forgive you, Ruth."

"And I forgive you," Ruth replied.

They strode past the sheriff's office. "How are you after three days alone?" Micah asked.

"Very glad to be out of the house and wishing I dared to go home to the ranch," Ruth answered. "I managed somehow. Although, I do need to talk to the school board. The wind goes right through the house. I ate, slept, and was spiritless in the easy chair which I pulled as close to the fire as I could without lighting myself on fire. Even then I got chilled if I didn't put wood on every couple of hours. If I got out of the chair, I put this shawl on to keep me semi-warm while I gathered wood or cooked."

Micah raised his eyebrows. "That needs to be fixed. Especially since this is supposed to be a cold winter."

Ruth nodded and stopped walking. "Here's the parsonage. Thank you for being so understanding."

"You're welcome."

"Godspeed finding Thomas."

Micah chuckled. "I'm almost positive he's at his house, but thank you. I'll see you around."

Later that morning, Ruth looked up at the sky as she left the parsonage. "Lord, is the weather going to hold? I pray that it does. I'd really like to get this school situation worked out and then go to the ranch."

"Howdy, Miss Brookings!"

Ruth looked around. She smiled when she spotted Jeremiah leaning on a shovel. "Good morning again, Jeremiah."

"What's happenin' with school?"

Ruth cocked an eyebrow. "Obviously I need to do a little more grammar review with some of my students. As for when school will start up again, I'm not sure. I have to talk to Mr. Jensen and possibly the school board."

Jeremiah shrugged. "Pa's in his office iffen you need to talk to him."

Ruth closed her eyes. "Jeremiah..."

Jeremiah grinned. "I know, don't use that kinda grammar. But you're so pretty when you get mad."

Ruth opened her mouth to protest and decided not to bother with a response, leaving the chuckling boy behind. After a short talk with the head of the school board, it was decided school would start when the snow was cleared from the roads of the students farthest away.

"I'll talk to the board and we'll get the cottage fixed soon, too," Mr. Jensen said. "I'm thinking someone didn't finish his job. Considering his reliability in other matters, I suppose I shouldn't be surprised. We'll see to it that all the students are informed about when school will start up again."

"Thank you," Ruth replied. "I'll be out at the ranch until the night before school starts up again."

"We'll announce it at church since most of the students and their parents go to church."

Ruth nodded as she stood up. "Thank you again, Mr. Jensen."

"You're welcome. Stay safe and warm on your trek to the ranch."

"I will," Ruth replied. She walked out into the fresh air. Mr. Jensen was a nice enough man most of the time, but the smell of the pipe he smoked was overpowering. The hair at the back of her neck stood on end and she wondered why. Trusting her instincts, she took a few quick steps toward the sheriff's office. As she passed a side street, a voice whispered, "What was Micah doing at your house so early this morning?"

Ruth's breathing and feet both stopped. She willed herself to move forward, to keep moving, but her legs refused to move. She knew the voice and refused to look at him. With an effort, she forced herself to breathe slowly and evenly. "I do not need to explain myself to you, Mr. Miller. But, he came to check up on me to make sure I was fine after the storm."

"Mm hm," Grover said. "If you want me to keep quiet about your liaisons with him, you'll need to give me something of yourself. Even just a kiss will do."

Ruth swallowed hard and the next words out of her mouth were harsh. "I would rather you tell everybody about it than even think once about kissing you."

"You might want to think about that. You could lose your job, your status as the perfect role model, and your last chance to marry anyone."

Ruth clenched her jaw. "The people of this town know better than that. I might lose my job, but kissing you would make me lose my chance to marry more than you spreading rumors would. And I don't have the status of a perfect role model. Excuse me, I need to get home."

Ruth's legs finally moved and she took quick, deliberate steps to the sheriff's office, opened the door, stepped inside, and leaned against the door when it shut.

Micah looked up and stared at her, but Ruth didn't even notice him.

"Miss Brookings?" Micah asked quietly. She didn't respond. "Ruth? What's the matter?"

The doorknob turned and someone tried to open the door. Ruth snapped out of her daze long enough to move out of the way. She stumbled to a chair and collapsed into it.

Micah kept an eye on her out of the corner of his eye while he waited for the intruder to come in.

"Sheriff, I was wonderin'..."

"Grover, what are you doing in town?" Micah asked.

"I got stuck in town when the storm hit."

"Have you been out to check on your kids?"

Ruth's head snapped up at the question.

Grover cleared his throat. "No."

"Make sure you do that as soon as you leave. Now, why are you here?"

"I thought, as sheriff and a member of the school board, you needed to know what the purty little schoolteacher is doin' most nights when she ain't teachin'."

Micah narrowed his eyes at Grover. "I don't know what lies you're about to spout off, and I don't want to know. Go home and check on your kids. Now. Or I'll lock you up."

Grover's eyes grew wide. "On what charges?"

"Child neglect. Now git! And don't you dare spread ANY rumors about Miss Brookings. Not that anybody would believe them anyway."

Grover snarled. "That's what you think." He stormed out of the office and Micah closed the door behind him.

Micah looked at Ruth. "What happened?"

"Him."

Micah sucked in a breath. "Would you like me to take you home?"

"Yes, please."

Micah nodded. "I'll go get Jeremiah, a sleigh, and a long-legged horse."

Ruth could only nod and Micah got concerned. "What did... Should I leave you here alone?"

Ruth shook herself and looked up at him. "I'll be fine. I just need to get home."

Micah pursed his lips together. "All right, but I'll be back soon and I'll send Jeremiah here shortly."

Ruth didn't respond.

Micah hurried outside, not realizing he'd forgotten his coat. "Jeremiah!" he shouted when he saw his son.

"Yeah, Pa?"

"Go to the office and keep Ruth company while I get a sleigh. We're taking her home."

"Why do I have to keep her company?"

Micah sighed. "Don't question, just obey."

Jeremiah shrugged. "Okay."

Five minutes later, Micah parked the sleigh in front of the sheriff's office.

Micah heard Jeremiah's shout of, "He's here!" and chuckled as he hopped off the sleigh, tying the horse to the hitching post. He hurried inside.

"It's too cold out there to go without a coat. Brr!"

Ruth stood up and blinked her eyes. "Why did you go outside without your coat?"

"I was too worried about getting you home to think about my coat."

"Oh."

Micah smiled and grabbed his coat. "Shall we go?"

"I'm ready!" Jeremiah exclaimed.

"You're always ready for something new," Ruth said. "I'm ready to get home."

Micah nodded. "Are you feeling better?"

"No. Just coping with it better."

Micah glanced at Jeremiah. "What happened?"

Ruth shook her head. "Not now."

Jeremiah looked first at his pa then at Ruth. "I think I'll go out and see if the horse wants a carrot."

Micah smiled. "Thank you, Jeremiah." After the door closed behind him, Micah said, "You don't have to tell me if you don't want to."

"That would be a great friendship," Ruth said with sarcasm. "I don't want to say it out loud, but I do want to tell you."

"Would you like a piece of paper?" Micah teased.

A slight smile showed up on her face. "No! I want it in writing even less. He saw you at the cottage this morning. He's trying to blackmail me to keep him from saying anything."

Micah's jaw dropped open. "How? Money?"

Ruth shook her head. "No. He wanted something else."

Micah cocked his head, but didn't question further. Micah held his hand out to Ruth and she took it. "Let's get you home."

Jeremiah was already in the middle of the seat and had the reins in his hands. "Star and I are ready to go, Pa."

"I see that. Thank you." He helped Ruth into the sleigh and tucked the blanket around her. "Will you be warm enough?"

"Yes, thank you," she replied.

Micah walked around the back of the sleigh and pulled himself in. "Do you need anything from your cottage?"

Ruth leaned back. "Yes, I do."

Micah nodded and directed the sleigh toward the cottage.

Ruth ran in quickly and grabbed her Bible, diary, and school assignments. When she returned, Micah clucked to Star and they glided along in silence for a few minutes.

"Would you please check on the Miller children when you get back to town?" Ruth asked.

Micah nodded.

"Why should he do that?" Jeremiah asked. "Their pa was there, wasn't he?"

"No," Micah replied. "He was in town when the storm hit."

"So those kids were all by themselves during the storm?" Jeremiah questioned.

"Yes," Ruth replied. "And even after the storm was done, Mr. Miller hadn't gotten out there yet until your pa practically threw him out of the sheriff's office."

"What?" Jeremiah exclaimed. "Why'd you do that, Pa?"

"He made crude comments in front of a lady and hadn't been out to check on his children yet."

"What's crude mean?" Jeremiah asked.

Ruth tried not to laugh. "You can take this one, Micah."

Micah cleared his throat a few times. "Crude is any topic or word that shouldn't be said to anybody, but especially in front of women and girls. And that will have to be enough of an explanation for now."

"Star is taking to this snow like a fish to water," Ruth said.

"Yes, he is," Micah replied. "That's why I chose him. He's one of your pa's horses and has never been one to shy from anything that I know of."

Ruth smiled. "Good."

"How much longer, Pa?"

Micah chuckled. "That depends on the snowdrifts. If it is drifted at all, we might have to stop to help Star. If it isn't, we could be there in about five minutes."

"I hope there isn't. I want to go out and see Peter."

"We can't stay long," Micah said.

"Not even till lunch?"

"No. I need to get back and help in town and check on the Miller children. And I don't want to be caught out here if there's another chance of more snow."

Jeremiah sighed. "Fine." He brightened suddenly. "Can I stay with them until Sunday?"

"No," Micah said. "First, you haven't been invited. Second, Sunday is almost a week away yet and you don't know if another storm might come up and snow you in at the ranch..."

"I don't mind," Jeremiah interrupted.

"I do. That is my final word on the matter, Jeremiah. You are not going to stay until Sunday."

Jeremiah crossed his arms. "But I could court Ruth for you and tell you everything she says and does and..."

Ruth choked. "No, your pa is the only Carson man who is going to court me. I won't have his son courting me."

Micah bit his tongue to keep from saying what was on the tip of his tongue. He knew he would regret it, so he let Ruth's reply stand.

Silence reigned in the sleigh until the entrance fence to the ranch came into sight. When Ruth saw the archway with the words "Double B Bar Ranch" carved out, she sank back into the seat and gave a happy sigh. Jeremiah sat up and bounced on the seat, alternately bumping into Ruth and Micah. Micah smiled at their reactions.

Three minutes later, Star pulled up in front of the porch. Micah climbed out and had barely walked one step before Jeremiah hopped out behind him and ran toward the bunkhouse.

Micah watched him as he walked around the sleigh. "I guess he's not coming in to say hello to your parents."

Ruth smiled for a second. "I guess not. Are you?"

"Do you mind?"

"No. You should probably hear everything anyway, both as sheriff and future beau."

Micah held out his hand and helped her out of the sleigh. They stood there, staring in different directions for a few seconds.

Ruth giggled nervously. "Now that we're here, I suddenly don't want to go inside."

Micah cocked his head. "Why not?"

"I don't know." She took a deep breath. "Let's go."

Micah kept her hand in his as he cleared a path for her to wade through. The door flung open before they reached the top of the porch steps.

"Ruth!" Harriet exclaimed as she gave Ruth a big hug. "You are all right! We were so worried about you! Let's get inside." She turned her head toward Micah. "Would you like to come in as well?"

"If it's all right, Ma'am."

Harriet smiled. "Of course it is. Come in." When she was inside, she yelled, "Daniel! Ruth's home with Micah." She lowered her voice. "Did you two come alone?"

"No, Mother. Jeremiah ran straight to the bunkhouse as soon as we got here." She cleared her throat as Daniel walked in and took her from her mother's arms to give Ruth a hug. When he released her, she pulled away. "I need to talk to you three."

She walked into the parlor and sat down on the edge of a chair. When the other three were settled in, she began. "Micah already knows pieces of this, but not everything. The blizzard was hard to get through. With the howling wind and being alone... If it weren't for my faith in God, I'm not sure I would have made it through." She then told them the rest that had happened that day, ending with, "...I told Grover I wouldn't and nearly ran to Micah's office." She stopped and looked around at each of them, looking at Micah last. "I don't remember much of what happened next until Jeremiah came in."

Micah cleared his throat and tried to keep his anger down. "Grover came in seconds after Ruth did and tried to get me to believe that Ruth was accepting late night callers while in town. As the sheriff and a member of the school board, he thought I should know. I turned the tables a little by defending her and asking what he was doing in town. His children spent the storm without a parent around."

Daniel shook his head. "I'll ride into town today to talk to Grover."

"Won't it be too late already?" Ruth asked.

"For what?" Daniel questioned.

"Well, folks might not believe the rumors, but I could still lose my job because of them."

"There's still half a year of school left. Who would they find to replace you? You may no longer be the perfect role model due to some rumors, but you'd be the best option."

"Annabelle could do it," Ruth said. "I would have to help her some to learn some of the teaching end of it, but she could do it."

"She's being courted, though," Micah said.

Ruth shrugged. "They might make an exception this time. I don't know."

"Let's wait and see what happens," Daniel said. "I'll talk to Grover tomorrow and I'm sure Micah already has."

"Yes, Sir, I have," Micah replied.

"Good. But having one more person saying something might help. Especially since I'm Ruth's father," Daniel said.

"I hope so," Ruth said.

"Are you going to stay for lunch?" Harriet asked Micah.

Micah shook his head. "As much as I'd like to, I shouldn't. I should be in town helping clean up and I still need to go out to make sure Grover's checked on his children."

Harriet nodded. "I understand."

Micah glanced at Ruth. "Now that you're home, you'll be fine, right?"

Ruth blinked and seemed to wake up even though her eyes had already been open. "Yes." She swallowed. "Yes, I am. I'll be fine. Thank you for bringing me home." She stopped and a shudder passed through her body as tears rolled down her cheeks and she hid her face in her hands.

Micah took one step forward before realizing he had no right to try to comfort her. He hurriedly stepped back as Harriet rushed to her daughter and pulled her into a tight hug. Daniel and Micah made eye contact and quietly left the room together.

"Thank you for checking on Ruth this morning, even if it has caused some problems," Daniel said.

"You're welcome. I just wish there was some way I could fix this."

"What if you went to Mr. Jensen and explained why the rumor might start flying around?"

Micah shrugged. "That might work. I'll see if I can do that later this afternoon. Right now, I should extricate my son from the bunkhouse and head home."

Daniel put his hand on Micah's shoulder. "You're welcome here any time. If you can come out tomorrow, it might be a good idea. With Joshua gone, Ruth doesn't have a protective older brother and you seem to have filled that void only in a slightly different way. Something tells me she would have preferred your comfort rather than her mother's right now. But I admire your self-control in resisting."

Micah felt his cheeks grow warm. "It was more like my conscience saying, 'Danger ahead!

Stop! Cease! Desist!'" He cleared his throat. "But thank you. Someday maybe I can be the one to comfort her if she needs it. In the meantime, we need to be patient while we wait to court. And then we have a lot to discuss. Edith and I had a short courtship and engagement. We also practically grew up with each other. I don't know if you prefer long courtships or not."

Daniel smiled. "If we feel you know each other enough and you know you are in love, Harriet and I are just fine with a short courtship. Martha and Matthew both had short courtships. Esther's was a bit longer, but they were married within a year of the courtship. It was only longer because David couldn't get up enough courage to ask my permission to marry her and then to ask her. I think he asked me a month before he finally asked her."

Micah laughed. "You're kidding!"

Daniel chuckled. "David was rather shy. Still is, actually. I miss him. When he did talk, you wanted to listen because he always said something that would either really make you think or was really important."

Micah nodded. "I had a friend like that in Chicago. He was impressive." Micah took a deep breath and let it out. "Would you tell your wife and daughter goodbye for me? I'll see if Jeremiah and I can come for lunch tomorrow if that's acceptable."

Daniel nodded. "That should be just fine. Thank you again for keeping an eye on Ruth when she's in town. In some ways, I almost hope she loses this job so I can stop worrying about her so much while she's living in town, and so you can finally come courting."

Micah half-smiled. "Me, too." He grabbed his coat off the hook and put it on. "I'll be seein' you."

"Goodbye, Micah. Stay safe."

Micah waved as he left the house.

CHAPTER EIGHTEEN

Harriet pulled Ruth into her arms and lap and held her tight. She didn't say anything, just held and rocked Ruth as she sobbed. When Ruth's crying slowed, Harriet kissed the top of her forehead. "Would you like to talk about it?"

Ruth lifted her head and looked around the room.

"Micah and your father both left us alone," Harriet assured her.

Ruth sighed in relief. "I don't even know why I started crying. Well, I guess I do know. As much as I like to be alone, I like to know someone is in the same house as me. And I can't be alone that long without some human contact. Being alone during the blizzard was horrible. Then to have *him* say that." She shuddered.

"What did he say exactly?" Harriet asked.

Ruth nodded. "He said, 'If you want me to keep quiet about your liaisons with him, you'll need to give me something of yourself. Even just a kiss will do.' Of course, I don't think he would ever be satisfied with just a kiss."

Harriet shook her head. "No, he wouldn't. Even though I know you like your job, I think it might be best if you do get fired. I don't want you staying there alone anymore."

Ruth pulled out of her mother's embrace and hugged herself. "I've had the same thought. But I don't want to leave the children without a teacher. I think Annabelle would be fine, but she hasn't had the training like I did. And I don't want to waste the money you and Pa spent on my training."

"If you don't lose the job, maybe you could have Annabelle stay with you."

Ruth nodded. "Maybe." She took a deep breath and let it out slowly as she stood up. "I need to do something to get my mind off of everything."

"It's almost time to start lunch, too."

"Is it all right if I go journal before I help you?"

Harriet stood up and put a hand on Ruth's shoulder. "Take all the time you need to journal, pray, and read Scripture. I've cooked lunch plenty of times without help; I can do it again."

Ruth gave her a half-smile. "Thank you, Ma."

Harriet pulled her into a quick hug. "You're welcome."

February 17, 1880
Later
Dear Diary,

The blizzard is over, I am exhausted, worn out, and feel horrible. I know I'm not supposed to complain, but I can't help it right now. I need to get some of my thoughts down or I will explode. Today, I've gone from ecstatic to horrified and shaky. A few months ago, Grover Miller asked to court me. I refused. Micah had to threaten him for him to leave me alone. He saw Micah check on me early this morning.

In a matter of days, I've gone from teaching to being stuck in a freezing house by myself to being blackmailed and practically propositioned. How in the world does this even happen? I still can't wrap my mind around the fact that he would dare do this. Maybe if I tell you everything, it will help. Although, telling Pa, Ma, and Micah didn't.

As I told you earlier, Micah showed up really early this morning to check on me. At first, I was thrilled that he would check on me. To know that someone cared so much about me... Well, then I had the thought that it was dangerous for him to be there. And I wasn't very kind with him and decided to go find him and apologize. I also wanted to talk to Annabelle.

Mayor Wilson was being rather rude to Micah when I got to the Wilson house, but at least I found Micah and the mayor told me where to find Annabelle. Micah walked me to the parsonage and we both apologized to each other. After he left, I joined the Jenkins family, Mrs. Wilson, and Annabelle. We had a good time talking and holding Rebekah. They all survived just fine. The men went out to help with the shoveling shortly after I arrived.

I was in a wonderful mood by the time I left. Being around people was just what I needed. But I was more than ready to go home to the ranch. First, I found Mr. Jensen and talked to him about school and the wind problems at the house. After that, I talked to

Jeremiah a little before I decided to go home. Before I got to the sheriff's office, Grover found me.

Before this, I had thought he was done thinking about me as a potential wife, but I guess not. Now I might lose my school teaching job just because Micah was sweet and decided to make sure I was all right. I can't even describe what I'm feeling. I'm horrified, shaky, tears in my eyes, my mind is blank, I can't think, I can't seem to want to do anything. I should be downstairs to help Mother, but I can't muster up the gumption to stop writing, get off my chair, and go down. All I want to do is sleep and hope it was all just a bad dream. But I know that won't help either.

I know I'm not supposed to be forming my opinion of Micah on my feelings, but it's really hard not to. We haven't even started courting yet, but we've known each other for years and have become really good friends. This afternoon, when he brought me here after Grover...I told Ma and Pa and him what had happened. After I was done, I broke down into tears. When I did,

Mother came to comfort me, but I wanted Micah. Is that wrong? Yes, I know it is, but... At least Mother's comfort was enough.

I know this is all disjointed, but that's how I feel right now. I feel like everything in my body is off somehow. I am so numb. I don't know what to do, think, feel, or anything. I've tried praying, but those prayers consist mostly of, "God, make these thoughts and memories go away. Please!" I know I'm supposed to pray for my enemies, but it's too raw yet. I just can't pray for him properly.

Does praying for his children count? Ever since I heard they were left alone during the blizzard, I've been praying for them. The oldest still home is only twelve! I wish there was something I could do for them, but unless I marry their father (which I wouldn't if he were the last man on earth), there's nothing I can do. Well, I can pray for them and pray he turns from the error of his way, I suppose.

Oh, Diary! I wish... I don't know what I wish. I wish a lot of things. I wish we hadn't come out here. I wish we hadn't met Jed. I wish Grover had learned how to be a gentleman. And yet, even as I wish those, I think of all that wouldn't have happened if those things hadn't happened. Anna, Jed, and Caleb probably wouldn't be Christians. Miles, John, and James would still be frazzled and running wild. Elizabeth would...I don't even want to think where she might have ended up. Same with Annabelle. I never would have met Annabelle or Micah. I wouldn't have grown into the woman I have become by God's grace.

Even with all that has happened, I can truly say it has all been for the best. Despite all the bad that happens, the good, in this case, outweighs the bad. I need to remember the words of the hymn,

He all my grief has taken,
and all my sorrows borne;
In temptation He's my strong
and mighty tow'r;
I've all for Him forsaken,
and all my idols torn
From my heart and now
He keeps me by His pow'r.

Though all the world forsake me,
and Satan tempt me sore,
Through Jesus I shall
safely reach the goal.

Lord, help me remember You are my strong and mighty tower and keep me by Your power. Help me remember the words of Psalm 91:

"He that dwelleth in the secret place of the most High shall abide under the shadow of the Almighty. I will say of the Lord, He is my refuge and my fortress: my God; in him will I trust. Surely he shall deliver thee from the snare of the fowler, and from the noisome pestilence. He shall cover thee with his feathers, and under his wings shalt thou trust: his truth shall be thy shield and buckler.

"Thou shalt not be afraid for the terror by night; nor for the arrow that flieth by day; Nor for the pestilence that walketh in darkness; nor for the destruction that wasteth at noonday. A thousand shall fall at thy side, and ten thousand at thy right hand; but it shall not come nigh thee. Only with thine *eyes shalt thou behold and see the reward of the wicked."*

You are my refuge and my fortress. In You I will trust. Cover me, Lord. I need Thee.

Harriet wished she knew what she could do to help Ruth, but the only thing she could think of was to pray. Even though she knew that was the most helpful thing to do, she'd always been one who liked to do something physical to help others. Since she couldn't, she bathed her daughter in prayer as the afternoon wore on.

As they sat down to lunch, Daniel asked, "Should we get Ruth?"

"No. She needs this time to write and pray."

He nodded. "Lord, I lift up my daughter. You know what she's been through more than we do. Give her Your peace and help her get through this tough time. Bless this food to our bodies and the hands that prepared it. In Jesus' name, amen."

"Amen."

The forks clinked on the plates as Daniel and Harriet sat in silence. "Did we do the wrong thing to let her teach?"

Harriet looked up. "No. I don't think so. God placed the desire on her heart. He wouldn't have done that if He didn't want her to teach."

Daniel sighed. "It's hard to see her go through this."

Harriet put her hand on his arm. "I know, but if she doesn't go through the hard things in life now, how much harder will it be for her later in life?"

Daniel reached his hand over his plate and patted her hand. "You are such a blessing to me, Harriet."

Harriet ducked her head and felt her cheeks warm.

"'Her children arise up, and call her blessed; her husband also, and he praiseth her. Many daughters have done virtuously, but thou excellest them all.' That is certainly true of you," Daniel said.

"Thank you, Daniel. I don't see it, but I also know you don't see just how wonderful you are either."

Daniel chuckled. "Exactly."

When it came time to go to bed, Ruth trudged up the stairs after a stilted dinner. None of the ranch hands knew anything about what had happened, but could tell something was wrong. Ruth forced her feet to move toward her bed and she sank onto the edge of her bed. "Energy. Motivation? Anything but this, God," Ruth muttered to herself. "Why? Why me? Why this? Why can't I just forget what he said and move on? Why, oh why, do I feel like my whole world has fallen apart? Elizabeth wasn't even a real Christian when Jed attacked her and she handled it so much better. And that was much worse than what Grover said. Why can't I handle it that way?"

Tears streamed down Ruth's cheeks and she did nothing to wipe them away or stop them from dripping onto her skirt.

"Heavenly Father, I know You are always there for Your children. And I know I just made an unfair presumption about Elizabeth. I know better than that. She wanted to kill herself, so I'm actually doing much better than she was; if you can call it that. And I have a mother to help me through this. Lord, I don't want to be like this anymore. Please help me forgive and forget. Help me learn to pray for Grover. I can't do it on my own."

With a shaky, sobbing breath, Ruth threw herself onto the bed and sobbed until a quilt square was soaked. As her tears slowed, Ruth lifted her head and she pushed herself off the bed. She was never more glad for her automatic routine than tonight. Without a single thought, Ruth got herself ready for bed, brushed her hair one hundred times, and pulled the covers down.

She slipped under the covers and blew out the candle. Laying her head on the pillow, she tried to close her eyes, but every time they closed, Grover's face was there. "God, I desperately need some real sleep tonight. Can You please keep Satan away tonight?"

Half an hour later, the clock downstairs chimed nine times and Ruth rolled over with a sigh. Her overactive mind was at it again. With another sigh, she closed her eyes and tried a trick Joshua had said worked for him sometimes, quoting verses in her head.

The next thing she knew, light streamed into the window above her and verses from Isaiah immediately popped into her head. With a smile, she threw the covers back and jumped out of bed. It was a new, fresh day, and she now had ammunition against any and all thoughts about Grover. Isaiah 40 was full of verses to comfort her through the day. As she dressed, she alternately chanted, said, and sang a few of the verses.

"Comfort ye, comfort ye my people saith your God...And the glory of the Lord shall be revealed, and all flesh shall see it together: for the mouth of the Lord hath spoken it...The grass withereth, the flower fadeth: but the word of God shall stand forever. O Zion, that bringest good tidings, get thee up into the high mountain; O Jerusalem, that bringest good tidings, lift up thy voice with strength; lift it up, be not afraid; say unto the cities of Judah, Behold your God! Behold, the Lord God will come with a strong hand, and His arm shall rule for Him: behold, His reward is with Him, and His work before Him. He shall feed His flock like a shepherd: He shall gather the lambs with His arm, and carry them in His bosom, and shall gently lead those that are with young."

As she brushed her hair, she contemplated the verses. "Thank You, Lord, for Your comfort and promises. I don't know where I would be if I didn't have You gently leading me on the paths You have for me. Even when it seems like You are making a mistake, I know You aren't. You always know exactly what we need, even if we don't know we need it. Thank You for Your mercies which are new every morning." She paused her brushing and looked in the small mirror. "Especially this morning, Lord. After the last few days, I...I actually feel like I can relax and do something with my life today. Yesterday, I was a mess and I'm not afraid to say it. Thank You."

Ruth set the brush on her dresser and braided her long, straight, brown hair, twisting it into a bun at the back of her head. With a nod to the mirror, she left the room and worked her way down the stairs to see what she had missed that morning.

CHAPTER NINETEEN

Micah and Jeremiah rode in silence back to town. Micah was lost in his own thoughts, and for once, Jeremiah didn't try to fill the silence until they saw the buildings at the edge of town.

"What'cha thinking about, Pa?" Jeremiah asked.

Micah jerked his head toward the sound of the voice and took in a sharp breath. "Lots of things."

Jeremiah bit his lip and gave his pa a glare out of the corner of his eye. Then a mischievous smile played on his lips. "Things like a certain young lady we left back at the ranch?"

Micah shot a glance at his son. "What is that tone of voice supposed to mean?"

Jeremiah smiled, but didn't respond.

Micah shook his head and rolled his eyes. "Fine. Yes, she was part of my thoughts, but probably not for the reason you're thinking. I wish we could have stayed for lunch."

Jeremiah straightened, knocking the blanket completely off of himself. "Why didn't we then?"

Micah sighed. "I have a duty as the Sheriff to be in town and available as much as possible when not taking some time off. After that storm, I'm needed in town. Plus, I need to check on the Miller children. And Ruth needs some time with her parents."

Jeremiah sighed and grabbed the blanket to put back on his lap. "I guess that makes sense. What else is involved as your duty?"

"Putting my job above my concern for the safety of those I love. At least in theory that's the case. However, if my family, or anybody, was being threatened by an outlaw, I would make sure they get to safety before I go out after him. I can always catch him later. What I can't do is bring the dead back to life."

Jeremiah nodded. "What were you thinking about that had to do with Miss Brookings?"

"That is none of your business."

"Why not?"

"Because I said so. Whoa!" He pulled the horses to a stop. "Here's where you get off."

"Micah!" a voice shouted.

Micah turned toward the voice and saw his deputy running toward him.

"Glad I caught you." Obadiah stopped running and tried to catch his breath. "Where to start is the next question."

Micah raised an eyebrow and jumped off the sleigh.

Obadiah took a deep breath. "Grover Miller was found in the saloon drunker'n anybody I ever did see. I threw him in jail none too gently to sleep it off."

Micah clenched his jaw and nodded tersely for Obadiah to continue.

"We got the streets in town mostly shoveled. Some men have started getting the roads away from town cleared. Mr. Jensen declared no school for at least another week while we get the roads all cleared. He also muttered something about schoolteacher trouble, but I didn't catch all of it, so I might be wrong. Um, oh yeah, and he needs help getting the schoolteacher's house fixed so wind doesn't go in and out so bad."

Obadiah took a deep breath. "We had two deaths."

Micah closed his eyes. "Who?"

"Emil and Luis Salvatorre. They were close to shelter, but didn't quite make it in time."

Micah inhaled and let it out slowly. "Do their families know yet?"

"Yes."

"Thank you for taking care of all this."

Obadiah shrugged. "It's my job. Oh yeah, I almost forgot, many of the ladies in town are making one large meal at the hotel for everybody whenever people can stop in to eat. It can be lunch, supper, or something in between. They figured since the storm had ever'body cooped up so long, it was a good time to spend together in town instead of just as families."

Micah took a deep breath and let it out. He raked his fingers through his hair as he looked up and down the street. "Would you mind taking your shift early?"

"I already kinda have. Why?"

"I'm going to go to the Miller farm and bring the kids home to stay at my place tonight. Then in the morning, I think I'll take them to the Brookings ranch until I decide to release their pa. Actually, could you do me one more favor?"

"Sure."

"Ride out to the Double B and tell Daniel he doesn't need to talk to Grover until Sunday."

"Talk about what?"

"He'll know what I'm talking about."

Obadiah shrugged. "All right. I'll be back in a shake of a lamb's tail."

As Obadiah jogged to the livery, Micah looked around for his son and saw him talking to John, James, Clem, and Chancy. "Jeremiah!" he yelled.

"Yeah, Pa?"

Micah beckoned for him and Jeremiah ran over, his friends trailing behind him. "I need you to go home and get the house ready for some guests. The Miller children are going to stay with us tonight and into tomorrow morning." A sudden thought came to him. "Stay here, I need to catch Obadiah quick."

He ran to the livery stable. "Obadiah!"

"Yeah?"

"Could you ask Daniel and Harriet if they're willing to let me bring the Miller children out there tomorrow?"

Obadiah tipped his hat. "Will do."

Micah waved his thanks as Obadiah spurred his horse into a gallop. As Obadiah faded into the distance, Micah turned and gave final instructions to Jeremiah. Jeremiah enlisted his friends' help and they all trooped off while Micah climbed back into the sleigh and made his way to the Miller farm.

Micah clenched his jaw and tried to keep his anger in check as he clucked to the horse. He could hardly believe what he'd seen at the Miller cabin and knew he had to keep as far away from Grover as possible for at least a day. And calm down before the children in the sleigh with him thought he was angry at them. He took a deep breath and very slowly let it out, praying for strength and calm.

"Are we in trouble, Sheriff?" the oldest boy asked.

Micah swallowed and took another deep breath, the anger rolling off him as he prayed. "No, Son, you aren't. Your pa's the one who's in trouble."

"What'd he do now?" a girl who couldn't be more than five asked.

Micah ran his tongue across his teeth and tapped his toes on the floorboards. "I can't say right now, Sweetheart. Maybe someday I can explain it to you, but not today."

"Why not?" the oldest boy asked.

Micah's grip on the reins tightened. "What are your names again?"

The oldest boy grinned. "I'm Otis, the next one is Olive, then comes Ellis, Mary, and Carter."

Micah nodded. "Like I said at your house, you five are going to stay at my house tonight and then hopefully the Brookings family will take you in until your pa is able to take care of you again."

"I'm cold," a small voice said.

Micah slowed the horse to a walk and tucked the blanket around the two little ones to his left. On his right, Mary snuggled in closer and laid her head on his lap. At first, he stiffened, unsure what

246

to do. Then he pulled the blanket back around her and put a reassuring hand on her head, a lump swelling in his throat. Carter gripped his left arm and Micah fought not to cry. Had these children been so deprived of the simple touch of a caring man that they would seek it from a man who was nearly a stranger to them?

"How old are you, Otis?" Micah asked as he encouraged the horse into a trot.

"Twelve."

"And your brothers and sisters?"

"Samantha, the only one not here, is sixteen and just got married. Olive's ten, Ellis is seven, Mary is five, and Carter is three."

Micah nearly choked when he heard how young Samantha was. "Did Samantha really want to be married that young?"

Otis cocked his head. "Yes, she did. She loves Lou. And I don't blame her for wantin' to leave Pa, either."

Micah nodded and decided to change the topic. "How'd you make it through the storm?"

Otis shrugged. "When we got home from school, we brought lotsa wood in. Olive cooked us some food when we couldn't go no longer and we huddled together in front of the fire to stay warm. Weren't too bad."

Mary shuddered and climbed into Micah's lap. Micah instinctively put an arm around her, warming and comforting her. "You didn't like it, did you, Mary?" Micah asked.

Mary shook her head, then flinched as if expecting to be reprimanded for her answer. Micah swallowed past the lump in his throat. *God,* he cried out silently, *what can I legally do to keep these kids away from their father? I can barely raise my own son. How would I be able to raise five more? Would Ruth even think about marrying me if she has to become an instant mother to six?* He shook his head. He couldn't think about that at least until they officially started courting.

"I didn't like it," Mary replied. "The wind scared me."

Otis's eyes went wide and he shot Mary a warning glance and shushed her.

Micah let go of Mary and put a hand on Otis's shoulder. "It's okay, Otis. She can tell me that. I'm not like your pa."

Otis stared at him. "What do you mean?"

"I won't get mad at her for answering my question honestly."

Otis blinked his eyes and stared at Micah with curiosity and doubt in his eyes.

Micah looked back at the road and saw they had entered town. He took his hand off Otis's shoulder and tucked Mary between his arms. "We're almost there, Kids," he announced.

"Where?" Ellis asked.

"To his house," Olive replied. "Weren't you listening to him?"

"Oh yeah," Ellis said. "I forgot."

Micah chuckled. "Do you remember Jeremiah from school?"

Ellis nodded. "He's nice."

Olive huffed. "Maybe to you he is, but he isn't to me."

Micah bit his cheeks to keep from smiling. "He's my son and you'll get to spend all of tonight and at least part of tomorrow with him."

"Yippee!" Ellis shouted.

Micah let his smile appear this time. At least one member of this group of children was excited. Otis and Olive seemed resigned to whatever fate came their way and Mary and Carter were simply starved for love.

Micah pulled the horse to a stop in front of the house that had always seemed too large. Now it seemed much too small. "Seven people," he muttered. "And who's going to make us something to eat?

"All right!" he said. "Here's our stop for the night. Everybody off the sleigh." He looked around. "On second thought, I'll get off and help each of you off. I'm not sure how slippery it is out here and we don't want anyone getting hurt."

Otis smiled shyly. "No, we don't." He waited for Micah to get off the sleigh before holding his hand out to Olive. "Ladies first, Dear Sister."

Olive rolled her eyes and Micah forced the laugh down. Olive needed to learn how to loosen up and be a little girl. Maybe Ruth could help her with that. When each of the children was off the sleigh, he led them inside the house. "Jeremiah!" he called.

"Yeah, Pa?" Jeremiah asked, coming out of the kitchen.

"Our guests are here."

"Hiya Otis, Olive, and Ellis," Jeremiah said with a wave. "These two must be Mary and Carter, right?"

Otis nodded as he stared around the entryway. As Micah watched him, he saw his house in a new light. After seeing the way the Miller family lived, his house seemed like a mansion.

"Pa, there's a meal being served at the hotel for everybody," Jeremiah said.

Micah opened his mouth and then shut it. "I nearly forgot that Obadiah said that. Is anybody hungry?"

Mary tugged on his sleeve with one hand while keeping a tight grip on his hand with the other.

"Yes, Mary?" Micah asked, looking down at her.

"I'm hungry," she whispered.

Micah knelt down in front of her and brushed a lock of blond hair off her forehead. "Me, too," he whispered. With a smile, he stood up and looked around at the six children. "Let's go eat."

"We can't eat at the hotel," Otis protested.

"Why not?" Micah asked.

"It's too expensive," Otis replied.

"This meal is free for everyone, Otis," Micah said. "The ladies in town made a meal for everybody. Since everybody was cooped up for a few days with no one but family, they decided to make today a social day."

Otis looked reluctant, but Jeremiah took matters into his own hands. "Come on, Otis. Don't be such a spoilsport. Plus it'll be tons better than anything Pa throws together. Let's go to the hotel and eat."

Otis chewed his lower lip, but didn't protest.

As soon as they entered the hotel restaurant, they were all hit by the most wonderful smell ever. Micah saw Obadiah shoveling food into his mouth and their eyes met. When Obadiah had finished his last bite, he hurried over to Micah.

"The Brookings' are happy to help with the kids. Ruth seemed especially excited for the distraction."

"Good. Thank you for going over there. Are you sure you can watch Grover tonight?" Micah asked.

"Yep, I can."

"Good. I don't trust myself to go near him." Micah turned to Jeremiah. "Could you and Otis take everybody and find a place for us to sit?"

"Sure, Pa."

Obadiah and Micah moved away from the crowd. "Why don't you trust yourself?" Obadiah asked in a hushed tone.

"After seeing those children today and what condition the house and farm are in, I don't trust myself not to lock him up and throw away the key. Either that or to haul him out of there and beat him until he's unrecognizable. That house is a disgrace. If Ruth thought her cottage was bad, this one was even worse. The fences are in such disrepair, a grizzly could go through them without batting an eyelash. His children are afraid of the simplest gesture of care. If you get tired of waiting tonight, see if you can find any laws against child neglect so I can have him locked away until Carter is old enough to be on his own."

Obadiah stared at him. "Are you all right?"

Micah clenched his fists and looked away. "Why do you ask?"

"I've never seen you so angry."

"I've never had this much reason to be angry."

Obadiah's eyebrows connected as his eyes narrowed. "Why?"

"I know I'm not a perfect father and I neglect Jeremiah more than I should due to my job. But Grover is a lazy, disgusting man, and I don't want to talk about it here."

Obadiah nodded. "I'll head back to the jail then and keep an eye on the man. He's probably still sleeping anyway."

Micah took a deep breath. "Thank you. I owe you one."

Obadiah took one look at the children. "No, you don't owe me anything. You'll have your hands full tonight. And I don't envy you that."

Micah felt a tug on his pant leg and looked down to see Mary trying to get his attention. "Yes, Miss Mary?"

"Are you going to eat with us?" Mary asked.

Obadiah waved. "Like I said..."

Micah glared at him. "Just watch the man and don't let me in there."

Obadiah saluted and nearly ran out of the hotel.

Micah bent down and picked Mary up. "I'm coming now, Sweetheart."

"Who were you talking 'bout?" Mary asked.

"Someone my deputy put in jail."

"What's a dep-a-ty?"

Micah opened his mouth and shut it. "Do you know what a sheriff is?"

Mary nodded, a solemn look on her face. "He locks Daddy up sometimes when he's too drunk to walk."

Micah swallowed. How old was Mary? Five? Even if she were ten, she shouldn't have to know about that. He tried to hide the sigh. "Yes, he does do that sometimes. Well, a deputy helps the sheriff when the sheriff has other things to do." Micah started toward the table Jeremiah and Otis had chosen.

"What's the sheriff doing tonight?" Mary asked, pulling on his beard.

"Eating dinner with two lovely young ladies, and four hungry young men," Micah replied as he put Mary in the chair next to her sister.

Micah looked around the crowded restaurant as he settled into a chair. "Lots of people here."

"May I join you?" a female voice asked. "It looks like the sheriff could use some assistance."

Micah glanced at the woman who spoke. "If you really want to help, Miss Wilson."

"Is there room for Mother, too? She's the one who suggested we join this table."

Micah was about to stand and offer his chair when Jeremiah beat him to it. "You can have my chair. I'll go find two more."

Annabelle smiled at Jeremiah. "Thank you, Jeremiah. That's very sweet of you." She sat on the chair Jeremiah had vacated and smiled at Ellis and Carter.

"Where is your mother?" Micah asked.

"She went to ask the ladies to bring some food to this table for you," Annabelle answered.

"Is that what I was supposed to do?" Micah asked. "I'm afraid I haven't had time to figure out what's going on let alone anything else."

Annabelle laughed. "Don't worry about it, Sheriff Carson. We've all heard about..." She glanced at the children and left the rest of the sentence unsaid. "Obadiah, Jeremiah, John, Clem, Chancy, and James also told many people about your generous offer to take care of these children until you could get them out to the Double B tomorrow."

"We're going to Miss Brookings' ranch?" Otis asked, excitement lighting up in his eyes.

Micah smiled. "Yes, you are. If the weather holds, we'll head over there in the morning."

Jeremiah returned with two more chairs and Otis scooted his chair closer to Carter while Micah stood up to rearrange the chairs the younger children were sitting on to make more room.

"Where're we going in the morning?" Jeremiah asked.

"The Double B Bar Ranch!" Otis exclaimed.

Jeremiah looked at his pa with wide eyes. "Again?"

"Mr. and Mrs. Brookings have offered to take care of the Miller children until their father can... Or rather, until I figure out what to do with their father," Micah replied.

"What do you mean?" Olive asked.

Micah sighed. "He's in jail right now."

"We have some food. Are any of y'all hungry?" a new voice interjected.

The words, "I am!" came from four mouths.

The four ladies carrying trays of food smiled.

"I always like feeding enthusiastic eaters. It makes me think I might actually be able to cook," Mrs. Hatchett said with a wink at Olive.

Olive blushed at the attention and whispered a thank-you as Mrs. Hatchett set a plate in front of her.

"Your cooking is always superb, Mrs. Hatchett," Micah said. "I should know. I eat here more often than I eat at home."

Mrs. Hatchett fanned herself as if blushing. "Oh you are a flatterer, Micah Carson. You just say that because you don't have Miss Brookings cooking for you every day. Now if anyone can cook, it's that young lady." She put a finger to her chin. "In fact, perhaps you should start courting her and marry her so you can stop being forced to waste your money eating my cooking."

Micah's face grew unbearably hot and he picked up his glass of water, taking a large gulp. "This water is superb," he said, trying to change the subject.

Mrs. Hatchett waved a finger at him. "You won't get away with that, Young Man. Is there any reason you shouldn't think about courting Ruth Brookings?"

Jeremiah piped up. "Yep. Because he's gonna as soon as school's out."

Mrs. Hatchett's eyes darted to Jeremiah and back to Micah while Olive giggled. "You're going courting and never told me?"

Micah swallowed hard, this time from fear. "No, Ma'am. I didn't. We wanted it to stay quiet."

Mrs. Hatchett's smile broadened. "Of course!" She leaned in and whispered loudly, "I'll be sure to keep my lips sealed. Enjoy your food." She sauntered off with an air of importance that Micah knew was faked.

Turning his attention back to the table and seeing everybody, including Mrs. Wilson, seated and waiting, he said, "Let's pray." When all the heads were bowed, Micah began, "Dear Heavenly Father, we thank You for this day. Thank You that the snow stopped. I pray for the snow to hold off at least until the Miller children safely arrive at the ranch tomorrow morning. Give me wisdom in dealing with their father. Thank You for this food and bless the many hands that prepared it. In Jesus' name, amen."

The children dug into their food as if they hadn't eaten much in days. Then Micah remembered they likely hadn't eaten much since before the storm. With a sigh, he turned to Mrs. Wilson. "Where is your husband?"

Mrs. Wilson swallowed the bite of potatoes. "Meeting with the town board. He doesn't think there is any reason for the town people to shovel the roads to the ranches and farms, but the board disagrees."

Micah tapped his fingers on the table. "Shouldn't I be there?"

Annabelle cleared her throat. "Mr. Jensen asked that as well, but my father said he knows your vote and will keep it in consideration. Plus you were rather busy."

Micah tried to smile, but it was a half-hearted attempt. "I suppose I was." He glanced at the children surrounding him. "And am." His smile grew. "At least the last part of the day should be better than the first. I hope."

Annabelle looked at him with curiosity in her large green eyes. She looked about to ask a question, but changed her mind. "Did you see

William when you brought Ruth home?" She picked at the lone green bean on her plate.

"No, I didn't..."

"I did!" Jeremiah interrupted. "He asked about you. I said you'd been out and about and went to the parsonage so you must've survived the blizzard."

Annabelle smiled shyly. "Thank you, Jeremiah."

"He also said he'd try to come see you as soon as he could," Jeremiah continued. When his message was delivered, he turned to Otis. "You'll like the ranch hands at the Double B. Peter's my favorite. He always has a funny story to tell. Wyatt and Flynn are quiet and serious, but they can be fun when they forget to think about it. William's shy, but very loveable. And he plays guitar and sings very well. Especially when he doesn't know anybody else is listening."

"Where will we stay while we are there?" Olive asked.

"I'm sure the ranch house will be big enough for all of you," Micah said. "If you thought my house was big, wait until you see theirs."

"Do you think Mary and I could stay in Miss Brookings' room?" Olive asked.

Micah raised an eyebrow. "You'll have to ask her when we see her."

Annabelle grinned. "I don't think she'll have a problem with it. She always wanted to have little sisters."

Micah looked up from his food. "She did?"

Annabelle nodded. "And if you're about done eating, you might want to get a couple of little ones home to bed." She nodded toward Mary and Carter who were almost asleep in their chairs.

Micah took one look at them, scooped the last bite of chicken into his mouth, and jumped out of the chair.

"Mother and I can take care of the dishes for you," Annabelle said with a laugh. "Good luck surviving the night."

Micah shook his head. "Thanks. But I'd rather have prayers than luck."

Mrs. Wilson patted Micah on the shoulder. "You have mine and Annabelle's prayers. And I'm sure Ruth, Harriet, and Daniel, and a host of other townspeople are also praying for you."

"Thank you," Micah said as he carefully picked up Mary and Carter. "Let's head back home and get everybody tucked in," he said to the other four.

"I'll stop by a little later," Mrs. Wilson said, "to see if you need anything else like extra blankets or pillows."

Micah turned his head. "Thank you, but that won't be necessary. I have more blankets and pillows than I know what to do with. I don't even know where, or how, I ended up with so many."

Mrs. Wilson smiled and waved as Micah left the hotel.

CHAPTER TWENTY

The next morning, Micah groaned as he lay in his bed and stretched. It had been too long since the sleepless nights when Jeremiah was a baby. He wondered briefly if Mary and Carter usually fussed that much or if it was the unfamiliar surroundings. He would have to ask Otis. In the meantime, he had to try to get out of his bed without squishing one or both of them.

It took him a couple minutes, but he got out of bed safely without waking either child up. He dressed hurriedly and strode down the stairs.

"Good morning, Mr. Carson," Olive greeted him.

Micah stopped in his tracks at the sight of his kitchen. It was scrubbed spotless and a griddle—the griddle he had never managed to get truly clean—was full of half-fried hotcakes. And, even with the hotcakes on the griddle, it looked cleaner than he had ever seen it. "How long have you been down here, Miss Olive?"

Olive smiled shyly. "I honestly don't know. I didn't look at the clock. Although, I think it's been at least an hour. It was still dark outside. That's all I know."

Micah glanced at the clock on the wall behind him. "I slept longer than I should have, too." He grimaced when he stretched his back. "I'm not used to getting up at night anymore. Unless I stay up while I'm at the jail or something."

Olive laughed softly. "They don't usually do that. I think the storm and everything else that happened, plus the care you've shown them, made them fuss more."

Micah nodded. When Olive went to flip the hotcakes, Micah asked the question burning on his lips. "How did you ever get that griddle clean?"

Olive flashed a smile at him and Micah barely caught the mischievous look in her eye before she turned back to the stove. "A woman never tells her household secrets to a man."

"Yeah, but I don't have a woman to help me clean the griddle."

"The way I hear it, you will by next fall."

"Maybe, but that's a long ways away yet. And she might not know how to clean a griddle."

Olive shook her head. "She'll know how to use the griddle so it doesn't need to be scrubbed the way I did it. And as long as you clean it right away after using it, you shouldn't have any more trouble with it."

Micah shrugged. "Are Otis, Ellis, and Jeremiah up yet?"

"I haven't seen 'em, but that doesn't mean anything."

"How come you're so grown up, Olive?" Micah asked.

Olive turned around and looked at him in confusion. "What do you mean?"

"You seem like you're at least fifteen, not ten."

Olive shrugged. "When Sam got married, I had to grow up fast. She taught me a lot before she got married and I had to be the woman of the house because Sam and I both knew, no woman in her right mind would marry pa."

"Why not?" Micah asked as he turned a chair around and straddled it, leaning his arms on the back of the chair.

"Everybody in town knows what Pa's like. Sam was worried no one would even wanna marry her because of him, but Lou didn't care. He was in love with Sam and wanted to get her away from Pa's..." Olive trailed off.

"Away from his what?" Micah asked.

Olive swallowed hard and refused to make eye contact. "He would sometimes do things to her she didn't like. Nothing too awful, but..." She turned back to the stove and took the hotcakes off the griddle, then poured some more.

Micah watched her, anger boiling up inside him. Another thing to add to the mental list of reasons Grover should never see his kids again. Especially with Olive already becoming such a beautiful young lady. "Lou is Clem and Chancy's older brother, right?"

Olive nodded.

Micah grinned. "I thought so. He was the first person to welcome me to town when I came in. I'm glad he married Samantha. I just wish you didn't have to be so grown up. You should still be playing with dolls and whatever else little girls do."

Olive's cheeks burned red. "It's okay, Mr. Carson. I like it this way."

Three pairs of feet stomped down the stairs. "Mornin', Boys," Micah said, keeping his back to the stairs.

"How'd you know it was us?" Ellis asked.

"Because Mary tiptoes around the house like it's made of glass and Carter wouldn't make that much noise all by himself," Micah said with a grin.

Jeremiah shrugged. "Whatcha makin', Olive?"

"Nothing for boys who can't use proper words," Olive replied.

Micah threw his head back and laughed. "You'll have to tell Miss Brookings that one, Olive."

Olive smiled. "I'll do that."

Otis snuck up behind his sister and stole a handful of hotcakes from the plate.

"Otis," Micah said in a warning voice, the smile fading off his face. "You can wait until the table is set."

Otis turned around with a scowl. At the sight of Micah's stern face, he turned around and put the hotcakes back on the plate.

"I'll let you boys set the table while I get Mary and Carter," Micah said as he stood up and headed for the stairs. He stared up the stairwell and took a deep breath. *Lord, what am I supposed to do with these children? And even more importantly, with their father?* He sighed as he stepped onto the landing between the bedrooms. *Please let there be some law I can use to take these children away from him. They can't stay with him and I can't break the law.*

With an effort, he pushed his bedroom door open. The sight of two little bodies sleeping peacefully on his bed brought a warm feeling to his insides. How long had it been since he stopped dreaming of having more children? Too long. He forced himself to step into the room and shake Mary and Carter awake. They both stretched and blinked up at him with sleepy eyes.

When her eyes came into focus, Mary smiled up at him. "G'morning, Mr. Sheriff."

Micah smiled and bent down to kiss her forehead. "Good morning, Sweetheart. Did you sleep well?"

Mary nodded.

"How about you, Champ?"

"I not Champ. I Carter," he said with a pout.

Micah chuckled. "I know your name is Carter, but you are also the Champion sleep boxer."

"What'th a thleep bok-ther?" Carter asked.

"Someone who boxes while he sleeps," Micah replied. Mary giggled.

"What'th bok-thing?"

"Someone who fights with other people with their fists. Come on, you two. Breakfast is a-waitin' and there are three hungry boys downstairs probably giving Olive a hard time."

It took him five more minutes to get them both dressed, but he managed it and congratulated himself on his triumph. Seven years out of practice and he could still do it.

When the two giggling children were dressed, he picked one up in each arm and threw them over his shoulder. "Time ta bring the sacks o' potatoes downstairs."

"I not 'tatoes!" Carter protested.

Mary didn't say anything because she couldn't stop giggling. With a chuckle, Micah hauled both of the little ones into the kitchen where the three boys sat around the table, waiting.

After breakfast, Micah asked Jeremiah and Otis to get the sleigh hitched up and ready. No more snow had fallen during the night for which Micah was very grateful. The Miller children seemed a little sad to leave, but Micah knew he couldn't take care of them and be sheriff at the same time while doing a good job with both.

The sleigh almost got stuck in a snowdrift once, but the horse labored through it. On the way to the ranch, Otis, Olive, Jeremiah, and Ellis talked amongst themselves while Mary and Carter snuggled up to him on either side. A sudden longing for more children of his own hit him. Why hadn't he remarried? Was it really because he still grieved the loss of Edith? Or was he afraid?

He took a deep breath and concentrated on driving. Thinking too much could get him into trouble. He needed to keep those types of thoughts to a minimum at least until he was engaged.

"The heart is deceitful above all things, and desperately wicked: who can know it?" Micah muttered to himself.

"What'd you say, Pa?" Jeremiah asked.

Micah chuckled. "Nothing to you, Son. I was just muttering to myself."

"Oh." Jeremiah looked back at his friends. "He does that a lot. Maybe when he marries Miss Brookings, he'll stop doing that."

"I heard that," Micah said. "And it isn't for sure that Miss Brookings and I will be married."

Micah could hear the smile in Jeremiah's voice when he replied. "I know, but it shore is fun to tease you 'bout it."

Micah shook his head and smiled. Jeremiah reminded him so much of Edith it sometimes hurt, but he would always love them both. Micah glanced down at the little ones by his sides. *Lord, if it is possible to love more than one child, it should be possible to love more than one woman in a lifetime, right?*

Micah pulled on the right rein to turn the horses into the Double B Bar Ranch. As they drew near to the house, the children all sat up straighter.

"That house is huge," Otis whispered in awe.

Micah chuckled. "I thought you might be surprised by the size. The Brookings' have done well and Daniel wanted to have a house large enough to house lots of people if the need ever arose."

"And Miss Brookings lives here?" Olive asked.

"Yep," Jeremiah replied. "There's four ranch hands, too, and they're great! Peter's especially friendly to kids."

Mary cuddled in close to Micah and he put an arm around her. "They're nice people here, Mary. You'll love them."

"Miss Brookings is waiting on the porch for us!" Ellis exclaimed.

"She must've heard the sleigh bells," Jeremiah said.

Micah smiled at their excitement as he saw the door open and Mrs. Brookings step out.

"Good morning," Ruth said in her quiet voice as they pulled up to the porch. "I understand we have five children coming to stay with us for a while."

"Hi, Miss Brookings!" Jeremiah exclaimed with a wave.

Ruth waved back as Micah pulled the horse to a stop. Otis and Jeremiah jumped out of the sleigh and Otis helped his sister climb out while Jeremiah helped Ellis.

"Good morning, Miss Brookings, Mrs. Brookings," Olive greeted with a sweet smile.

Ruth squeezed Olive's shoulder as she walked to the sleigh. "Micah, would you like to hand little Carter down to me?"

Micah nodded and held onto the boy until he was sure Ruth had a good hold on him. When that was done, he jumped down and beckoned for Mary to come into his outstretched arms.

Harriet ushered everybody into the warm house. As they entered, Micah watched the reactions as the Miller children stared around the entryway. This was the least fancy room in the house and they were already in awe. He wondered how they would react if they'd seen the house he'd grown up in.

"Would you like to do the introductions, Micah?" Harriet asked.

Micah shook his head slightly to clear the cobwebs. "Of course. Mrs. Brookings, in age order we have Otis, Olive, Ellis, Mary, and Carter. Correct me if I'm wrong with the ages, Otis. They're twelve, ten, seven, five, and three." Micah smiled when Otis nodded.

"My, my," Harriet exclaimed. "You're all practically grown up."

Mary snuggled close to Ruth. "I not." She pointed at Carter. "Neither is Carter. Daddy calls us babies all the time."

Ruth knelt down and gave Mary a hug. "I don't think you're a baby. You're almost old enough to go to school even. And we can't have any babies at school."

Mary giggled. "The older girls would get too distracted with babies at school."

Ruth grinned. "You're right, they would."

"Jeremiah..." Micah started.

Jeremiah looked at him pleadingly. "We don't have to leave already, do we, Pa?"

Micah tapped his foot. "We should. I don't want to leave, but I need to give Obadiah a break."

Jeremiah grinned. "Then let's not." He turned away as if that ended the discussion, but Ruth took a quick step toward him and tapped him on the shoulder. He glared at her. "What?"

"I don't think I really need to say it, do I?" Ruth said.

"You ain't my ma and this ain't school," Jeremiah said.

Micah closed his eyes. "Come on, Jeremiah. It's time to get home. Your disrespect will get punished when we get home."

Micah said goodbye to everybody and led a reluctant and defiant Jeremiah outside. Mary watched them with wide eyes. "He's not going to beat Jeremiah, is he?"

Harriet knelt down in front of Mary. "No, Mary, he's not. Micah will use the Biblical principle of the rod of correction to help Jeremiah realize there are consequences for his actions. It will sting for a while, but Micah won't be doing it too hard."

Mary shuddered. "I wouldn't want him to do it to me."

Harriet smiled and hugged the girl. "I wouldn't want to do it to you, either. But sometimes it's necessary. Only if you're a bad girl, though."

"What'd 'Miah do?" Ellis asked.

Harriet took a deep breath. "He was disrespectful to his father and Ruth. The Bible tells us to obey our elders, especially our parents."

Ellis cocked his head and looked at her. "What'll you do if we don't obey?"

Harriet pursed her lips. "I'm not sure yet. Mr. Brookings and I will have to discuss that."

Ellis nodded.

"How would you all like to go see the horses?" Ruth asked.

"What horses?" Otis questioned.

"This is a horse ranch," Ruth answered. "We have lots of horses here. Although, you won't be able to see most of them because of the snow."

Otis's eyes lit up. "You have horses? Let's go!"

Ruth looked them over. "You all need to get a few more layers on if we want to go very far. Let's see if we can find a few scarves, hats, and mittens."

After taking Jeremiah to the woodshed behind the house and leaving him at the parsonage, Micah returned to his office. He gave Obadiah the rest of the day off.

"You're sure?" Obadiah asked. "I won't have to clean up any messes back there, will I?"

Micah chuckled. "I've calmed down. I still want to give him a good talking-to, but I think I can stay self-controlled."

"You better."

Micah sobered. "Do I need to deal with anything else?"

"Mayor Wilson said Thomas returned all in one piece no thanks to you."

Micah sat in the chair behind his desk. "I forgot about him."

"I figured you had other things on your mind. Other than that, the only thing you might want to do is stop by the Salvatorres' to pay your respects."

Micah nodded. "Thank you, Obadiah."

"Take care, Micah."

"I will."

Flynn cleared his throat as he approached William in the barn.

William turned and smiled. "Hey, Flynn. Sorry you got stuck in the line cabin the whole blizzard."

Flynn shrugged. "It was fine. Did you put the Bible in there?"

William chuckled. "Yes, I did. I figured if someone got stuck out there, they'd appreciate something to read."

Flynn sat next to him on the haystack. "Thanks. I read a lot of it. Things finally started to make sense."

William glanced at Flynn. "Like what?"

Flynn picked up a piece of straw and stuck it in his mouth. "Why I shouldn't wait for my deathbed to accept God's gift. I read Ephesians and when I got to Ephesians 2, I recognized some verses and then came to verse ten where it says, 'For we are His workmanship, created in Christ Jesus unto good works, which God hath before ordained that we should walk in them.' If I'm not mistaken, that means God has things he wants me to do after I accept His gift. Right?"

William nodded. "That is correct."

Flynn let out a breath. "Good. So, how do you know what He wants you to do?"

William looked around. "How does a horse know where his master wants him to go?"

"By letting his master tell him."

"Yep. First, you need to let God lead you to the cross and empty tomb. And now that God no longer speaks directly to people, you do what He says in God's Word: Study it and meditate on it day and night."

Flynn's eyes widened. "How do you do that?"

"Which part?"

Flynn waved his hand. "The last one. I already did the first in the cabin with God."

William grinned. "I wondered what was different about you. The last part you do by reading the Bible, praying, and applying what it says to do and not to do."

"Oh. Okay. And what about these works?"

"That's something between you and God. Sometimes it will mean sharing the Gospel with someone, helping someone, or any number of things."

"Hm." Flynn thought for a few minutes. "Thank you, William."

"Anytime, Flynn. Thank you for listening to God."

Flynn smiled up at William as he stood up. "I'm glad I did. Now all I have to do is convince my brother to do the same thing."

William chuckled. "Just don't force it on him if he doesn't want it."

"I know. I won't."

CHAPTER TWENTY ONE

"Micah told me about Grover Miller," Miles said.

Daniel nodded.

"And the children are staying with you?"

"Until Micah lets Grover out of jail."

"What if Grover doesn't want the children back?"

Daniel narrowed his eyes and looked around the snowy yard. "What are you thinking?"

Miles looked up at the sky. "Micah's looked and there are no laws against the neglect Grover has shown. The Bible clearly states that we should take care of orphans and widows. Even though their father is still alive, since he is absent most of the time, I would consider the Miller children to be orphans."

Miles shifted his feet. "I've talked to the other elders as well as Mayor Wilson. We all agree some of us should talk to Grover and tell him he either needs to change and take better care of his children or we'll take the children away from him.

If he doesn't want them back, or doesn't change, would you and Harriet be willing to take them in?"

Daniel took a deep breath. "I'll have to talk it over with Harriet and pray about it."

Miles smiled. "I thought that would be your answer. Let me know when you decide and I'll take a couple elders with me to talk to him. Considering what happened with Ruth and the fact you're taking care of his children..."

Daniel nodded. "I understand."

Miles slapped his shoulder. "Thank you, Daniel. What's it like having five young children around again?"

Daniel raised his eyebrows and smiled. "Hectic. Our children were further apart in age, but these kids are very well behaved. Almost too much so, actually. I get the feeling they were beaten into submission."

Miles grimaced. "Micah mentioned that, too. He said there were a few times that night he wanted to give Grover a beating of his own. It's sad how some people don't realize how what they do affects their children in many different ways."

Daniel nodded. "Mary and Carter stay as close as they can to either Harriet or Ruth whenever possible. It's like they need to stay close to make sure they won't disappear. Mary and Olive share Ruth's room and after the first night, Ruth asked me to take the trundle bed out for now because

Mary joined her in her bed anyway. We'll have to gently break her of that before Ruth leaves, but for now..." he let his voice trail off as his eyes caught sight of a group of men walking toward them.

"What is it?" Miles asked when he saw the look of surprise and resignation on Daniel's face.

"The school board is coming this way."

Miles turned to look. "Why would they want to talk to you?"

Daniel stared at him. "You really haven't heard?"

Miles shook his head.

"Micah checked on Ruth as soon as the blizzard was finished and Grover saw him at her door."

Miles closed his eyes. "And they are going to take that man's word for it?"

"Micah told Mr. Jensen about it, too. He also made sure to say that it was only for a couple of minutes and Ruth didn't open the door more than a crack, but..."

Miles flexed his hand. "I wish people wouldn't gossip or believe every rumor they hear. If they didn't, we wouldn't have to worry about this getting out there and life would be a lot simpler."

"I agree," Daniel whispered as the men reached them.

"Mr. Brookings," Mr. Jensen said.

"Yes?"

"Is your daughter somewhere around?"

Daniel looked around the churchyard. "I'm sure she is, I just don't know exactly where."

"No matter," he replied. "I'm sure you can pass it on. We've discussed the situation with Micah and Grover and come to the decision that Annabelle Wilson will be our teacher for the rest of the year. We would like Ruth to help Annabelle for the first few days until Annabelle is more comfortable teaching."

Daniel held up his hand to stop the man from talking. "I can pass this on to Ruth, but I think she deserves to hear it straight from your mouths. One or more of you, along with your families, are more than welcome to join us for our noon meal."

Mr. Jensen looked around at the school board members. When no one volunteered, he clenched his teeth together. "I'll find her here and tell her."

"Just make sure there aren't a lot of people around," Daniel said. "The more private you can make it the better."

Mr. Jensen narrowed his eyes. "Why?"

Daniel took a step forward and stared right into the man's eyes. "This situation shouldn't even have been made public and she shouldn't have to quit teaching simply because Micah did what he, or any other decent man—especially a sheriff—would have done for any unmarried woman living by herself during a blizzard. Just because one man claims it was more than that means nothing. Especially when that same man has threatened her and refuses to leave her alone."

"All the more reason for her to be out of town," Mr. Jensen replied. "Where is she?"

A movement in the corner of his eye caught Daniel's attention. "Over there," he said, pointing toward the group of children surrounding Ruth as she sat on the steps of the church and talked to them.

Mr. Jensen nodded. "Only two of us should probably go." He looked at the group. "Carl, would you please come with me?"

Carl nodded.

"I'm coming, too," Daniel said.

Carl looked at him, puzzled. "No need for that."

"I insist," Daniel said. "I want to make sure you don't hurt my daughter."

Mr. Jensen stiffened. "We wouldn't touch her."

"That's not what I meant," Daniel said. "You don't have to touch someone to hurt them. She loves teaching those children and she's going to be hurt enough that you don't want her to teach anymore without you saying something else that could hurt her even more. I'm going with you."

Mr. Jensen looked at Daniel with a raised eyebrow before nodding. "Fine." He turned on his heel and the three men walked to where Ruth sat on the steps.

Daniel saw Ruth stiffen when she saw the group walking toward her. She turned a questioning look to him and he saw the pain in her eyes as she stood up and said a quick goodbye to the children. The children had all scattered by the time the three men reached her. Ruth took two short steps to shorten the distance between them.

"Good morning, gentlemen," she said with a bright, but fake, smile. "What can I do for you?"

"After much discussion," Mr. Jensen said, "the school board has decided Annabelle will finish off the school year as the teacher. You will assist her for a few days until she is acclimated to the position. At that time, you can stay safely at your home on the ranch."

Ruth fought to control her breathing and keep a blank mask on her face. "May I ask why?"

Carl Fischer scratched his forehead. "We require our teachers to be of upright and moral character. Even a hint is enough to put their reputations at risk. A concerned parent informed us of the early morning visit from Micah and then Micah himself told Mr. Jensen. Because your reputation has come into question..."

Ruth held up a hand and Daniel saw the rare flash of anger in her eyes. "Because of one person's report, you decided to fire me? I have a guess who it was, too. Do you realize...?" She took a deep breath and closed her eyes. "Never mind. I'll do as you say. When is school starting again?"

"Next Monday," Mr. Jensen answered.

Ruth clenched her jaw and nodded before turning to her father. "Can we go home please, Pa?"

Daniel looked to Mr. Jensen and Carl and offered his arm to Ruth. She took it as they walked away from the two men. "Where are your mother and the children?"

"Home," Ruth said as they walked across the yard.

Daniel turned a confused look to his daughter. "Why?"

"Mary and Carter were getting tired and hungry. I suggested she take them home and you and I could walk home."

Daniel smiled. "Let me guess, you have something you want to talk about."

"I did," Ruth replied. "Right now, though, I just want to go home, lock myself in my room, and pour my heart out to my diary and pillow."

Daniel saw Miles mouth the words, "Should I try to talk to her?" and waved him off with a grateful and sad smile. "You could pretend I'm your diary."

"I think better on paper," Ruth replied.

"You could still try," Daniel said as he led her onto the road home. "I'll keep a good hold on your arm so you can walk and cry at the same time if you need to."

Ruth bit her lips and leaned her head on his upper arm. "I love all those children so much. I've poured myself into teaching them everything I can. Did you know I got Tate Winters to actually like school? He's sixteen and always hated school. With God's help, I found a way for him to like coming.

"And then there are the Miller and Hale children. Both families need so much and I wish I could anonymously give something to the Hales to help them. They are such a sweet family and have simply come up on hard times with Mr. Hale unable to find a steady job. Did you know Paul was thinking about quitting school so he could get a job?"

Ruth sighed. "I just don't want to lose all this. I know it will make things easier on you, Ma, and me. And Micah could finally come courting. But..."

Daniel reached his hand over and touched her arm. "I know, Sweetheart. I can't believe they took Grover's words for absolute truth. They should have trusted Micah and you more than a silly rumor no one will believe."

Ruth stopped and Daniel turned to her, concerned. "Have they talked to Annabelle yet?"

"I don't know. Why?"

"She told me today, she was hoping for an April or May wedding. She can't do that if she's teaching. And I know she won't want to take the job from me."

Daniel looked down the road in both directions. "Would you like to go back and talk to her?"

"No, it can wait until tomorrow. If she does take the job, I'll need to talk to her anyway." Ruth forced herself to turn toward the ranch.

"Was there something else you wanted to talk about?" Daniel asked.

"Yes, but I don't remember what it was."

Daniel chuckled. "Well, if you think of it, let me know."

"I will, Pa."

"Can I go with you, please?" Mary asked.

"I'm sorry," Ruth replied. "I need to go to town alone today."

"What are you doing in town?"

Ruth smiled. Mary had attached to her immediately and seemed to follow her everywhere. "I need to go see my friend, Annabelle."

Mary bit her lip and cocked her head. "The mayor's daughter?"

Ruth nodded.

"She's different now," Mary said. "Why is that?"

Ruth took a deep breath to try and keep herself patient. "She asked God to help her change the way she was living. She asked Him to forgive her sins and help her keep from sinning more."

"Oh. Okay. Have a good time with your friend."

Ruth shook her head as Mary walked away. Mary was a perceptive child who would take almost any answer as the gospel truth if she trusted the person who answered her. "Lord," Ruth prayed as she stepped outside, "help me not answer Mary's questions with error. She trusts me more than she probably should and that is a scary thought. Thank You for sending these five precious children into our lives, even if only for a short time."

Twenty minutes later, she arrived at Annabelle's door. She hesitated as she reached the first step to the porch, but she didn't have the chance to pretend she never came because the door flung open and Annabelle rushed out.

"Oh, Ruth! I prayed you would come today. Come inside, please."

Ruth blinked in surprise as a stocking-footed Annabelle came down to the last step on the porch to grab her arm and pull her. "What's the matter?"

Ruth asked. "And why are you out here without shoes or a coat?"

Annabelle pulled Ruth into the parlor before finally stopping and wringing her hands. "I'm sorry, Ruth, but Mr. Jensen stopped by this morning and ever since he left, I've been a mess, shaky, mad, horrified... Oh, I don't know!" She collapsed into the chair behind her and buried her head in her hands.

Ruth sent a short prayer for help as she shrugged out of her coat and gloves, laying them carefully on the settee. "Tell me what happened and why you are acting like this."

Annabelle looked up with tears rimming her eyes. "Mr. Jensen said you'd been fired and I was being asked to take your place. I tried to be calm about it and told him I would have to pray about it. I also told him I would probably be married in April or May and was being courted by Will. His response was, 'We don't have any other choices. You at least live with your parents in town and can be chaperoned at all times.'

"It was awful! I didn't know what to say. I still don't know what to say. I can't take the job, but if I don't, who will teach the children?"

"Annabelle, can you please look at me?" Ruth asked.

Annabelle tipped her head up and tried to keep eye contact with Ruth.

"I think you will make a wonderful temporary schoolteacher. If the school board is all right with your courtship and impending marriage, you should take the job. You are the only person in town I would trust to take the position."

Annabelle looked into Ruth's eyes. "Really?"

"Really. I think you should take the job."

"I want to talk to William first, though," Annabelle said.

Ruth smiled. "That is an excellent idea. I happen to know he is on barn duty this morning. Shall we go to the ranch? We can talk about lesson plans, too."

Annabelle's forehead wrinkled. "Did Mr. Jensen say something about you helping me for the first few days?"

"I think I'll only be needed on Monday and possibly Tuesday, but yes, he did."

Annabelle bit her lip. "Fine. Let's go."

As they passed the sheriff's office, Ruth heard her name. She looked back and saw Micah hurrying toward them.

"I'm glad I caught you. How are the Miller children doing?" Micah asked.

"They're fine," Ruth said, her forehead wrinkling.

Micah chuckled. "You know that's not why I stopped you, don't you?"

Ruth raised an eyebrow but said nothing.

"Hi, Annabelle. I hear you're going to be the new schoolteacher," Micah said.

Annabelle stiffened. "Who told you that?"

Micah frowned. "I don't remember. Why?"

"I hadn't told Mr. Jensen I would for sure do it." Annabelle clenched her hands into fists. "And I certainly didn't tell him he could tell everybody I was going to be the teacher."

Micah shook his head. "I'll try to stop the rumor if I can, but there's probably nothing I can do about it."

"Thanks," Annabelle replied. "I probably will be the new schoolteacher, but I don't want to get pushed into it. And I want to ask William before I commit to anything."

Micah nodded. "Good idea." He turned back to Ruth. "Will you be home on Wednesday evening? Since there's no school this week and you won't be teaching anymore, I thought maybe Jeremiah and I could come over."

Ruth smiled. "Isn't it a little early for that? Should we wait until the rumors die down?"

Micah scowled. "We probably should, but this is the best time of year for me to go courting."

Ruth bit her lip. "I'll ask Pa and Ma and when William walks Annabelle home, he can give you their answer. Would that work?"

"That would work just fine. Thank you, Miss Brookings," Micah replied, touching a finger to his hat.

Ruth nodded and followed Annabelle out of town.

"He's smitten with you," Annabelle said as soon as they were out of earshot.

Ruth's face burned. "Do you really think so?"

"No," Annabelle said with a grin. "I know so."

Ruth ducked her head and bit her lip. "I think he still grieves for his first wife."

"I'm not so sure. I think your friendship with him the last couple of years is helping him get over that."

Ruth shrugged. "We're supposed to be talking about school."

Annabelle groaned. "I don't want to."

"I know, but if you're going to be ready to teach school on Monday, there are quite a few things you need to know. I already started making a list of the children you need to keep a careful eye on and a few other suggestions and tips."

"How did you find time to do that?"

"Pa took the Miller children outside to build a snow fort yesterday afternoon and Ma and I got some letter writing done. I only had one letter to write, so I started on the list afterwards."

Annabelle nodded. "Fine. What do I need to know?"

"First, do you want to hear any of this before you talk to William?"

"Probably not. It would be kind of pointless if William thinks I shouldn't do the teaching."

Ruth sighed. "True. Then what else would you like to talk about?"

Annabelle grinned. "You and Micah Carson."

Ruth laughed. "We aren't even courting yet. How about you and William instead?"

"But it sounds like you'll be starting on Wednesday," Annabelle teased. "And I'm not going to be selfish and talk only about myself. I want to hear what you think about finally getting to court."

Ruth shook her head. "Nope. I'm not going there. One 'rule' Pa has for all of us while courting is to not get emotionally attached until we are engaged. For Martha that was hard, but she did it and it was beautiful."

Annabelle's eyes widened. "I cannot imagine doing that. I would fail miserably."

Ruth laughed. "I know you would. Not everyone can and that is fine. But you are more of a dreamer and you know you're going to get engaged as soon as William gets up the courage to ask your father and then you."

Annabelle laughed. "I suppose. But I want more details, Darling. Would you marry Micah if he asked you to marry him a month from now?"

"No," Ruth replied. At Annabelle's startled expression, she smiled. "I don't know enough about him yet and won't even a month from now. I'm still trying to figure out what God's desire is for me in my choice of a husband. I don't trust my feelings because feelings come and go unpredictably and I want to keep my whole heart safe for my husband, whoever he may be."

Annabelle's face grew sober. "Hm."

Ruth glanced at her friend. "Are you all right?"

"Yeah. Why?"

"I expected a longer reply than that."

Annabelle smirked. "Just because I talk a lot doesn't mean I always have something to say about everything."

"Howdy!" a voice in front of them called.

The two young women looked up to see William walking toward them. "Hi, William!" they exclaimed together.

"You two headed to the ranch?" William asked.

"Yes, we were," Ruth replied. "Annabelle needed to talk to you about something."

William frowned. "About what?"

"Were you headed somewhere important?" Annabelle asked.

"No," he replied.

Annabelle beckoned to him. "Would you mind joining us, then?"

William grinned. "Escort two lovely young ladies through the treacherous snowdrifts? Might be too hard." He winked at Annabelle and offered each of them an arm.

"The snowdrifts aren't that treacherous," Annabelle stated.

William chuckled. "I know. I was teasin'. What did you need to talk to me about?"

Annabelle swallowed hard. "Ruth's being fired as schoolteacher and I've been asked to take the position."

William whistled and ran his fingers through his hair.

"Yeah. I don't know exactly what that means for our courtship and everything yet, but Mr. Jensen at least sounded like he was fine with us courting since I'll still be living with Father and Mother."

"That sounds like a double standard," William said. "He wouldn't let Ruth and Micah court."

"I also didn't live with Pa and Ma during the week," Ruth said. "And he's rather limited on choices for single teachers."

William cleared his throat. "What if we decide to get married before the school year is over?"

"I don't know."

William sighed. "I think I'd like to have a talk with Mr. Jensen before I give you my opinion."

Ruth stopped. "Should you two head back into town then?"

Annabelle shook her head. "You need to ask your parents about Wednesday so Will can give Micah his answer. We're almost to the ranch anyway."

"What answer?" William asked.

"Micah wants to start courting Ruth on Wednesday," Annabelle replied with a grin.

William smiled. "Let's get back to the ranch. I should ask Mr. Brookings if I can take some of the day off anyway. I have a feeling Mr. Jensen isn't going to be easy to talk to."

"Is he ever easy to talk to?" Ruth asked.

Annabelle grimaced. "Not that I've ever seen."

"What does your father think about you becoming a teacher?" William asked.

"I don't know. He won't say anything one way or the other," Annabelle replied. "Mother thinks it will be fine, but she's also concerned about the courtship and possible marriage. I think she's more afraid you'll get impatient and not want to court me anymore since I won't have as many open evenings for you to come calling."

William shook his head and smiled. "She needn't worry about that."

Annabelle shrugged. "I know, but she worries a lot and nothing I say can stop her."

"Here we are," Ruth announced. "Home, sweet home. And not a moment too soon. I'm cold!"

The three of them laughed as they traipsed through the front door.

CHAPTER TWENTY TWO

After dinner on Wednesday, Harriet and Daniel shooed Ruth and Micah into the parlor. "We'll take care of the dishes, and get the children to bed. I'm sure Jeremiah wouldn't mind hanging out in the bunkhouse."

Jeremiah grinned. "Nope, I wouldn't. Can Otis come with me?"

Daniel nodded. "Go ahead."

Micah and Ruth sat in silence for a few minutes.

Micah cleared his throat. "I guess a good place to start would be how we came to know Christ and what our childhood was like."

Ruth nodded.

Micah took a deep breath. "I'll go first. I grew up in a hypocritical family. My parents went to church, but didn't live a Christian life at all. I was a naughty child who got away with everything. We were rich and acted like it. I was the perfect, spoiled rotten kid. I picked on everybody at school, refused to do homework, teased the girls, and anything else you could think of. I was probably worse than Clem, Chancy, Jeremiah, and John combined."

Ruth chuckled. "That's possible?"

Micah smiled. "Yes." He cleared his throat and gathered his thoughts. "My parents fought a lot and I often hid in the hallway listening to them. They never talked about divorce because his parents would have cut them off of all the money they gave us if they had. My first taste of real Christianity was the summer I was sent to live with Father's parents. They were rich, too, but they were actually true Christians. We went to church anytime the doors were open, prayed at every meal, studied the Bible at different times during the day, and Grandpa led a family devotional time.

"In July, there was a week of revival meetings. The speaker wasn't overly dynamic and all fire and brimstone like they usually are, but he was still good. We went to every single meeting. By the time Thursday rolled around, I really did not want to go. The things the preacher said were too convicting and I didn't want to do what he said. I couldn't humble myself that much and let God take over my life.

"My grandparents dragged me to the meetings under much protestation. During the meeting that night, I felt like he was talking directly to me.

Every single word he said was directed toward me. It was horrible. I slunk down on the bench, but that didn't last long because it was very uncomfortable.

"When the preacher did the altar call, I knew I needed to go up there. I needed what he'd been talking about. I just couldn't do it. So I prayed right there instead. All I did was pray a simple prayer, 'Lord, I believe, help my unbelief. I know I've sinned horribly. I'm sick of it. Help me learn to trust You and do what You want me to do. Amen.'

"My grandparents didn't have any idea what had happened. In fact, I think they had been hoping I would respond to one of the altar calls and when I didn't, they were disappointed. As the weeks went on, though, I changed slowly and participated more in family devotions. Grandpa finally asked what had happened to me. I told him about the prayer, and both he and Grandma cried for joy.

"When the summer was over, I dreaded going back home. I wanted to stay with Grandpa and Grandma forever, but I knew I couldn't. Father and Mother needed to hear about God, too. When I got home, I told them I was a Christian now. Mother's first reaction was, 'You already were. We had you baptized when you were a baby.' I explained what I meant and they thought I was crazy. I shrugged it off and let my actions speak for me.

"I wasn't perfect, of course, but my parents did see the obvious changes in my life and to my surprise, Father was the first one to ask me more. A few months later, Mother asked both Father and I about the changes she had seen, especially in my behavior. Our home wasn't without its problems, but we had God working in each of us, so those problems were resolved in a much better way." He paused for a few seconds. "And I think that's about it."

"Are you sure?" Ruth asked.

Micah blinked. "Um, yeah, I'm sure."

Ruth smiled. "I'm teasing you, Micah. I wasn't expecting your testimony to be so long."

Micah shook his head. "I see. So yours is shorter?"

"Yes, it is. I grew up in a Christian home with four older siblings. I was seen as the good girl of the family, but that's just because I was too shy to do anything too terrible. At least outwardly. Inside, I hated one of my sisters and one of my brothers, but they never knew about it.

"When Joshua was eight, he trusted Jesus as his Savior and immediately told me about it. I got caught up in his excitement. I was six and I understood what I needed to do and why. After that, I learned to forgive my two siblings and our relationship changed. I told my parents right away as well. Of course, they were happy to hear it, unlike your parents." Ruth bit her lip. "I think that's about it. I think I had a pretty normal childhood. Well, as normal as a shy girl can with four loud, energetic older siblings."

Micah smiled. "We've been Christians close to the same amount of time then. I was thirteen when I trusted Jesus and you were six, so I would have trusted Him about three years before you."

"That is strange to think about."

"What do you think about having five younger siblings for a few days?"

Ruth smiled. "I love it. I've always wanted younger siblings. I just wish we didn't have to give them back."

"I wish you didn't either. They seem much happier here."

"I agree."

Daniel and Harriet walked into the room. "Jeremiah and Otis are having a lot of fun out in the bunkhouse," Daniel said.

Micah grunted. "I'm not surprised."

"Did we miss anything?"

Ruth nodded. "Micah's testimony. It was very interesting."

Harriet sat down on the settee. "Why was it so interesting?"

"Probably because it was so different from hers," Micah said.

"No, that's not why," Ruth replied. "It was interesting because he is only about three years older than me as a Christian and he became a Christian under protest."

"What?" Daniel asked.

Micah chuckled. "I think she means that I didn't want to that night, but God worked on me and I accepted His gift anyway."

"I'm glad God did that," Harriet said.

"So am I," Micah replied. He glanced at the clock. "I should probably go home. Even though tomorrow isn't a school day, Jeremiah doesn't do well without sleep."

Daniel nodded. "We had a few children like that. Especially Martha."

Ruth's eyes widened. "She was horrible! If she didn't get at least eight hours of sleep, there was no living with her at all."

Micah chuckled. "I cannot imagine having a sister like that."

"Did you have any sisters or brothers?" Harriet asked.

"No, I did not," Micah answered. "And I am grateful for that. I would have loved a sister or brother, but with the way my parents were and the way I was, I don't think it would have been a good thing. God knew what He was doing making me an only child." He stood up. "Thank you for a wonderful meal and for letting me come."

Daniel, Harriet, and Ruth stood. "It was our pleasure," Daniel said.

Harriet led the way to the door. "Goodbye, Micah. Have a safe trip home."

Micah stepped out onto the porch. "Thank you. Lord willing, I will see you all on Sunday."

"Goodbye, Micah," Ruth said.

Daniel and Ruth stood together on the porch watching as Micah disappeared around the house to get his son. "Well, what did you think?" Daniel asked.

"About what?"

"About Micah."

"The same as I have before. He's a wonderful man and a very good friend."

"Nothing more?" Daniel questioned.

"When Martha and Esther were being courted, I remember you telling them not to get emotionally attached until they were engaged. So how do you expect me to answer that question?"

Daniel chuckled. "That's true."

"Is it bad to struggle to not become emotionally attached?"

Daniel shook his head. "No, it isn't. I think it's normal, especially since you've known Micah for quite some time and he is now paying special attention to you."

"Yes, but he was Joshua's friend until a couple years ago, not really mine."

"But he did talk to you, me, and your mother sometimes."

Ruth nodded. "I suppose."

"If you ever find yourself relying too much on your emotions toward Micah, let me or your mother know."

Ruth smiled up at her father and snuggled into his side. "I will, Pa."

After a soul-refreshing Sunday, Ruth packed her things for the last time. This time it was in preparation to help Annabelle teach school and she would only be gone two days. It had been decided early the week before that she would stay with the Wilsons instead of in the cottage near the school.

"Where are you going?" Mary asked.

Ruth sighed. "I'm going to help my friend learn how to teach school."

"Why?"

"Because I am no longer the teacher and she is going to be the teacher starting tomorrow."

"How long will you be gone?"

With a chuckle, Ruth replied, "I'm not sure. I hope to come home on Tuesday afternoon with Otis, Olive, and Ellis, but I don't know for sure."

"When's Tuesday?"

With a grin, Ruth patted Mary's head. "Today is Sunday night. Tomorrow is Monday night." She held up one finger. "And the night after that is Tuesday night." She lifted up another finger.

"Two nights without you?" Mary asked, a frown furrowing her face.

Ruth knelt down and pulled Mary into a tight hug. "Yes, Darling, but Olive will be here and she can help comfort you."

Mary put her arms around Ruth's neck. "But I want you to be here."

Ruth choked on the lump in her throat. "Want to know a secret?"

Mary nodded, her head thudding into Ruth's shoulder.

"I want to be here, too, but Annabelle needs me right now. And I will be back."

"Mama didn't come back," Mary said. She tightened her arms around Ruth and started to sob.

The breath Ruth was about to take got stuck halfway as the words sank in. "Oh, Mary." Tears sprang to her eyes and she blinked them away. "Cry it all out, Sweetheart."

A minute later, Mary's sobs turned into sniffles as Ruth rubbed her back and held her tight. "I miss Mama," Mary said.

Ruth closed her eyes. "I know you do. I would, too, if my mama died."

"Daddy wasn't so mean before Mama died," Mary said. "And he never left us to go to the saloon." Mary stepped away from Ruth's hug. "Why does Daddy drink so much?"

Ruth sighed. "I don't know. I think he's trying to forget."

"Forget what?"

"His grief for his wife."

"Oh." Mary paused. "Is that why he doesn't like Olive?"

Ruth started. "What?"

"Is it because she looks so much like Mama?"

Ruth closed her eyes and tried to picture what Mrs. Miller had looked like. Mary was right, Olive was a miniature version of her mother. "That's possible." She stood up. "I really need to go now, Mary. Mother will be here and so will Olive. They can give you what you need while I'm gone, all right?"

Mary tilted her head and looked up at Ruth with large, tear-filled eyes. "Okay."

Ruth bent down and gave her a kiss on the cheek before carrying her bag out of the room to say goodbye to the rest of the family.

"You did a wonderful job, Annabelle!" Ruth exclaimed.

Annabelle looked at Ruth as if her hair had suddenly turned green. "I did not. You had to rescue me too many times to count..."

"It was only four times," Ruth protested. "And I didn't really even need to save you from anything. You would have done just fine."

"I doubt it."

"You're too hard on yourself," Ruth said.

Annabelle glared at Ruth. "No, I'm not."

"You should have seen me on my first day. I would have loved to have someone else there to rescue me. But the children are all very forgiving and probably don't even remember all the mistakes I made that first day. If it weren't for the fact that you would never forgive me and might kidnap me, I would go home right now and let you teach alone tomorrow."

"Yeah, I wouldn't want you to be an accessory to your own kidnapping and land us both in jail. Then where would the children be?" Annabelle asked, fighting against the giggle welling up inside her.

Ruth glanced at her and they both burst into a fit of giggles. When she caught her breath, Ruth said, "I can see Micah's face right now. He would be dumbfounded and shocked. Then he'd make us wait in the office while he scrubbed the jail cells down completely to make them halfway livable."

Annabelle sighed. "Oh my! I can't recall the last time I laughed that hard."

Ruth smiled. "Me, either."

"Really?" Annabelle asked. "With Joshua as your brother, you haven't laughed that hard recently? He was here for Christmas, remember?"

Ruth shook her head with a smile. "I remember. Joshua can be funny, but most of his jokes are old and most of his stories now are about work, not some made-up ones."

Annabelle nodded. When they arrived at her house, she paused on the porch. "You really think I can do this?"

"Remember what Mr. Jensen said? You only need to be the teacher until they can find, and hire, a replacement."

"But it's almost the end of the school year. And where are they going to find someone who's willing to come out here to the middle of nowhere?"

Ruth moved past Annabelle and opened the door. "Can we go inside? I'm cold."

Annabelle shrugged and followed her in.

While she took her coat, scarf, hat, and gloves off, Ruth answered her friend's question. "I'm sure there's someone out there who didn't get a teaching job and is willing to sacrifice his or her comfort to come out here and teach these poor, neglected heathens."

Annabelle stared at Ruth. "Heathens?"

"That's how most Easterners think of us. We don't live in the 'civilized' world, so we must all be heathens."

Annabelle cocked an eyebrow. "Interesting." She breathed heavily. "If you're sure I can do this..."

"I'm more than sure. I know you can do it."

"Fine. But you're still staying here tonight and helping me tomorrow, right?"

"Yes, but tomorrow I can leave after school, right?"

"Why?"

"I told Mary I would hopefully be able to walk home with Otis, Olive, and Ellis."

Annabelle smiled. "That little girl is attached to you, isn't she?"

Ruth grinned. "It seems like it."

"What happens if she has to go back to her father?"

Ruth slumped against the wall. "I don't know."

"And even if you do get to let them stay with you, what happens when you get married?"

"When?" Ruth protested and looked up and down the hall. "How about if?"

Annabelle shook her head as they headed upstairs. "Nope. When."

Ruth laughed. "You're crazy."

"I know. But you love me anyway. And I'm not crazy to think you'll be married soon. I've seen the way William looks at me and the way Micah looks at you. He might not realize it, but he's in love with you."

Ruth shrugged. "If you say so."

"What? Don't you want him to be?"

"I want to hear it from him, not you. And not until the day he proposes."

Annabelle furrowed her eyebrows. "Why?"

"I don't want to get emotionally attached before we get engaged."

"All right." Annabelle sat silently on her bed for a minute, deep in thought. She took a deep breath and exhaled loudly. "What do we need to do to prepare for tomorrow?"

"Same thing I told you to do after school every day."

Annabelle groaned. "Get tomorrow's lesson plans ready."

"Exactly. Now get to work, Slave."

"Yes, Massa."

The room erupted into a series of giggles.

"Ruth! Wait up!"

Ruth turned and paused when she saw Micah hurrying toward her.

Micah looked at Otis, Olive, and Ellis. "You three can go on. I only need a minute and then Miss Brookings will catch up to you."

Otis looked from Ruth to Micah and back again. Ruth gave a short nod and Otis led his siblings toward the ranch.

"What is it?" Ruth asked when they were out of hearing distance.

Micah shifted. "I'm letting Grover loose this evening. Miles, another man from church, and I will talk to him before we let him go. We're going to talk about his care for his children and lay down the law about that. If he doesn't want the children yet, we'll let him go on his way. If he does, Grover and I will come out to the ranch tomorrow morning."

"Will he know where they are?"

"No."

Ruth nodded. "Thank you for the warning. Can you send someone to let us know if you are coming tomorrow?"

"Good idea. I'll send someone. I also won't be coming out tomorrow night. Hopefully Friday, though. I...I just want to be here tomorrow night. It's been a couple of weeks since he's had a drink and I wish I could say he's cured..."

Ruth nodded. "I understand. I better go now or I'll never catch up to them."

Micah grinned. "Actually, they're waiting for you just around the bend."

Ruth chuckled. "They really are sweet."

"I hope for their sakes their father doesn't want them back yet."

"Me, too. As sad and heartbreaking as it would be, I think it would be for the best."

"Bye, Ruth. Lord willing, I will see you on Friday."

Ruth waved and hurried to catch up to the Miller children.

CHAPTER TWENTY THREE

With a heavy heart, Micah picked up the keys and walked the short distance to the jail cell. He put the key into the lock and slowly turned it. The man inside the cell didn't move until the lock snapped open. The man rolled over slowly and blinked up at Micah with squinted eyes.

"Come on out, Grover," Micah said. "I'm letting you go. But before you leave, we need to have a talk with you."

"We?" Grover asked.

Micah beckoned for him to follow. Grover hesitantly stepped past the bars that had kept him locked up since just after the blizzard. He followed Micah and paused in the doorway to the office. The door to the outside was blocked by Pastor Jenkins, Oscar Johnson, and deputy Obadiah Smith.

"What do you want?" Grover asked, crossing his arms and leaning against the doorway.

Miles Jenkins took a step forward. "We need to talk to you about your children. If there was a law against child abuse and child neglect, you would still be in that jail cell. Since there isn't however, God's law requires us to take care of the orphans and widows. Your children aren't orphaned, but they may as well be as often as you leave them. You have a choice: stop leaving your children on the farm and take care of them, or let them get the care they need from someone else. They are with a family right now who is willing to look after them if you choose not to."

Grover shifted his gaze from one man to the next and back again. "You are serious?"

"Yes," Micah answered.

Grover shook his head and pushed himself away from the wall. "In that case, let someone else take care of the imps. I don't care."

Micah stiffened and clenched his jaw to keep the words from flying out. He shouldn't have been surprised, but hearing it in such strong words straight from the man's mouth just made him mad.

Miles pursed his lips together. "Fine. I would encourage you to take this time alone to seek God. If you'd like, I can come out and talk with you about Him."

"You sayin' I ain't livin' right, Preacher?" Grover asked, a glint in his eyes.

"You wouldn't have been in jail if you were living right," Miles responded.

Grover huffed.

"Don't cause any more trouble," Micah warned. "I don't want to arrest you again."

Grover sneered at him, but didn't say a word.

Micah motioned for Obadiah to move away from the door and let Grover leave. As he left, Obadiah grabbed Grover's arm. "Just a friendly word of advice. Stay away from the saloon."

Grover glared at the deputy without a word and stepped around him.

Micah, Miles, Oscar, and Obadiah watched him leave the office.

"Did we do the right thing?" Micah asked.

Miles turned to face him. "Yes, I think we did. Aside from keeping him locked up illegally, there was nothing else you could do."

Micah sighed as he walked around his desk and plopped into the chair. "I know. I just have this feeling that he's not done messin' up yet."

Miles nodded grimly. "I know what you mean. Well, I better get home."

Micah sat up straight. "Would John and James want to go to the ranch with Jeremiah to deliver a message for me?"

"Sure. Clem and Chancy are at the house now, too. They're supposedly studying together. Is it okay...?"

Micah interrupted him. "That's fine. Safety in numbers."

Obadiah guffawed. "With those five? They're more likely to get into trouble than stay safe."

"That is also possible." Miles chuckled as he thought about it.

Micah shrugged. "It'll be fine. I hope. Thanks for coming by, Oscar and Miles."

"Glad to do it," Oscar said. "Even though I didn't say anything."

Micah smiled slightly. "Just having someone besides the lawmen and preacher probably helped."

Oscar nodded. "See ya around."

Miles followed Oscar out, but paused in the doorway. "Shall I send the boys here to get the note or does Jeremiah already have it?"

"Send 'em here, please," Micah said.

"Will do."

After Miles left, Micah sighed again. "Here's hoping we have a quiet afternoon and evening. For that matter how about a quiet week?"

"With Grover out?" Obadiah asked. "I doubt that."

"Thanks for the vote of confidence, Deputy," Micah groused.

Obadiah grinned. "No problem, Boss. I'm gonna get some shuteye before my evening shift."

"Alrighty. Thanks for interrupting your beauty sleep."

Obadiah waved his hand at Micah in disbelief. "So long."

"What is that?" Clem asked.

"What?" Jeremiah replied.

Clem pointed ahead at a dark spot in the snow and Jeremiah, John, James, and Chancy all squinted their eyes to see better.

"I don't know," John said.

James jumped up and down and ran closer, signing something as he ran. John stared at his brother's hand while hurrying after him. "A dog?" he finally asked. "You think it's a dog?" He reached the spot where James stood. It was a brown and white dog with floppy ears and a long coat of fur.

"Come here, Boy," Clem called when he caught up. The puppy stared at them with unblinking eyes, but didn't move. The five boys tried everything they could think of to get the puppy to come to them. They were about to give up when they heard someone yelling.

"Hi, guys! What are you doing there?"

Jeremiah glanced toward the voice. "Hi, Otis. We found this puppy and we're trying to get it to move so we can try to find its owner."

Otis walked up to the group and looked the direction they were pointing. He grinned when he saw the puppy. "That's because I trained him not to go to anyone besides me or Samantha. I didn't want anybody hurting him." Otis crouched down behind the snowbank and out of the dog's sight. "Come here, Shep!" he called.

Jeremiah and the other boys watched as the puppy's ears perked up and he slowly stood on his legs. Otis gave a low, drawn-out whistle with a few complicated trills, and the puppy took a few more hesitant steps forward before lunging full tilt through the snow and jumping on top of Otis.

Otis laughed as Shep knocked him down and started licking his face. "Get off me, you big baby. I've told you no licking. Ugh!" Otis pushed Shep off him and stood. Shep sat at his master's feet and stared up with adoration in his big brown eyes. Otis's eyebrows drew together. "Where have you been, Shep? What happened to Samantha?"

John looked from owner to dog and back to the owner. "Samantha was in town today, so maybe Shep came with her and decided to try to find you."

"Maybe," Otis sighed. "I'll have to bring him back. See ya later." He started toward town. He paused and turned. "Oh. Where are you all headed?"

"To the Double B," Clem said.

"Could you tell Mrs. Brookings where I am, please?" Otis asked.

"Sure," John said.

Clem looked at the setting sun. "How about Chancy and I come with you since Samantha's house is on the way to our house. I wouldn't mind seeing Lou again and we should head home, anyway."

Otis smiled. "Thanks. I'd like that."

Ruth bit her lower lip. She knew she should ask the question she'd been dying to ask, but her mouth was dry and her heart beat erratically.

"I can tell you have a question for me," Micah said. "What is it?"

Ruth swallowed to try to moisten her mouth. "How did you know?"

Micah grinned. "You get a certain look on your face when you have a question."

"Hm. Well, I'm not sure I should ask it."

Micah leaned back in the chair and crossed his arms. "Why not?"

"You might not want to talk about it."

"Try me."

Ruth licked her lips. "What was Edith like?"

Micah took a deep breath and held it for a second before letting it out. "That is a complicated question."

"Why?"

"I don't want you to feel like you need to measure up to her. You and Edith were very different and I'm very different now than I was when I married her."

"Yep," Ruth said. "You're definitely a lot older now. Though, I'm not sure if you're wiser."

Micah threw his head back and laughed. "Miss Brookings, you are getting into dangerous territory there."

Ruth flashed a mischievous smile at him and kept her mouth shut.

Micah shook his head and slowly sobered. He studied his hands for a few seconds while he thought. "Edith was a gentle, vivacious woman. Jeremiah reminds me of her a lot, actually. She was passionate about everything, especially if she had a strong opinion about it." He chuckled. "I remember one time when a woman at church criticized the way she disciplined Jeremiah for something during the service. Keep in mind that Jeremiah was only about two at the time. Edith made sure this woman knew she was welcome to try to keep Jeremiah quiet and still during the two-hour long service if she wanted to."

Ruth smirked. "That sounds like something Anna would do."

Micah glanced up at her. "You're right, it does." He searched the wall behind Ruth. "Edith was one active and energetic woman. She loved being the wife of a wealthy man, not because of the money, but because she could serve others with it. She was raised wealthy and had been involved in charity work from childhood and continued right on with those charities even after Jeremiah was born."

Ruth blinked and leaned forward. "You were wealthy?"

Micah swallowed hard and cleared his throat. "Um, yeah. I was. Actually, I still kind of am."

"Kind of am? You either are or you aren't."

Micah shrugged. "Fine. Yes, I am."

"Why did you never tell anybody?"

Micah sighed. "I don't really want anyone to know. The banker knew since I transferred my money here, but he's sworn to secrecy. I wanted people to accept me for who I am rather than for my money. And I don't really want to be seen as that eligible of a bachelor."

"True," Ruth said. "Does Pa know?"

"Um, I'm not sure. Probably not. Why?"

Ruth shrugged. "He might want to know."

"I'll tell him before I leave, then. Now I think it's time for you to answer a hard question. Is there anything you've always wanted to do, but couldn't because you were female or didn't have the money?"

Ruth's eyes widened. "That's a hard one." She rubbed her forehead and stared at the corner where the ceiling and wall met. "I don't think so. The only thing I've really wanted to do that I can't is to help the poor and orphaned more than I am able to. What about you?"

Micah chuckled. "I should have known you'd turn the question back around on me. Hm...I've always wanted to have more kids, but that dream kind of died with Edith. And I never thought I could love another woman enough to marry her. I'm still not quite sure I can."

Ruth raised an eyebrow. "What about Pastor Jenkins and Anna's sister-in-law, Maggie?"

Micah shrugged. "I suppose those are good examples. It's hard to think that way. I've been widowed for almost six years and my life is so different from what it was in Chicago when I was married. I don't know what to think, I guess I need to let God guide me."

"That would help. When I asked Pa about it, he said love feels different for everybody, so you can't even go by that."

Micah grunted. "That sounds about right."

324

They were silent for a few seconds.

"What did you do before you became a deputy? I know Joshua suggested you, but I don't really know what you did before that."

"Oh boy," Micah chuckled. "I did a little bit of this and a little bit of that. The Lancasters had me do their bookkeeping for a while right away and I'd worked for a bank before, so I asked Carl if he needed a teller or someone like that. He did, so I worked there part-time. I also wanted to do something outside since that was one reason I came West in the first place. I wanted to get away from the routines back home and do something different. So I rented some farmland from an older couple who wanted to live in their house, but couldn't farm anymore. I did a halfway decent job farming the first year.

"Mr. Harper gave me advice and I did better each successive year until I decided to quit my job at the bank. Carl's son was ready to take over for me anyway. Then I met Joshua and he conned me into becoming a deputy."

A laugh burst out of Ruth. "He conned you?"

"I don't know what else to call it!" Micah protested.

"How about gentle persuasion?" Daniel asked as he walked into the room.

Micah bit his lip and squinted one eye. "I don't think so, I think it was more of a con. Anyway, by that time, I owned the land because the Harpers gave it to me when they died."

"You own a farm?" Ruth asked. "Why do you keep so many secrets? And why don't you live on the farm?"

"The big farmhouse seems too empty for just two of us," Micah said. "I don't intentionally keep secrets. I just don't offer information if there's no need to."

Daniel cocked an eyebrow. "Is there something else he's been keeping quiet that made you ask that question, Ruth?"

Ruth crossed her arms and stared at Micah. "I think Micah should answer that question."

Daniel turned his gaze to Micah and Micah cleared his throat a few times, pulling on the collar of his shirt as if it were choking him. "Well, I, um...I have quite a bit of money from when I worked in Chicago. By Western standards, I would probably be considered rich. I've just...kept it quiet so money hunters don't come after me."

Daniel nodded slowly, his face a mask of neutrality as he lowered himself into a chair. "Does Jeremiah know this?"

"No."

"Are you ashamed of the money?" Daniel asked.

"No."

"Are you the one who keeps making anonymous donations to the church?"

Micah raised his eyebrows. "Would I tell you even if I was?"

Daniel smiled. "Probably not. This certainly puts things into perspective a little more."

"I didn't intentionally keep any of this from you," Micah said quickly. "I honestly didn't even think about it. I've invested some of my money and it's either staying steady or growing. I've quietly helped a few people start businesses."

"And this farm?" Daniel asked. "Are you planning to farm when you retire from being sheriff?"

"Either that or do something like what the Harpers did. Rent the land and live off the money I've saved. The sheriff job has kept me supplied enough to live comfortably."

"If you get married and have kids, will your money be enough?" Daniel asked.

"For a while. I would probably keep half my farmland to farm myself. I wouldn't mind teaching Jeremiah how to farm."

"Wouldn't you get bored if you don't work anywhere?" Ruth asked.

"Not if I can do what I want to with the farming and other things."

"Like what?" Daniel questioned.

Micah cleared his throat. "If I get married and my wife agrees to it, I've thought about adopting some older children from the orphanage in Helena and having them farm the land I keep and give them a home and parents to guide them to the Lord and through life."

Ruth stared at Micah. "You would do that?"

Micah nodded. "Why not?"

Ruth opened and closed her mouth. "I don't know, I just wasn't expecting that to be your answer."

Micah shrugged and glanced at the clock. "I guess tonight's been the night of surprises. As much as I don't want to, I should go. Jeremiah's not very happy I didn't bring him with me today and is probably not listening to Mrs. Tucker."

Daniel nodded. "I wouldn't mind getting some shuteye myself."

Micah stood up and stretched. "Thank you for the stimulating conversation, Miss Brookings. I'm glad you thought to ask that first question."

Ruth smiled as she stood up. "I'm glad, too."

Daniel looked between the two of them. "I hope you can bring Jeremiah out next time. Do you want to come later this week?"

Micah shook his head. "I would love to, but I told Obadiah I wouldn't make him work four nights this week."

"We'll talk on Sunday then," Daniel said.

"Yes," Micah replied. "Thank you for having me over tonight."

The three walked to the door together and after Micah had his coat on, Daniel opened the door for Micah and Ruth to step out onto the porch, then closed the door gently.

Ruth hugged her shawl closer. "Thank you for being so open tonight."

Micah smiled. "You're welcome. It's nice to know that someone knows what I really am and that I have money, without having to worry about you telling people. I'm also grateful for your questions about Edith. I've never known quite how to bring her up, but now I feel like I can talk about her without hurting your feelings at all."

Ruth shivered. "You're welcome."

Micah took a deep breath. "I need to let you get back inside. Goodbye, Ruth. I will see you on Sunday."

Ruth smiled. "Goodbye, Micah." She watched him walk to his horse and mount up before turning back into the house to talk to her waiting father.

"What question did you ask that he was so grateful for?" Daniel asked as soon as she stepped inside.

"I asked him what his first wife was like," Ruth replied. "That's also how I found out he's wealthier than he looks."

Daniel shook his head. "I still can't believe Micah is wealthy. Or that he farmed without most people knowing it. Although, when he was farming, we were either not here yet, or getting the ranch ready."

Ruth laughed. "You're right. I'm still not sure what to think of the revelation." She looked around. "Where's Mother?"

"She decided to take some personal time with the Lord. She used to do it right after breakfast, but her schedule has been thrown off by all the changes."

Ruth nodded and took a deep breath. "I think I'll go to bed. I'm tired."

Daniel patted her shoulder. "I love you, Ruth."

"I love you, too, Pa."

CHAPTER TWENTY FOUR

Micah sighed. It had been a week since he'd released Grover. The Miller children now knew their father didn't want them. Tears stung Micah's eyes as he recalled the look in Otis's face. He may not have liked his father, but being rejected by a father was devastating to anyone, especially to a twelve year old boy.

At least Otis had Mr. Brookings now. And he knew Harriet and Ruth would help as well. Micah smiled as he twirled the pencil through his fingers. Only tonight and tomorrow to get through until he would get to see Ruth again. *Lord, why do I want to see her so badly all of a sudden? I've only called on her four times now. I shouldn't be so preoccupied by thinking about her so much. It could cost me my life considering the job I have.* He groaned. *For that matter, how can I consider marrying her when she could so easily become a widow a week after marrying me? At least what I have in the bank would support her.* He sighed. He had no right to even consider marrying a woman, let alone Ruth.

Crack. Micah jumped up, knocking his chair to the floor and pulling his gun as he rushed to the door. The report of the gun still echoed off the buildings as his mind realized this was the first gunshot in town since he had become sheriff. Micah slowly opened the door and scanned what he could see of the dark street. He stepped cautiously onto the boardwalk and kept up a continual scan. The streets were clear, probably due to the late hour and whoever had been out had scurried for cover. He saw a man back out of the saloon and race for a horse.

Micah took a shot at him to try to slow him down, but the man didn't even hesitate.

"Hey! That's my horse!" a man yelled from the batwing doors.

Micah ran toward the saloon. "What happened?"

The man who had yelled gestured toward the inside of the saloon. "That man just killed Aaron Cooper in cold blood. Aaron wasn't even armed. And then he stole my horse!"

Micah stepped past the man into the saloon, the doors swinging back behind him. Micah looked around the saloon as he approached the body. He was indeed unarmed and had been shot in the back.

"What happened?" Micah asked.

The bartender stepped forward. "Grover had been drinking an awful lot and I told 'im he couldn't have no more. He kinda went a little crazy when I told 'im that. He started threatening all the men if they didn't buy him a drink. Aaron was the loudest speaker against him. He probably figured Grover wouldn't shoot 'im because he was unarmed."

"Grover pulled his gun," another man cut in, "and when Aaron turned away from him, shot him in the back."

Micah knelt beside the body. "I didn't even know Grover had a gun. I've never seen him carry one before." He looked at the group of men huddled around him. "Morton, could you please saddle Jericho?" Morton nodded and hurried outside. "Make sure you take good care of Aaron's body. We'll have to notify his family. If I'm not back by mornin', tell Obadiah to send the telegram and have Jeremiah go out to the Double B."

As he stood up, his heart grew heavier. How could a man kill someone just because he didn't get enough to drink? If it were water and water was scarce, he might understand, but alcohol?

"I'll do my best to bring him back," Micah promised.

The batwing doors swung behind him as he left. Morton arrived with his horse as Micah stepped out of the saloon onto the boardwalk. He nodded his thanks to the man and swung into the saddle. Micah dug his heels into the horse's sides and galloped toward his house to grab his gear and some food.

When his supplies were packed in the saddlebags, he spurred his horse after Grover, his heart sinking and dread filling his every pore. Some men might thrive on the adventure of the unknown, but he had a son to think about and a young lady he wanted to marry.

He shook the thoughts out of his head and concentrated on the task at hand. He'd seen the direction Grover had gone, but had no idea where he might go. The moon guided his way for another half hour, but when the already faint light began to fail, Micah stopped for the night in a small grove of trees. He built a small fire and lay down to sleep. He would need all the rest he could get.

The next morning, Micah woke as dawn lit up the morning sky. When the light was good enough to follow Grover's trail, he set out. Grover had taken no precautions to hide his trail, but he'd also been able to ride all night.

Micah kept his horse at a steady canter unless the trail became too hard to follow. At noon, he let Jericho take a short rest next to a running stream. The horse Grover was riding was getting tired and would soon drop from exhaustion. Micah pushed his way through the snow on foot and up a small hill. He scanned the area carefully. The ranch to the west looked to be the most likely place for Grover to steal another horse from.

He half walked, half slid down the hill back to the place he'd left Jericho. Mounting up, he cut across the ranch and reined in at the house. He jumped off his horse and was met at the front door by a burly man.

The man looked him up and down and his eyes rested on Micah's badge. "Somethin' wrong, Sheriff?"

"I'm looking for a murderer and horse thief who may have stolen one of your horses."

The man nodded. "Yep. He left his beaten down horse here and took one o' mine. We took care of his horse, figurin' it to be stolen. "

Micah nodded. "Thanks. What kind of horse did he steal from you?"

"A white 'un. It'll be hard to see against this snow. He's also one of our fastest runnin' horses." The man looked at Micah's horse. "Yer horse looks 'most done in, too. Why don't you stable yer horse here and borrow one of ours?"

Micah smiled. "I'd be mighty obliged. How long ago did he steal the horse?"

The man tilted his head and thought. "Before dawn, but after two in the morning. I was up about two and the horse was still in the corral."

Micah nodded his thanks.

"Pedro!" the man shouted.

A young Mexican boy ran toward them. "Sí, Señor?"

"Take this horse and saddle Flighty. When he's saddled, take real good care of the sheriff's horse."

Pedro grinned. "Sí, Señor!"

"Flighty?" Micah asked as Pedro disappeared around the house.

The man motioned for him to follow. "Come in and warm yerself. I've got some coffee on. You may's well have a cup while you wait."

Micah followed the man inside to the kitchen and watched as he poured coffee into a large tin cup.

"Thank you."

The man settled into a chair across the table from Micah. "My wife gave Flighty his name. She thought he was a she and the horse didn't seem to want to listen to anything but his own way of thinking. But he's our fastest horse and can run for days if need be when paced out right. Alternate cantering and galloping with an occasional trot and you'll have a horse to ride the river with."

Micah grinned. "I'm hopin' not to have to ride a river."

The man chuckled and reached his hand across the table. Micah shook his hand.

"The name's Adam Milton."

"Micah Carson."

"Pleasure to meet you. I hope you catch your man. We don't need men like that roaming the country and I wouldn't mind having Snowball back. He's one of our best studs."

Micah nodded. "I'll definitely do my best. When I catch him, I'll return your two horses and pick up mine and the other stolen horse."

"I'll be prayin' for you," Adam said.

Micah drank the last swallow of the bitter coffee and stood up. "Thanks for the coffee, horse, warmth, help, and prayers. I appreciate it."

Adam stood up. "Glad to do it. Now go catch your man."

Micah grinned. "Yes, Sir."

Adam followed him out the front door. "Good boy, Pedro! Mr. Carson, meet Flighty. Flighty, meet Micah Carson. Be good to him, Flighty."

Flighty whinnied in response and Adam chuckled. "That horse is smart, Micah. Watch out for him."

"I will. And thanks again!" Micah said as he swung into the saddle and got the horse moving back toward the trail.

Micah paced Flighty using Adam's suggestions and covered nearly twice as much ground that afternoon as he had in the morning. As the sun set over the mountains, Micah searched for a place to stop for the night.

Once his camp was set up and the coffee heating, he chewed on his beef jerky and tried not to think about anything but his mission. Every time he closed his eyes, however, Ruth's face popped into his mind. He finally gave in and allowed himself to think some things through out loud.

"Ruth is intelligent, beautiful, and loves children. She is a devoted Christian and has a servant heart. She would make an excellent wife. For me? I don't know." He looked at Flighty and noticed with a start that he was looking at him. "What?" Micah asked, raising an eyebrow. "Doesn't anybody at your ranch talk to themselves?

"Where was I? Oh yeah. I don't deserve her, but I can't stand the thought of someone else marrying her either." He sighed. "Before I think about proposing though, I need to talk to Daniel Brookings about how risky this job is. If I even make it back alive from this."

Micah rested his chin in his hand and stared at the flames. "It's been three days since I saw her and I already miss her." He lifted his eyes to the stars. "God, what am I supposed to do?"

CHAPTER TWENTY FIVE

The Brookings family, guests, and ranch hands had just sat down to eat when the front door burst open and a young voice shouted, "Mr. Brookings?"

Daniel and Peter shoved their chairs back at the sound of the distressed and breathless voice and ran through the doorway.

"Jeremiah?" Daniel asked. "What's going on?"

Jeremiah fought to catch his breath. "Is everybody here?"

Daniel nodded. "Yes, we were about to eat supper. Where's your pa?"

Jeremiah straightened. "Can I talk to you, Miss Brookings, and Mrs. Brookings alone, please?"

"We can watch the kids," Peter said.

Daniel bit his lip. "Thank you." They walked into the kitchen. "Ruth, Harriet. Jeremiah would like to talk to us alone." He looked at the Miller children and ranch hands. "You go ahead and eat, just save some for the rest of us, all right?" He tried to smile.

Ruth and Harriet followed Daniel into his den where they found Jeremiah already sprawled on one of the chairs.

"What happened?" Daniel asked as he sat in his chair across the desk and Harriet and Ruth sat in the chairs to either side of Jeremiah.

"Grover Miller shot a man in the back in the saloon and ran off." He swallowed hard and swiped at his eyes. "Pa went after him and asked that I stay here till he gets back."

The blood drained out of Ruth's face. "Why did he shoot the man? Is the man...dead?"

Jeremiah looked over at her. "Yeah. He's dead. Mr. Miller was refused more to drink and he shot the first man to turn his back on him. At least, I think that's how it went."

"I knew that man was trouble, but I didn't think he'd ever do something that foolhardy," Daniel said.

Harriet reached over and rested a hand on Jeremiah's arm. "Do you mind sharing a room with Otis, Ellis, and Carter?"

Jeremiah's eyes went wide. "No, Ma'am." He hesitated. "Are you going to tell them?"

Daniel and Harriet exchanged a glance. "Yes, we will, but not until after supper. Ruth, I think you should do the dishes alone while Jeremiah tells the ranch hands and your mother and I tell the children."

Ruth nodded. "Yes, Pa."

Daniel sighed. "Well, I suppose we should get back to our supper."

Harriet nodded. "We should also try to cheer up a little."

Daniel forced himself to smile. "I'll try, Darling, but it'll be awfully hard."

"I know," Harriet replied. "But think about all the fun we'll have with five more children to raise."

Daniel's smile became more genuine. "A total of ten children to raise in our lifetime? I dunno, that might be too many."

"How about the range of ages?" Harriet asked with a laugh. "Matthew's what? Thirty-two? And Carter is two?" Harriet shrugged. "That's only a thirty year age span."

Ruth chuckled. "Oh my. Ma, I didn't know you had it in you."

"For what?" Harriet asked. "You didn't know I could do math that well?"

Daniel laughed. "I think she means having kids for thirty years."

Harriet raised an eyebrow. "At least I didn't have to have these last five myself. I think that would have been a little much."

Ruth smiled as she stood up. "We better get back in the kitchen." She walked to where Jeremiah sat slumped in the large armchair, ignoring her parents. "Jeremiah." He looked at her. "Your pa will be fine. He's smart and fast with a gun."

"What if that man ambushes him?" Jeremiah asked, looking up at her with tear-filled eyes.

Ruth pulled Jeremiah into her arms. "All we can do is pray for God's protection and trust his instincts."

Jeremiah clung to Ruth for a minute before taking a deep breath and letting it out slowly. Ruth let go and stepped away from the embrace as Jeremiah wiped his eyes dry. "I'll try."

Ruth took his arm and they walked into the kitchen together.

After a quiet supper, Daniel asked the Miller children to join him and Harriet in the living room. Jeremiah stayed in the kitchen to talk to the ranch hands and help Ruth with the dishes.

"What is it?" Otis asked, eyes wary.

Daniel tried to smile. "Have a seat, please."

The two girls sat on one chair while the three boys crowded onto a settee.

Daniel cleared his throat and held his wife's hand. "As you know, your father was let out of jail about a week ago. Some of the men from church told him what he needed to do if he wanted you to live with him again. He chose to let you stay here."

Mary's face lit up. "Do we get to stay here forever?"

Otis grunted. "I doubt it. He'll change his mind sooner or later."

Daniel held his hand up. "He no longer has a choice. He did something very bad and when Sheriff Carson catches him, he will be punished for it."

Olive scooted forward on the chair. "What did he do? Will he be in jail for a long time?"

Daniel and Harriet exchanged glances. "He did something really bad and will hang for it."

At the announcement, it felt like the air had been sucked right out of the room. Harriet saw the tears forming in Olive's and Mary's eyes and hurried toward them, pulling them into her arms.

Otis sat rigid as a board in his seat and Ellis looked confused.

"Where are we going to stay?" Ellis asked.

"Mrs. Brookings and I will let you stay here as long as you want to. If we can, we might even adopt you."

Otis's head snapped up. "Why?"

"We love all of you," Harriet said. "You are all precious to us and we want you to be part of our family forever, without you wondering if you're really part of the family."

Otis nodded and Daniel wondered what he was thinking. He knew the boy was a deep thinker and would need lots of time to think things through before he truly adjusted. In many ways, Otis reminded him of Ruth.

Daniel's thoughts were interrupted by Olive. "What about Samantha? Does she know?"

Daniel shook himself. "I don't know. I'll have to ask Jeremiah. If she doesn't know yet, I'll go to her house tomorrow."

"Can Shep stay here if you adopt us?" Otis asked.

"Who's Shep?" Harriet asked.

"Shep is Otis's dog," Mary piped up. "He's cute."

"Where is he now?" Daniel asked.

Otis shrugged. "Sam's taking care of him. When she got married, I asked her to take him until Dad stopped drinkin' so much."

Daniel nodded. "What kind of dog is he?"

"An Australian Shepherd," Otis said, a smile flickering at the corners of his mouth. "He's real smart and only obeys me or someone I tell him to obey."

Daniel tapped his fingers on the arm of his chair, thinking hard. "Would you be willing to train him to help on the ranch? I've been wanting a guard dog, especially when the girls are here alone."

The smile that popped on Otis's face could have filled the whole room. "I know he can do that."

Daniel smiled. "How about you come with me tomorrow morning, Otis, and we can get Shep and check on your sister."

A quiet knock on the doorframe interrupted them. "Can we come in?" Ruth asked.

Mary jumped out of the chair and ran to her, grabbing her hand and pulling her into the room. Ruth laughed. "I guess it's fine with Mary, how about the rest of you?"

Harriet beckoned. "Come on in, Jeremiah and Ruth."

"Daddy did something really bad," Mary said.

Ruth squatted. "I know he did. What do you think about it?"

"Is Daddy going to hurt when he gets hanged?"

Ruth shuddered. "I don't know, Sweetheart."

Ellis bounced up to Jeremiah. "Otis gets to bring Shep here tomorrow!"

Jeremiah looked at Daniel with confusion on his face and Daniel shrugged.

"Do you know if Samantha has been told about her father yet?" Daniel asked.

"No, I don't know," Jeremiah replied. "What's this about Shep?"

"Mr. Brookings and I are going to tell Samantha and bring Shep back with us to stay on the ranch," Otis said.

Jeremiah nodded and looked around, seeming to be lost.

"Mr. Brookings," Otis asked, "can Jeremiah come with us?"

Daniel smiled and nodded.

"Thank you, Sir!" Otis exclaimed. "Are we done in here?"

Harriet looked at Daniel.

"Yes," Daniel replied. "But please feel free to talk about your dad if you want to. Mrs. Brookings, Ruth, and I are willing to answer questions and listen to you if you need to talk about things."

Ruth walked over to the settee the boys had been on. "I think it's time for bed for at least one little one." She smiled as she lifted the sleeping boy out of the chair. "Jeremiah? Would you like to help me get Carter ready for bed?"

Jeremiah shrugged and followed her out of the room.

Once upstairs, Ruth lay Carter on the bed Otis and Ellis shared. "How about you carefully take his clothes off while I get his nightshirt?"

Jeremiah's eyes widened, but he nodded and did as she asked.

When Ruth came back to the bed, Carter was still sleeping. "Can you please pull the trundle bed out from under the bed?"

"Sure." Jeremiah pulled the small bed out while Ruth slipped the nightshirt over Carter's sleeping body. Ruth smiled as Jeremiah folded the covers down so Ruth could put Carter under the blankets.

When they left the room, Ruth put a hand on his shoulder. "Thank you for helping me, Jeremiah."

"I don't have anything better to do," Jeremiah said.

Ruth took a few more steps down the hall and turned to face him. "Jeremiah, you know you can talk to me about anything, right?"

Jeremiah nodded.

"Can I take a little time to talk to you?"

He nodded again.

"Let's go to Pa's study so this can be a little more private." Ruth led the way, praying Jeremiah would follow her.

In the study, Ruth sat in the chair closest to the books, leaving the chair by the window for

Jeremiah. He lagged behind a little, looked around the room, and slouched into the chair.

"What's bothering you?" Ruth asked when he had settled into the chair.

Jeremiah shrugged.

Ruth sighed. "Is it your pa?"

Jeremiah shrugged again.

Ruth bit her lip. "Do you know what I miss most tonight?"

Jeremiah shook his head.

"Looking over the next day's school assignments and anticipating a short visit from you and your pa." Ruth closed her eyes and leaned back in the chair. "When I think I might never see your pa again..."

"Do you really think Pa might die?" Jeremiah asked in a small voice.

Ruth took a deep breath and tried to keep her voice steady. "I pray not, but if Mr. Miller is desperate, there is that possibility. One thing I do know is that your pa will do his very best to stay alive and bring Mr. Miller back with him."

Jeremiah breathed a sigh of relief. "Thank you. I just keep thinking through all the possible bad things that could happen. I don't wanna lose my pa. I already lost my ma. I can't lose him, too."

Ruth slipped off the chair and perched on the edge of the seat Jeremiah sat on. She put an arm around his shoulder. "Keep praying for his safety,

Jeremiah. God will help you through whatever comes."

Jeremiah nodded and shrugged out from under her arm. "I better get ready for bed." He paused at the door. "Do you think Otis will share his clothes with me? I didn't think to bring mine."

Ruth smiled. "I'm sure he will. And mention it to Pa in the morning. You three can stop by your house to get some on your way to or from Samantha's house."

Jeremiah smiled. "Thank you, Miss Brookings."

"You're welcome, Jeremiah."

CHAPTER TWENTY SIX

The tracks were fresher on Saturday and Micah looked around more thoroughly. He was getting close. Did Grover know he was being followed? Micah watched the trail carefully and kept his eyes and ears alert. If Grover was aware of the sheriff following him, he would probably try to ambush him. And if that were the case...

Micah scanned the land in front of him. There were too many hiding places. A faint tendril of smoke caught his eye. Micah rode toward it cautiously. The fire had been recently abandoned. Micah sat on his horse, thoughtfully looking around. What was Grover up to?

As the terrain registered in his mind, a thought hit Micah. Being the ignorant outdoorsman he was, Grover had gotten himself trapped in a box canyon. Some canyons had walls a horse could climb up. Others had more than one way in and out. A box canyon had neither. Micah slid off his horse and tied Flighty loosely to a nearby tree.

Dodging behind rocks and leafless bushes, Micah crept forward across an open space, his eyes darting back and forth. Out of the corner of his eye, he saw the flash of sunlight on a gun barrel. He dove to the ground, scraping his hands on the loose rock hiding under the snow. The echo of a gunshot echoed off the canyon walls and Micah listened to make sure the shot hadn't caused an avalanche.

In another instant, his rifle was to his shoulder, a bullet in the chamber. Shooting at Grover from this angle wouldn't work unless the man thought he'd hit Micah and showed his face. Micah kept his eyes on the rock and surrounding area the flash had come from. When he saw no movement, he started to belly crawl forward.

He had only moved a few feet when he heard the click of a gun hammer above him. Without looking up or thinking about what he was doing, Micah swung the butt of his rifle up. The motion surprised Grover and knocked the pistol out of his hand. Micah stood up as he swung the rifle and by the time the pistol was out of Grover's hand, the barrel was pointed at the murderer.

"Hands in the air, Grover."

Grover slowly raised his arms and at the last second, launched himself toward Micah. Micah stepped to the side and Grover fell onto his back in the snow.

Micah put his right foot on Grover's stomach and pointed the rifle at his chest. "Stay put or I'll put a bullet in you."

Grover grunted and scowled. "Why'd you follow me? I won't ever go back to that town. You could've let me go."

Micah shook his head. "I can't let a killer go loose. And your children would always be wondering if and when you might come back."

Grover gritted his teeth. "Keep my kids outta this."

Micah pursed his lips. "I can't." He lifted his foot and nodded. "Get up and walk slowly to the horse."

They walked to Flighty and Micah took the coil of rope off the saddle horn. "Back against the tree."

Grover grunted, but obeyed. Micah snaked the rope around his wrists and pulled them around the tree, tying it tight. When he was finished, Grover glared at him, but Micah ignored the glare.

"Keep a close eye on him, Flighty. I've gotta find the other horse."

Micah worked his way to the rock Grover had shot from. Just as he'd thought, the horse was there. The horse was a little skittish, but compliant enough. He picked up the reins and led Snowball to where Flighty kept watch over Grover. When Flighty came into sight, Micah became the follower rather than the leader as Snowball and Flighty became reacquainted.

Micah ground-staked Snowball and went through the saddlebags to make sure Grover hadn't hidden anything in them. When he was sure there wasn't anything in them, he untied Grover. "Get on the horse."

Grover crossed his arms and leaned against the tree.

Micah pressed his lips together. "Move now or I'll tie you up here and leave you to the wolves." He wouldn't actually do anything like that, but Grover didn't need to know that.

Grover climbed on the horse and Micah tied him to the saddle. He took the reins in his hands and led Snowball to Flighty. "You ready to ride, Flighty?" Micah asked. Flighty whinnied in response. "I bet you want some oats. I'm sure your owner will have plenty of oats for you when we get back to your ranch."

Micah swung into the saddle and turned the horses around to go to Adam's ranch. As he rode, he kept quiet. Saying something to Grover would be a bad idea right now. He went over the entire scene again. How had he not noticed Grover walking up to him? He had almost been killed.

Micah gritted his teeth. *God, thank You for protecting me. Help me to be more attentive next time. Or keep there from being a next time. I know*

Jeremiah is probably worried sick about me like he always is. Give him comfort. Let him know You are there for him even if I'm not. Lord, please help the Brookings family be patient and understanding with him.

That night, they camped out in a small grove of trees. Micah untied Grover until he was off the horse, then tied him to a tree. He fed Grover and helped him drink some water. He knew Grover hated every second of it, but Micah was beyond caring.

Before dawn made its presence across the plains, Micah stirred up the fire and got a pot of coffee heating. He took out the last of his jerky and biscuits and fed half of them to Grover after he'd eaten the other half.

The two men were silent as they mounted up. As he led the stolen horse and outlaw to Flighty's ranch, Micah kept his eyes alert as he scanned the landscape. He was always amazed at the beauty of God's creation.

Just before the sun reached the pinnacle of the sky, a ranch house loomed up in front of them.

"No," Grover whispered. "Why're you bringing me here?"

"To return my borrowed horse and your stolen horse, and also to pick up my horse, and the other horse you stole," Micah said.

"They'll lynch me."

"No they won't," Micah answered in a harsh voice. "If they do, I'll arrest them and they know it."

A man stepped onto the porch as they approached and Micah recognized him.

"Howdy, Adam!" he shouted.

"Looks to me like you caught yer quarry," Adam replied with a smile.

"That I did," Micah said. "He gave me a little trouble and nearly got the drop on me, but I got him."

"God was watchin' you."

"Don't I know it," Micah replied. "I was almost killed twice, but God protected me."

"Praise the Lord!" Adam said. He nodded toward the white horse. "Looks like you found Snowball, too."

Micah nodded. "Yep. How did he get that name, anyway?"

Adam shrugged. "He's white and runs faster'n a snowball rolling down a hill."

Micah shook his head. "I don't think I should introduce you to my friend Joshua Brookings. He would probably have too much fun trying to name all their horses as...uniquely as you have."

"Brookings," Adam asked. "He the kid who became sheriff?"

Micah nodded. "Yep."

"What's he doing now if you're sheriff?"

"It's kind of secret, I think," Micah replied in a quiet tone, glancing at his prisoner.

"Ah. Well, shall we let your prisoner down?" Adam asked.

Grover glared at Adam. Micah chuckled as he climbed off his horse.

"Thank you for letting me borrow Flighty. I don't know what I would've done without him."

Adam waved his hand in dismissal. "Don't mention it." He turned his head to the side. "Pedro!"

The Mexican boy ran toward them. "Sí, Señor?"

"Go get Mr. Carson's horses saddled and take care of Flighty. Give him lots of oats. He deserves them."

Pedro grinned. "Sí, Señor."

"Come up on the porch," Adam invited.

"Don't mind if I do," Micah said.

"What about me?" Grover asked. "Do I have to stay here trussed on top of this horse?"

Micah glanced over his shoulder. "Until Pedro comes back with the horses, yes, you do."

Grover slumped over.

"He's a little belligerent," Adam mentioned.

Micah shrugged. "Wouldn't you be belligerent if you'd had the drop on a guy and he took your legs right from under you?"

Adam nodded. "Probably. Do you need anything else before you head out? How's the food and water supply?"

"I can't take any more from you. You've already fed my horses, or those in my responsibility, and lent me one of your horses."

Adam crossed his arms and cocked an eyebrow. "Consider it a friend helping a friend. We don't live so far away that we can't see each other once in a while. In fact, I may start getting my supplies in Castle City from now on so I can visit my new friend. So consider it good for the town and helping out the community. It ain't much anyway. Besides, your horses ate less food in three days than mine would've in two."

Micah smiled. "In that case, I will gladly accept some food and water for the journey back. Thank you. I would appreciate the visits. I think my son, Jeremiah, would love to meet you, too, so feel free to come and stay the night if you'd like sometime."

"You're married?" Adam asked as he stood up. "You can answer that question in a minute." He opened the door. "Felicia, could you please put together a few sandwiches and some other food for the two travelers?" He paused for a response.

"Gracias." He closed the door and sat back down. "Now where were we? Oh yes, I'd asked if you were married."

"I was," Micah replied. "My wife died about seven years ago. I came out here shortly after her death."

"And you never remarried?"

"Not yet."

Adam fought to keep the grin off his face. "Not yet?"

Micah tugged his hat down and felt his ears grow warm. "I'm courting a young lady right now and..." He glanced at Grover who suddenly looked alert. Micah lowered his voice. "I'm thinking about marrying her, but I need to do some more praying about it and ask her pa first."

Adam slapped Micah on the shoulder. "Good for you! And what's going on with the outlaw? Why don't you want him to know?"

"It's complicated. If you come visit maybe I can tell you more someday." Micah stood up as Pedro came around the corner of the house leading the two horses. "Gracias, Pedro."

"De nada, Señor Carson," Pedro replied.

Adam patted Pedro on the head. "Please go inside and see if your mother has finished packing the food."

Pedro nodded and hurried inside.

Micah smiled. "If you come to my place, would you be able to bring Pedro with you?"

Adam rubbed his chin. "Why?"

"Pedro and Jeremiah are about the same age and Jeremiah could use the influence of a hardworking young boy."

"I'll ask Felicia when I'm about to leave. It should be fine, though." Adam stepped off the porch. "Now, let's get the outlaw transferred onto a different horse."

"Sí, Señor Boss man," Micah said with a grin.

Micah untied Grover and steadied him as he slid off the horse.

"Can I use the outhouse?" Grover asked.

Micah nodded and followed Grover to the back of the house.

By the time they got back, Adam had stuffed Micah's saddlebags with food and refilled their canteens.

"This canteen," Adam said, holding the canteen with a ribbon tied around it, "has hot chocolate in it. Which is why the ribbon is on it."

Micah laughed. "Can you thank Felicia for me, please? It's been a long time since I've had hot chocolate."

"Me, too. I'm wondering where she's hidden it."

"Maybe I should give it to you then."

Adam laughed. "Naw, I'm sure she's got some inside for me." He stepped backward onto the porch. "Safe travels, Micah. I'll try to come to town in a few weeks."

When he had mounted, he waved. "I look forward to it. Thanks for everything." Micah clucked to his horse and the two travelers were on their way back to Castle City.

The journey back was long, chilly, and quiet. Too quiet for Micah. He liked action, noise, distraction. Especially distraction. If he was distracted, he couldn't think as much. Thinking could be a good thing sometimes, but right now all he could think of was Ruth. *God,* he prayed silently, *I know You placed this love in my heart for Ruth and I truly do thank You for it. But, I can't be distracted by thoughts of her right now. Please keep Satan from distracting me. In Jesus' name, amen.*

Micah scanned the terrain. It was rocky with some small hills, but otherwise, he saw nothing amiss. Not that he expected anything to be. The snow was blinding in the sunlight and he tried not to look around too much. The last thing he needed to get was snow blindness.

As dusk started to fall, Micah rode into town. Obadiah met him in front of the sheriff's office. He took one look at Micah and waved him off. "I'll take care o' this. You go to the Double B and see yer son and future wife."

Micah's head snapped up. "What?"

Obadiah chuckled. "Just ignore what I said and go."

"I'll go, but I'll be asking you about what you said when I have a little more energy to do so."

Obadiah shrugged and walked up to the horse Grover was riding. "Decided to steal the worst horse in a ten mile radius?" he asked.

Micah didn't stay around to hear more. He pointed Jericho's head to the west and the Double B Bar Ranch.

CHAPTER TWENTY SEVEN

The kitchen was a flurry of movement as Ruth, Olive, Mary, and Harriet hurried to get supper on the table. Samantha and Lou were coming for supper and the day had been full of adventure. A horse had gotten stuck in the snow and all the children had wanted to help or watch. It had taken a long time to get the horse out and by the time Harriet realized what time it was, it was too late to make the supper she had planned.

The girls had rushed back to the house and were just finishing up the quick meal when the men and boys came in.

Mary ran up to Jeremiah. "Will the horsey be okay?"

The left side of Jeremiah's mouth lifted. "Yeah, he'll be fine. The snow got him a little cold, but we've got a blanket on him in the barn."

"Should somebody stay out there to sleep with him to keep him warm tonight?" Mary asked.

Jeremiah laughed. "I don't think that would work. We'd need someone twice as big as my pa to do that. And horses sleep standing up most of the time."

Mary's eyes widened. "They do? How do they do that?"

Jeremiah shrugged. "God made 'em that way."

Otis chuckled. "'Miah, I think you have an admirer."

Jeremiah looked at Otis over his shoulder. "Huh?"

Otis nodded toward Mary. "Mary doesn't warm up to just anybody and she'd normally ask me all those questions."

Jeremiah glanced between the sister and brother. "Why would she like me so much?"

Otis shrugged. "I dunno. Ask her."

Jeremiah raised an eyebrow and looked at Mary. "Why do you like me so much?"

Mary shrugged her shoulders. "You're funny."

"I'm funny?" Jeremiah was incredulous.

Ruth rolled her eyes. "Jeremiah, how can you not know that you're funny?"

Jeremiah blinked his eyes and bit his lip. "I don't know."

A knock at the door interrupted the conversation and Otis leaped forward. "It's probably Sam and Lou! I'll get it!"

Ellis and Carter trailed after Otis.

"Mary, Olive, if you want to go greet them, you can," Harriet said.

"That's okay, Mrs. Brookings," Olive replied. "I don't mind."

"Jeremiah! Miss Brookings! Come see who it is!" Otis shouted.

Jeremiah and Ruth looked at each other a split second before they hurried through the doorway.

"*PA!* You made it back!" Jeremiah exclaimed as he ran to Micah.

Micah pulled Jeremiah into a tight hug and spoke into his hair. "I missed you so much, Jeremiah. It's good to see you again." Tears pooled in his eyes as he looked toward the doorway where Ruth stood watching them.

Ruth glanced around for the Miller boys, but Otis must have brought his brothers back into the kitchen without her noticing.

Micah took a shaky breath. "It's good to see you both again. And those rambunctious Miller kids." He smiled. "I think they were expecting someone else, though."

"Their sister and brother-in-law are coming for supper," Ruth replied. She kept her back against the wall trying to keep her relief from showing too much. "Did you catch Grover?"

"Yes. Obadiah got him into the jail cell after insisting I come straight out here."

"Was it hard, Pa?" Jeremiah asked.

Micah looked away. "Yes, it was. He nearly killed me. But I'm sure everybody wants to hear it, so if it isn't a problem for me to stay to supper..."

Ruth smiled. "Has it ever been a problem in the past when you drop by unexpectedly?"

Micah grinned. "No, I guess not."

Boots hitting the porch outside caught their attention and Micah turned around and opened the door before the couple could knock. "Come on in, Mr. and Mrs. Lancaster."

"Sheriff?" Samantha asked. "I thought you were out hunting Pa."

Micah winced. "I was until a day and a half ago when I caught him. He's in jail now. I just got back."

Samantha nodded and her husband, Lou, spoke up. "What's he going to be charged with?"

Micah glanced around. "Murder and two counts of horse thieving."

"Two?" Lou asked.

"He stole a horse from town as well as one from a ranch along the way."

Lou nodded.

Ruth stepped forward. "Would you like to join us in the kitchen? I believe supper should be ready by now. And I know some children who are very anxious to see the two of you."

Samantha smiled. "Thank you, Ruth. I can't thank you and your parents enough for taking them in. I would have, but I don't think Lou and I could raise them well."

Ruth took Samantha's arm and led her into the kitchen. "I'm sure you would have done just fine, but I know Pa and Ma understand and are more than willing to raise them."

The five of them walked into the kitchen and Samantha and Lou were immediately surrounded.

When Daniel walked into the kitchen a few minutes later, the noise level had died down some. He walked up to Micah and clasped his shoulder. "It's good to have you back, Son."

Micah swallowed, not having expected to be called "son." "It's good to be back."

Daniel looked at his wife. "Is supper ready?"

Harriet nodded.

Daniel smiled and walked up to the group of noisy people. "I hate to break this up, but it's time to eat."

Olive smiled as she pulled her older sister to the table. "I helped make supper tonight."

Samantha giggled. "I'm glad my cooking lessons paid off."

After everybody was seated and the prayer of thanks had been said, Jeremiah started the conversation. "Pa, were you going to tell us how you caught Mr. Miller?"

Micah cleared his throat. "That might be a topic better saved for after supper." He hesitated.

"And I'm not sure Ellis, Mary, and Carter should hear it."

Harriet bit her lip. "It may be difficult, but I think they should hear it."

Daniel looked around the table and nodded. "I agree. Harriet and I can talk about it with them later."

Micah shrugged and took a bite of his mashed potatoes. When he had swallowed, he said, "All right, I'll give you the short version. I spent three days trailing him. On the second day, I came to a ranch and Adam Milton allowed me to borrow a horse from him. Only I asked, unlike Grover.

"About noon the next day, I caught up to Grover. He'd gotten himself boxed in and tried to ambush me. He almost got me with his first shot, but by God's providence, I got off the horse just before he fired. I slid along the ground to sneak up on him, but he must've anticipated that and snuck up on me. He stood over me, lifted his pistol, and pulled the hammer back. The hammer action was the only thing that saved my life. I reacted swiftly and swung my rifle up to knock the pistol out of his hand. After that, it was a matter of getting him back here without him causing trouble. He tried to, but it didn't work."

Samantha sighed. "I always hoped he would come around someday."

"So did I," Ruth said.

"I think we all did," Daniel mentioned. He turned to Micah. "Adam Milton. The name sounds familiar."

"He's a rancher about a half day's ride from town. He ranches mostly cattle, but also some horses. He's got some horses with strange names." Micah chuckled. "Snowball and Flighty are the two I met."

"Let me guess," Jeremiah said, "Snowball is white and Flighty is really fast?"

Micah grinned. "Yep. Snowball is fast, too. As fast as a snowball rolling down the hill."

Groans were elicited from around the table.

After a few minutes of eating in silence, Lou spoke up. "Otis mentioned you were open to adopting all five of the children."

Daniel nodded.

"Can I ask why?" Lou asked.

Daniel smiled. "We believe they should feel like part of a family and have a real mother and father. But we don't want them to forget their real parents either, and will encourage them to talk about their parents as much as they would like."

"Thank you," Samantha whispered.

Harriet shifted in her chair. "You two are welcome to come here as often as you like. We don't ever want to be accused of keeping you away."

Lou grinned. "That is most generous of you, Ma'am. I'm sure we'll take you up on that offer. I, for one, wouldn't mind some advice on raising children. My pa already told me I've gotta figure it out on my own."

Samantha nodded. "And his mother isn't much better. Of course, if you don't..."

"We would be honored to give you advice," Harriet interrupted. "Nothing we've done to raise our children is a family secret. Although, we're far from being the perfect parents." She wrinkled her eyebrows. "But does this mean what I think it does?"

Samantha turned as red as her sweater and nodded.

"You're gonna have a baby?" Otis asked.

"Yes," Lou said with a grin. "We are."

Mary squealed, toppled her chair over, and ran over to give her oldest sister a hug. "Can I hold the baby when it's borned?"

Samantha pulled Mary into her lap. "Yes, you may. And if Mr. and Mrs. Brookings let you, I might even have you and Olive stay with me for a few weeks after the baby is born."

Harriet smiled. "That sounds like a wonderful idea. I think we could spare them for a while."

Daniel nodded. "And, Lou, if you ever want your brothers to help you out, feel free to ask."

"Thank you," Lou said. "Sam helped me in the fields last summer, but this year I'm not going to let her, so I might need the help."

"From all of us?" Ellis asked.

"Yep," Lou replied. "You and Otis would be great helpers. Carter might even be able to help with a few things."

Carter clapped his hands. "Me help."

Samantha smiled as she tousled his hair. "I'm sure we'll find something for you to help with."

Harriet stood up to clear the table. "Daniel, how about you take the guests and children to the parlor to visit while Ruth and I clear the table?"

Micah raised his hand. "If you don't mind, Mrs. Brookings, could I help Ruth clear the table while you visit with your guests?"

Harriet glanced at Ruth who nodded. She set the platter down with a smile. "That would be fine with me. I don't mind getting out of work." She turned to Samantha and Lou. "Would anybody like some coffee while we retire to the parlor?"

"I'll take some," Lou said.

"No, thank you," Samantha replied.

"Pa..." Jeremiah started.

"No," Micah said sharply.

"You know I would take some," Daniel said.

"Two coffees then," Harriet smiled. "I'll be right in there with them."

When everybody except Ruth, Micah, and Harriet left, Ruth stood up and picked up the platter of meat off the table. She took it into the kitchen and was about to leave when Harriet and Micah walked in.

"You two behave yourselves in here," Harriet warned with a wink.

Micah smiled. "Yes, Ma'am."

Ruth blushed. "I will, Ma."

Harriet nodded and left the room, steam trailing behind her from the two cups of coffee.

Ruth went to the table and stacked the dirty plates in a pile.

Micah joined her and gathered the silverware. "How have you been this week?"

Ruth paused, a plate halfway to the stack. "It's been a very strange week. First, no teaching. Second, having the Miller children here, then you being gone half the week. I like my routines and felt totally lost because all my normal routines were gone. I didn't go to school, we had extra people here, and I hardly saw you at all. The best part was that I could talk to Pa and Ma when I wanted to without having to walk to the ranch from town." She put the plate on the stack and sighed. "I hope next week is better."

Micah put the silverware on top of the plates and picked it up. "I hope so, too." He put the stack on the counter while Ruth took the dishes of food off the table.

"There were good things that happened, too," Ruth said. "Mary is so adorable. She wants to go everywhere I go and do everything I do. I love having five younger siblings after going so long without any. Having Jeremiah here for a few days was nice, too."

"Really?" Micah asked, his eyebrows rising.

Ruth smiled and poured the warm water from the pan on the stove into the dishpan. "Yes. He behaved well and the two of us had a couple of good talks the first night he was here."

"About what?"

Ruth handed Micah a clean plate to dry. "You. He was worried Grover would...you know..."

Micah dried the plate and put it in the cupboard. "Does he really worry that much?"

Ruth swirled the dishrag in the water. "I don't know if he usually does, but he did this time."

"What did you tell him?" Micah asked.

Ruth watched the dishes she washed carefully. "I told him what I missed most that night and how worried I was and how I knew you would do your best to use the brains and skills you have to get back to us alive. I also told him we needed to trust God to bring you back."

"You were worried, too?"

Ruth nodded. "Why wouldn't I be?"

Micah shrugged. "I don't know. I just... I didn't know for sure if you would, I guess."

Ruth bit her lip. "You're one of my best friends. Of course I would be worried about you." She turned her attention back to the dish she was washing. "How was your week? Besides the obvious."

Micah chuckled. "I had a lot of time to think. I came to some realizations while I was riding after Grover. I had to go slow so I didn't lose his trail. I hated being gone so long. That was the first time I had to chase after someone for such a long time. Now I wonder how Joshua can handle being gone from his family so much with such a dangerous job."

Ruth smiled. "He's got a different personality than you do. He likes to go on adventures. You seem to like being around your family more than going off on adventures."

"Especially adventures that nearly kill me," Micah said, a wry smile on his face.

"Were you really that close to dying?" Ruth asked.

Micah rubbed the plate dry until there wasn't a drop of water left. "Yes, I was. He really came close to orphaning my son."

Micah stared at the wall in front of him and his hands stilled. "I know he would be well cared for, but he's already motherless and I know that bothers him. I said I didn't know he worries so much about me, but I don't think that's quite true. He's like Edith. When she worried about something, she would bury herself in some sort of mission or project. 'Miah's version of worry is to misbehave or cause mischief.

"I don't want him to turn out like I did when I was his age. I don't even know if he's ever truly accepted Christ as his own Savior." Micah turned a tortured gaze to Ruth and found compassion and comfort in her gaze. "I know I can't force him to become a Christian, but sometimes I wish I could know for sure."

"Have you asked him?"

"Yes. He shrugs and says he doesn't know. When I asked if he knew how to know for sure, he nodded and that was the end of it."

"He's smart enough to figure it out," Ruth said. "I will pray for him more, too."

"Thank you," Micah whispered, looking down. He sighed and leaned back against the counter. Ruth watched him out of the corner of her eye. "I'm glad Grover was sullen and quiet on the way home. I thought about a lot while I tried to find him, but I thought about even more on the way back. Some things I still need to think about more, but I did have a few ideas for my farm."

Ruth turned to him. "So did I."

"You did?"

Ruth dipped her chin down. "I know I don't really have any right to, but..."

Micah smiled. "Go ahead."

"Well, you remember how I told you I wanted to help the Hales out, but couldn't?"

Micah nodded.

"What if you hired Mr. Hale to manage and run your farm so it doesn't go dormant? As sheriff, you don't have time to continue to farm the land and the Hales need something to get them on their feet."

A smile played with Micah's mouth. "I had the same idea."

Ruth laughed. "Great minds think alike, I guess."

"I guess." Micah put the last plate away and took the dishrag away from Ruth to wash the table off. "I have a slightly odd question. Have you ever wanted someone to court you, but he never asked?"

"No," Ruth replied as she scanned the kitchen for any stray dishes. "Have you ever thought about courting someone and not asked them?"

"Nope."

"Not even before you knew Edith?"

"Nope. Edith was my sweetheart even in our last couple years of school. I never thought about courting anyone else until you."

"Why me?" Ruth asked.

Micah rinsed out the dishrag and squeezed the water out of it before answering. "You're the one who challenged me to think about marrying for Jeremiah's sake. I thought you were crazy at first and started to avoid you because I hated to admit you were right. Jeremiah did...does need a mother. What you said about him this evening is just one more proof of that. Thank you for being here for him, by the way."

Ruth ducked her head. "You're welcome."

"As for why I chose you, after avoiding you for a couple of weeks, I realized how much I missed our talks together. As I considered that, I thought about other things. We'd become really good friends. You were the first really good friend I had had since Edith died and I prayed asking God if He was leading us into a deeper relationship with each other. The weeks I waited for your father to talk to you and for you to think about it were torturous. After so many weeks in prayer myself, I was convinced we were supposed to court and the wait was hard. I couldn't believe how hard."

"And you don't regret it? Even after having to wait even longer to court me?"

"No. Do you?"

Ruth shook her head. "No, I don't. Even if we decide not to marry, I wouldn't trade these last couple of months for the world."

Micah grinned and turned to pick up the dishpan. "Where do you usually dump this?"

"Away from the path outside," Ruth replied.

She walked ahead of him to open the door. When he came back in, he handed the empty dishpan to Ruth. "We should probably go into the parlor before your mother starts to wonder what's taking us so long."

Ruth smiled. "Probably."

Micah held out his hand and Ruth shook her head. "I'm not supposed to hold hands with a young man until we're engaged."

Micah nodded and gestured for Ruth to go first. "After you, Miss Ruth."

Ruth curtsied. "Thank you, kind sir."

CHAPTER TWENTY EIGHT

"Do you know when Ruth's birthday is, Jeremiah?" Micah asked as they walked home that evening. "It's coming up pretty soon, isn't it?"

Jeremiah nodded. "Kind of. Mary and Olive were talking about it. They're trying to figure out some sort of surprise for her birthday." He scuffed his toe on the frozen ground. "May twenty-seventh. So it's still a bit away yet."

Micah nodded. "Thank you."

"Why are you wondering?"

Micah ignored his question and kept walking.

"Pa?" Jeremiah ran after him. "Why did you ask?"

Micah sighed. "I wanted to know so I can make sure I have my birthday present ready for her."

Jeremiah grinned. "What'cha gonna give her?"

"None of your business, Jeremiah," Micah said.

Jeremiah scowled. "Why not?"

Micah shook his head and remained silent.

Jeremiah shrugged and followed his pa home.

"Mr. Hale?" Micah asked as he stepped into the Hales' barn a few days later. "I wondered if we could talk about something?"

"I'm not in trouble, am I?" Richard Hale asked as he looked up from the bridle he was fixing.

Micah chuckled. "No, Sir, you aren't. I have a business proposition for you."

"I'm listening."

"How would you like to become a farm manager? I have a farm that hasn't been worked for two planting seasons and I'd like to someday have the farm take over my sheriff's income when I decide to hang up my gun and sheriff's star." Micah held up his hand. "Before you say yes, hear all the facts."

Richard smiled and clamped his mouth shut.

"That's better," Micah said with a wink. "Some of this is only if other things happen. If I get married to Miss Brookings, we would both like to adopt some older children from the orphanage and teach them various things. If this happens, I would like the boys especially to work on the farm with you. You would help teach them different aspects of farming. I would definitely help with that as well. The girls, I'm not sure about yet. We may just stick with boys for now, but I haven't thought that far ahead yet. What do you think?"

Richard Hale stroked his beard. "I like your ideas."

"Are you up for the challenge?"

"Can my boys work on the farm, too? I'd like to teach them alongside the orphans if I can."

Micah nodded. "That would be perfectly fine with me."

"Do you mind if I ask a question?"

"Go ahead."

"Do you really make enough as sheriff to adopt and support growing kids?"

Micah chuckled. "No, I don't. But I have money from previous jobs."

Richard smiled. "All right, I won't ask any more questions about that. When can I start?"

"As soon as you can see enough of the ground to start working it. And if you need any equipment, let me know and I'll either tell you where it is or get it for you."

Richard nodded. "That sounds like it'll work. Thank you, Micah. I really appreciate this opportunity."

"I'm glad I could help out."

Micah shook hands with him and headed back toward town, praising God for His bountiful care.

"Can we quiz Miss Brookings and Mr. Carson tonight?" Otis asked.

Daniel Brookings looked across the desk at him. "What do you mean?"

"Olive, Ellis, and I have come up with a list of questions we think Mr. Carson and Miss Brookings need to answer for each other."

Daniel smiled. "Oh really? This sounds interesting. I think it's a good idea. Can I see the list?"

Otis shook his head.

"Very well. Yes, you may."

"Thank you, Mr. Brookings."

After supper, everybody traipsed into the parlor. "I'm a little nervous about this interrogation," Micah said.

"If I didn't know the Miller children, I would be, too," Ruth said.

Mary snuggled up onto Ruth's lap and Carter did the same in Micah's.

"Are you two ready?" Otis asked.

Ruth and Micah exchanged a glance. "I'm as ready as I'll ever be, I guess," Micah said.

Otis cleared his throat. "The first question is 'What do you do when you get mad at someone else?'"

Micah chuckled. "I think Jeremiah could answer this question better than me."

Jeremiah rolled his eyes.

"I try to pray and cool off before I react, but that doesn't always happen. If it doesn't, I usually yell at the person I'm mad at."

Ruth bit her lip. "I don't usually get mad at people very often. But I try to just get away from them and pray for them. I do sometimes say something right away if needed, though." She shuddered as Grover Miller came to mind again.

Olive stepped forward. "What is your favorite animal?"

"Cats," Ruth said quickly.

"Depends on what it's for," Micah answered. "For transportation, horses. For guarding livestock or the house, dogs. For rodent control, cats."

"Sure, you had to get all practical," Ruth teased. "I just went for the animal I prefer to spend time with."

Micah grinned. "Sorry, Ruth."

"No you're not," Jeremiah said.

Micah rolled his eyes. "Shh."

Ruth laughed. "I already knew you weren't really sorry, Micah." She turned back to the Miller children. "Who has the next question?"

"Me," Jeremiah said. "How many children do you want?"

Ruth's eyes widened and her face grew warm. "Micah can answer this one first."

"Thanks, Ruth," Micah said insincerely. "However many God wants to give me. After I get married. One child has been good, but I wouldn't mind having more."

"How many more?" Jeremiah asked.

"I don't know. I've never really thought about it. If I could choose, which I can't, I guess I'd say four more. But, more or less is fine, too."

Ruth stuck the needle in the shirt she was mending. "I think five children is a good amount, but that's because that's what I've always been around. However many God wants me to have, would be my real answer."

"Does five include me or not?" Jeremiah asked.

"That's up to God," Ruth replied with a wink.

Jeremiah huffed. "That's not fair."

"Your question isn't fair, either," Micah protested. "We have no way of knowing how many children God wants us to have, or even if we're going to get married."

"You'll get married," Jeremiah said.

"How do you know?" Micah asked.

"You have to," Jeremiah answered. "I want a mother, you need a wife, she needs a husband, and the Brookings need the room now that they have five more kids in the house."

Harriet held up her hand. "We do not need the room, Jeremiah. There is plenty of room here for all of them."

Jeremiah scrunched his nose. "Fine. I still think they'll get married."

Micah shrugged. "We'll see."

Otis cleared his throat. "If you had a thousand dollars, what would you do with it?"

Micah sank back into the chair and pulled Carter closer as the little boy's eyes drifted shut. "Find some way to help orphans. I'd also give a good chunk of it to the church."

Ruth smiled. "Give at least two hundred dollars to the church and the rest I'd give to the poor and needy in the community."

"Nothing for yourselves?" Jeremiah asked.

"I don't need any more money," Micah answered.

Ruth nodded. "Me neither."

Olive looked at the list Otis held and grinned. "If you could go anywhere in the world, where would you go?"

Ruth shifted Mary in her arms. "To visit my family in Illinois."

"I've always wanted to see the Alps in Switzerland. Especially now that I have seen the mountains here in Montana. I want to see how the Alps compare."

"I hate to be the one to break this up," Ruth said, "but there's at least one little one who needs to get to sleep."

Micah glanced at the clock. "And we should get home, too, since it takes a while to walk all that way." He stood up and stretched.

"Do we have to, Pa?" Jeremiah protested.

"Yes, we do. You need to get rested for school tomorrow."

"I could always skip school."

"No."

Jeremiah pouted and waved to everybody. "Bye, everybody. I'll see some of you at school tomorrow."

Otis clapped him on the back. "You'll appreciate being forced to go to school someday."

Jeremiah rolled his eyes. "When?"

Otis shrugged. "When you're older and using what you've learned in some high falutin' job somewhere."

Jeremiah scoffed. "All I want to do is grow up to be a cowboy. I don't want 'some high falutin' job somewhere.'"

"You might change your mind, though," Otis said.

"I doubt it." Jeremiah followed his father and Ruth who were already at the door talking quietly to each other. "What are you two whispering about?"

"None of your business," Micah said.

"There's nobody up there to chaperone you two, so of course it's my business," Jeremiah replied.

"No, it isn't," Ruth answered. She put a firm hand to Jeremiah's back and pushed him toward the door. "Now get on home to get some sleep so you can be well rested at school tomorrow."

Jeremiah sighed. "Fine. It was nice being here. Thank you for the wonderful supper and for saving me from Pa's cooking."

Ruth laughed. "You're welcome, Jeremiah. I'm happy to save you from his cooking."

Micah shook his head. "It's not that bad, is it?"

"Naw. It's just fun to tease you," Jeremiah said.

"Well, teasing boy, let's head home before it gets too dark to see the road," Micah said. "Thank you for having us over again, Mr. and Mrs. Brookings. And thank you for the interrogation, Otis and Olive."

"We still have more questions for you when you have a chance to come back," Otis said.

"I'll keep that in mind," Micah said.

"They aren't that bad," Olive said. "So don't be afraid to come back."

Micah chuckled. "Thank you for reassuring me, Olive. Goodbye!"

CHAPTER TWENTY NINE

"I wonder what she'll be like," Olive said, holding onto Ruth's hand.

"I have no idea," Ruth replied. "Even Micah didn't get to see the letter. I just hope they thought about James."

"Me, too. If not, I'm sure Mrs. Jenkins will give them a good talking-to."

Ruth chuckled. "I wouldn't be surprised if she did."

The stagecoach pulled up next to them and Ruth and Annabelle exchanged glances.

"I hope she's better than I was," Annabelle said.

"You were a wonderful teacher," Olive said. "Maybe not quite as good as Miss Brookings, but you were better than some we've had in the past."

"You make it sound like you're ancient, Olive," Annabelle said with a laugh.

Olive shrugged.

Ruth nodded. "They're about to open the door. We should probably behave."

"You know? I just thought of a question," Annabelle said.

"What?" Ruth asked.

"If your reputation is ruined so much you can't be a teacher, why did they ask you to be one of the people to greet the new teacher?"

Ruth shook her head. "I don't have a clue. I wondered the same thing, but since I wanted to meet her, I decided not to ask."

"Oh, and do we know for sure the teacher is female?"

Ruth blinked. "Um, I guess not. I don't even know a first name or a last name. I didn't think to ask and Mr. Jensen didn't tell me."

"We're about to find out," Olive said.

The stagecoach door opened and a long ostrich feather peeked out of the door followed by a woman wearing a fancy traveling suit. She looked up and down the sidewalk and right past Ruth, Annabelle, and Olive. With a sniff, she turned to the driver. "My trunk can stay here until I find the man who was supposed to meet me here."

"Who would that be, Ma'am?" the driver asked. "I could probably help you find him."

"Grover Miller."

Olive gasped. "What would Pa have to do with someone like her?" she whispered.

"I don't know," Ruth whispered back. With a gulp, she stepped forward. "Excuse me, Miss. I couldn't help but overhear what you said." She glanced at Annabelle. "Take care of the schoolteacher please," she whispered.

Annabelle nodded and Ruth took the woman's elbow, leading her away from the stagecoach. "If you don't mind me asking, what business do you have with Grover Miller?"

"I don't see why that has anything to do with you," the woman exclaimed.

"Well, you see, my parents currently have custody of his children."

The woman gasped. "What? Why doesn't he have them?"

Ruth led the woman over to a bench in front of the stage office. "He's in jail."

The woman narrowed her eyes. "For what?"

"He murdered a man and stole two horses during his escape."

The woman put a hand to her throat and stared at Ruth with wide eyes. "Why?"

"The bartender refused to sell him any more alcohol."

The woman leaned back against the building and closed her eyes. After a few seconds, she held out a hand to Ruth. "I'm Eleanor Miller, Grover's sister. And yes, I am a spinster."

Ruth smiled. "Ruth Brookings."

Eleanor nodded in acknowledgement. "I am here to see two men, actually," Eleanor continued. "My brother and the head of the school board. I am the new schoolteacher."

Ruth bit her lip. "Your brother is at the sheriff's office across the street. And the head of the school board, Mr. Jensen, asked Miss Wilson and me to greet the new schoolteacher."

Annabelle raised an eyebrow at the sound of her name. Olive took a tentative step forward.

"What is going on, Miss Brookings?" Olive asked.

Ruth looked at Miss Miller. "Olive, this is your father's sister, Eleanor Miller. She would be Aunt Eleanor to you. Miss Miller, I apologize you were not informed about your brother. We had no idea he had any living family."

Eleanor waved her hand in the air and stood up. "There was no way for you to know, Miss Brookings. My brother was disowned more than fifteen years ago. I tried to keep in touch with him, but I honestly didn't even know for sure if he still lived here or not. How many children does he have?"

"Six, but your oldest niece is married."

"Six? My goodness. Can I meet them?"

Ruth smiled. "Of course. How about we get you settled into your house and then you can come to the ranch and meet my parents and the rest of the children?"

"I get a house?"

Ruth shrugged. "It's more of a cottage than a house, but yes, you do."

"And which one of you was the teacher?" Eleanor asked.

"Both of us," Annabelle replied. "Ruth was until someone started spreading untrue rumors about her, then I took over in mid-February."

"Rumors, eh?" Eleanor asked, shaking her head. "I don't know why anybody believes those. Most of the time they're too outlandish to believe."

"I agree. But I don't really mind too much," Ruth said. "It's sad that I can't teach the children and I do miss them, but this way, my beau can come calling before summer."

Eleanor smiled. "That is true. Now, where is this cottage of mine?"

Ruth pointed in the general direction of the cottage.

"Miss Brookings," Olive interrupted. "Do you think Sheriff Carson would be willing to carry the trunk?"

Ruth laughed. "What do you think, Olive?"

Olive grinned. "I'll go ask him and meet you at the cottage."

"Thank you, Olive," Ruth replied.

Eleanor watched Olive scurry across the street to the sheriff's office. "Is she always that helpful?"

"Almost to a fault," Ruth answered.

Annabelle, Eleanor, and Ruth walked to the cottage. "Is there anything you would like to know?"

Eleanor looked around. "The town itself seems pretty self-explanatory. It's smaller than I'm used to, but I don't mind. How many children attend school?"

"On a good day, there will be twenty-five to thirty," Annabelle answered. "If the weather is at all iffy, you may only have ten. Many of the children come from outlying farms and ranches and their parents are very cautious."

"Good," Eleanor said. "I would rather have to catch a few students up than have half my students buried behind the church."

Ruth smiled. "I think you will fit in just fine here. Although, if all your dresses are that fancy, you may be a little overdressed."

Eleanor looked down at her dark gray dress with pearl edging and light gray lace. "This is probably my fanciest dress. I wanted to make sure I made a good impression on the head of the school board."

"Well, you certainly made an impression on one of your students," Ruth said with a giggle. "Olive was very impressed."

Eleanor pursed her lips. "I apologize."

"Don't," Annabelle replied. "I've made my share of interesting impressions. Sometimes I do that just to keep the children distracted from misbehaving. And I, personally, will enjoy having someone else to talk to about fashion. The only other person in town who really cares about the newest fashions is my mother."

Eleanor laughed. "I would love to talk with you about fashion, Annabelle. Ah. This must be the cottage."

Ruth walked up to the door. "It will be strange to think of someone else living here."

"Ruth would live here from Sunday evening to Friday afternoon," Annabelle informed Eleanor. "The ranch was just a little bit too far for her to make the trek every day."

"That must have been hard," Eleanor said.

"It was," Ruth answered as she pushed the door open. She shivered as she walked in. "Perhaps we should have started a fire while we waited for the stagecoach."

Eleanor shook her head. "It's just fine. All I'm going to do right now—well, as soon as I get my trunk—is change out of this dusty dress and then walk to the ranch with you to meet my nieces and nephews."

"Howdy, Miss Brookings, Miss Wilson, and new schoolteacher!"

Ruth spun to see Jeremiah. "Hello, Jeremiah. Eleanor, this is one of your problem students. Not usually, but he can be. Jeremiah, Miss Miller."

"Miller?" Jeremiah asked, a distrusting look coming quickly to his face.

"She's Grover's sister," Ruth said hurriedly, "but I have yet to see anything that reminds me of him. Could you please go to Samantha and Lou's and ask them to come to supper tonight? Samantha's aunt Eleanor is here and would like to meet them."

Jeremiah scrunched his nose. "I suppose I can. Can pa and I come, too?"

"That's up to your father," Ruth said as Micah came in.

"What's up to me?" Micah asked.

"Can we go to the Brookings' for supper, please?" Jeremiah begged.

"Why?" Micah questioned.

"Because I'll be there," Eleanor said. "As will Samantha and Lou." She gestured for Micah to put the trunk down in the bedroom. When he came back in, she held out her hand. "Eleanor Miller. And yes, I am related to Grover. I'll be over to scold him tomorrow morning. I'm his older sister."

Micah tried to keep a straight face, but couldn't hide his smile. "I'm Micah Carson, the sheriff, but I think you already figured that out."

Eleanor nodded and pointed to Jeremiah. "Your son is still waiting for an answer."

"We'll see if Obadiah can stay at the office."

"Yippee!" Jeremiah exclaimed. "I'll be back in a jiffy!"

Eleanor shook her head. "I can see why he would be one of the troublemakers."

"There's four of them," Annabelle said. "And they're all ten. There are a couple of twelve year old boys who are a little bit of trouble sometimes, too."

Eleanor smiled. "I'll handle them. Now if y'all don't mind," she put on an affected southern drawl, "I'd like to get out of my dusty clothing."

Micah nodded. "It was nice meeting you, Miss Miller. I think you'll fit perfectly in town and particularly in the schoolroom."

Eleanor laughed. "It was a pleasure meeting you as well, Sheriff Carson. Despite your son being one of the troublemakers."

"With me as his father, would you expect anything less?" Micah asked with a wink.

Annabelle laughed. "I guess not. Sometimes I wonder who's worse. Goodbye, Miss Miller. If you would like to talk about anything school related, just ask anybody to direct you to Mayor Wilson's house. I'm available except during school hours. And some evenings."

Eleanor nodded. "Thank you. I might stop in to observe tomorrow and then chat with you tomorrow after school."

Annabelle smiled. "That will work for me. It was nice meeting you." She stepped out the door, following Micah.

"I'll wait for you outside, Miss Miller," Ruth said.

"Thank you, Dear. I won't take long with it being so cold."

Ruth smiled as she closed the door behind her.

"When I heard the name Miller," Micah said, "that is not what I expected."

Ruth shook her head. "When she said she was looking for Grover, you could have pushed me over with a feather. At first I wondered if he wrote to a mail order bride. I don't know what I would have done if she had been."

Micah shuddered. "I don't know what I would have done either. Well, I suppose I better go see if Obadiah can take over this evening." He tipped his hat. "Probably see you later, Miss Brookings."

Ruth waved as he left. She looked at the porch swing. "There you are." She sat next to Olive. "I was wondering what happened to you."

"Do you think Aunt Eleanor will want to take us from you?"

Ruth sighed. She had been dreading that question. "I don't know. I hope that when she sees how much you love being with us, she'll decide we should continue caring for you. Or she may not even want to take care of you at all. Schoolteachers don't really make enough to raise five children. But, I'm also very sure she'll want to make sure you are all happy where you are before she decides anything."

Olive nodded. "I hope she lets us stay with you. She seems nice, but I like it on the ranch. And I think it's better for the boys, too."

"I agree."

Ruth and Olive swung in silence until the door opened and Eleanor stepped out. She wore a simple, dark blue dress with flared sleeves with a tiny bit of lace at their edges.

"Is this better?" Eleanor asked.

Ruth smiled. "Yes, it is. Are you sure you're up to walking all the way to the ranch?"

Eleanor nodded. "I've been sitting in that stagecoach for days. I am more than ready to get some good exercise. My legs need to get stretched."

"Good. Let's head out there, then."

March 13, 1880
Dear Diary,

We met the Miller children's aunt Eleanor today. She is very nice and will make a wonderful schoolteacher. The children were cautious at first because they weren't sure if she might end up taking them away from us. She set their minds at ease almost immediately.

"I wouldn't dream of changing anything unless there was some reason I needed to. I don't believe any changes need to be implemented, so I won't."

After that, the Miller children enjoyed learning what their father was like as a boy and everything else Eleanor shared with us. Samantha and Lou joined us shortly after we arrived and Eleanor has already promised to be the best aunt and great aunt she can be. She claims she's going to spoil her little grand niece or nephew. That made Samantha blush.

Somehow—and I'm guessing it had something to do with Otis, Olive, and Jeremiah—Eleanor found out that Micah is the young man courting me. So when he arrived for supper, she had a lot of fun teasing us, too. I think she may have guessed it even from the short time she had seen us in the same room together, but I also believe Otis and Olive told her. Oh well. We survived the teasing. It's not like we don't get it from other people.

Peter, Wyatt, and Flynn were really subdued tonight at the table. I'm not sure why, unless Eleanor intimidated them. William didn't seem any different, though, and of all of them, I would have thought he would have been. Hm. Of course, he's been courting Annabelle for a while now, and all three members of the Wilson family can be rather intimidating, so maybe he's gotten used to it.

All together, I think we laughed most of the night. Eleanor fits in perfectly with our group of friends and she also had plenty of fun stories about Grover. Apparently Grover grew up in a wealthy home. You never would've guessed it from the way he's lived. He was disowned when he nearly killed a man, stole some money, and then expected his father to bail him out of jail. Instead, his father made him stay *in jail as long as the sentence was set for, disowned him, and gave him some money to get out of town. He's never seen his father since.*

Eleanor did say she planned to telegraph her father to let him know the latest about Grover. I hope and pray Eleanor and their father can help Grover find the Lord before he is sentenced to hang.

To change the subject, I'm anxious to see where this courtship leads. I'm trying very hard not to get attached to Micah yet, but it's really hard. I know there are things we haven't discussed yet that we need to, but I truly believe I am ready to say yes to marrying him.

Lord, help me be patient and not want to rush things.

CHAPTER THIRTY

With the March flurries came Grover Miller's hanging. Daniel and Harriet Brookings kept the Miller children home from school the day of the hanging as well as the following week. Mary and Carter didn't understand what was happening, but Otis, Olive, and Ellis all knew that their father was dead. After the hanging, Miles held a brief service before Grover was buried on Boot Hill behind the church.

Over the next few days, Otis, Olive, and Ellis were very quiet. Grover Miller had been hanged on a Friday. On the next Wednesday, while Mary and Carter were lying down, Ruth and Harriet sat down to talk with the other three.

"I know you are really sad right now," Harriet began. "I can't imagine what you are feeling. Remember that we are here for you if you ever need a shoulder to cry on or someone to talk to. If you want to talk about your parents, we would love to hear about them."

Ellis climbed up into Harriet's lap and gave her a hug. "Why'd Daddy kill that man?"

Harriet put her arms around Ellis and rocked him gently. "I don't know, Ellis."

Olive snuggled closer to Ruth. "Will we see Pa in heaven?"

Ruth drew in a deep breath. "I don't know. I know your Aunt Eleanor talked to him and that your grandfather wrote him a letter about it as well. Nobody knows if he did anything with it."

"Didn't Pastor Jenkins talk with him, too?" Otis asked.

"Yes, he did," Harriet replied.

Otis sighed. "Why do I feel so bad when I didn't even really like Pa?"

Harriet took a deep breath. "I had the same problem when I was a little older than you. My daddy didn't do anything like killing a man, but he wasn't a kind father. I can't remember even one kind word he ever said to me, my sisters, brothers, or mother. He never struck us physically, but he was always critical of everything. I didn't like my daddy, but when he died, I felt horrible and sad. I think it's because he's still your father, even if he wasn't a good one. He's the man who took care of you and that gives him a special spot in your heart."

Otis pursed his lips together. "I suppose. Can we go back to school tomorrow?"

"If you would like to, yes," Harriet said.

"I do," Otis said.

"Me, too," Olive echoed.

"I don't," Ellis said.

"I guess the O's will go to school tomorrow, then," Ruth said. Olive's mouth turned up in a slight smile.

"I'm gonna go study a little," Otis said.

Harriet nodded. "All right."

March snowed into April. On the second Saturday of April, Ruth hurried to Annabelle's house.

"I'm here!" she announced as Annabelle opened the door.

Annabelle enveloped her friend in a big hug. "I can't believe I'm getting married tomorrow!"

"Me either," Ruth said. "You look terrible."

"I know I do. There are so many details I've been worrying about..."

Ruth put a finger to her lips. "Let me get my things off, then you give me your list and I'll worry about the list while you go upstairs and take a short nap. You won't be a very good bride if you start off the marriage half asleep."

Annabelle smiled weakly. "I don't deserve a friend like you, Ruth."

Ruth shrugged as she took her coat, scarf, and mittens off. "Now, where's your list?"

Annabelle led the way into the parlor where ribbons and other decorations were strewn around the room.

"Oh my," Ruth said.

"Yeah. How in the world am I going to sleep...?"

"You will sleep," Ruth interrupted, "because you know Ruth Brookings, one of the best organizers in Castle City, is here ready to organize this mess and get your list taken care of." She held out her hand. "Your list, please, Madam?"

Annabelle stared at Ruth in shock, then glanced around the room and spotted a piece of paper on the table. "Here you go. I hope you can read it."

"Thank you, I'll manage. Now get to bed and don't worry about anything more. I have everything under control here and already told Father and Mother I would not be home today. If anybody is going to lose sleep tonight, it will be me. Go!"

Annabelle raised an eyebrow.

"I know. I'm not usually this bossy, but when my best friend looks this terrible and doesn't appear to be listening, I have to get bossy." Ruth grinned as she teased her friend.

Annabelle smiled tiredly. "Thank you, Ruth."

"You're welcome." She cocked her head.

"I'm going!" Annabelle protested as she turned around. "Are you sure...?"

"I'm positive. Get up there before I have to drag you up the stairs."

Annabelle disappeared from Ruth's sight.

"Now to start by organizing this mess. Then I'll start on the list."

April twelfth dawned, cool, white, and slightly warmer than the day before. Annabelle stretched as she looked up at the ceiling. "This is the last time I'll wake up in this bedroom. I'm getting married in..." she looked at the clock beside her bed, "just over five hours!"

She heard someone groan nearby. "Sorry, Ruth. Did I wake you up?"

Ruth rolled over. "Not really. I was kind of awake already." She stood up and looked out the window. "It looks like a beautiful day for a wedding."

"Yes, it does. There's even a fresh dusting of snow to cover up the ugly melting snow."

Ruth smiled. "You look much better now than you did yesterday."

"Thanks to you," Annabelle said. "I never would have thought to do all those shortcuts."

"I was happy to help. Even though you'll be living kind of far away on the property, you'll still be closer after you're married than right now."

Annabelle grinned. "I can't wait!"

Annabelle jumped when someone knocked on the door.

"May I come in?" The muffled voice of Mrs. Wilson came through the door.

Annabelle rushed to the door and flung it open. "Come in, Mother."

"How's my girl this morning?" Mrs. Wilson asked.

"Well, I slept in more than I intended."

Mrs. Wilson laughed. "I see that. Are you and Ruth going to be ready for church on time?"

"Yes, Mother."

Ruth finished brushing her hair. "If you'll excuse me, I think I'll go to the room next door to get dressed."

Mrs. Wilson smiled at her. "That is just fine."

Ruth grabbed the clothing she had laid out the night before and gently closed the door behind her.

"Any second thoughts?" Mrs. Wilson asked.

"None."

"But you're nervous and scared?"

Annabelle ducked her head. "Yes."

"That's normal. When I married your father, I couldn't eat a thing that morning. But I knew I loved the man dearly and couldn't imagine life without him, so I pushed myself through and made it. Twenty-three years later, I get to see my only child get married to the man of her dreams."

Annabelle chuckled. "I'm not sure he's exactly the man of my dreams, but my dreams were so fanciful that no one could have fit into the mold. Not even Prince Edward of England. Besides the minor detail that he's probably old enough to be my grandfather."

Mrs. Wilson shook her head. "William is now the real man of your dreams though, right?"

"Yes, Mother."

Mrs. Wilson patted Annabelle's shoulder. "Good. Do you have any questions for me before the morning rush?"

Annabelle took a sharp breath in and chewed her bottom lip. "I don't think so. I think we discussed everything we needed to a couple nights ago."

Mrs. Wilson pulled Annabelle into a tight hug and held on. "I'm proud of you, Dear."

Annabelle put her arms around her mother. "Thank you, Mother."

"You have turned into a beautiful, godly young lady any mother would be proud to have, even if I don't quite understand some of your convictions."

Annabelle squeezed her mother. "Thank you."

Mrs. Wilson pulled away. "I need to let you get dressed. Ruth will be here to help you get ready for the wedding, right?"

"Yes, Mother."

"Good. I don't think my nerves would allow me to help. As much as I want to."

"Having Ruth's steady nerves will be wonderful after church. We'll manage."

Mrs. Wilson took one last look at her daughter before leaving the bedroom.

About a month after Annabelle's wedding, Micah saw Ruth walk past his office. *Lord, is she going to be in town long enough? I certainly hope so.* "Obadiah, I'm going to ride out to the Double B," he said.

"What fer?" Obadiah asked. "Didn't I just see Ruth walkin' past?"

Micah averted his eyes. "I'll be back in an hour or so."

He walked out of the office before Obadiah could question him further and headed to the livery to saddle Jericho. During the ride to the ranch, Micah tried to calm his nerves. It wasn't like he'd never done this before. But that had been almost fifteen years ago. And he hadn't been nearly this nervous. Why, then, was he so nervous this time?

Micah glanced around to see if anybody was nearby. Seeing nobody, he prayed out loud, "God, I know this is what You want me to do, but I'm so nervous I feel like running all the way to Chicago and never coming back. I want to marry Ruth, I really do, but asking Daniel if I can ask Ruth sounds downright scary. And I don't even know why. Why am I so scared to ask him? Why would he say no? If he had an objection to me, he would have stopped our courtship a long time ago. After all, we've been courting for about three months now."

He sighed. "I don't know what's going on, God. Ever since I came back with Grover, I've been out of sorts, confused, and jittery. I can't seem to do anything right! Is that what happens when you're in love? But I've been in love before and didn't feel this way."

Micah wrinkled his forehead. "And now I'm talking to myself. Maybe I lost my sanity somewhere on the chase to find Grover."

"Or maybe you're just doing the best you can as you ride all by yourself toward somewhere," a voice cut into his musings.

Micah's head jerked up. "Oh. Hi, Peter."

"What are you muttering to yourself about? Besides doubting your sanity."

Micah chuckled humorlessly. "Nothin'."

"Ah," Peter said. "I get it now."

Micah continued riding while Peter rode up next to him. "You get what?"

"Why you're mutterin' to yourself."

Micah cocked an eyebrow. "What do you think it is?"

"Wahl..." Peter stalled. "Ruth's in town, so you're not comin' to see her. You're nervous as all get out, you're muttering to yourself, and you're doubting yer sanity. All that could add up to just one thing."

Micah waited for him to say what it was. After a minute of silence, he looked over at Peter. "What's that one thing?"

"You're gonna ask Daniel Brookings for permission to marry Ruth."

Micah was silent.

"You aren't insane, by the way," Peter said just before he dug his spurs into the horse's side and galloped away, flinging snow at Micah.

Micah stared after him until Peter and his horse were just a speck on the horizon. Then he shook his head and turned onto the walkway to the ranch house. He stopped and hitched his horse to the post and took a deep breath. After swallowing hard, he rapped his knuckles firmly on the door.

"Good morning, Micah," Harriet said as she opened the door. "You just missed Ruth."

"I know, Ma'am." Micah bit his lip. "I came to see Mr. Brookings if he's available."

Harriet smiled. "Of course. He's in his study."

"Thank you, Ma'am."

Harriet patted his shoulder. "You're welcome, Micah."

Micah walked past her to the study. He tapped on the door.

"Come in," Daniel said in a clipped tone.

Micah cracked the door open. "Am I interrupting something?"

Daniel muttered to himself as he looked at the papers in front of him. When he looked up, his face lit up. "Not at all! Come on in, Micah. You're just what I needed. I'm in the middle of my least favorite job in the universe. A distraction is perfect. Have a seat."

Micah strode to the chair across from Daniel and plopped into it.

"What can I do for you this morning?" Daniel asked.

Micah took a deep breath. "Ruth and I have been courting for a little over three months now and if I'm rushing things too much, please tell me." He swallowed. "When I was chasing after Grover, and then in the weeks since then, I have done a lot of thinking. Some about what to do with my farm, and some about my life. Since then, after my close shave with death, I've done even more thinkin'. If I would've died back there, I realized my greatest regret wouldn't have been not seeing Jeremiah grow up, but not marrying Ruth. I love your daughter, Mr. Brookings. I guess what I'm trying to say is, can I marry Ruth?"

"Are you sure you know enough about her, and your feelings for her, to know for sure you truly love her and that it's not all about your feelings, which will fade?"

Micah nodded. "Yes, Sir."

"How do you know that?"

Micah swallowed. "The most important things are that she loves God more than me, is a Christian, loves Jeremiah, Jeremiah loves her, and the love I have for her is similar to the love I had for my first wife. It isn't lust, it's a love that will last through the tough times and the good times. More importantly, God put that love there."

"And do you love God more than you love Ruth?"

Micah didn't hesitate in his answer. "Yes."

Daniel nodded. "Well, I know you can provide for her, and that you and Jeremiah love her. My wife has been wanting this marriage for a while as well. The only other question I have is how do you plan to spend enough time with Ruth so she doesn't feel neglected? The job of a sheriff is very time consuming."

Micah leaned back in the armchair. "Obadiah and I would have to work that out for sure, but I'm almost positive he prefers working more at night than in the morning; I just don't like making him do that all the time. If he's willing, I'll work until suppertime, and he can work until breakfast. I'll probably have to work through the night occasionally, but hopefully not too often. If it gets to be too much for her, or me, I'll resign and let someone else take over as sheriff."

"And do what?" Daniel questioned.

"Farm."

"I thought the Hales were taking over the farm."

Micah nodded. "They are. At least until they can get back on their feet and figure out what else to do. My long-term goal would be to retire from the sheriff position and become a farmer, adopt some orphan boys to help me out, buy more farmland, and make it into a big production. If this can all happen in a timely manner, I'd probably even still keep Mr. Hale as farm manager and employ other people from town who need the jobs, as well as adopting as many of the unwanted boys and girls as we can handle."

"Many of those orphans will be troubled children and most likely be bigger than Ruth."

Micah tapped his fingers on the arm of the chair. "I know. That's the only problem with my ideas. Before I do anything, I'll have to talk it over with Ruth and probably be pretty choosy with the first orphans I...we adopt. For the first few orphans, I can adopt only the good kids and try them out first." He bit his lip. "I know I haven't thought through everything yet."

Daniel smiled. "I didn't have everything thought through when I married Harriet, either." He chuckled. "In fact, we had known each other for less than a year, courted for three months, got married, bought the farm with money we borrowed from the bank, and had three children in less than five years. Joshua and Ruth were surprise babies, to be honest. Harriet had two miscarriages the year after Esther turned one. Four years later, Joshua showed up.

"Needless to say, nothing really went as I planned for my life. I wanted to get rich quick with the farm and move everybody out to Montana within a year. Almost thirty years after we were married, we finally saved up enough money to move out here, but without three of our children." Daniel held eye contact with Micah. "Let God lead you where He wants you to go, Micah. He'll work out the details."

"Yes, Sir. That is advice I've tried to live by my whole life. Sometimes it doesn't happen, though."

"I know. I don't always follow it either. One last question. About your silence to Ruth after she challenged you to find a wife, do you do things like that often? I'm especially concerned that you didn't attend church for a few weeks."

Micah gulped. "No, Sir. I don't usually do that. I usually handle it better. However, I will ask that you keep me accountable if I ever appear to be doing it again."

Daniel nodded. "I will certainly try."

"Does this mean I have your permission to ask Ruth?"

Daniel grinned. "Yes. You're the only man around here I would have trusted my daughter with."

"What about William?"

"I would have trusted him with her, but not as a married couple. They're too similar and love each other as brother and sister, nothing more."

Micah nodded. "Thank you, Mr. Brookings." He stood up and Daniel followed suit, stretching out his arm. They shook hands. "I'm thinking about asking her on her birthday, but I haven't figured out exactly how I want to do it yet."

"We'll try to keep the plans flexible around here, but figure it out soon. Mary and Olive would like to do some sort of surprise party."

"Hmm, I wonder if I could talk to those two alone and see what the three of us can come up with." Micah tapped a finger to his chin. "I'll have to think about this. Could you give them a heads-up that I'll be talking to them soon?"

Daniel nodded. "Maybe they could go into town with Otis and Ruth next Saturday to visit you and Jeremiah."

"Good idea," Micah said. "Let's plan on that for now."

Daniel gripped his shoulder. "It'll be good to have you in the family."

"Remember not to tell her yet."

Daniel laughed. "I won't. I'll tell my wife, but I'll try not to tell Ruth."

"Thank you."

"You're welcome. I'm sure we'll see you around."

"Yes, you will."

Micah waved to Harriet as he let himself out of the house and headed back to town, an extra bounce in his step.

CHAPTER THIRTY ONE

The sun shone brightly into the bedroom. Ruth stretched as she opened her eyes. "Oh my!" She sat up quickly and looked around the room. Olive and Mary were nowhere to be seen. "How late is it?" She hurried into her dress and rushed down the stairs.

"You're just in time for breakfast," Olive said with a smile. "I hope it's all right that we didn't wake you up. I wanted you to be able to sleep in on your birthday."

Ruth smiled back. "Thank you. I did panic a little, but now that I think of it, this is one of the first mornings with sun the last few weeks. Seeing all that light made me think it was later than it really is."

Mary giggled. "That's funny."

"Can I help with anything, Olive?" Ruth asked.

Olive looked at her. "No. It's your birthday and we have big plans for you. All of which are a surprise and don't require you to work." She narrowed her eyes. "I think you should probably change into one of your better dresses, too. You won't be doing anything dirty, so you don't need to wear that ugly thing."

Ruth looked down at her brown filigree work dress. "What's ugly about this?" She looked up and saw the laughter in Olive's face.

"It isn't necessarily ugly, just not as pretty as your light blue lawn," Olive replied.

"Is that a hint, Olive?"

Olive grinned. "Yes, it is."

"Isn't it a bit chilly out yet for that dress? My lawn dress is meant as a summer dress."

Olive shrugged. "If you wear enough petticoats underneath and your shawl when you go outside, you'll be fine."

Ruth shook her head. "Very well then, I will go change into my blue lawn dress."

Ten minutes later, she was back downstairs. "What's next, Boss?" she asked Olive.

"Sit over there and wait for your breakfast meal to be served," Olive ordered.

Ruth cocked an eyebrow and Harriet, who had come into the kitchen while Ruth was dressing, saw it. "Don't worry, Ruth. I know all their plans and approved each of them."

Ruth shrugged and sat down on the decorated chair Olive had pointed out. She fidgeted while waiting. If there was one thing in the world she hated, it was sitting around doing nothing while others worked. Knowing Olive and Mary had planned to do this surprise and didn't know how much she hated doing nothing, she tried to be content watching them work.

As she watched, she decided her mother must have given them a few hints on what to make. The breakfast was her favorite: biscuits with sausage and gravy. The only thing that would make it better would be Micah... She shook the thought out of her head. It might be Wednesday, but that didn't mean he would be able to come for breakfast. And he shouldn't be expected to come just for her birthday breakfast anyway. They weren't even engaged!

"Won't you be late for school?" Ruth asked Olive.

"Nope. We started plenty early and your pa's driving us in today."

"He is?"

"Yes," Mary answered. "And Carter and I get to ride with them, too."

Ruth's forehead wrinkled. "Why?"

Olive smiled. "You'll see."

Ruth glanced at her mother who simply smiled and set the table.

Ruth counted the plates as Harriet set them down and then double-checked the counting. There were two extra plates at the table. There were two extra chairs as well. Just as she was about to ask about it, boots clomped in the lean-to and the ranch hands and her father entered the kitchen.

Daniel walked around to Ruth and Ruth stood up, throwing her arms around his neck.

"Happy birthday, Ruthie Girl," Daniel said, hugging her close.

"Thank you, Pa."

"It's hard to believe my little girl is twenty already."

"It's hard to believe that *I'm* twenty," Ruth laughed.

Daniel stepped back. "I suppose I should share you with the rest of your birthday guests."

"Happy Birthday, Miss Ruth!" Peter, Wyatt, and Flynn said.

Ruth beamed at them. "Thank you." She was about to say something else when something caught her attention out of the corner of her eye. She blinked in surprise. "Micah? Jeremiah?"

Jeremiah ran over to her and gave her a hug. "Happy birthday, Miss Brookings! Were you surprised?"

Ruth stared at him and glanced up at Micah. "Yes," she stammered, "how did you...?"

Micah walked over and put a hand on Jeremiah's shoulder. "Let's all sit down and eat this scrumptious meal." He glanced at the clock. "It's already getting rather late."

"Mr. Brookings is driving us into school, though," Jeremiah protested.

"It still takes more than five minutes to drive there," Micah said. He turned to Ruth. "Happy birthday, Ruth."

Ruth smiled shyly. "Thank you."

They all sat down and the table was abuzz with happy chatter throughout the meal. Ruth didn't say much, but she smiled a lot. As Harriet, Olive, and Mary hurriedly cleared the table, Ruth breathed a prayer of thanks to God.

"Ruth, do you mind if I go to town with your father and the children?" Harriet asked.

Ruth furrowed her eyebrows. "No, why would I?"

"Micah was hoping to stay and take a birthday walk with you. I didn't know if you would prefer I stay at home or not."

Ruth bit her bottom lip. "If you and pa are fine with it, I am, too."

Daniel clapped his hand on Micah's shoulder. "I trust you with my daughter. Don't betray that trust."

Micah swallowed and held eye contact with him. "Yes, Sir."

"And relax a little or she'll suspect something," Daniel whispered.

Micah sighed and took a deep breath.

"Everybody to the wagon!" Daniel exclaimed. "Well, everybody except the ranch hands, Ruth, and Micah." He winked at Ruth. "Have a good walk with Micah, Ruth."

Ruth felt her cheeks warm, suddenly suspicious. "I'll try, Pa."

The house emptied quickly as everybody departed for their destinations.

"Let's go outside," Micah suggested. "I know it's a bit chilly, but it's still nice out there."

Ruth looked around the kitchen. "Mother would probably tan my hide if I did the dishes today anyway. Let me go get my shawl and then I'll be ready."

Micah nodded and clasped his hands behind his back, trying to relax.

Ruth ran up the stairs, her heart beating rapidly and her stomach full of butterflies. "God, why is he here? Why did everybody leave? Mother can't need something that badly from town, can she? Or does she just want to spend some time alone with Father?" She grabbed her warmest shawl and draped it over her shoulders. "Well," she said to the reflection in the mirror, "I guess there's only one way to find out." With a firm nod of her head at the reflection, she turned on her heel and made her way down the stairs.

"Ready?" Micah asked as she stepped off the last stair.

"Yes, I am," Ruth said with a smile. "Lead on, Sheriff Carson."

The right side of Micah's face quirked up. They were both silent as they walked out of the house and down the path to the creek.

"The sun is beautiful today," Micah said as they reached the creek.

Ruth nodded. "Yes, it is."

They walked along the creek, the silence stretching between them. As they reached a bend in the creek, Micah cleared his throat and turned to face Ruth. "Do you remember how I told you I had a lot of time to think when I was going after Grover?"

Ruth looked up at him and nodded.

"Well, a lot of that thinking was about you and me." He looked toward the trees and took a deep breath. "Ruth, I've known for over a month that I was in love with you, but I knew it wasn't the right time to ask. And that time alone, especially after almost dying, I realized I didn't want to live another day without you at my side. If I had died that day, the one regret I would have had would have been not telling you how much I love you and not marrying you." Micah knelt down on one knee and looked up at Ruth. "Ruth Brookings, will you marry me?"

Ruth gasped. After her mother left, she'd suspected this would happen, but it still surprised her. "Before I answer that, there is one question I've been too scared to ask."

Micah stood up and nodded.

Ruth's eyes darted around everywhere except near Micah. "I know you will grieve the loss of Edith your whole life, but can you honestly say you will do your best to see me as I am and not compare me to her?"

She lifted her eyes to his and Micah resisted the urge to stroke her cheek when he saw the look of pain and love combining on her face.

He cleared his throat. "Yes. With God's help, I will try to do that. I know you are very different from Edith and I respect that. I know I cannot say, do, or act the same way with you as I did with her. It will take adjustments on both our parts should we get married, but God will sustain us."

Ruth smiled and the pain vanished from her face. "Thank you, Micah." She bit her lip and took a quick breath. "My answer is yes."

Micah reached into his pocket and dug something out. "This is my mother's engagement ring. I had wanted to use it for Edith, but Mother wouldn't part with it at the time. When she died a couple years after Edith and I married, I saved it to pass down to my oldest daughter, if I had any." He looked at Ruth. "If I hadn't met you, I would have passed it down to Jeremiah."

Ruth beamed as Micah slid the ring on her finger.

Micah held her hand tightly. "Now we can pass it down to our oldest daughter, if God blesses us with one."

Ruth looked away, suddenly feeling shy.

Micah took her chin in his hand and tugged on it gently. "Mrs. Micah Carson. It has a nice ring to it and fits you perfectly."

Ruth smiled and bit her lip. "It makes me sound old."

"No, it makes you sound regal," Micah teased.

"Regal?" Ruth protested. "How do you figure that?"

Micah shrugged. "I dunno. It was just a fun word to use."

Ruth laughed. "You're incorrigible."

Micah bowed. "Thank you, M'lady."

Ruth giggled. "So now that we're engaged, you have to become courtly instead of coming courting?"

Micah looked thoughtfully at the clear blue sky. "Yes, that sounds about right."

"I wish the line cabin wasn't so far away."

"Why?"

Ruth shrugged. "I want to tell Annabelle."

Micah looked across the pastures. "It isn't that far, is it? Not as far as town, for sure."

Ruth cocked her head. "I suppose not. You wouldn't mind?"

Micah smiled. "Not at all."

After they finished a quick visit with Annabelle, Micah and Ruth returned to the house. Micah helped Ruth take her shawl off and hung it on one of the hooks by the door. Ruth stepped into the kitchen and looked around. "Well, I suppose I could get lunch started."

"Nope," Micah said. "We're supposed to meet your parents for lunch at the café."

Ruth turned around and stared at Micah. "They're staying in town that long? What are we supposed to do during that time?"

"Well, we do have a wedding to plan," Micah said. "Your mother suggested we figure out who we want to stand with us, when we want to get married, and where we want to..." he cleared his throat, "...honeymoon, and other details like that."

"All right," Ruth said. "I'll go get some paper and a pencil. Can you find the parlor on your own?"

Micah shook his head and grinned. "I might be able to manage."

For the next hour, they talked and discussed their wedding, laughing, teasing, and being serious. As they figured out some of the last details they could think of, Micah looked at the clock in the corner.

"It's a good thing we're almost done. We need to head to town soon."

Ruth sighed as she looked at the sheets of paper in front of her. "I can't believe we're actually doing this. And that we're planning to be married in three or four weeks. It seems so far away and yet so close, too."

Micah took a deep breath. "I know."

Ruth bit her lip. "Who all knew you were proposing today?"

"Your parents. I think Obadiah guessed it when I asked him to come in so early today, but he won't say anything."

"So Jeremiah, Otis, Olive, Ellis, Carter, and Mary have no idea why you stayed here?"

"Otis and Olive probably figured it out. I'm not sure about Jeremiah, though."

Ruth grinned. "Are you coming for supper tonight?"

"Yes." Micah chuckled. "Are you thinking what I'm thinking?"

Ruth shrugged. "I don't know. What are you thinking?"

"I'm thinking we make them notice the ring."

Ruth shook her head. "Olive will notice as soon as she gets home from school."

"Fine, then everybody will know except Jeremiah and we make him notice it."

"That would be mean!" Ruth protested.

"We'll be sure to tell him after supper if he hasn't noticed by then."

"I still think that's mean."

Micah shrugged. "Fine. Shall I tell him before we come for supper?"

"No, I want to see his face."

"So as soon as we get back here?"

Ruth nodded. "If that's fine with you."

"Sure. This way I can torment him on the way here."

"Just don't hint too much so he guesses."

"I'll try not to. And we should get to the café."

Ruth stood up and straightened the pile of papers, setting them on the coffee table. "I'm ready. Well, as soon as I get my shawl."

Micah stood up. "I'll go get it and bring it to the front door for you."

"Thank you, Micah."

Once they were dressed for the weather, they started down the road toward town. "Where will we live once we're married?"

"I'm not sure. The farmhouse isn't that far from town, so I don't think it would be a problem for us to live there, but I'm also not sure it's in good enough shape to be moved into right now. I'll go out there tomorrow to see what condition it's in. If we adopt a couple orphans on our honeymoon, we'll probably want to live on the farm right away instead of in town. My house in town is good-sized, but not that big."

Ruth nodded. "I don't think I've ever seen the inside of either of your houses."

Micah glanced at her. "Hm. I think we should change that before the wedding."

"I agree. I'll have to start packing my things to move to whichever house we decide to live in, too."

Micah breathed in deeply. "So many details to work out. Are you sure we can do all of it in four weeks?"

"We'll have plenty of help," Ruth said. "This is a slow time at the ranch, so I'm sure Pa will have the ranch hands help us as much as we need."

"And I'm sure Obadiah will be more than happy to watch the town and office while I help, too."

"Why's that?"

Micah grinned. "He's been trying to marry me off ever since he became deputy. He practically pushed me out the door this morning."

"Shall we stop by the office to show off the ring to him before we go to the café?"

Micah chuckled. "Good idea."

They reached the edge of town and Ruth looked around. "The streets look dead."

"Happens sometimes."

Ruth shrugged. "Here's the sheriff's office."

Micah reached across and opened the door. "Obadiah!" he shouted.

Obadiah peeked his head above the desk.

"What are you doing under there?" Micah asked.

"Cleaning the bottom of the desk. I was bored. What are you doing here?"

Ruth waved her left hand in the air.

"What's that, Miss Brookings?" Obadiah asked.

"Just a little birthday present Micah gave me," Ruth said with a smile.

"When's the wedding?" Obadiah grinned.

"We have a couple of dates picked and have to talk it over with Mr. and Mrs. Brookings," Micah answered.

"Just let me know and I'll work my schedule around it so you two can be gone for a week."

"A week?" Micah asked.

Obadiah nodded. "You two deserve a week-long honeymoon."

Ruth felt her cheeks grow warm. "We'll see."

Micah glanced outside. "I hate to break this up, but we're supposed to meet Mr. and Mrs. Brookings."

Obadiah waved them away. "Don't worry about me. I've gotcha covered."

"Thanks, Obadiah," Micah said.

Micah and Ruth walked back outside and down to the café. "Ready for this?" Micah asked.

Ruth bit her lip. "Ready as I'll ever be, I guess."

Together, they made their way into the café. They stopped inside the door and waited for their eyes to adjust. Micah smiled when he saw Mary waving her arms at them.

With a gentle push on Ruth's back, Micah led her over to the table where Carter, Mary, and Mr. and Mrs. Brookings sat.

"We wondered where you were," Mrs. Brookings said.

"We stopped by the sheriff's office to prove Obadiah correct," Ruth answered.

Harriet smiled and stood. She pulled her daughter into a tight hug. "Let's see that ring." She lifted up Ruth's left hand. "Micah, this is gorgeous! The emerald set in between two diamonds matches the silver band beautifully."

Micah cleared his throat and shuffled his feet. "It was my mother's engagement ring."

Harriet squeezed Ruth's shoulders. "I'm happy for you, Ruth."

"Thank you, Mother."

"What about?" Mary asked.

"Micah asked Ruth to marry him," Daniel explained, "and she said yes."

"What does that mean?" Mary questioned.

Micah pulled out a chair for Ruth and she sat in it. "It means that in a few weeks, Ruth and I will say our vows like Annabelle and William did a couple weeks ago. And then Ruth will come to live with Jeremiah and me."

"Will she ever come back to live with us?" Mary asked, a frown furrowing her face.

Ruth put a hand on Mary's arm. "Not to live with you, but I will definitely come visit as often as I can."

"I don't want you to get married," Mary protested.

Micah chuckled. "I'm sorry to hear that, Mary, but I think you'll get used to it."

Mary pouted. "I doubt it."

Ruth looked at her mother.

"Mary," Harriet said, "I know you don't understand this now, but someday you will. Right now, let's just have fun eating lunch together and celebrating."

Daniel raised an eyebrow. "Did you two pick a wedding day?"

"We have two, actually," Micah answered. "We thought we should pick two just in case one didn't work for some reason."

"Good idea," Daniel replied. "What dates did you pick?"

"June twenty-eighth and July fifth," Ruth said.

"What day of the week are those?" Harriet asked.

"Sunday," Micah replied.

Harriet nodded. "Would you prefer the closer date?"

"Only if we can all be ready by then," Micah said. "I need to check out the farmhouse and see what condition it's in. I haven't checked it since the snow started to fall."

"You'll be living in the farmhouse?" Harriet asked.

"Especially if we adopt some orphans right away," Ruth replied. "Micah doesn't think the house in town is big enough for more than three people."

"And," Micah cut in, "I also think it would be better for any orphans we adopt to be out in the country where they can roam around a little more and not get into quite as much trouble."

Daniel nodded. "That is good thinking. When would you get the orphans?"

Ruth smiled. "We're talking about at least looking into the possibility on our honeymoon."

Harriet raised an eyebrow. "Are you sure you want to do that? It might be a good idea to get used to married life before you adopt. It would probably be a little easier on Jeremiah as well. I know he wants this change in his life, but he might not adjust as well as you hope he will."

Micah took a deep breath. "I hadn't thought about that. Thank you, Mrs. Brookings."

The waitress came over. "Are you ready to order?"

"Hello, Sally," Ruth said. "I think I'm ready."

Everybody nodded. Five minutes later, Sally left to fill the order.

"How many of the wedding plans do you have finished?" Harriet asked.

"All the ones we could think of," Micah replied.

"Excellent!" Harriet exclaimed. "I look forward to seeing what you came up with."

"I hope you don't mind, but we're going to have the children involved heavily," Micah said.

Daniel raised his eyebrows. "How so?"

"Jeremiah and Otis will be two of our groomsmen, and Olive and Mary will be two of the bridesmaids," Ruth said.

Harriet smiled. "How many of each are you having?"

"Joshua or William will be the other groomsman and Annabelle is the other bridesmaid," Micah answered.

"Why Joshua *or* William?" Mary asked.

Micah smiled. "Because I don't know if Joshua will be able to get away or not. If he can't, I'll ask William instead. Although, that is another reason we chose two dates. We're hoping that if Joshua can't do one, he can do the other."

Daniel nodded. "I hope he can make it."

"Me, too," Ruth said. "It wouldn't seem right to be married without Joshua here."

"We'll get in touch with him," Harriet said. "If need be, we could even probably have everything ready for an even earlier wedding."

Sally came back with their food and they all dug in after a prayer of blessing. The conversation settled down, but didn't die completely as they ate.

After the meal, Micah stretched. "I suppose I should head back to the sheriff's office and get some work done before dinner."

"And I have a dinner to make," Harriet said.

"And Ruth has two children to keep entertained while Harriet and I are busy," Daniel teased.

Micah chuckled. "Somehow I don't think she'll mind."

Ruth smiled. "No, I won't." She stood up and helped Mary wipe up. "Not at all." She tweaked

Mary's nose and Mary giggled. "And I don't think Mary will mind, either. Carter won't care since he'll be napping. What does Mary think about reading a book this afternoon?"

Mary stood on the chair and flung her arms around Ruth's neck. "Yes, please!" she said, snuggling her head into the crook of Ruth's neck.

Ruth smiled and tilted her head toward the little girl. *Thank You for this precious gift, Lord,* she prayed.

Micah helped Daniel get Carter ready and they all walked out of the café together.

"I'll see you this evening," Micah said. "I can't guarantee what time I'll be there."

"We'll plan supper for six," Harriet said. "Supper isn't terribly time-oriented tonight, so if you're a little late, it won't be too much of a problem."

"Thank you, Mrs. Brookings. I'll see you then." He touched a finger to the brim of his hat. "Mr. Brookings, Mary, Carter, I'll see you all later. Ruth..." He cleared his throat. "Thank you."

Ruth looked down. "You're welcome."

Micah took a deep breath and forced his feet to move away from the Brookings'.

"The wagon's just up the street," Daniel said as he led the way.

Harriet moved up next to Ruth. "Do you want me to take Mary?"

"No, thank you. I'm fine carrying her."

"Are you happy?"

Ruth looked up at her mother. "Oh yes. I'm very happy."

Harriet smiled. "Good. It is sometimes hard to tell with you."

Ruth sighed. "I know. I'm sorry."

"Does Micah know about that?"

Ruth blinked her eyes. "I don't know. We should make sure he does."

Harriet raised an eyebrow. "Yes, we should."

"I'll take Mary," Daniel said, "and then hand her up to you when you get up there."

Ruth nodded. "Thank you, Pa."

"For what?"

"Everything. The way you raised me, the way you have always protected me, how you have always guided me on the paths that would lead me closer to God, and I'm sure there's much more."

Daniel hugged Ruth. "You're welcome."

Ruth handed Mary to Daniel and climbed into the wagon before helping Mary get up and sit on her lap. Harriet climbed up next and took Carter in her lap.

"This is one way to make sure we stay warm," Harriet said with a chuckle. "Hold a child in your lap and your lap is guaranteed to stay warm, and you get to help keep them warm as well."

Ruth laughed and Daniel clucked to the horses. "To home we go. Unless you ladies needed to go somewhere else?"

Harriet shook her head. "Haven't I done enough shopping for one day?"

"I don't know. Have you?" Daniel teased.

"I think so."

"What all did you get, Mother?" Ruth asked.

"Some things for your birthday and other things for the wedding."

Ruth's head snapped to look at her mother. "You were that sure I would say yes?"

"There was no doubt in my mind that you would say yes," Harriet said. "You may hide your emotions sometimes, but you don't hide them all the time. This was one time I was absolutely sure of your answer."

Ruth smiled. "What all did you get for the wedding?"

"Just a few odds and ends I thought would be helpful. We can go through them after I get supper started."

"Sounds like fun," Ruth answered with a smile.

They rode in silence the rest of the way to the ranch and each of them went their separate ways.

CHAPTER THIRTY TWO

After ten telegrams and replies were sent out, Joshua finally gave them a date in June he would be able to come for the wedding. It was a week earlier than Micah and Ruth had chosen, which gave them only three weeks to get everything ready, but with all their friends and family helping as much as they could, everything was ready on June twenty-first.

The day of the wedding was rainy, cold, and dreary, but Ruth didn't care. Her brother was there and she was getting married. With butterflies diving and swooping around her insides, Ruth hurried into her Sunday dress and fingered her wedding dress one last time. She looked around the bedroom and smiled at the two little girls who had taken over her room. This room would no longer be hers at the end of the day.

"God," she whispered, "You have blessed me so much. Thank You. I know it's raining and some people like their wedding days to be sunny and gorgeous, but thank You for the rain today. I love the sound of rain pattering on the roof. It might be chilly, but what would June in Montana be without a chill in the air?" She smiled. "Ma's idea for adjustable sleeves was wonderful."

She quietly opened the door and stepped into the hall. Creeping downstairs, she entered the kitchen and lit the oil lamp in the middle of the table. With a sigh, she tried not to think of all the good times she'd had in this kitchen and how much she would miss it all.

"But I'll have my own kitchen to make new memories in," she told herself.

"Talking to yourself already?" Harriet asked.

Ruth spun around and hugged her mother. "Yes and no. I was just scolding myself."

Harriet pulled back. "About what?"

"How much I'll miss this kitchen and all the memories here. I reminded myself that I'll have my own kitchen to make memories in soon."

Harriet let out a shuddering breath. "I can't believe my baby is getting married."

Ruth ducked her head. "Well, you have five more babies now."

Harriet chuckled. "At least these five don't seem to be quite as much of a handful as the other five were."

"I wasn't that bad, was I?"

Harriet shook her head. "No, you weren't. You were the perfect child, at least on the outside, but there were times you did rebel, just not as verbally as your siblings."

Ruth smiled. "I suppose we should get breakfast started."

"It's your wedding day, you don't have to make breakfast," Harriet said.

"I want to," Ruth replied. "Otherwise, I'll go stir crazy. Everything is at the parsonage and ready for the wedding, so we don't even really need to do anything except get ready for church and get to town."

Harriet shrugged. "If you insist."

"Plus, I really want to cook one more meal in this kitchen."

"You're welcome here anytime," Harriet mentioned, a twinkle in her eyes.

Ruth laughed. "I know, Ma, but I'm not sure I'll have the time. I'll have a husband, son, and my own home to care for. And if we end up adopting right away, there will be those children to care for as well."

Harriet opened the small icebox and pulled out the eggs, milk, and a block of cheese. "I was teasing."

"I know."

"Ruth?" A little voice spoke from behind them.

Ruth turned away from the stove. "Good morning, Mary. What are you doing up so early?"

"I couldn't sleep."

"Aw. Why not?"

"You weren't there."

Ruth hurried to Mary and gave her a hug. "You do remember this was my last night living here, don't you?"

Mary nodded her head against her chest. "I still missed you."

Ruth pulled Mary tight. "Olive is still there."

"I know, but it isn't the same." She sighed. "And I know what you're gonna say. I have to get used to it."

Ruth smiled. "You took the words right out of my mouth."

"Eww!" Mary protested.

"How would you like to help make breakfast?" Ruth asked.

She giggled. "Can I crack the eggs?"

"Of course you can! Pull up a chair and Ma will get you the bowl."

"Ruth," Harriet said, "would you like to make some hotcakes to go with the eggs?"

"I would love to."

Half an hour later, the smell of frying bacon, hotcakes, eggs, and boiling coffee filled the kitchen. Ruth glanced at the clock. "Do we need to go wake people up?"

"The smell will wake them soon, if it hasn't already," Harriet said. "But, I know one little girl who should get dressed for church. Can you handle everything in here?"

Ruth smiled. "Yes, Ma. I think I can manage to flip all the hotcakes and pour new ones."

Harriet shook her head. "Very funny, Ruth." She kissed Ruth on the cheek. "I love you," she whispered.

"I love you, too."

As Ruth poured the last of the hotcake batter onto the pan, she heard boots clomping in the lean-to and lighter feet coming down the stairs.

"Good morning, Ruth!" Peter exclaimed. "It's a wet, chilly day for a wedding."

"Are you getting married, Peter?" Ruth asked with her back to him.

"Ha! Nope, you are."

Ruth grinned and turned around. "That's right, I am. And I don't mind the rain a bit. I like to hear the sound of the rain on the roof."

"Good," Peter answered, "because it doesn't look like it'll stop any time soon."

"Hi, Ruth, Peter, Wyatt, and Flynn," Otis said. "The others will be down in a few minutes. Carter had some problems getting dressed this morning."

"It takes five people to fix the problem?" Ruth asked.

"No," Otis replied, "but Olive was taking care of Mary's hair and Ellis wanted to watch Mrs. Brookings help Carter."

"What about Pa?" Ruth asked.

"Pa is now downstairs," Daniel said. "He was making sure his tie was straight." He made his way through the crowd of people and hugged and kissed Ruth. "How's the bride this morning?"

Ruth felt her cheeks grow warm. "Nervous, but good."

"No second thoughts?" Daniel asked.

"No, Pa, none," Ruth answered. She turned and flipped the hotcakes. "If everybody will take a seat, breakfast will be on in a few minutes."

"Yes, Ma'am," Flynn responded.

Ruth shook her head and laughed.

When the church service was over, Ruth, Harriet, Annabelle, and Anna hurried to the parsonage to prepare Ruth.

"How are we going to get you over to the church without ruining your dress?" Annabelle asked. "The rain has created mud everywhere."

"Pa said he would come in twenty minutes to carry me to the church," Ruth said.

Harriet's eyes widened. "When did he do that?"

"As we were leaving."

"Are you sure he can do that?" Harriet asked.

Ruth stepped into the parsonage. "Are you saying I'm too heavy for him?"

Harriet chuckled. "No... Well, I guess that is what I was thinking. Now that I look at you, though, I know you won't be."

"Esther or Martha would be a problem since they're almost as large as Matthew and Joshua, but not me."

Anna smiled. "Let's get you ready and then worry about it."

Ruth hurried into the room Anna had given her to change in and quickly changed into her wedding dress. As she slipped it on, she looked it over in the mirror. The white lawn material had light blue flowers running through the full skirt and the bodice had a white lace overlay to contrast slightly with the skirt. The sleeves, which Ruth chose to wear long for the wedding, had the option to be made shorter and still fashionable. With the short sleeves, it would just look more puffed than straight.

After Ruth had been in the room for a few minutes, a knock came on the door.

"Do you need to be buttoned up yet?" Annabelle asked.

"Yes, please," Ruth replied.

Annabelle slipped into the room and looked Ruth up and down. "You are absolutely lovely! Micah isn't going to know what hit him."

Ruth giggled. "I don't think so."

"Why not?"

Ruth shrugged. "I just don't."

Annabelle started buttoning the dress. "How's it feel to be getting married today?"

Ruth licked her lips. "I understand what you went through now. I'm so nervous, but I still know this is the right thing to do. I'm also excited and scared. How can you have so many conflicting feelings at the same time?"

Annabelle chuckled. "I have no idea, but I think it must be a bride thing because I felt the same way until I saw William. Then they all disappeared except the excitement."

Ruth shuddered. "I hope that happens to me, too. Only seeing Micah, not William."

Annabelle playfully slapped Ruth's shoulder. "You better not feel that relief when you see William."

Ruth laughed. "I won't. I probably won't even see William at all."

"Oh! I love how you included the Miller children in your wedding. Olive and Mary look so cute in their new dresses!"

Ruth smiled. "Thank you. I'm glad Micah agreed to have them in the wedding."

Annabelle slipped the last button into the buttonhole. "There! Let's see how you look." She spun Ruth around and looked her up and down. "Absolutely stunning!" She sighed. "The only thing I don't like about you getting married is that now you're going to be the one living far away from me."

Ruth ducked her head. "I know. But we can still visit each other."

"If we can find the time to do it as we both set up new households."

"Yes, but at the moment, you don't have any children, so you should have plenty of time, right?"

"Theoretically, yes. Actually happening? Not necessarily. But I do see your point. You'll have Jeremiah to take care of, too."

Ruth nodded. "I suppose we should go out and see what Ma wants to do to me next."

"Yes, we should." Annabelle took a few quick steps to the door and opened it, letting Ruth go first.

When they reached the parlor, Anna and Harriet stopped talking. "Ruth, that dress is perfect for you!" Anna exclaimed.

"Thank you," Ruth said, her cheeks warming.

Harriet blinked the tears out of her eyes. "You are beautiful, Ruth. Now, here is something old and borrowed." She handed Ruth a pearl necklace. "This was my mother's and both Mother and I wore it for our weddings." Harriet stepped behind Ruth and clasped the necklace on. With a deep breath, she came back into Ruth's view. "This is a gift from your father and me." She pulled out a brooch. "This is your something new and something else blue. I know your dress has blue on it, but I figured two blue things wouldn't hurt." She smiled.

Ruth took the brooch from her mother and fingered it. The brooch was in the shape of a cross with diamonds lining it and a blue stone in the very middle that matched the flowers on her skirt. Ruth looked at her ma with tears in her eyes. "Thank you. If I forget, please thank Pa for me, too." She flung her arms around Harriet's neck. "Can you please put it on for me?"

Harriet nodded, unable to speak, and gently pinned the brooch onto the right shoulder of Ruth's dress.

"Now all you need is your veil," Anna said.

"I'll go tell everybody at the church you're almost ready and send Mr. Brookings over," Annabelle offered.

"Thank you, Annabelle," Ruth said.

Between Harriet and Anna, they got the veil adjusted perfectly just before Daniel knocked on the front door.

Anna hurried to let him in and left as he came in to let Harriet and Daniel have a few minutes alone with Ruth.

Daniel walked into the parlor and stopped in the doorway. "When did my little girl grow up to be so beautiful?"

Ruth swallowed hard. "I don't know, Pa. Right now I feel like I'm too young to even be thinking about marriage."

Daniel strode to her and gave her a gentle hug. "You aren't. You may not feel like you are ready, but I truly believe you are."

"Thank you, Pa."

"Now, shall we go get you married to Micah?"

Ruth smiled and pulled her parents into a group hug. "Yes, let's."

"Can we pray first?" Harriet asked.

"Of course," Daniel replied. "Dear Heavenly Father, Thank You for always being there for us when we need You. Today, we have the privilege to witness the marriage of Ruth to Micah. Lord, as they begin their new lives together, give them grace, wisdom, and peace. They are both still young and they are entering their marriage with many differences and also with a ten year old young man who will most likely cause some extra friction in their marriage. Lord, I know You are with each and every one of them and pray that You will continue to guide them both. In Jesus' name, amen."

As Daniel carried her through the mud, the words of the last verse of "Lily of the Valley" played through her head.

He'll never, never leave me, nor yet forsake me here,
While I live by faith and do His blessed will;
A wall of fire about me, I've nothing now to fear,
From His manna He my hungry soul shall fill.
Then sweeping up to glory to see His blessed face,
Where rivers of delight shall ever roll.

He's the Lily of the Valley,
the Bright and Morning Star,
He's the fairest of ten thousand to my soul.

Thank You, Father, she prayed silently, *for promising to never leave us, nor forsake us. Thank You for giving me twenty years with my parents and for their care in raising me. And most of all, thank You for always being a wall of fire about me* so that I have nothing to fear. You are my God, help me to always remember that You are always with me.

NOTE TO THE READER

You may have noticed that Jeremiah's salvation is never resolved in this book. That was done on purpose. I like to write my novels as close to real life as possible. We do not always know if someone is truly a Christian or not and that's what I chose to do with Jeremiah. I will be publishing a novella early next year that has Micah, Ruth, and Jeremiah in it, so if you would like to know more about them, be on the lookout for the novella, *Take My Life.*

Please share this book with a friend.

Please recommend this book.
Good books are meant to be shared. If you enjoyed this book, let a friend know about it.

Please post a review.
Reviews are important to authors and helps other customers find books and make the decision whether or not to buy them. Reviews are especially helpful to Indie authors such as myself. Please take a few minutes and leave an honest review on http://amazon.com and/or http://goodreads.com. Thank you!

Please read more in the series.
This is the fourth of five novels in the series.

PREVIEW

Keep reading for a special preview of the upcoming novel from author Faith Blum! (Some details in the sneak peek are subject to change.)

Hymns of the West #5
The Solid Rock

Coming in late spring 2016!

Joshua pushed the door open and breathed deeply. "There's nothing like the distinct odor of men slaving away in a confined place mixed with rotting coffee grounds and ink."

"You always make it sound so pleasant," Paul Greene said, an amused smile on his face. "Mr. Pinkerton will be with you in a moment."

A tall man stepped out of the door behind the secretary. "Actually, he'll be here right now. Come with me, Joshua."

Joshua nodded to the secretary and followed Robert Pinkerton into his office.

"I have a case for you. I believe it will fit with your moral objections as well as your skill set."

Joshua raised an eyebrow. "What is it?"

"We have an agent in Cheyenne, Wyoming, who has been investigating some strange events for more than ten years now. He is close to the end and has been kidnapped."

Joshua leaned forward. "How long ago?"

"He was kidnapped yesterday. His daughter sent us a telegram."

"Why me?"

Robert smiled. This was one reason he loved working with Joshua. "You know the area better than most agents and you have been quite successful tracking down criminals on fairly cold trails. You read fast and think well on your feet. I can also trust you not to flirt with Mr. Harris's daughter. I hear she's unmarried and quite lovely."

Joshua's head jerked up from his examination of the Oriental rug. "Harris. Would the daughter's name be Elizabeth?"

Robert shuffled a few papers on his desk and skimmed one. "Yes, it is. How did you know?"

"We met about four years ago when I was the sheriff in Cartersville, which is now Castle City. Is there anything else I need to know?"

Robert skimmed the papers in front of him. "Knowing Edward Harris, he'll have kept notes of his investigation and hidden them well."

Joshua nodded with a smile. "I can see him doing that."

Robert stood up and Joshua followed suit. They shook hands. "Good luck to you and Godspeed."

"Thank you," Joshua replied.

SPECIAL THANKS

This is usually the hardest part of the book to write. How do you say thank you to everybody who has impacted your book? How do you make it interesting when you've said almost the same thing in each book you have published? Instead of doing either of those, I'll simply spout off as many of the names as I can think of. These people either impacted something in the book, were part of the editing process, or were otherwise involved in making *Lily of the Valley* what it is today.

Amanda Tero, Janell Rogers, Patricia Gallie, Andrew Abraham, Lydia Blum, Gail Blum, Naomi Blum, Perry Kirkpatrick, Kelsey Bryant, Aubrey Hansen, Joel Greene, Pastor George and Bev Jaderston, Janet Weihrouch, Travis Perry, Sheila Odom Hollinghead, and many more who I'm sure I am forgetting. Thank you all very much for everything you did whether it was doing a word war with me, beta-reading, proofreading, formatting, or just keeping me moving along because you wanted the next book. Thank you, thank you, thank you from the bottom of my heart.

ABOUT THE AUTHOR

Faith Blum started writing at an early age. She started even before she could read! She even thought she could write better than Dr. Seuss. (The picture doesn't show it well, but there are scribblings on the page of *Green Eggs and Ham*). Now that she has grown up a little more, she knows she will probably never reach the success of Dr. Seuss, but that doesn't stop her from trying.

When she isn't writing, Faith enjoys doing many right-brained activities such as reading, crafting, writing, playing piano, and playing games with her family. One of her dreams is to visit Castle City, Montana someday to see the ghost town she chose for her characters to live in. She currently lives on a hobby farm with her family in Wisconsin.

There are many ways to connect with Faith online. All of them can be found in one convenient place: http://FaithBlum.com. On her website, you can find her on various social media sites as well as her blog.